I0593388

Journals of The
EARTH
GUARDIANS

SERIES 3

Journals of The
EARTH
GUARDIANS

SERIES 3

L.C Webb

Copyright © 2022 by L.C Webb.

All rights reserved. No part of this book may be used or reproduced in any form whatsoever without written permission except in the case of brief quotations in critical articles or reviews.

This book is a work of fiction. Names, characters, businesses, organizations, places, events and incidents either are the product of the author's imagination or are used fictitiously. Any resemblance to actual persons, living or dead, events, or locales is entirely coincidental.

2023 COLLECTIVE EDITION
ISBN – 978-0-6458878-3-9

Published by The Knights Corner Publishing
knightscornerpublishing@gmail.com

CONTENTS

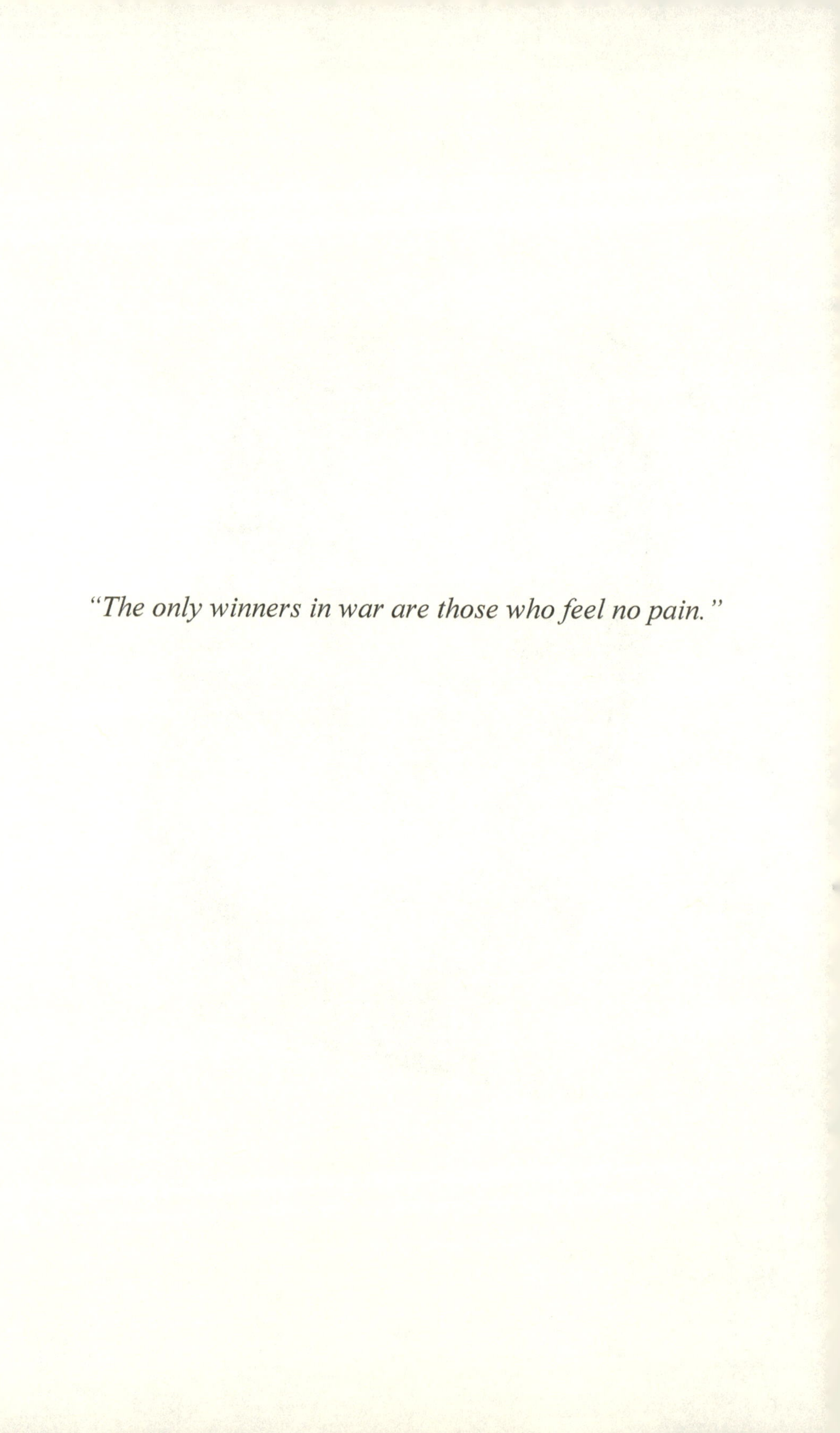

"The only winners in war are those who feel no pain."

CHAPTER 1

The Aftermath

Journal entry by Lila Winters

Well, this is a nice feeling to have. It's 4.30 in the morning, and I'm doing laps in the Eden hotel pool trying desperately not to think about anything and everything.

After the success of the Canadian mission, the team was on a high, and I was thrilled to be able to help set up our New York based team with Henry and Jennifer. It took us a couple of weeks, but I helped them to screen all the volunteers from our Agronomique's rescue who were willing to join the fight against The Board.

Being an Animal and Nature guardian definitely came in handy because I was able to sense the true nature and intent of the applicants as we screened them. — Some of them were only applying because they wanted revenge. But that is not why our team exists.

Well... not the only reason.

Quite a lot of the rescued guardians and humans wanted to return home, and I couldn't blame them, but I did tell them to be vigilant and to be on guard. And since all of them know exactly what The Board is capable of, quite a few of them have gone into hiding. So once all the rescued guardians were safe and my team had finally returned home to Melbourne, it felt like we were all still in recovery mode. But it's more like everyone's just trying to take that moment to enjoy life before the next metaphorical axe falls.

I'm beginning to think these morning swims are not very effective to distract me. But I'm getting pretty good at challenging myself. I've been swimming in the hotel pool every day at a ridiculously early hour since our return last week, and I'm now able to swim the entire length of the pool twice without coming up for air.

I was just about to push myself to three laps when I heard footsteps along the pool's edge, and I know that it isn't any of my team — because ridiculously early hours of the mornings are just not their thing. In knowing that, I kept my head below the water, sinking down to the bottom of the pool as the shadow appeared at the ledge. I waited at the base of the pool, trying to make out who was standing there, but I was running out of air and had to make a choice.

Thinking out my options, I planted my feet on the base of the pool then pushed up with all of my strength, bursting out of the water at full-speed to land on the ledge of the pool next to the stranger then I moved into a high-spin kick, aiming for the back of the person's head.

It wasn't until the last second that I realised it was Billy Jonas, one of our new team members, and also the one who cottoned on to the game I was playing when I was trying to rescue him and the others from the Agronomique's facility. But just before my foot connected with his head, he moved at full-speed to catch it then held it in a bit of shock, staring at it.

"Billy?" I questioned, catching my breath while staring up at him. "What the hell are you doing here?"

He looked at me and took a breath, apologizing in a very odd, kind of Canadian, somewhat American accent, "Sorry, I didn't think anyone would be awake this early."

From the looks of it, he'd just finished a work-out in the gym with his sweaty shirt and gym bag sitting on one of the deck chairs. I started to feel like maybe I had overreacted – just a little. But I'm still a bit on edge and irked. "Well, it is 4.30 in the morning... You don't usually have people awake at this hour."

"Yet here we are," Billy so blatantly stated with his eyes darting from my foot that he was still holding quite close to his head, and then to me, before kindly lowering my foot to hand me a towel. "That was a pretty sweet move. Where did you learn it?"

"I taught myself," I replied, accepting the towel from him to wrap it around me.

As I looked back up, I caught him staring at the many scars I bared all over my body from being treated like a lab rat and soldier, and many other things that I'm trying not to think about. But Billy stared at one scar in particular. He moved closer to me and brushed his hand along my collar bone where a now healed scar is. It's from a bullet wound that I got on the last rescue op. – To rescue him.

My body tensed under Billy's hand causing him to pull his hand away, apologising again. "Sorry... I was just... admiring the healing process."

He awkwardly turned away, scrubbing his fingers through his now dishevelled hair. The hair that he's trying to grow out, now that he no longer has to look like a military man. He used to have short back and sides, but not anymore. Instead, his dark-brown almost-black hair is just long enough to see that it curls a little, especially when he leaves it scruffy like that.

Interesting. – I sense Billy's emotions of curiosity. – Which is an emotion I'm not used to sensing when people look at my scars.

"Well, that's a new one." I tittered, wrapping the towel around my waist to pull on my jumper, and ready to leave.

He looked back at me again, curious, and asked, "What do you mean by 'a new one'?"

I huffed a little and rolled my eyes at him. "Well, most people can't stand to look at me… Whenever they see the scars, most of the time I sense their guilt, their anger or their empathy… But I've never sensed curiosity from them before?"

"Sorry," he said again, turning to look at me. "It's just you've been a curious wonder to me since the moment I met you… especially because you can… you know…"

With a slight peak at his lips, he snapped his fingers, creating a tiny fireball that he held at the end of his index finger. Then he tossed it into the pool to extinguish it.

Ah right. – There's that I suppose. I did show him during the rescue op that I could play with fire and all. – But at this point, I'm secretly glad I haven't revealed all my abilities to him. – It's safer this way.

Now having the confidence to look at me directly, Billy glanced down at the scars then moved to stand in front of me again. "Well, if it helps, I just want to make sure you know... that when I see these scars..."

He paused, beginning to highlight some of the not-so-nice, jagged scars on my body then looked into my eyes and smiled. "I don't feel guilt... I feel honoured, that a person who has clearly been through hell, is still willing to stand up and fight for me, and for everyone else... You are the reason I joined this cause. I watched you take a beating and never fight back. Because you knew what would happen if those soldiers lost to you. So please don't ever feel like you need to hide those scars... They are the marks of a true warrior."

Hmm? – He's beginning to remind me of Alex a little. He too is accepting of the scars to a point. – But it's nice to hear from another person as well.

I quickly realised Billy and I had gotten way too close for my standard liking, and instantly tensed, moving away as I cleared my throat and rushed to grab my bag.

"The pool's all yours... enjoy the swim," I mumbled while hastily walking out of the pool room.

When I got up to my apartment, everyone was still sleeping. So I very quietly raced at half-speed to shower and change, and ended up sitting in my study office with a banana in one hand and a protein shake in the other. I'm actually pretty pleased with myself, to be ready to start the day before 5.30 am, and hopefully I will have all of these stacks of paperwork sorted and sent off before the team meets for a jog through the city in a few hours.

Sure-enough, by using my nifty super-speed, I was able to do just that. – I did slow down just a tad to go thoroughly over

Billy Jonas's application form for a security position on my team. And I may have felt a little smile on my lips when I read through his answer for the 'reason for application' question.

Finally, I got to the last piece of paperwork and my smile disappeared as my hair streaked white along the front strands of my honey-blond hair. In my hands, I hold the divorce papers that Matt had given me just before I left for the Canadian mission.

I had already signed them, but I have not yet given them back to him. And I'm still not overly happy that the casualty of this – war – is our marriage. But deep down I know this is right for him.

After all, this is what he wanted.

Journal entry insert by Alex Woods

I'm feeling very refreshed this morning. Confident that we have all now fully recovered from Canada. Even Lila's acting more like herself. – And her taking back the role of head of security is an absolute load off my shoulders, because paperwork is just not my thing. Lila even told me that last week, when I so very happily handed over the back log of papers and forms that had accumulated while she was 'missing'.

To be fair. – I was distracted by her when I originally tried to get to them. – So the fact that I tried should have been enough.

Today we're going for a team jog around the city because of the safety-in-numbers thing. – Keeping in mind that we did just tick off a powerful and dangerous organisation, and all that jazz. – You know, we kind of need to be careful now.

I knocked on Lila's apartment door at 7am on the dot to walk with her to the lobby. But when she opened the door, she didn't look like her usual self. She looked like she had been crying.

"Lila, what's wrong?" I moved closer, wiping one of the tears from her cheek.

"It's nothing, I was just having a moment," she whimpered before walking to the elevator.

But it's clearly not nothing and judging by the emotion of heart-break oozing from her, and her now streaked white hair, I bet that 'nothing' has something to do with Matt. – Lila hasn't officially told anyone about the divorce yet, but we all know about it. – And what that means for their family dynamics is anyone's guess at the moment.

Personally, I just wish Lila was open to me about it, and it really does hurt when she keeps brushing me off like this. Add to that, I still haven't gotten the chance to talk to her about everything that happened before we went to Canada. – When I unintentionally blurted out that I love her. But I take comfort, remembering what she said to me when I last confronted her. She said that I was perfect, and that she knows in her heart that I will always be the person she trusts to be there for her, no matter what.

That is undeniably true. – I'm not going anywhere.

While we stood in the elevator, Lila glanced at me a few times but said nothing. – Which again is an ouch. It wasn't until she received a text message that read, "You've been targeted," that she actually looked at me to show me the text. And yep. – I'm starting to reach boiling point, knowing she clearly has no plans to stay in the hotel where it's safe.

"Lila, I think we should go back to the apartment," I griped.

"What, why?"

"Oh, I don't know, maybe it's because you've just pissed off the enemy and painted a big target on your back, and you're in danger... Shouldn't that be a good enough reason?" I bickered and huffed, turning to see her smiling, and giggling at me.

"Alex, we're always in danger. It's one of the many perks of our job... If we hide, it means they've won. And I will not let them claim our freedom through fear and intimidation."

ARGH!!! – I hate it when she's right like this. – But I love it when she giggles.

"Fine... Will you at least tell me why you were crying before?" I frustratedly asked.

She straightened her body before looking back at the elevator door, and replied, "Allergies."

And that is total <u>bull</u>. But because the elevator doors are just about to open on the ground floor, I know not to push the issue.

Not yet anyway.

As the doors opened, I felt my stomach start to churn when I saw Billy standing there, waiting to go up to his apartment. He said Lila's name with a cocky smile as he cleared his throat. "Hi... um, Lila, I just wanted to apologise again about this morning. I didn't mean—"

"Don't worry about it," Lila casually interrupted.

Wait. – What the hell happened this morning? – And why is this the first I'm hearing about it? – And why is there so many questions?

Lila followed me out of the elevator but stopped Billy before he stepped in. "Hey, the teams going out for a run, did you want to join us?"

No. – I would very much not like him to join us. – I would like him to stay home. But I don't get a say in this because instead he said, "Sure" with a giddy grin.

So I tried to be polite and joked, "Try to keep up."

His grin got wider as he sniggered back. "That won't be a problem."

We then both followed Lila's lead to where the team was waiting and talking with Shane and Jessica, who were sitting at the reception desk. – Jess is currently teaching Shane the ropes of the reception duties now that he works at the hotel as a concierge.

Our running group this morning now consists of Adela, Tyme, Katie, and Terrence as well as some of our human security team Chase, Michael, and Roy. But before we left, Lila spoke quietly, reminding us of the rules and the dangers.

"Remember, don't wander off and no super moves," she urged then started us on a slow jog through the city towards the Melbourne botanic gardens.

We were all doing pretty well as we followed the footpath along the Yarra River, and everyone was keeping a good running speed. – Even Billy. But because he's new to the team, he ran alongside the only person he knew, and that was Lila. We kept a steady pace, with some being a little competitive. Until we got to the corner of Alexandra Avenue and Anderson Street, where there was this strange and strong gust of wind that stopped us.

The wind was so strong that we needed to shield ourselves from the dust and pollen. Lila had stopped under a large tree and before she realised it, the branch of the tree snapped and was heading straight down towards her. So at full-speed, Billy raced to pull Lila out of the way, and then shielded her from the debris of leaves and sticks by towering over her as his arms enveloped her.

Aw damn. – My gut's churning now.

"Are you okay?" he asked while looking her over for any injuries as the rest of the group rushed to aid her.

Lila stood up tall as she stepped away from Billy, and thankfully stood back next to me, clearing her throat as she regained her bearings. "Yeah, thank you, Billy... But for future reference, we try not to use our abilities in public unless we absolutely have to... And yes, the branch is a decent size, but it wouldn't have hurt me that much... Remember I'm tougher than I look."

Billy glanced over at me and may have noticed my clenched fist as he replied with a little chuckle, "I'll try to remember that."

A few of us helped Lila to move the branch to the side, clearing the path for other pedestrians, and I swear she wasn't kidding when she said the branch was a decent size. – It required three of us using our super strength to move it. So after realising that, I'm really not that upset that Billy pulled Lila out of the way when he did, because I'm pretty sure it would have killed her. But it does have me wondering why Lila is playing that little fact down. Instead, she just stood there, dusting off the dirt and branches from her pants while smiling at the team.

"Alright, we'll finish up at the shrine then head up to the Pancake Parlour for breakfast, my shout," she offered, trying to bring the team morale back up before she started running with the group again.

I needed to hold back for a second, watching them run a head as I grinded my teeth and clenched my fist into an even tighter ball. But Terrence noticed it and stayed back with me, asking if I was okay.

"Yep, just fine," I grunted as I started running alongside him to catch up with the group.

Journal entry continued by Lila Winters

When the team finally ran up the steps of the Shrine, I'd actually become pretty competitive with my brother Tyme as we raced to the top. And because I'm such an awesome big sister, I let him win.

The smile on his face when he reached the top, beamed from ear to ear as he turned around to give me a celebratory hug and announce his victory to the world. However, the team couldn't celebrate with him, with most of them reaching their fatigue limit as they stop to take a breather and stretch out their aching muscles.

I stood at the top of the steps stretching out my torso as if I was yawning and soaking in the autumn sun, gazing at the city view. – Which I will add is amazing. Especially with the play on colours of reds and yellows with the hint of green still hanging in there as autumn starts to settle.

Billy was soaking in the views on the other side of the steps, so I walked over to join him and commented, "Well, you certainly proved you can keep up."

He glanced back and grinned at my approval. "It would have been nicer to go faster though."

I laughed a little, leaning back on the brick ledge to relax, and crinkled my nose a bit as I looked at him. "Sorry, but the rules are there for a reason."

He turned to lean next to me and quizzically sighed, looking over at the Victorian Army barracks just opposite us when he questioned, "Do you think they know?"

I followed his gaze then chuckled at the irony. "Plausible deniability... It goes a long way for our government sectors."

He nodded, understanding my non-committal answer, and asked again but this time with a bit of fear in his voice, "But how do you stay so calm?"

Hmm...? – Where was this coming from?

Maybe he suspects the tree branch wasn't an accident. – Which if I'm being honest, it wasn't. But I'm positive no one else saw the scorch marks at the end of the branch where it was severed. So I think I'll play ignorant.

"What do you mean?" I asked with a puzzling look.

He shook his head, almost confused at my ignorance, and explained, "You run through Melbourne like a normal person, and you have no idea if you're walking... well, in this case running into a trap or not. I mean how do you know that tree branch wasn't intended to kill you."

Ah. – I was right. – He did smell a trap.

"Was it?" I cheekily grinned, still playing ignorant, which I suspect is not helping with Billy's own fears as his nostrils begin to flare. And he placed his hands on his hips while shifting into a stand-offish demeanour.

He looks kind of funny, and I really couldn't help but laugh at him, causing him to smile back at me. In the end, I caved, giving him some advice.

"The General..." I stopped there needing to correct myself. "I mean Richard had a saying when I was younger... Treat your enemies as if they were your friends..."

Billy sighed realising what I was saying and finished my sentence, "That way you'll always be one step ahead." He then cleared his throat and started to relax again, adding, "He used to give that speech to us too... But I never understood it."

"It's about knowing your enemies as if you would your best friend," I explained, still with a slight chuckle. "For example, Alex and I are friends, but only a true friend would know what his strengths and weaknesses are... Just like he knows what mine are."

"And what are they?" Billy asked with a brazen grin.

Still chuckling, I leaned in closer to him to cheekily whisper in his ear. "Alex knows that my favourite colour... is not pink."

Billy pulled his head back just a little to see my face while holding back his laughter and eyeing me in disbelief. That is until I winked at him, causing both of us to break into hysterical laughter.

When we eventually managed to compose ourselves again, I went on to explain, "The point is... at the moment our enemies operate in secret, so for us, a public area is always safer."

He nodded then asked, "But what do you do when you're alone?"

I could sense the fear he was desperately trying to hide, so I confidently replied, "Always have a plan B... Take this morning for example. I assumed I'd be swimming alone, but when I realised I wasn't, I knew exactly what to do... And that was hit first and ask questions later."

Leaning back on the brick ledge next to me again, Billy began to smile, genuinely this time. "Yeah, about that. I was wondering if you would teach me that sweet move you did... jumping out of the water and all... That is if you're not too busy."

Hmm...?

I'm not overly confident at the moment about what to say. Considering this whole time that I've been talking to Billy, Alex has been standing at the ledge opposite us, and I can definitely feel the territorial jealousy pouring from him, and is most likely eves-dropping on my conversation. As is Terrence.

In thinking the request through properly. – I'm simply trying to boost team morale and make the new guy feel welcome, as well as ensure he is up for a fight if and when that time comes. So I agreed to train Billy, and he became so ecstatic that he asked to start at my ridiculously early hours tomorrow morning.

As expected, Alex appeared behind me, wrapping his arm over my shoulder while he condescendingly smiled at Billy. "Sorry, Billy, I've got to steal Lila for just one second... But the others are heading up to Melbourne Central for breakfast. You should follow them, so you don't get lost."

Before I could object to Alex's plan, he wrapped his arms around my waist, lifting me up, and then took off at full-speed. I didn't fight Alex. But I'm certainly not going to make it easy for him either, so he ended up having to run with me partially blocking his view, with my legs wrapped around his waist and my arms crossed in front of me as I angrily glare at him.

He ran fast then stopped on one of the hidden paths just past the Fern Gully rest house. And I barked as he placed me down. "Alex, you know the rules! No running in public."

The problem is, he seems too distracted to listen to me. Scrubbing his hands through his now messed up, short brown hair as he grunted, "What the hell was that?"

I huffed but stayed silent, keeping my arms crossed, still glaring at him. Leading him to gripe, "Lila, what's going on between you and Billy?"

"Urgh! Nothing is going on, Alex... What's going on with you?"

Now frustrated and needing to vent, Alex clawed his fist into the tree, pulling some of the bark away, trying to take a few calming breaths. When suddenly, Terrence ran up at full-speed. – And I don't know how he does it, but his dark-brown mid-length hair is always perfectly combed and parted. And for some annoying reason, when he runs, it doesn't get messed up, and it _frustrates_ me. – He stopped right next to Alex, and I want so badly to mess up his hair just to annoy him, like they're both annoying me.

"Lila," he curiously spoke. "What happened to you this morning down at the pool?"

Again, I growled, this time at Terrence and glared at the fact that he also broke the super's rule. But he glowered back at me with determination, so I caved. "Urgh... I promise you, Terry, nothing happened... I was swimming and I saw Billy watching me. I got scared and I hit him... That's it."

I looked over at Alex who seems to be fuelled with a mix of emotions. – And I am really struggling to keep up with all of them. I tried to comfort him, placing my hand on his shoulder, and for the first time, he pulled away from me.

"Alex, talk to me," I begged.

"Talk!" He scoffed, scowling at me. "Lila, I've been waiting weeks for you to talk to me... That's all I've ever wanted you to do. And it hurts because I thought you trusted me... Your so-called true friend!"

"I do trust you," I insisted back.

"THEN WHY DIDN'T YOU TELL ME ABOUT THE DIVORCE!?!" he angrily roared. – And that is a first for him too.

Woah. – Alex has never yelled at me like that before.

I didn't know what to say, and I peered back at Terrence who also seems to be waiting for an answer, causing me to stutter, "I... I didn't think... I didn't want to... um."

Terrence interrupted my stutter to tell me that my hair had turned completely white, and I snapped with the obvious. "Yeah it does that."

"BUT IT'S NOT SUPPOSED TO DO THAT!" Alex yelled at me again, turning away from me to take some calming breaths. "Look, I get that you can't control it... but that's what I'm here for. I have always been willing to help you control your animal instincts... And you know I can feel your pain. It eats away at me every time I see you, and you keep me at arm's length."

My heart ached, and I stared down at the ground, knowing everything he was saying was true. But still I couldn't tell him. I can't tell him anything because I don't want to hurt him. I know Alex loves me, but I don't want to give him false hope. Because my feelings for him are confusing. – Just like my feelings for Terrence.

I can't do it. – I respect and love them far too much to ever want to hurt either of them.

"Lila," Terrence uttered as his blue-green eyes looked into my blue eyes. "This isn't about Matt, is it?"

He placed his warm hand on my cheek to wipe away the tears then pulled back in confusion and sadness, staring down at his stone-bracelet when he asked. "Lila, why are you afraid of us?"

That caught Alex's attention, and he turned to finally look at me and see the fear in my eyes as I cried and stared into his angered hazel ones. I let out another whimper, trying to compose myself before I explained, "I'm sorry I didn't tell you... I was afraid... And I still am... I'm scared that if either of you knew about the divorce that somehow our friendship would change, and I don't know if I want it to... I have so many confusing feelings raging through me, that the only consistent things in my life are you two. And I can't lose that... Alex, I'm so sorry. I didn't mean to hurt you."

Feeling ashamed of my actions, I tried to hide my sniffles when Alex moved at super-speed to wrap his arms around me. I couldn't help but cry into his neck as he held me up and whispered to me, "You will never lose me, Lila... I already told you that... No matter how many moods you throw at me... Got that?"

I took in a shaky breath and nodded while my head was still buried in the crook of his neck. Then eventually, I peered up to see Terrence. I was about to tell him I was sorry as well, but he stopped me.

"Don't even say it," he demanded with such a caring voice. "Lila, I promise I will never let anything get in the way of our friendship. Because I don't ever want to lose you... Not again."

Feeling incredibly happy, I pulled Terrence in for a group hug. But then we all laughed as the beautifully tender moment was interrupted by the sound of my stomach growling. As he chuckled, Terrence lifted his head from mine and added with a sly grin. "You know if we're super quick, we should be able to make it to the Parlour house in time for breakfast."

I rolled my eyes and agreed to his madness, "Alright, but we're taking the alleys."

Yet before I started to run, I turned to both of them with a cheeky grin. "But if I beat you there, you're both buying me ice cream."

They agreed to the bet, so we ran out of the park at super-speed racing towards Melbourne central.

By the time the rest of our team had actually arrived at the Pancake Parlour, Alex, Terrence, and I were already at a table with two bowls of ice-cream in front of me. I was nice enough to share some of the ice-cream with Alex and Terrence. — But not much. — We kept fighting with our spoons over who gets the next scoop.

The moment came that all three of us dreaded, and it was absolutely hilarious when Adela sat down at the table with her arms crossed, eye-balling all of us. Causing Alex to eventually break with a mouth full of ice-cream, pointing at Terrence as he claimed, "It was his idea."

I couldn't hold it in and broke into giggles, struggling to keep the ice-cream in my mouth, all while Billy, Katie, and Tyme sat down at the table next to Chase, Michael, and Roy. And Chase was the first to comment.

"That doesn't look like a very healthy breakfast, Lila."

I chuckled at him while swallowing my mouthful. "You're just jealous that you can't have a sexy bod like mine and eat like this... Besides technically this is my lunch... I have been up since 4."

Chase looked back at me in stunned silence as the waiters served a dozen stacks of pancakes on the table for everyone, and I looked over the stacks to him with a cheeky grin.

"I'm just that good." I boasted while trying to hold back my amusement. Then everyone in the group smiled at me and broke into laughter as we all got stuck into the pancakes and enjoyed an awesome breakfast-almost-lunch.

CHAPTER 2

The Bottled Stuff

Journal entry by Lila Winters

I didn't get back to the apartment until after lunch, but I thought it would be nice if I brought back some glazed donuts for when Matt, Danny, and Ruby return from school, kinder, and work. I wasn't expecting anyone home, so I jumped in fright when Matt greeted me at the door. I was distracted when he approached me because I'd only just realized that the fallen branch this morning had torn my pant leg. – And I'm pretty sure these are my last pair of gym pants that aren't torn to shreds, stained with blood, or falling apart from over-use.

"Frac! Matt, you scared me," I gasped, trying to stop myself from dropping the donuts. He then walked back with me to the loungeroom but stayed eerily quiet. – Which is odd??? – I'm sensing an angered emotion from him, so I questioned with extreme caution, "Matt, is everything okay?"

He stood opposite the coffee table and scowled in a fury as he asked, "Why?" while holding up the divorce papers.

Completely confused by his question, I replied, "It's what you wanted."

"Yes, but I didn't expect you to sign it." He glowered at me as if his heart was breaking.

"I'm sorry." I puzzled still very confused. "I signed it the day you asked for it... I just never got the chance to hand it back to you. You know because of my impending flight..."

Hang on???

Slowly realising something, I grew very angry and raised my voice slightly. "Wait, if you didn't want a divorce then why the hell did you ask for one?!"

Matt moved to stand in front of me, holding my arms as he pleaded, "Because I wanted you to choose us. To choose me... I want you to realise that I'm the better option."

"But are you?" I questioned, pulling my arms away from him.

He couldn't answer it, he just stood there speechless. – And to be honest I'm glad my hair was already white before we started this conversation.

"Are you really the better option? Am I really yours...? Matt, our relationship is being strained by our marriage, and both of us can see that... We are two very different people from when we first got married. And I know part of you hates the fact that I am what I am... And while as interesting as I am to you, because of that, you were made to believe I was dead. You now have to go to work with a bodyguard, and the children don't go anywhere without Max's security team in tow... Matt, because of what I am, you and I have grown apart... I mean, you can't even look at me the way you used to."

I gazed at Matt, waiting for him to rebuke any of what I'd said, but he just stared at the floor in silence. So I continued, "Matt, I love you and I know you love me. But it's not the kind of love you stay married for and you know that... or at least part of you did when you filed for divorce... You deserve better than me, Matt... You deserve someone normal."

He slowly let his tears fall, conceding to what I was saying, so I pulled him closer to hold him as he sobbed. Then after a while, he mumbled, "What's going to happen to us?"

Eerr...? – That's actually a good question.

Before I could answer it, I needed a moment to think through our current options. – On one hand, living with your ex-husband is not necessarily normal, and it could get awkward if and when he does decide to... move on. But on the other hand, it would be a hell of a lot easier to keep an eye on him and to protect the kids if we just kept things the way they are.

I like that idea better. So I took a deep breath and hoped to God he'd go for it. "The living arrangement we have at the moment seem to be working, with us staying in separate rooms and all. And it seems to work for Danny and Ruby. That is, assuming you don't hate me, and you're still happy to remain friends with me... If that's the case, we do nothing, and nothing has to change between us."

Matt liked the idea and straightened up as he dried his tears, muttering, "That's good. Family first... I like it."

Instantly, I started to feel all of the horrible feelings I was desperately trying to bury, and I hated it. Because signing a piece of paper was nothing compared to handing Matt back my wedding and engagement rings. It left my body feeling tingly and almost numb. – Because now our marriage is really and truly over.

Journal entry insert by Adela Eden

Tyme and I were in the lobby, coming back from a pretty awesome lunch date from one of the downstairs restaurants, and part of me is feeling a bit fluttery inside. This guy is actually pretty damn decent and it's sometimes hard to believe how we ended up in each other's orbit.

He was just about to give me one of his amazingly sweet kisses with those gorgeous and totally kiss-worthy lips when he spotted his sister storming out of the elevator towards the door. It piqued both of our interests since it was Lila's rule to not leave the hotel without back-up. Tyme rushed to stand in front of her, calling her name, but she looked like she was off in her own world.

"Hey, Lila, where are you off too?" he asked with that husky American accent, eventually getting her attention when he raced to stand in front of her.

Lila pulled a clearly fake smile, and I could tell she was holding back tears with her hair still white. - Her natural hair is almost the same as her brothers, only a little darker, with Tyme's being a sandy blond. But seeing her wolf-white hair made it easy to figure out where Lila had just come from.

"As hard as it is to believe, I need to go shopping," she spoke with a hint of a sniffle.

That statement caught my dad's attention as he walked in from the street, after his daily drive around town in his favourite sports car. "Shopping...? Now that's a word I rarely hear from you."

Lila turned to him, trying not to huff as she replied, "It's nothing major. I just need some new pants and some other stuff... Matt and I have arranged a sci-fi movie night. So we need supplies."

I don't think Lila was expecting anyone to notice that she was hiding a black rotted apple in her hand, that I suspect wasn't rotted before she got into the elevator. - But I did.

Still, I stayed quiet and listened to Tyme be the amazing brother that he is, and ask, "Have you got someone to go with you?"

"I'll be fine on my own," Lila sniped as she moved to walk around him.

Moving faster, Tyme grabbed hold of Lila's free hand, and Wow. - She glared at him as if she was about to pummel him into the next state. So I thought I'd step in, to avoid the sibling squabble. "I'll go with her... I need to get my hair done anyway."

Lila looked back at me and gave me the death stare, but also seemed somewhat grateful with a slight peak at her lips as she yanked her hand away from her brother, growling, "There... happy?"

Aw. - Now my poor Tyme looks all sad and pouty faced with his curly blond hair drooping forward as he hung his head, watching Lila storm out of the hotel. It's adorably cute of him, leading me to quickly pull him in for a hug as I whispered to him. "It's not you... Trust me. Just give me a few hours with her, and by the end of the day, I'll have us both invited to her sci-fi night. And if I'm right, that will be way more fun than shopping."

That made him happy again, and I finally got my kiss before I rushed to follow after Lila.

We decided to catch a tram up through the city and went shopping in the arcades. We were careful and took the alleys to avoid the main streets. And Lila was even nice enough to stop at one of my favourite hairdressers, which just so happens to be not on the main streets at the other end of China town.

When we walked into the hairdressers, my friend, Becky - who is my favourite hairdresser was there. She already had a client with her, so we had to wait. But not before she stopped and marvelled at Lila's amazingly and ridiculously long white hair as it draped down past the base of her back. And just to rub it in, when Becky asked who Lila's hairdresser was, she replied, "It's naturally white," with the worst eye-rolling I've ever seen.

I mean seriously. - Can this woman be any more unsatisfied at the fact that she can change her hair colour with just a thought. - And I get the fact that there are moments when she can't control it, but still... it looks awesome.

As we sat in the waiting area, Lila and I flipped through the stack of magazines until I finally broke the pensive silence she was in. "You gave him the papers today, didn't you?"

She kept flipping through the magazine, and let out a great long breath then nodded, obviously not looking happy. But I have an idea about that.

"So, you're officially a free woman," I stated with a tentative grin.

Again Lila sighed. "Define a free woman when you need a bodyguard to buy pants and popcorn."

I leaned over the chair, hoping to get Lila's attention as I replied, "Good point... but in saying that, I have an idea to get you out of the moody funk you're in."

Still refusing to look at me, Lila just kept flipping through the magazine as she grumbled, "And what would that be?"

Wow. - Isn't she just a perky ray of sunshine today.

"Well..." I beamed with excitement. "It's a tradition when the women in my family get divorced to go all out with a complete make-over. So why not join in the fun... Go all out... with a new hairstyle and a completely new wardrobe. Then at the end of the night, we burn all your old clothes."

That last part caught Lila's attention, and I think she was trying to gauge if I was serious or not when she asked, "Just how many women in your family are divorced?"

My brows furrowed as I thought through the many numbers. "Pretty much all of them."

"Wow... that really sets the benchmark for you." She sniggered, and then very sternly looked at me as she added, "If that's the case... I just want to make sure you know... that if you break my brother's heart, you know exactly what I can and will do."

I grinned and nodded. "I know... so how about that make-over?"

She took one look at my eager and persistent smile then caved, agreeing to my insanity.

YES! – I got Lila to cave.

Becky put Lila in the chair first and coloured her hair with streaks of purple and green to break up all the white. – And to match the purple and green stone-vine bracelet that Terrence gave her. The colouring took a while because of how long her hair is, but I just know that when it's done, she is going to love it. Then when Becky finished putting my foils in to touch up my red streak, Lila dared me to go bold and add a second colour as well.

I chose blue. But as Becky went to the go make up the new colour dye, she stopped with a gasp. "Oh my gosh, I think next stores getting robbed."

I heard Lila sigh, listening to Becky's assistant gawking and stating the obvious, "We need to call the police."

And I may have grinned a little when Lila groaned, getting up from her chair to remove her protective apron. She then handed it to the assistant while politely pulling the broom from her hand.

"Can I borrow this?" she asked before snapping the head off the broom. But it wasn't like she was giving them a choice,

seeing how she was already walking out of the store and into the other store that was being robbed. - And she looked hilarious with the foils in the hair.

Becky glanced back at me and shrieked, "Should we go and help her?"

I shook my head, slouching back in the chair and kept grinning, "She'll be fine, just give her a minute."

Obviously, my casual attitude did not rub off on Becky as she looked back and gawked with her assistant through the window. They watched as Lila used the broomstick to knock one of the robber's guns out of his hand before hitting both of the robbers in the face with one swing of the broom-handle, causing them to fall to the floor unconscious.

Lila then used electrical cords to hogtie them together until the police arrive. And again, it looked hilarious - especially when Lila collected both of the guns and waved to the store owner before she walked back into the hair-dressers, placing the guns on the counter in front of her. - After she completely dismantled both of them. For everyone's safety of course. - Then with a grunt in her voice, she handed the broom handle back to Becky before sitting back down in the chair.

"Feel better?" I casually asked, still flipping through the magazines.

I could tell Lila was grinning just a little as she buried her nose in her magazine again and mumbled, "Not really."

All of a sudden, Becky had a whole new level of respect for Lila and was super helpful as well. I wasn't sure if it was because she was scared or a new admirer for Lila, but either way I'm absolutely positive that I'm going to need a new hairdresser after this.

After the hairdressers, I convinced Lila to take a gamble and buy a whole new wardrobe. So by close of business, we were carrying home a fruit-load of shopping bags. I even got

Lila to laugh. But I still hadn't managed to get her out of the gloomy mood she's still in. That is until we walked down the wrong alleyway to go home, only to be greeted by 2 Fire guardians, 2 Animal guardians, and 1 Land guardian who created a silver sword from the handful of coins she held in her hand.

Now that's cool.

I wasn't scared. I just grinned and commented, "This'll work... do you think you can take 'em?"

With angered determination, Lila dropped her shopping bags to the ground and retorted, "That's a stupid question."

She was so right. But one of the guardians had way too much confidence and scoffed, "You should give up while you can, girls. You're clearly out-numbered."

Muffling my laugh, I smiled and scoffed back, "Then I should warn you... you're fighting a girl who just got dumped."

Everything then went so fast as Lila moved at full-speed fighting all five guardians. I occasionally got a few hits in, but it was merely to throw them back into Lila's line of rage, all while I continued to talk to her.

"So do you think this will be enough to get you out of this moody funk?" I shouted over the fighting and in between punches.

"Since when are you so concerned about how I feel?" she bellowed back, knocking one of the guardians to the ground, unconscious with a nasty black eye.

"It's not just me. All of us are concerned," I shouted again, knocking the second one unconscious for her.

"What's there to be concerned about? I told you I was fine!" She vexed then turned to me and shouted, "Make yourself useful... in my bag there's four epi-pens."

"You know we should really create a name for this cure you've created?" I yelled back as I rummaged through her bag. I pulled out the epi-pens filled with the Neuritamine cure, injecting them into our unconscious new friends before I added, "And that is total bull, you're avoiding your emotions instead of dealing with them, and that fake smile you hide behind is not fooling anyone!"

The next thing I knew I was dodging a sword being thrown above my head and embedding itself into the wall behind me.

Okay. - Not entirely sure who threw it at this point.

"I'm not avoiding my emotions!" Lila yelled as I threw the last two epi-pens to her for her to inject them into the tiger and the oversized lion, causing them to fall to the ground and morph back to their naked human selves.

The last guardian, the cocky one, was a bit harder to take down. But Lila's cool leaf bracelet grew tendrils, trapping him where he stood. When suddenly, Alex and Terrence appeared at full-speed. Alex punched the last guardian in the face as Terrence quickly pulled an epi-pen from his pocket to inject into the guardian's shoulder. Then while still in a huff, Lila stood amongst the fallen guardians, now with a bruised cheek and cut lip, seething at me.

"I'm not avoiding my emotions," she grumbled.

I looked down to see Terrence's and Lila's matching stone-bracelets glowing as both Alex and he stood there in shock, hoping for some answers. But I wanted some answers of my own and I could tell I was getting through to Lila, so I snipingly questioned, "So tell me then, how did you cope with your fake father rising from the dead and beating the crap out of you? And how are you really coping with the divorce? And it would have been nicer for you to talk to your brother about this, instead of biting his head off like you did... I'm also curious what you're planning to do or say if Alex or Terrence want to know these answers as well. Or if heaven forbid, they want to ask you out on a date?!"

I peered back at Alex who looked like he was freaking out watching as Lila's eyes flickered black and her ears began to turn wolf-like as she growled, "What's your point?!"

So I very eagerly growled back, "My point is that the more people you push away, the harder it is for you to keep your guard up. Sooner or later you're going to get tired of fighting, and someone is going to break through that icy wall of yours, and there's a good chance you won't like who it is."

"That will never happen!" She growled again. "I don't feel anything for my fake father. I've always known he was a jerk. I got off that train a long time ago... And yes, I suck at being a sister, but I've only had 3 months to get used to the gig... And as for my relationship with Alex or Terrence, I trust both these men with my life, so yeah, I would trust them with my heart as well. But you are the last person I'd ever want to talk to about my divorce with, considering you were the one in bed with him!"

"And I said I was sorry!" I rebuffed.

"I know!" Lila shouted, raising her voice to match mine. "Everyone is always sorry, as if everything is miraculously fixed when you say it!"

Lila suddenly became so angry and wailed in frustration, running at full-speed to kick the concrete base of the street-lamp post, shattering it into rubble. In shock, she just stood there slightly out of breath then looked back at me and laughed, realising what I had done.

"Okay. Now I feel better... Thanks."

Yes! – Another win for me.

This time with a genuine smile, Lila happily turned to Alex and Terrence, who were still confused at the sight of her and still wanting answers.

"Lila, please tell me you didn't go looking for trouble," Alex worriedly begged.

She chortled at his question while dragging the unconscious guardians to the side of the alley to rest them up against the wall. Then as Lila pulled out the sword that was embedded in the wall, she replied, "What are you talking about, Alex...? Trouble always finds me."

Alex looked across at the guardians as they began to stir awake then back at Lila's fresh bruises and the smile across her face, shaking his head in bewilderment. "I don't think that's something to be happy about."

It didn't stop her from giggling as Lila gave both Alex and Terrence a kiss on the cheek as she explained, "I'm happy because I know you two will always be there for me, if and when the trouble does find me."

Very briefly, I noticed Alex and Terrence grin at that answer, watching as Lila turned to help two of the guardians to their feet.

Oh Gosh. - Those two are both so into that girl that it's hilarious watching them fight their urges.

Lila grunted as she held up the two barely conscious, naked animal guardians, taking Terrence's jacket from him to wrap around one of them while giving her jumper to the other. She then instructed Alex and Terrence to help with the last three. And I already had my priorities, gathering up the shopping bags before we raced back to the hotel with our new guardian friends in tow.

Once we had the new guardians safe at the hotel, and appropriately dressed, we left them in Chase's and my dad's very capable hands as Alex, Terrence, and me followed Lila up to her apartment to watch sci-fi movies all night with Tyme and Matt. But things may have gotten a little more out of hand than I expected. Because we ended up burning all of Lila's old clothes, and surprisingly Matt helped. - I think the night ended up being very therapeutic for both of them.

Journal entry continued by Lila Winters

I woke up at the standard time of 4am. – Well, for me anyway. And to be honest, the sight I woke up to had me laughing on the inside. We'd all fallen asleep watching Star Trek: The Original's marathon, and both Alex and Matt had fallen asleep holding the popcorn bucket. I had fallen asleep snuggled up next to Terrence as he took up the length of the couch with his arms wrapped around me, and Adela was snuggled up next to Tyme. – And they are just so cute together.

Oh frac.

As I glanced around the apartment, I realised the travesty of the entire night, and that was the sight of all my old clothes in the fire-pit on the balcony outside, completely burnt to ash. – And I mean _all_ of them. – I brushed my hands through my hair, remembering that I had promised to train Billy this morning. Then I looked back to see all the many shopping bags left at the apartment door, praying that Adela had the foresight to buy me some bathers.

It turns out she did, just not my usual style bathers. But it's what I have, so I got changed and quietly made my way down to the pool room where Billy was already waiting for me. He looked a little nervous as he waited by the pool. Then when I walked in, his mouth dropped open, and his brows raised an inch as he stared at my new white two-piece bikini that did the cool criss-cross thing around my hips – which I think was the only reason why I liked them.

Mental note. – Never go shopping with Adela when you're in a 'moody funk' as she puts it.

"Wow. New... new bathers?" he stuttered with a slight grin.

"Yeah." I awkwardly played with my fingers. "Adela found out that I was officially a free woman yesterday, and thought it was the perfect excuse for me to get my hair done and buy a whole new wardrobe... And then she burned everything else while my ex-husband helped... Not that I had much to burn... Most of my clothes were torn or blood-stained."

Aw Frac. – I'm rambling, and I'm probably scaring the poor man. – And Billy probably doesn't even care either.

"A free woman?" Billy puzzled and shook his head. "Um... when did you get divorced?"

Huh? – Maybe he does care.

I walked over to put my gym bag and towel down next to his, about to answer his question. But he quickly stopped me as he appeared next to me, pulling my face up to look at the now fading bruise and tiny cut on my bottom lip.

"Should I ask?" He looked concerned while gently tapping on my lip.

I cheekily grinned, pulling my chin away from his hand. "Just ran into some hunters while shopping yesterday. But I won and they're now on their way back to their homes and families... And as for the divorce... um... Matt asked for a divorce the day I left for Canada. So technically, I've been a 'free woman' since then. But... it was a long time coming before that."

His brows furrowed and he looked really sad. But he also noticed I was holding back tears, so he moved closer to rest his hand on my arm. "Lila... we don't have to do this if you're not up for it."

"No, I'm okay." I sniffled, wiping the tears away to smile at him. "This is actually the first time I've been able to talk about it with someone... I mean the rest of the team knows. But they found out before I was ready to actually tell anyone, so they've been kind of walking on eggshells around me for the last few weeks... Which only made it more awkward. I don't even know why I'm talking to you about it."

"Maybe... it's because you like me," he cheeked with a brazen grin.

"Maybe." I tittered as I shook my head. "Are you ready?"

With a smile, Billy nodded then followed me to the opposite side of the pool where I explained, "First we're going to practice out of the water, so just do what I do."

I stood at the edge of the pool and knelt down into a runner's start position then waited for Billy to copy before I added, "Now, you need to focus all the energy you have in your body and push it down to your feet. Then when you're ready, jump to the other side."

After taking a deep breath, I jumped to the other side of the pool, landing on the ledge where I waited for Billy to copy. And he did, taking a deep breath in before he jumped with all his might to the ledge next to me. But not quite. His feet landed on the corner of the ledge, and it caused him to lose his balance, falling back towards the water.

I reached out and grabbed his hand before he fell too far, pulling him up towards me and holding him close for him to gain his bearing. – Oh Wow. – I'd forgotten how tall he is until now. I could feel his chin gently brushing against my forehead when his eyes darted down to the water, and then to me as he thanked me, leading me to nod with a demanding smile.

"Again."

We took it in turns, jumping from one side of the pool to the other. Then after more than a dozen times of success, we moved on to landing in fight mode. Each taking turns to jump to the other side of the pool to fight the other, both trying to tap each other's shoulders.

Alright yeah. — I'm actually starting to have a lot of fun with him.

When Billy was confident enough, we took the lesson into the water and swam to the base of the pool together. But it took Billy a bit more time, because he struggled with the concept of breathing out as much air as he could in order to sink to the bottom. He eventually got the idea, when he finally planted his feet at the base of the pool next to me. Then we both pushed to the surface of the water at full-speed, landing on the ledge of the pool next to each other.

Still at full-speed, I moved to kick Billy in the chest, but he caught my foot mid-swing again and held it there as I ordered, "Remember to think about what your next move will be. And it needs to be something your attacker will never expect to come from you... For example, right now, my next move would be to use your hand as an anchor, spinning my other foot up to kick you in the back of the head and complete the turn, thus freeing my currently caught foot."

Billy stared at me, amazed and stunned, pausing for a moment, almost as if he were contemplating wanting to see that. Instead he mumbled, "Alright then."

His eyes suddenly glowed a fiery red while holding tight to my foot, and steam began to evaporate off Billy's body before he turned to push us both back into the pool. Then as we landed in the water, his body glowed a vibrant red, heating the pool and causing the room to become filled with steam.

With a massive grin on my face, I swam to the surface of the water along with Billy, and breathed in the humid warm air while laughing at his interesting counter move.

"Okay... I wasn't expecting that."

I miserably failed to stop my giggles as I waded around, enjoying the now pleasantly hot water. It kind of felt like we were in a spa, and I let out a relaxing breath when Billy randomly grabbed hold of my hand, pulling me closer to press his lips against mine. His lips were incredibly soft, and they lingered in the very long, very steamy kiss with his hands curled around my wrist and waist. Then when he let go, he pulled away to look at me, and I really didn't know how to feel.

He nervously stared at me, waiting for a reaction. And to my surprise, I copied him. I wrapped my arms around his shoulders, running my hands up into his dark wavy hair to kiss him back just as passionately, loving the tender feel of his lips on mine as I deepened the kiss.

My body tensed, and I groaned with pleasure as I felt his hands trace the length of my back. Then in the heat of the moment, I pulled him closer, pressing my chest against his very muscly and well-defined body to continue the kiss. – And damn he's a good kisser. He was even mindful about the cut in the corner of my bottom lip, favouring the other side.

Eventually I pulled away to breathe, and he confusedly smiled at me, briefly glancing at my legs that somehow became locked around his waist and still aren't moving.

His lips slowly tilted up on one side, and he sounded impressed. "Okay... I wasn't expecting that."

Frac – neither was I.

"I… have to go." I mumbled in a confused panic, and then raced out of the pool at a ridiculously fast speed. And it wasn't until I was in the elevator that I stopped to take another breath. I felt hot. I felt out of sorts, and I felt very, very confused as I held my bottom lip and gasped, "What the hell just happened?"

CHAPTER 3

Murder Mystery

Journal entry by Tyme Knight

These last three months living at the hotel have been amazing. I now have a sister, who is awesome and teaches me how to be awesome as well. And last Saturday we had a second sci-fi marathon, but it was just Lila and me with her husband Matt. – I mean ex-husband. – That Saturday we stayed up all night watching Lila's favourite superheroes, like Superman and Wonder Woman. But it was hilarious when there was an epic fight scene, because Lila would always scrutinize how it could have been done better or how the story was unrealistic.

That, and she apparently hates the two-minute-kiss scenes. – The one where the world is falling apart around them, but the hero still has this imaginary two minutes of not dying while kissing someone they barely know. – I tried to speculate that maybe they might have been Time guardians like me, but she didn't buy that one.

Today is going to be pretty amazing as well because Lila has agreed to go out to lunch with me, and I'm going to officially introduce her to my dad. – Our dad, William. He's been staying in my apartment since... well, since Terrence let him out of the tree he trapped him in on New Year's Day. – Which I'm still really pissed at him about. And Lila got upset at him too but understood Terrence's reasoning. Neither of them would tell me why, just that Terrence was protecting Lila, and that was apparently a good enough excuse for my dad, so I'm going to accept it.

It's currently the early hours of the morning and as I lay in the bed trying to sleep, I was abruptly roused by Adela sleeping next to me. She was having what looks like a horrific nightmare, screaming, "No... please... No!" with her hands out in front of her. And for some reason, she was struggling to breathe with strands of her long brown hair sticking to her sweaty cheeks and neck.

Strange??

I called her name and tried to gently shake her awake, and when she finally did wake up, the bed was covered in ice with her just about to throw an ice shard at the wall.

"ADELA!" I screamed, breaking her out of her trance.

She looked over at me as I knelt amongst the ice that had accumulated on the bed then she broke into tears. So I shuffled closer to comfort her. "Hey, just breathe, okay... It was just a dream."

But with a heavy breath, she shook her head and pulled away from me, fearfully saying, "No, that wasn't a dream." Then she rushed out of the apartment.

I followed Adela through the hotel and into the elevator as she explained, "I've had this kind of dream before when Lila was missing last year and had fallen into the ocean... At first, I thought it was Lila's ghost coming back to haunt me, but it was more than that."

I wasn't sure what to say, and I just looked at her while still stunned and half asleep then looked at my watch, realising it was 3 in the morning. Yet the early hour did not affect Adela as she went on to explain how all guardians have the ability to communicate through their element if they were strong enough and knew how to.

"Wait... So your saying Lila's a Water guardian?" I asked while trying to rub the sleep from my eyes. Again, Adela just looked at me in silence until I asked with more seriousness. "Wait... is she? How could she not tell me this?"

I was baffled and slightly annoyed, causing Adela to move closer to me when she noticed me pouting. "Tyme, your sister's a hybrid with more than one element... The more elements she reveals to people, the more she's deemed as either a threat or a more valuable target... Don't take it personally. She's just trying to protect you. The only reason I know is because she accidentally made it snow while she was training on the roof-top garden a few months ago."

Damn. – I feel gutted. – I can't believe my sister's keeping secrets from me.

I was still in a bit of a trance when I followed Adela towards Lila's apartment, and she banged loudly on the door. It wasn't long before Lila yanked open the door, half asleep and still in her pyjamas, griping, "What the frac, guys... You know, I don't wake up for another hour."

"Wait, you wake up at 4am?" I gasped in more confused shock.

Letting out a sigh, Lila gently rubbed the sleep from her eyes as she watched Adela barge through her door, straight past her to rush into Lila's study.

"Well, good morning to you too," Lila sarcastically grumbled with a slightly fatigued smile on her face. Then she looked back at me and properly smiled, opening the door further to let me in. "Good morning, Little Brother."

Wrapping her arm around me, Lila commented on my cute pyjamas. Smiling because they're the pyjamas that she had bought for me. – In my favourite color blue. – She then pulled in for a side cuddle while resting her sleepy head on my shoulder as we walked back to the loungeroom to sit. And while she got comfortable, I brushed some of the hair out of Lila's face and commented on the color. – Very much liking the purple and green streaks to break up the lack of color.

"So... still got the white hair."

"Yep." She pouted then clapped her hands, causing the overhead lights to turn on as she replied, "And I don't think it's going away anytime soon... Turns out living with your ex is harder than it sounds."

With a yawn, Lila laid her head back down on my shoulder and closed her eyes, still taking those last few minutes to fully wake up. I love that she's so comfortable around me like this, but I also want to confront her about not being honest with me. – The problem is I don't think 3am is really the best time for that. So I let Lila rest, and she snuggled into me while we waited for Adela. – And we waited for a while, with me and Lila almost falling asleep on the couch.

"Tyme," Lila whispered, sounding nervous. "Can I tell you something, and you promise not to judge me or react weirdly. And promise not to tell anyone else."

Oh my gosh. – She wants to be honest with me.

I quietly agreed then listened to her very sleepily whisper, "Billy kissed me last Tuesday, and... I kissed him back."

"Okay?" I mumbled, very surprised at that secret, and can understand why she wants me to keep it. But I thought I'd question, "So... did you like it?"

Before Lila could answer, Adela hurriedly emerged from the study, carrying the stack of missing guardian files with her. She placed them down on the coffee table, fully gaining the attention of both me and my still snuggly sister, causing Lila to begrudgingly sit up properly. She then leaned forward and grumbled, "Adela it's 3.30 in the morning… What is this about?"

"Somebody's been murdered," Adela stated.

"In the hotel?" Lila worriedly questioned with her body becoming tense as she looked back at me, and I shrugged my shoulders, feeling just as clueless.

"No. I don't know where, but I know who she is," Adela replied, continuing to look through the folders at the profile pictures.

Lila yawned again, confusedly staring at the folders. "Adela, that's the stack of rescued guardians… Are you saying someone we rescued has been murdered?"

There was an eerie silence as Adela peered up quickly at Lila then went back to searching the files as she explained, "I had a vision of someone being drowned… She was being held under the water by a dark shadow… But I've seen the victim before. I remember her."

She then stopped and jumped victoriously handing a folder to Lila. "That's her. That's the woman I saw."

Still slightly sleepy and sceptical, Lila opened the file and leaned back on me so I could read it as well. It was one of the guardians we rescued from Canada. – Lauren Bithol. She came back with us to Melbourne because she had family on this side of the world.

"Adela, are you sure she was drowned," Lila asked while reading through the profile info.

Seeming nervous and tense, Adela became insistent. "Positive, I know what I saw."

I tilted my head forward to look at Lila's puzzled face and asked, "Why, what's wrong?"

She glanced up at me still puzzled. "Lauren Bithol is a Water guardian. Why would she drown? Not only that Lauren was really strong in her element. Stronger than you, Del. It doesn't make sense for The Board to kill her... she's more valuable to be recollected."

Adela became more agitated, probably scared Lila wasn't believing her. But Lila sighed and stood to her feet, handing the folder back to Adela. "Well, it says here her family lives out in Blackburn. If you want, we can do a house call... check everything's okay?"

That seemed to have made Adela happy and she nodded her head as she hugged Lila, thanking her before she took slow calming breaths. As Adela calmed, I spotted Lila's eyes glowing a beautiful golden colour. Then when Lila let her go, Adela was almost calm again.

"Lila, you know you're not supposed to use your animal thing on me," Adela griped.

Lila's eyes glowed a shade of gold again, looking directly into Adela's eyes. "Adela it's almost 4 in the morning, and your freaking out has caused a thick cloud of fog over the city to the point where I can't see the building next to us... Now if you want us to make it to Blackburn in one piece, you're gonna need to calm down... And if you don't do that, I can always convince your mind that you need to hibernate instead."

Begrudgingly, Adela rolled her eyes and started taking more calming breaths as she walked back out of the apartment to go get ready. All the while Lila walked out onto the balcony. She was there for a mere few seconds when suddenly the fog cleared up, revealing the city night lights of Melbourne again.

Woah. – That was... cool.

I heard Lila yawn again, disappearing at half-speed into her room, and then reappeared dressed and ready to go in her new yoga pants and a long knitted red skivvy, applying the last of the foundation crème onto her face and hands to cover the visible scars. – They're not as bad as they once were. Most of the scars have faded to a pale white, but I know why she covers them. – It helps the other staff and hotel guests feel more comfortable around her, which I find both sad and admirable at the same time.

She stood in the loungeroom and ran her hands through her long hair while she stretched out her body, and in being a kind brother I stood up and started to make us a tomato and cheese toastie to share. As I pulled out the ingredients from the refrigerator, I noticed she was slightly more awake than before, so I started talking in the hopes to spark up a conversation about her secret abilities.

"I didn't know you could do that."

"Do what?" Lila puzzled, smiling back at me when she realised what I was making.

"Well, getting Adela to hibernate for one, and you just made the fog disappear."

She sat down at the kitchen bench, staring at me with a little smile. "Um... for one, I can't make people hibernate... Our kind don't produce enough of the hibernation protein in order for it to actually be effective. It would have taken me hours at best to get her to just sleep... And as for the fog, I thought you already knew I was a Water guardian... Remember I accidentally made it rain when you took me sightseeing in New York."

Oh Right. – I actually didn't know it was her when that happened. – Huh? – Maybe she's not keeping secrets from me after all.

I finished making the toastie and broke it in two, handing one half to her as I stood on the opposite side of the bench. But she then looked at me curiously.

"What?" I asked.

"You're mad at me... Why?"

"How could you possibly know that?" I replied, a little squeamishly.

In seconds, she appeared standing in front of me with a cocky grin, and glowing gold and green eyes as she whispered, "Because of what I am, silly brother."

She stayed staring at me for a few more seconds then stood back with realization across her face, and her grin completely gone. "That's why you're mad at me... You're mad at me because of what I am."

I looked at the ground in a sense of frustration at the fact that she could so easily read me.

What else can she do? – Damn it! – Why am I even thinking this way.

I didn't know what to say, and she looked like I'd hurt her or like I was judging her. And I wasn't or at least I'm not trying to. But I need to say something. – Anything.

"There's just a lot about you that I don't know." I pouted.

Seriously? – That was the best I could think of? – Come on, Tyme, suck it up.

There was a moment of very tense silence until Lila smiled back at me. "Isn't that the whole reason why you're here... to get to know me? I mean I know you originally came here looking for your dad and that I was a happy extra, but—"

"No, Lila, please don't think of it that way," I pleaded as I held her hands.

"Why not...?" she rebutted a little defensively.

Um? – I don't think this is going well for me. – Especially because she's moving away from me as she speaks.

"Tyme, you've known about me longer than I have. And yeah, I'm not knocking the fact that since we've met, you've been an awesome brother... Saving my life gives you a lot of brownie points. But it's been over three months... And now, the moment I finally start feeling comfortable around you to be who I really am, you're afraid."

Oh Crap. – I've done this all wrong. She's only known me for three months, and I'm angry that she hasn't told me all of her deep dark secrets. – What the hell's wrong with me?

"I'm sorry," I whispered.

Great. – I made my sister cry. – 4am in the damn morning and I made her cry.

She turned away from me, leaning on the other bench, trying to compose herself. Then eventually, she sniffled. "I know you're sorry... because I can sense that, and I'm sorry about that... If you want, I don't have to use my abilities around you anymore... If that makes you feel more comfortable."

What! – No.

That is not at all what I want, so I moved closer, wrapping my arms around her. And I am not letting her out of this hug until I have the chance to explain. "No. Lila, that's not what I meant. I want to know more about you...Ugh... I want to know what you are...Ugh... I'm mad because you don't talk to me about this part of your life... and I desperately want to be a part of it."

I felt Lila's body start to relax in my hug, and I'm pretty sure she could sense that I was genuine in my plea, because she happily returned the hug then stayed in my arms while we both finished our toastie-halves.

"Okay." She whispered and looked up at me with a smile. She then darted to the apartment door and held it open for me, now with a cheeky grin again. "Come on, your girlfriend's waiting for you. And I think she's expecting you to be dressed."

"She's not my girlfriend." I sighed, following Lila out the door, curious as to why she just abruptly stopped the conversation and our hug.

I felt confused, but before Lila closed the apartment door, she quickly stopped me and held her hand up towards the roof of the apartment. As she did, the light in the apartment was absorbed into her hands, leaving the apartment dark again.

Holy Crappers – She's a guardian of electricity too.

Lila turned back to see my amazement, and with a grin, she winked before walking into the elevator. "Tyme, just some sisterly advice for you... If you're sleeping in the same bed as someone, you should really define the relationship first."

Ah, sisterly advice. – Why does she have to be so awesome?

Journal entry insert by Lila Winters

We decided to drive out to Blackburn, instead of run. But by the time Adela, Tyme, and I got to Lauren's house, there was already a police car parked outside. And because we drove Adela's blue Lamborghini, I thought it would be best not to park right outside and draw unwanted attention to us. Instead, Adela parked down the street and we walked.

We stood opposite the house when we saw two police officers standing at the door, talking to Lauren's parent.

"You were right, Del," Tyme whispered.

We had to stop for a minute and keep a distance when I realised my old – yet newly rekindle friend, George Nell was the lead detective on the case.

"Fruits," Adela mumbled. "I was really hoping I was wrong... Hey, what's George doing here? I thought he was in the Melbourne district."

I had to shush my brother and Adela while I tried to listen in to George's conversation. But it was hard to do that over the surrounding noise of trucks and cars passing us on the street.

"Is there any reason as to why your daughter was out so late?" George asked.

Mr Bithol shook his head. "No, but she's been acting really strange since she got back from her missionary work in North America."

"What do you mean by that?" George added.

"I think she was paranoid... And so was her mother," Mr Bithol replied. "Her mother's name is Karen. We never married... And they were both doing missionary work in North America, but Karen never came back. The last time Karen called, Lauren kept mumbling something about the guardians and that we all had to be careful about who we talk to."

Oh Frac.

George stopped his questions there, staring up at the man who was still trying to comfort his wife, and then repeated in almost disbelief, "Guardians?"

He began to look around and peered over his shoulder to see me, still watching from the distance on the other side of the road. But before he could turn to walk over to me, Adela and Tyme had pulled up in the Lamborghini for me to get in, sending a text message to George as we drove off that read: "Golden Arches."

I waited in the car park of the Blackburn McDonald's, leaning on the hood of Adela's shiny blue sports car. And the looks I got from people walking past were quite obviously impressed, especially the teenagers who were supposed to be on their way to school but were stopping in for a morning snack.

A dark-grey unmarked police car pulled up in the car park next to me, and George stepped out of the car, shaking his head as he leaned on the bonnet beside me.

He glanced back at Adela and Tyme who were having a late breakfast and coffee inside the store while keeping a watchful eye on me from the window.

"Please tell me you were just out on a morning stroll," George sarcastically questioned yet almost sounded hopeful.

I peered across to him, arching a brow and replied just as sarcastic, "In Blackburn?"

"Lila, this is serious. Can you tell me where you were last night?" he demanded, turning his body to face me.

Ah right. – He's jumping straight into the interrogation mode. Still, I'm happy to play by his rules, so I very calmly replied, "Trust me, George, it wasn't me or my team."

He groaned, clearly annoyed at me. "I'm trying to trust you, Lila... But you don't make it easy for me when you don't tell me about these... guardian things."

I sat back and thought for a second with a slight grin at the irony. "You know surprisingly I had a similar conversation with my brother this morning."

He shook his head in a huff, refusing to react to the pleasantries of this conversation, so I went back to playing by his rules and got straight to business. "I need to know what happened to Lauren... And before you ask, yes, she was one of us."

George stayed quiet for a few moments of thoughtful contemplation then eventually broke. "Her body was found this morning at Albert Park, back in the city... There was no bruises or injuries or any sign of a struggle. The coroner thinks it's an accidental drowning or suicide... But I'm guessing you're here to tell me otherwise."

"She was a Water guardian," I replied.

"And what does that mean?" He rolled his eyes in a huff.

Wow. – He is definitely not a morning person.

Still, I replied, "It means she had the ability to control and manipulate the water around her. The elements don't usually work against their guardians... Not unless they're told to."

"Oh gosh... you make it sound like the water has feelings." He sniggered. Then he looked at me and waited for me to respond, but I didn't because his statement was true — but not relative to the problem. So he huffed again. "That still doesn't explain why you're here or how you knew she was dead."

I stood to my feet, glancing around to do a quick sweep of the car park then whispered, "Adela had a vision of Lauren in trouble this morning. She was being held underwater by someone. The only reason we're here is because we may be responsible for the danger she was put in."

While still scanning the perimeter, I pulled out two pieces of paper with a list of all the guardians we had rescued that currently reside in Australia. I then explained, "That is a list of the guardians we rescued on our previous mission that have either been sent home to their families or relocated. Lauren was one of them."

George took a moment to read through the list but then fell eerily quiet, looking something up on his phone before he worriedly sighed. "Then we have a problem."

With a growing concern, he handed me back the list and started pointing to names, explaining, "Kirsten Brooks, she was on the news on Sunday, died in a suspicious house fire in Sydney... Paul Watson was attacked by a shark while surfing on the Gold Coast... and Luke Salders died in a car accident caused by a minor land slide on the Hume Highway. And all of these deaths occurred in the last two weeks."

In the background, I heard Tyme's voice whisper, "They're being hunted... but they're not collecting them."

Aw Frac. — This is definitely not good.

I looked back at Tyme through the McDonald's window, and then down at the ground to try and think through our options.

"Oh... no," George worriedly sighed, pulling away from the car and standing defensively. "I know that look. No, Lila. Just no... Now I know I have no hope in stopping you with whatever it is you have planned, but I need this one to go by the book."

He took a moment, scratching his head before he reluctantly asked, "I want you to work with me on the case."

Well, that's a new one.

His demand was not expected, and it led me to question, "You want me to help you investigate?"

I honestly think he's lost his marbles, and to make things worse, Tyme was still talking to me through the window, loudly disagreeing with the idea, making it hard for me to listen to two conversations at once.

"Yes." George nodded. "But we do this my way, and you follow my orders... Please."

He stared at me, looking very agitated as if he were preparing to fight me on this until his last breath. But in being in a cooperative and friendly mood, I replied, "Okay."

And just to put me in a sour mood because I really can't stand that whole talking in unison thing, it gets worse when three people do it, as George, Tyme, and Adela all gasped, "What?" With some being louder than others.

Ouch!!!

I held my ears in a bit of pain, glaring back at Tyme while replying to George. "George... this isn't like finding a missing person like my team is used to. My kind are being hunted but not to be collected... There being slaughtered by their own elements... Guardian or not, the faster these killers are caught, the safer everyone will be. And I'd be wasting time arguing with you about this... Chances are the killer has already chosen their next target."

I was on a train of thought, but I could sense my brother's disgruntled mood from here. So when I turned back to look at Adela and Tyme, who both obviously did not seem overly confident with the plan as they frowned at me through the window, I griped back at them, "We don't have a choice... Del, call the team, let them know what's going on... and tell them to use security code C."

In confusion, George gawked at me then looked back through the McDonald's window at Adela and Tyme as they nodded while preparing to leave.

"They can hear you from out here?" he questioned in shock.

"Yes," I answered then continued to talk as I climbed into George's car. "George and I will head up to Albert Park to check out the crime scene. Adela, drop your car back at the hotel and meet us there... Remember code C."

"Understood," Adela replied from the front seat of her car, causing George to jump at the sight of her sudden appearance. – And Tyme also appearing next to Adela probably didn't help his confusion.

I'm also getting the slight feeling that George is still trying to get used to me, because I heard him as he got into his car, mumbling under his breath, "This chick's freaky as hell."

I'm assuming he still hasn't figured out that I can hear him, so I stayed quiet as he drove back to the city, mumbling to himself.

Journal entry continued by Tyme Knight

This is a very stupid idea. But I know I have no hope in convincing my sister not to involve the human detective. And when we arrived at Albert Park, Adela made me promise to follow the rule of code C. – That means no super-powers in public or where any human might see us.

We stood under a picnic gazebo on the other side of the lake to Lila, trying to keep a distance, and we listened in as the detective led Lila along the running track and then stop at a grassy area that is now muddy and swamp-like.

"This is where we found her," the detective stated.

Lila scanned around the area and asked, "Do you know what she was doing out here?"

He shook his head. "Her father said she left the house around 6pm last night but didn't say where she was going."

"What was she wearing when you found her?"

The detective then pulled up a photo from the iPad he was carrying, and stated, "Here... She was wearing her sports gear... Most likely going for a run."

As we sat listening to Lila and the detective's conversation, Adela noticed that I was impatiently tapping my fingers on the picnic table, and have looked at my watch for like twentieth time.

"Is there somewhere you need to be?" she queried.

"No." I pouted. – Because it was so not true.

Adela chuckled, realising exactly why I was moody, other than the fact that I woke up at 3am. "That's right... You and Lila were supposed to meet up with your dad today, weren't you?"

She laughed even harder when she pointed out my nose crinkling. – Apparently it looks cute. – That, and my sister does the same thing. But her laugh is not helping my mood, so I sat back and sulked. Leading Adela to highlight, "Tyme, you know she's never going to accept him if you keep forcing the issue."

That's easy for her to say. – She has a dad. – Meanwhile my dad's cooped up in my apartment, moping because he feels like a screw-up.

"Hey, here's an idea, what if you talk to her for me," I pitched with a hopeful grin.

She cocked her head, staring at me in disbelief. "Are you serious?"

"Yeah." I nodded, continuing the pitch. "Look, you've met my dad. He even cooks your favourite dinner when you stay over. You could tell Lila that he's not a bad guy and that all he wants is a chance."

Unfortunately, Adela didn't go for it and she shot me down. "Tyme, as your friend... I have to step in here... play it smart and don't force the issue. Think about it... It's only been a few months and already she treats you like you've always been her little brother. Falling asleep on your shoulder and everything... She even lectured me to be nice to you while we have our little fun."

Little fun?

Great. – It seems Adela and I are just friends with benefits and not anywhere close to boyfriend and girlfriend like my loving sister thought we were. – And I kind of did as well. But hearing that made me more moody, and I sat in a silent sulk again when Alex and Terrence strolled up in a fairly obvious mood as well.

"Finally." Adela griped at them in a huff. "It took you guys long enough. What did you do, stop for ice cream or something?"

"Mmm, ice cream," Alex sneered back in a temper. "Now there's a good idea, and it's probably been the only good one you've had all morning."

"Alex, be nice." Terrence sighed but had to step away when he received a phone call.

It only gave Alex clear ability to arc up. "No... Screw being nice. You guys let Lila join an investigation to find a murderer who is... as you so casually put it on the phone <u>HUNTING</u> us! Have you lost your freaking mind? She's a sitting duck over there."

"Oh, and like you would have been able to stop her!" Adela shouted back.

"No!" Alex also shouted while pointing to Lila on the other side of the lake. "But I wouldn't be stupid enough to let her do it on her own!"

"HEY!" Terrence shouted to get all of our attention. "Lila's on the phone. She needs Adela's help... and she also says... Alex, stop being a fraccing ass, please."

Instead of being an ass, Alex silently fumed, leaning on the table as Adela made her way around the lake. But I swear that picnic table nearly snapped in two when Alex saw Billy walking up to stand next to Lila.

Wow. – Now that is a jealous man. – Glad I'm not telling him what happened last Tuesday.

Journal entry insert by Lila Winters

I don't think George is happy that I travel with an entourage. But considering it's my kind being hunted, I want us to be together if and when everything goes sideways.

"George, I want you to meet Billy. He was in... er... a similar situation to Lauren, and were both... from the same site," I explained. – And Frac did I sound cagey.

I heard Billy titter under his breath, glancing at me as he shook George's hand to greet him. But then George got straight down to the questions.

"So did you know the victim or were you just... well, you know?"

Billy glanced at me again to see if he should answer or not, so I nodded to him and added, "He knows." But I then pretended to canvas the area as I whispered under my breath, "Not everything... just what we are and what I do... to a certain point."

In hearing that, Billy answered, "Yes, I knew Lauren. She was on the same... training round as me."

While George continued to coax around for more background information, I noticed something in one of the nearby puddles that was beginning to dry up. It had some broken twigs crushed into what looks like a partial boot print.

"Hey, Billy," I called. "Do you think you could discreetly dry this out for me?"

I pointed to the puddle of water, and he placed his hand on the ground next to the water. His hand glowed just a little, causing the puddle to evaporate, revealing a clear outline of a large boot print all while George watched on, completely fascinated.

"How the hell did he do that?" he queried.

"George, now is not the time to play twenty questions. We have a killer to catch," I replied in the hopes of speeding this conversation up. Preferably before Alex pops a muscle in his neck while grinding his teeth way too hard.

Frac damn. – He sounds so loud in my ears.

George held up his iPad to take a photo of the boot print, and while he measured the length and depth of the boot print, he mumbled, "I'll need to send this to my team to profile. But from my guess... we're looking for a man's size 14 boot and weighs about 110 to 130 kilograms."

"No, that can't be right," Billy interrupted shaking his head. He then looked around at the park landscape, explaining, "Lauren was a fighter and a darn good one... She was also very quick on her feet. I don't think someone that big would have been able to catch her."

George huffed while looking up at Billy, still very sceptical as he crossed his arms. "Okay, what if she knew the guy and didn't think he was a threat?"

"Maybe," Billy replied. "What's more likely is someone was carrying her, and she was probably already dead at the time."

Well frac buckets. – George is now really sceptical and possibly suspicious of Billy, leading him to ask, "How could you possibly know that?"

As I nervously pulled the sleeve of my skivvy down to cover the fact that I was 'think fidgeting,' I noticed Billy staring at me with a grin. He looked me up and down then answered slightly distracted as he stared at me. "I don't know about you, but if I was going to kill somebody as strong and as fast as

Lauren, I wouldn't have done it in such a public place. Whoever did this wanted the body to be found."

"Like a trail of bread crumbs," I added, getting very worried that we had just stupidly walked into a trap. – Which would be very bad for Alex's over-protective ego. – And who I can clearly hear mumbling curse words under his breath because Billy keeps staring at me.

"Now who's reaching?" George scoffed as he watched Billy look for another puddle of water.

"Lila, how much do you weigh?" Billy asked as he randomly scooped me up into his arms.

Woah. – Here we go.

"Er...? I don't know... around 75...ish. Why?"

He carried me towards another puddle and replied as he walked through the middle of it, "Because, you and Lauren look to be about the same height and size."

He then put me down on the other side of the puddle before placing his hand down on the ground to evaporate the water, and reveal a very similar boot print right down to the size. "You're looking for another guardian... These boots were standard issue at Agro... I mean where Lila found us. There's just one problem," he noted, and walked back to the original boot print before continuing to explain, "Guardians who were trained by... eerr..." Again he hesitated, quickly looking back at me and shrugged. "You know who... are a hell of a lot stealthier than your average Joe. We wouldn't be stupid enough to walk through a puddle. So you're right, Lila, this hunter's leaving bread crumbs."

Well Frac. – That's just what I needed to hear. – NOT.

Finally, Adela made her way around the lake, walking up to stand next to me and complained while glaring directly at me. "Code C sucks. You know that, right?"

Now George was completely confused, looking at me for an explanation, so I added, "No super-moves unless absolutely necessary."

He nodded, looking like he agreed with the idea. So I thought it best to continue, "Del, I need more information on what you saw last night. You said before that Lauren was being held down, and you couldn't see the attackers face. But tell me about the water. Was it dark, muggy, clear? Did you see any plants or objects?"

She took a second to think back on her vision and replied, "Light. I saw a light, and the water looked clear and blue."

"Like a swimming pool?" George suggested.

"And I think we found our next bread crumb." I sighed before looking back at the Melbourne Sport and Aquatic Centre just across the park.

We started to walk towards the centre, and as we did, I heard Tyme sigh from across the lake, "And we're walking."

Yep. – I can just tell that my team is super excited about this idea. – NOT.

CHAPTER 4

When Life Hangs In The Balance

Journal entry by Billy Jonas

I'm really glad Lila called today, especially after what happened between us last week. And yeah, I know the circumstance right now isn't the best but being able to help and do something productive is really fun. – I was starting to lose my mind being cooped up in that hotel. Not that I'm knocking the freedom I get in return.

There's also the added benefit of spending time with Lila. And if I'm being honest, I haven't been able to stop thinking about our kiss all week, and I'm kind of hoping we can do it again. But I need to get the timing right, and solving a murder is probably not the best time to ask her out on a date.

"You didn't train in the pool this morning," I casually stated as I walked next to Lila toward the swimming centre.

"Eerr... Yeah. Adela and Tyme rocked up at my door at 3 this morning. So I'll have to train later tonight instead. You're welcome to join if you'd like."

"Really? And here I thought you might be avoiding me."

"Says you..." She peered up at me and smilingly shook her head. "My training schedule has not changed. Yet you seem to be entering the pool room just as I leave... So tell me, who's avoiding who."

Darn. – She had me there.

I looked around and walked a little slower, appreciating that she matched my speed to create some distance from George and Adela. Then I spoke at a soft whisper, not wanting Adela to hear our conversation. "I guess I was just worried. You looked a little freaked out last week... and... I didn't want you to tell me that it was a mistake. Or that you regret it."

She averted her gaze, also looking around before she spoke, "I don't regret anything... While yes it was unexpected, I had an amazing time last week. For the first time in a long time, I was able to just have fun and be myself... And you looked like you were having fun as well."

"I had a fantastic time, and I thoroughly enjoyed every second of it."

Her smile grew curious as she queried, "Then why are we whispering about it?"

Hmm? – A fair point.

Standing a bit taller, I peered up to where Adela and George were walking, and then back across the lake to where Tyme, Alex, and Terrence were walking. – With them needing to walk away from the swimming centre to get around the lake. I then sounded a bit coy when I spoke. "I may have noticed... that you have a few men in your life that are..."

"Over-protective?" She tried to finish my statement, and I nodded while trying not to tell her what I was really thinking, leading her to giggle as she agreed.

Darn, she has a cute laugh. – Don't do it, Billy. – Now's not the time to ask her out.

I cleared my throat and gave her a smile as I walked a little faster to catch up with her detective friend and Adela. When we had re-joined them, George continued to ask more questions, pretty good ones actually.

One of his questions caught me off guard, when George asked about the tribal marking I have on the side of my neck just behind my ear, commenting that it's the same marking as Lauren's. He then pointed out Adela's mark behind her ear before noting that he'd seen it on Alex and the others in the team as well.

I answered that it was a birthmark that all guardians get when they come of age. But when George glanced across to see Lila's neck, he asked, "Where's Lila's then."

Hmm? – That's odd. – She is definitely of age.

In my confusion, I stared at her neck, and without even thinking, I ran my fingers along the skin of her neck where the mark should be, assuming she had covered it with the foundation she was wearing to mask her scars. But there was nothing.

"I'm sorry to say this, Billy, but it's not a birthmark," Lila explained, sounding very apologetic as she moved her neck away from my hand. "It's actually a branding that The Board uses to discern whose guardian belongs to who... Not all guardians have that kind of mark though. Terrence and I were branded with something a little different. Not as visible but just as permanent and well known to The Board...When I married, I lost my original branding, so they branded me with the same mark you have. But during my escape from... eerr... where they held me, I managed to get rid of it. Although, I'm still trying to figure out how."

Ah-huh. – I'm feeling really cheesed off right now. – And I'm struggling to hold my temper.

My eyes glowed a fiery red as I tried to contain my fury of being branded like some farm animal. But I'm really struggling here. Then in my silent rage, I felt Lila's soft hand in mine, and all of a sudden I felt calm. I peered across to see her walking with me with her eyes glowing a strong gold to help keep me calm. – But to be honest, just her holding my hand did the job.

I think George realised that, that topic was a touchy one because Adela was also upset and self-conscious about the mark on her neck. Instead, George brought the subject back on to the investigation. "So if it's true that we're following a trail of bread crumbs... who were they left for? They can't have possibly known that you guys were going to be brought onto this case."

Lila sighed in deep thought while walking alongside me, still surprisingly holding my hand. "There are only two other rescued guardians who came back to Melbourne with us other than Billy. Do you really think they wouldn't have checked up on each other?"

"So what....? They were just throwing down the bread crumbs, hoping one of you would surface?" George asked cynically.

Oh Darn.

"SNIPER!" I shouted, quickly spotting the red laser brush across my face and then dodged at super-speed, pushing Lila away from me as we both watched a tranquiliser-dart race past me and into George's leg. – And holy darn crap. – We're in trouble now.

George fell to the ground and Adela moved to catch him, putting herself in the firing line and getting shot with a tranque dart as well. I looked across, amazed at how Lila acted as the distraction, dodging three more darts while I moved to pull Adela and George to safety. But I then heard the sound of a different weapon being fired. The sniper was clearly a Water guardian, because the next thing I saw was a shower of sharp ice crystals hurtling towards Lila.

She moved at super-speed to dodge them but didn't know where to go. So Lila flew up, jumping onto a huge spiral of leaves, and then plummeted past me to pull me up onto the leaves as well.

"You won't have much time!" she explained while focusing on raising the leaf platform higher. "When we reach the sniper's level, create a firewall and push him back."

In following her orders, I readied to do just that then as soon as we got high enough, I threw over a dozen fireballs, one after the other onto the roof of the swimming centre, creating a wall. And it worked. The shooting stopped and the ice crystals disappeared.

Unfortunately, Lila failed to mention that she got hit by one of the tranque darts before she created the platform, and was seconds away from falling unconscious. I didn't realise it until it was too late, and I watched in horror as she fell off the leaf platform, plummeting towards the ground when suddenly one of the nearby tree branches grew to catch Lila before she hit the cement.

She stayed awake just long enough to bring the leaf platform lower to the ground for me to jump off. Then she hung almost lifeless from the branch as it gently lowered her to the ground. I raced to see if Lila was okay, but I immediately eyed the blood on the cement where she fell and just knew the branch wasn't fast enough. I looked back to see if Adela and George were in a safe place, both still asleep, then I knelt down to inspect Lila, gently pulling her up to look for any injuries.

It was incredibly hard to breathe as I held her, and when I found it — damn it was bad. Lila had hit her head, and there was a large gash hidden amongst the white and green hair above her ear.

I still have that blue-rose epi-pen in my pocket that each of the team members were given just before we left the hotel. But I can't give it to her now. She would risk infection if the wound isn't cleaned first. Instead, I hurriedly scooped Lila up into my arms to carry her into the swimming centre, moving at super-speed to ensure no one would see us.

I am aware of the code C rule. — But I'm doing this. — And I'll apologise to her later.

When I eventually found the first aid room, I kicked open the doors and screamed at the first aider to get out as I carried Lila in, and I laid her down on the bed so that she was on her side. I then darted around the room to find the supplies I needed.

"Hold on, Lila... I got ya," I whispered, still struggling to breathe.

A commotion of people rushing past the first-aid room caught my attention, so I briefly peered out into the corridor to investigate before returning to my search. Apparently, the centre's being evacuated because a bomb threat had been called in. And it isn't a hoax because when I opened the supply cupboard to get some gauze, I found it. A bomb. – Poorly designed but still just as dangerous.

Okay, Billy. – Keep your cool. – You can do this.

My thoughts were a little distracted by the unconscious woman on the bed behind me. So to calm my nerves, I cleared my throat, trying to take a deep breath in as I carefully melted the plastic components of the time panel before melting down the electricals simultaneously. But as I took a moment to breathe out, I heard him. – The hunter, addressing me through the speaker-system, and it became clear that he was watching me through the security cameras.

"Well done, Billy... But you know there's more than one, don't you? You've seen them before... You could stop this whole place from going up in flames and save that pretty little thing on the table if you want... All you have to do is surrender. I'll be waiting by the blue water when you decide your fate."

While contemplating my lack of options, I stared back at Lila looking so beautiful and fragile as she slept, and instantly I knew what I had to do. Very carefully, I brushed the hair away from Lila's head wound, and cleaned it as fast as I could before injecting the epi-pen into her thigh. Then I kissed her forehead and whispered, "Thank you, Lila... For everything."

Journal entry insert by Alex Woods

By the time we had made it around the lake at our ridiculous human speed, things had gotten way out of hand. People were evacuating the swimming centre in a fraught state, and police cars were just arriving on the scene.

I raced over to where Adela and George were lying as Tyme darted around calling for Lila, and we could hear the desperation in his voice. He then called my name and appeared next to me at full-speed almost hyperventilating.

"Alex, there's tranquilisers everywhere, and I can't find Lila... And Terrence found blood on the cement."

Oh Crap. – I do not work well under pressure. – Not when the love of my life is missing. – Think, Alex, what would Lila do?

I quickly thought of an idea then ordered, "Tyme, insert your epi-pen into Adela's leg. Quickly, before the police arrive."

He fumbled around in his pocket to pull out the healing tonic, then pressed it into Adela's thigh. I did the same for the one I had into George's leg just seconds before a police officer stepped up behind us. We then discreetly put the epi-pens back in our pockets before stepping aside for the officer to call in an ambulance, and we continued to step away and regroup with Terrence.

I stared at the many people still racing out of the front entrance, and at the police officers standing by and assisting in the evacuation, quickly realising there was no way we'd be able to get into the building with-out anyone seeing us.

"Tyme, can you phase us?" I whispered.

He shook his head and became more frustrated. "Not without at least a dozen people noticing… And then you'd still have the issues with any closed doors."

Yep. – That won't work.

Instead we casually backed away from the building, ducking through the crowd in the hopes to find another way in. We raced around the back of the building to find the loading door, only to see it being guarded by over a dozen very obvious guardians. Mainly because I recognise some of them from the Agronomique's rescue op.

Damn. – They can't have possibly been collected this fast. – Could they?

"Err… I'll take the right and you take the left?" Terrence asked, glancing at me, hoping I'd know what to do.

And damn it, this is usually Lila's thing. – I really need to think. – Right, Lila usually tells me to trust my instincts, so I nodded to Terrence then shouted, "Tyme, take the strays and whatever you do, don't die!"

Journal entry continued by Billy Jonas

I was careful and slow as I opened the doors leading into the swimming pool, taking calming breaths all while trying to find the courage, not knowing what I was up against. As I stood by the pool-side, I scanned the area and found Nigel Thornsbury, a Water guardian I knew from Canada. He's old but he knows his way around the water, and I'm pretty sure he was also Lauren Bithol's elemental mentor. – That is before Lila's team pulled their rescue stunt and freed us all.

He sat up in the spectators stand, resting his hand on one of the many active bombs. – On my way into the pool room, I spotted 16 more bombs, all with a remote detonator, and I'm going to assume the remote is the one he's clutching in his hand.

"Nigel... Should have known it was you... Are you here to kill me?" I queried while weighing up what my next potential options would be.

Yet he shook his head disappointingly. "Once again you fail to see the bigger picture, Billy... I'm not here to kill you. I'm simply sending a message."

"A message...? To who? These people have done nothing," I replied, slowly inching towards him.

"Exactly..." He stood to his feet and seethed, "They have done nothing! All while the governments of this world lie to them... And they will not stop hunting us until we are all mindless drones or dead."

Slowly, Nigel directed his gaze up to the diving-board where Andrew Banks appeared at super-speed, standing at the edge of it, holding an unconscious female body in his arms.

Oh darn! – It's Lila. – I shouldn't have left her alone.

Her body hung limp in Andrew's arms, with the blood from her head wound staining and mixing with the purple and green of her long white hair as it sways beneath her.

"Lila!" I gasped, turning to save her.

But before I took another step, Nigel spoke again. "Uh-ahh... No-no. Take one more step and Andrew drops her..."

With an evil grin, Nigel raised his hand to the pool water, creating an iceberg with sharp, body-impaling shards growing out the top of it, and it rested in the water just beneath the diving board where Lila hung. He then continued to speak, "And as she plummets to her death, this building will be blown to shreds."

In sheer confusion, I turned and scowled at him. "She saved your life and this is how you repay her!"

"Did she? Did she really save me!" he shouted with anger. "She may have given me my freedom back, but my life had already been destroyed. I have been left with NOTHING!!!"

He glared back at me while taking a few calming breaths, adjusting his demeanour to negotiate. "So here I am... offering you a choice to join us in our revenge... I know you're in the same boat as us, Billy... With nowhere to go and no one to love, with your life completely empty."

His words were true. – I have been left with nothing. – But is it completely true?

As I thought about it, I stared back at Lila, feeling torn. She'd shown compassion to me and shared her friendship and her home. And she gave me a cause to fight for. — Yet without her, all of that means nothing.

"And if I say no?" I asked, turning back to Nigel but still kept an eye on Lila.

"She dies…" Nigel's nostrils flared as he whispered, "Tick-tock, Mr Jonas… we are after all on a time limit here."

Still with that grin, he very casually glanced back at the bomb before he began to walk to the top of the spectators stand.

Aw Darn

I need more time to think. I need another plan to save Lila and save everyone outside. But I'd run out of time when Nigel sniggered, "No… well… you've made your choice then."

My fear rose and my entire body tensed, watching Andrew let Lila's body go directly above the iceberg as Nigel pressed the button, setting off the bombs before running off at super-speed.

"NO!!!" I screamed, seeing Lila fall as the bombs exploded around us.

Suddenly everything froze. — The flames billowing from the many bombs around the centre that were detonated just stopped. Even Nigel and Andrew were frozen where they stood. And Lila had stopped mid-air, seconds away from being impaled.

I watched still in fear and slight amazement as Alex, Terrence, and Tyme appeared at super-speed into the room. Then Terrence followed Tyme up onto the diving-board and held

Tyme's feet as he hung off the board, trying to grab hold of Lila.

"I can't reach her!" Tyme screamed in desperation, noticing that Lila's body was still moving just that little bit. — As if she didn't completely freeze like everything else did.

Alex turned to me, demanding I get out of here, but I stopped him to explain, "No, I can help... I can absorb the blast and put it in the water."

"Do it!" he ordered while looking around at the impending destruction.

But I frustratedly shook my head. "I can't, not until Lila's safe. If she's anywhere near the water when the blast hits, she'll die."

"Guys... I can't hold time for much longer!" Tyme shouted, still trying to reach for his sister.

The fear in him was all over his face, and we all looked at Alex for our next orders when he shouted, "Tyme, Terrence, get clear of the water. Billy, I'll grab Lila... but as soon as I move her, time will unfreeze, and you will need to be fast... got it?"

I nodded my head, and instantly Alex ran at super-speed, jumping off the ledge of the pool towards Lila. So while still at super-speed as well, I reached out my hands, using all the strength I had to summon the fire towards me. Then in that moment when Alex reached Lila's body as it hung in mid-air, pushing her to the other side of the pool with him, the plan went off in seconds.

The fire that raged throughout the building came blazing towards me before I directed the flames into the water of the pool. The pool's temperature then rose, and the water boiled, creating extremely hot, searing steam that began to fill the building.

Still moving at super-speed, Tyme, Terrence, and I followed Alex as he carried Lila through the building, trying to escape the steam. But our skins were red hot from the heat, so as we ran out of the front doors at super-speed, I shouted to all of them to head to the lake. — It was the only thing I could think of to cool us down. And that was where Alex led us as we all jumped into what felt like the ice-cold waters of Albert Park Lake.

Holy Darn. — That's cold.

When my head breached above the surface of the water again, I gasped for air, looking around to see Terrence and Tyme break through the surface of the water as well. But Alex didn't and neither did Lila.

Tyme shouted Lila's name in a panic, and even Terrence and I were starting to panic. But within seconds, Alex burst up from the water pulling Lila up with him. — Thankfully, she's now wide awake, but gasping for air and in shock from the cold as she tries to hold on to Alex for dear life.

Very slowly, we made our way to the other side of the lake, all a little sluggish as we climbed out. And Terrence and Alex helped Lila out before we all rested on the ground, staring up at the grey clouds, panting with the feeling of exhaustion looming over us.

"I take it... we didn't win?" Lila wheezed with a hint of amusement in her voice.

She then sat up to look across the lake at the chaos of people in the evacuation area, and the frenzy of police and firefighters surrounding the swimming centre. Along with the steam and fog pouring out of the windows and doors of the building.

With concerned determination, I gradually crawled over to sit next to Lila, and then fumbled around in her hair to check if the gash had closed up. And it — kind of — stopped bleeding at least.

While I was still inspecting her wound, Lila peered over her shoulder to look at me and quietly wheezed with a raspy voice. "Am I going to live, Doctor Jonas?"

I was a little taken back at the fact that she knew I was a doctor. Then with a giggle, she winked at me as her lips peaked to one side, waiting for my answer. I nodded as I helped Lila to her feet, but then stayed close to her as she very sluggishly walked over to Alex and Terrence, tapping them on the legs before she helped her brother to stand.

"Come on, guys... I'm hungry." She sighed with a crackling voice. "And one of you is going to need to buy me dinner... Because I'm pretty sure I left my wallet in George's car. And as much as I want to, I don't think he would be too happy about me smashing all of his windows."

We all laughed at Lila when we noticed her actually contemplating that thought. Then Terrence agreed to buy dinner for the group as we began walking along the footpath back towards the city.

Journal entry insert by George Nell

I woke up in the emergency room of the Alfred hospital in the middle of the night. There were monitors and cords attached to me, and one of my colleagues, Vicki, sat at the end of the bed reading a magazine.

She filled me in on the bomb threat and what she knew of the incident. And it was no surprise that what she knew made absolutely no sense to her. She did, however, tell me that Adela was still sleeping a few beds over from me, so I made my way down to see her.

I found Maxwell Eden sitting with her, and as I stood at the end of Adela's bed, Maxwell stood to greet me. "Detective, how are you feeling?"

"A little headache but I'm okay. What about her?"

Maxwell walked closer to talk at a lower level and reply, "According to Lila, she got hit with two darts... So hopefully a good night sleep will do it."

I glanced around to make sure no one was listening, pulling the curtains closed before I asked. "Did Lila catch whoever was behind this?"

"In a way," he answered. "He's in the room next door... But he doesn't look too good. When the police found him, he was raving about his revenge, and he kept screaming, 'I will kill any guardian that stands against us'... Thankfully the police just think he's a loon. But he has burn blisters covering 60 percent of his body with the majority on his face and arms."

"Crikey... What the hell did Lila do to him?" I gasped, tensing in shock.

But Maxwell shook his head, trying to explain, "That wasn't her... Her team actually prevented this mess from becoming a disaster. The entire centre was rigged with explosives that would have caused a lot of damage when they exploded. But the team managed to make it look like a misfire."

Holy crickets. – How the heck did they do that?

I sat down in the chair still in a bit of shock, trying to absorb everything when amongst the silence, we heard the mumbling sounds coming from the bed next door. It sounded like our new criminal friend had a visitor. One he was not expecting.

I heard him mumble the name, "Katty." Then a few seconds later we watched as she made her silent exit down the hallway back into the waiting room. She looked mid-thirties with long dark-brown hair tied back into a ponytail. With a long face and sharp blue eyes. And she looked like a model, wearing ridiculously high heels.

In his curiosity, Maxwell quickly popped his head into the next room then called for a nurse as he gasped, "I... I think he's dead."

CHAPTER 5

Mr Connors

Journal entry by Lila Winters

So, it turns out I started another war. And I can't blame Nigel for wanting revenge, but he took it out on the wrong people. – Targeting innocent civilians crosses a line.

Within hours of George being released from the hospital, he was at my door, rambling on about how Nigel was dead and that some woman named Katty killed him. And for some reason, George was convinced she was a guardian. But there wasn't a lot I could do to help him. I had no idea who she was, and she wasn't on the missing guardian database that I'd created for the New York or Melbourne teams. So he left my apartment feeling a little tense and I think scared.

Thankfully, over the following couple of days, things began to ease and George reported no suspicious deaths and neither did Adela. – So maybe the war ended before it got started.

Or at least I hope so.

Today we're planning another rescue mission, because Terrence had received word that his adoptive mother, Odele Connors, is hosting a gathering of The Board's CEOs at her holiday mansion in the wine-country of the Yarra Ranges. During this gathering, all of the CEOs, and their guardian bodyguards, and collections will be there as security. So the plan is to break into the house tonight, plant some lily and rose seeds throughout the house and garden, and then watch from a safe distance as the party continues.

We're all up in the conference room at the moment, mapping out the plan. And Terrence was awesome enough to draw up a blueprint of the house for us.

For tonight's mission, our team consists of Alex, Terrence, Adela, Billy, and Katie. Tyme did offer to help, but I don't want him on these kinds of missions until he's had a bit more experience in fighting, especially because his ability is also a rare kind that Odele has not yet collected. – There are still more of his kind than mine, but they're just smart enough to not get caught.

As I laid out the house blueprint on the conference room table, Terrence explained to the team, "There's always two guards posted on the front and side entrances."

"Guardians?" Billy asked.

"No, humans," Terrence answered. "Odele doesn't like using Board guardians for personal use. She only trust those in her private collection for non-Board purposes... In saying that."

He then placed four surveillance pictures of his collected brothers and sisters on the table next to the blueprint, and explained who and what they were. "Keith, most of you would know is a Fire guardian. My youngest sister Izzy is a guardian of Wind. Anna is Land, and Robert is Water."

Alex shuddered a bit before he added, "Don't forget that personal secretary of hers... She's a sparky one."

Billy huffed, leaning back in surprise. "Wow, your mother likes to collect. All she was missing was Time and a family pet."

To that Terrence casually replied while glancing up at me, "Um, not really... Animal guardians are more useful to The Board out in the field. So Odele doesn't keep them in her collection... No offence Alex... and Lila."

"None taken." I smiled, feeling a little cheeky and holding back a laugh, remembering when Odele contemplated the idea of Terrence and me marrying.

Needing to shake that thought from my head, I cleared my throat and straightened my demeanour before I asked, "Terrence, these are your family. Do you think any of them would be convinced to join our side? I recognise Anna. She was the one back at Agronomique's that ordered Billy not to shoot me?"

In hearing that, Billy instantly grunted, feeling a little uncomfortable with that memory. So I thought I'd ease his nerves and cheekily grinned at him. "Don't worry, Billy, I know you weren't planning on shooting me. You were too busy trying to figure out what game I was playing... That and you found me very... fascinating."

Yes! – I got Billy to smile again, now thinking of a completely different memory. – Possibly the memory that occurred a little later in our first encounter. – Which probably wouldn't make Alex happy.

Either way I had to get back on topic, so I turned back to Terrence and questioned him again. But he shook his head and replied, "I doubt any of my siblings would change sides if they had the choice. Being part of Odele's collection does offer an enticing sense of security and luxuries that other guardians don't get."

Billy's brows raised as he curiously asked, "So why did you choose to join the rebellion over the dark side?"

"Nuh-huh, we're not rebels." I cheekily pouted, wanting to correct him. "We're more like... Jedis who are super cool, and everyone wants a piece of us. And as for Terrence, he joined my team because I'm just that awesome... aren't I, Terry?"

While smiling up at Terrence, I crinkled my nose, and he shook his head as he chuckled under his breath, "Yep, she's that awesome."

I don't know why, but I'm in a bit of a playful mood tonight, and I giggled, biting my bottom lip to hide my smile as I cheekily poked Terrence in the ribs. He tittered as he rested his arm over my shoulders, and then stuck his tongue out at me.

Oh. – The nerve of this man.

In playful shock, I gasped at him then tried to get back to the plan while still discreetly poking him in the ribs, trying to get him to giggle as I spoke.

"Anyway... if we do end up running into any of the brothers or sisters, they will be treated like every other guardian and be given the choice... Whether they take it, is up to them."

Aw Frac. – I had to take my hand away from Terrence, and I got all serious again as I pointed down to the blueprint to highlight certain access points and areas to cover.

"We'll pair up and take separate entrances to cover more ground... Alex and Terrence, you take the east wing. Adela and Katie, you go in through the west. And Billy and I will take the top floor and work our way to the middle."

Very briefly, I glanced over at Alex when I sensed his uncertainty, but he didn't say anything. He just sat back and huffed. So I continued. "Remember, no one is to know we were there. So get in, drop the seeds and get out. Got it?"

Everyone nodded in agreement – except for Alex, so as the team all started filing out of the conference room, I caught Alex's hand and pulled him back to talk in private.

"Hey... are you okay? You didn't look like you were happy with the plan... Is there something I'm missing?"

He pulled his lips in tighter and his brows lowered into a scowl as he questioned, "Lila, why didn't you partner Billy with Adela or Terrence?"

Okay? – I wasn't expecting that question. I kind of thought he already knew why. But I'm happy to explain anyway. "Because Katie would be safer with Adela... She's still on probation, remember? And you and I both know Adela can hold her own with her."

"Yeah well, what about Billy? He's new to this operation," he grumbled back.

Ah-huh. – Clearly something's bugging him.

I moved closer to Alex, and took a few moments to understand his emotions before I replied, "That's exactly why he's been partnered with me... And I partnered you with Terrence because he's going to need one of us with him... This mission might be really hard for him, and I know I can rely on you to keep Terrence focused."

Gently, I cupped my hand against his cheek, pulling his face down towards mine so he would actually look at me and understand. "Alex, I know you're upset that I didn't partner with you. But you are the only one I trust to lead this team to safety if something were to happen to me. Which is why I don't partner myself up with you... I promise it's not because I'm avoiding you. You're stuck with me remember? No matter what mood I throw at you."

He nodded then wrapped his arms around me, pulling me close to him as he mumbled, "Yeah... I remember."

Mmm. – I am loving this hug.

I looked up, continuing to smile at Alex as he tilted his head down to see my eyes, causing the fringe of his scruffy brown hair to fall forward and cover his eyes. So gently, I brushed it to the side for him. Then while still holding me in his arms, he leaned down and kissed me. – And I'm not sure, but I think I like it.

Until I didn't. – I could feel my animal instincts taking over as the rage that I kept at bay started seeping out. Alex watched as my eyes turned black, and in fear for his safety, I hurriedly pushed him away from me.

"No..." I gasped and stepped away from him, desperately trying to get control of my emotions again when my hands suddenly lit up with flames surrounding them.

Oh Frac! – Lila, you need to calm down. – Now!!!

I took some slow deep breaths and focused, causing my black eyes and the flames to disappear. But I instantly felt so much guilt in me because I just knew that I'd hurt him. I could feel Alex's heart aching, and I looked back at him, trying to hold back the tears as I whimpered, "Alex... I'm sorry."

But he wouldn't listen. He was too emotional and scrubbed his hands through his hair, turning away from me as he stormed out of the conference room.

Frac. – That just went terribly.

Journal entry insert by Alex Woods

We borrowed one of the hotel's hire cars – a Hyundai Imax for the drive out of Melbourne. Terrence sat in the front passenger seat, guiding Adela as she drove along the windy roads of the Yarra Ranges, and Lila and I both offered to sit in the back row of seats, which left Billy and Katie in the middle row in front of us.

Lila and I stayed very quiet, sitting next to each other. But every now and then I would glance over, only to see that long white hair acting as a curtain to hide that beautiful but gloomy face of hers. Occasionally I would see Lila twirling her fingers around one another. – As if one hand was trying to catch the other. And though it's amazingly cute when she does that, it also meant she was nervous or lost in thought or that something had gotten to her. – And today that something was me.

Right now, I'm really struggling to control my own emotions of confusion and anger and jealousy and love. Lila knows that I love her, but I can't get close to her without her pulling away, and that hurts because each time she does I sense her fear.

Why...? – What is it in me that she's scared of?

Suddenly, Adela went around a sharp bend on the road, and Lila was taken by surprise and was jerked towards me. She moved to put her hand down and accidentally landed on my hand. But my emotions are a mess, and there's no way I want her to sense any or all of them from just a simple touch. So I pulled away, unintentionally sending the wrong message to her.

"Sorry," she mumbled under her breath as she turned away from me again, and rested her head in her hands.

I can sense that she isn't happy. – I made her un-happy. – I didn't want things to go this way, and I know I need to say something. But by the time I worked up the courage to say anything, we'd arrived at our destination.

Damn it.

Adela parked the car just off the road amongst some trees, and when we all got out, Lila waved her hand, calling the surrounding trees to pull down their branches and cover the car so that only someone who was looking for it would be able to find it.

She then turned to the group, taking a deep breath and questioned, "Does everyone know what to do?"

We all nodded in confirmation before she added, "Stick to radio silence where possible, and if things go wrong, we all meet back here... Good luck."

Again, we nodded then ran off in different directions.

Journal entry continued by Lila Winters

Billy and I were approaching the mansion from the south, using the cover of the surrounding trees. But we had to stop just opposite a beautifully manicured garden, and I pulled Billy back, pressing him up against one of the trees to avoid the light of the moon revealing us.

I very carefully pointed out the security cameras on one of the nearby fence pillars that stood between us and the house. Then I tapped on my ear-mic to whisper, "Guys, there's scanning cameras scattered throughout the premises. And if they're the ones I think they are... they'll be able to detect us at full-speed. Wait for the right moment and then move."

I tapped my ear-mic again to switch off the mic then looked up at Billy, who was patiently waiting for my instructions as I pressed him against the tree.

"It looks like this is a full rotation camera," I whispered, scanning the area for any guards or counters. "Once the camera hits its 7 o'clock view-point, we're going to run as fast as we can and jump the fence. But there won't be much time before the rotation meets us again, so we're going to need to stand up against the pillar that the camera's resting on. Okay?"

He nodded silently, and we took a deep breath, watching the camera, then at the right moment I whispered, "Now."

Moving at full-speed we ran to jump the fence, and once we were on the other side, Billy pressed his back up against the pillar and I stood next to him. Then to help, he wrapped his hand around my waist, holding me close against the side of his body. And I carefully peered up to watch as the edge of the camera turned past its 12 o'clock view-point then continued on.

I took a relaxing breath, signalling Billy to let me go but ordered him to stay close just in case. – I'm confident he knows what he's doing on these kinds of missions. But he is still the newbie on the team, so I have to treat him that way. And he just understood me, happily following my orders.

Very quietly, we ran at a half speed, dodging bushes and shrubs until we reached the side of the mansion, then we jumped up onto the balcony of the second level. We stayed low and crept along the tiles towards the glass doors for me to peer inside the darkened room.

"Clear," I whispered.

Billy knelt next to me, and pulled one of the bobby pins from the long fringe of my hair that was skilfully keeping it from covering my face. He then held up his pocket knife, using them both to pick the old lock of the glass door. And I watched in amazement as he opened the door for me.

"Well that was handy," I whispered as we crept inside.

Once we saw no cameras in the room, we stood to our feet, and Billy folded the bobby pin back up, handing it back to me as he quietly joked, "What can I say... I'm a handy-man."

He then brushed his fingers along the front of my white hair that had fallen forward, and he tucked it behind my ear for me as he commented, "You're not wearing your hair up tonight."

I bit my bottom lip, feeling a little sad and shy, not wanting to tell him why my hair wasn't up. – That it's because I wanted to hide my shame and tears from the world on the drive here. – That I wanted to hide from Alex.

Noticing my sadness, Billy let out a sigh, taking the bobby pin from me to clip it back into my hair as he said. "I like your hair this way. You look more relaxed... It also reminds me of when we first met... All your missing is the pointy ears."

His lips peaked with a cheeky grin, and I rolled my eyes trying not to smile. But I miserably failed as we started hiding the flower seeds around the bedroom. – Under the mattress, in the air vent and behind some of the many books.

We were just about to walk out of the room when Billy grabbed me, pulling me into the closet with him where he pinned me against the closet wall with his hand on my mouth for some reason. He quickly closed the closet door but left it ajar as we heard heavy footsteps walking into the room.

Carefully, I peered out to see the very recognisable, messy mid-length light-brown hair and scruffy jeans, and knew exactly who it was. – It was Keith, carrying books and listening to very loud music on his headphones.

Aw Frac.

Billy confusedly looked at me as I stared up at him. – He was probably wondering why I was frisking his pockets. Until I pulled out one of the epi-pens I gave him. He then kind of relaxed a little and waited for my next orders.

But before I could think of a plan, our comms went off and Adela whispered, "Guys, we have a live bomb in the kitchen."

"Yeah, so do we," Alex replied.

A Bomb? – HOLY FRACCING FRUIT CAKES!! – This was not what I was expecting to go wrong on this mission.

It got even worse when Adela added, "I've got one minute on mine."

FRAC!!!

"We need to pull back now," Alex demanded.

In a hurry, I moved my head to pull my mouth free from Billy's hand, tapping my ear-mic to respond, "Go... We'll be right behind you... We've just got to get past Keith."

I was quickly shushed by Billy when he heard the music of Keith's headphones stop and change songs. I then heard Terrence in the ear-mic, and he sounded panicked. "Lila, where are you?"

"I think we're in his bedroom closet," Billy replied, tapping on his earpiece.

Unfortunately, neither of us realised that Keith's music had stopped, and he pulled the closet door open, staring at us while holding a fireball in his hand.

Double frac!!!

As I looked out at Keith, I innocently grinned. "Hi, Keith, it's nice to see you again."

There wasn't much time left before we all go boom, so I needed to form a plan quickly. And I think Billy knew what I was going to do when we looked at each other in agreement. We both ran at full-speed out of the closet, grabbing hold of Keith as we ran towards the balcony glass doors.

We had only just made it to the balcony when I injected the epi-pen into Keith's leg. Then as we jumped, the house exploded, sending us flying across the garden and showering us with debris. - Argh!! - My body tensed in pain as I felt a shard of glass pierce into my back, next to my shoulder blade, limiting my arm movement. But I still stayed focused and held Keith in front of me to protect him as we landed.

Aw Frac, this hurts.

The moment we hit the ground, Keith and I rolled together along the grass, snapping the glass shard flush against my back, and I screamed out my pain as Keith landed on top of me. He scowled at me in a state of rage and fear, then stood to his feet shouting, "What have you done!"

While still in a world of pain, I looked over at Billy who had a broken piece of wood impaled into his lower leg, making it hard for him to get up. He suddenly disappeared and reappeared on top of me, rolling me out of the way as Keith hurled a fireball at the ground where I lay. I screamed in more agony as I landed again then Billy stood to his feet, bearing through his pain as he tried to defend me.

I knew I had to help him, so I pushed through the pain as my eyes glowed green, calling the branches from a nearby bush to wrap around Billy's leg, acting as a brace and stopping the bleed. In doing so, it gave him more movement as he deflected the fireballs and created some of his own.

That's pretty much all I had in me. – The rest is up to him.

Journal entry insert by Billy Jonas

I don't know what Lila just did, but when those branches wrapped around my leg, it stopped the bleeding and the excruciating pain as well. It also gave me the strength to stand in front of Lila, protecting her from the never-ending rain of fire coming from Keith Connors, until finally the backup arrived.

At super-speed, Alex ran up and tackled Keith to the ground. And while he and Terrence dealt with him, I turned my attention back to Lila. Her lips were shivering as she winced, taking slow breaths.

"Don't move me. Not yet... I'm pretty sure there's a piece of glass in my back... and it's pretty deep." Her tears fell, and she looked scared as she stared up at me, trying to explain, "I can stop the bleeding and stabilise the shard, so it won't move. But it also means I won't be able to move... coz it's gonna pinch the surrounding nerves."

I nodded, listening to Lila's instructions. But she started to shiver more as we overheard Keith accusing Terrence of blowing up their house. She cringed in pain again, and I tried to hold her hand to comfort her but it was lifeless. – Which means she most likely severed a nerve.

"Lila, just hold on. We're going to get you to the hospital," I said with worry.

"No," she whimpered, shaking her head as more tears fell from her eyes. "You won't be able to move me unless I stabilise it... and if I do that, I can't go to the hospital. They'll know what I am. It has to be you... You have to do it... Please, Billy."

Oh Darn. — She's asking me to do the surgery myself. — Um… right, I can do that. I guess. — Or at least I think I can do that.

Lila waited for me to nod and agree to her request before her eyes glowed an amazing bright green, causing the vines from her leaf-bracelet to grow. They wrapped along her arm then down around her torso and up around her neck. Then when the vines stopped growing and were tightly knitted around her, Lila's body went limp and the glow in her eyes disappeared as she fell asleep.

While having a mild freak out at what Lila just ordered me to do, I turned to see Keith unconscious on the ground with Terrence standing over him, yelling at Adela who was holding a frying pan as she yelled back at him.

"He had a fire ball. What did you want me to do?" she grumbled.

"HEY!" I shouted, gaining their attention. "I need some help over here!"

Instantly, Alex appeared kneeling next to Lila and felt the blood seeping into the grass.

"She doesn't have much time," I said, lifting up her torso to inspect the damage and held her up for Alex to inspect the wound as well. The sight and severity of the wound led him to curse and gasp Lila's name in worry as he eyed the sliver of glass embedded in her back.

Now, I know I'm still the newbie but I had my orders, so I demanded, "We need to get her back to the hotel."

"What!" Katie shrieked. "She has a piece of glass in her back, and you have a stick running through your leg. You both need a doctor."

"I can fix it!" I shouted. "I used to be a doctor... Whatever it is Lila did to herself was done to give me more time to get her back to the hotel. Now unless you want to disobey her orders and give me a new one, somebody help me get her to the damn car!"

Alex wasted no time, carefully pulling Lila up into his arms, and then waited for Terrence and Adela to help me to my feet before we ran at a half speed back to where the car was hidden.

On the drive back, Alex and I sat in the middle row of seats with Lila resting between us. Alex supported her head as she lay on her side across both of us, and I monitored her vitals, checking her breathing and heart rate. We struggled a little when Adela drove around the bends at a ridiculous speed, but her driving got us back to the hotel in a record-breaking time.

Maxwell and Tyme were waiting for us up in the conference room and had collected all of the supplies I needed. – Or at least what they could get at this very late hour. We all rushed into the conference room, and as soon as Alex laid Lila face down on the conference table, Terrence held his hand above her back and looked at me and Alex while hesitantly explaining his plan.

"The second I remove these vines she's going to wake up and feel everything, so I'm going to try and pull Alex and her into the dreamland to make her sleep... Alex, I need you to use everything you have to keep her asleep. And Billy, don't waste a second to get started."

Alex and I both nodded before Terrence's eyes glowed green, and the vines retracted and pulled away from Lila's body. The second they did, she woke up and her screams filled the room, so Alex grabbed hold of Lila's uninjured hand, and Terrence used the vines from his bracelet to wrap around Alex and Lila's arms, locking them together. Then both Alex and Lila's eyes glowed a dark gold as they fell asleep on the table.

As soon as her screaming stopped, I got to work, using office scissors to cut open her skivvy. Then I used whatever Max and Tyme were able to get from the pharmacy and first-aid room to start cleaning the wound.

Okay, Billy, you can do this. — She's trusting you to do this.

It's taken me just over an hour now to remove and clean all of the broken glass from Lila's shoulder. And she wasn't kidding. It was very deep. It was one large shard that had broken into multiple pieces, very wide and long, damaging quite a lot of her surrounding tissue as well as the nerves beneath her shoulder blade.

While I worked, Terrence disappeared somewhere, mumbling something to himself, and Tyme had fallen asleep at the end of the table next to his dad. — Apparently his dad's not supposed to be anywhere near Lila, but Tyme refused to let him leave, so William stayed and watched from the end of the table as I continue to work on who I have now learnt to be his actual biological daughter.

Right. — No pressure here.

I had only just started on Lila's sutures when her eyes opened, and she stared at the bloodied glass shards that are now resting on a kitchen plate next to her head. But when she started to move, I had to stop her by pressing down on her lower back to hold her still.

"Hey... I'm not done yet. Try not to move."

She peered over her shoulder at me and breathlessly moaned, "Okay," then relaxed back down on the table. But her eyes then glowed gold as she said. "Hello William."

Wow. – How the heck did she know he was there?

Very timidly, William walked up to stand where Lila could see him and knelt down to talk to her. "Hello Lila."

Surprisingly, Lila didn't seem to mind his presence like the others predicted, but I did notice her eyes flicker black just briefly before she spoke, "William, can you take Tyme to bed, please. He's not going to get very good sleep at the end of the table."

"Lila, you know he's not going to leave you," William replied. "He's worried about you."

"I know..." Lila rasped with barely any breath. "But I'm worried about him, and I'm the big sister. So I overrule him... Please, do this for me."

William took a moment to think and almost looked sad as he nodded to her request. Then he went to pick Tyme up and walked him out of the office as he very sleepily protested.

"Thank-you," Lila rasped a little louder as William closed the door behind him.

I continued to stitch up her wound, occasionally glancing down at Lila as she remained so incredibly still. – It was amazing. The entire time she spoke to William, she didn't flinch when I pierced the sewing needle into her. But even now she's still staying so quiet and calm.

"Are you in pain… can you feel this?" I asked, slightly worried about the nerve damage.

"Yes…" She breathed slowly. "And I can feel my toes and my fingers… But I think the hand Alex is holding is going dead."

I let out a sigh of relief, and stopped the stitching for a second to grab hold of the green vine, and turned it to ash before helping to gently move Lila's hand down to her side. She let out a groan but tried not to move as she smiled and relaxed onto the table again, and I got back to my sewing, fascinated at how still she remains for me all while completely awake.

"How are you not flinching… or moving?" I questioned.

"You told me not to." She grinned but also looked like she wanted to laugh as she added, "Rule 2."

I smiled at her as I finished off the last stitch and whispered, "Pain can be your friend."

Now that the stitching was done, I placed the wound dressing on her and started cleaning away the bloody towels that surrounded her.

"All done," I whispered before sitting down on the chair next to her.

"Thanks, Doc," she cheekily rasped, looking over at me. "So what do I owe you?"

I leaned forward in the chair and thought for a second. "How about dinner?"

"What?" She puzzled while trying to sit up.

As she moved, her now ruined top fell off her, so I slowly stood up, struggling a bit from my own pain as I helped her to put my jumper on to keep her covered. — And she looks so small wearing it. — I then nervously repeated, "Would you like to have dinner with me? I'm asking you out on a date."

I held onto Lila's hand as she sat on the edge of the table trying to get her balance, and she groaned from her pain as her nose crinkled up. "Yeah, I know what you said... It's just, I haven't been asked out on a date in... a long time."

I noticed her glance back at Alex as he slept hunched on the table, and saw her hesitate as she bit her bottom lip and thought about it.

"You can say no," I suggested, tilting my head sideways to see her face, trying to get some kind of indication from her.

Then while still biting her lip, she turned back to me, but when her eyes met mine again, she smiled. "Um, I'd rather say yes... A date actually sounds like fun."

Holy darns, she said yes. — I was not expecting her to say yes.

"Um... great." I beamed with joy while slowly and gently pulling her limp hand up into an arm sling.

As I did, Terrence walked into the room, carrying two glasses of blue liquid in his hand and looked relieved and happy when he handed Lila a glass.

"Hey, you're awake," he whispered.

"Yeah, turns out Billy has magic hands," she replied, taking a large gulp of the blue liquid and pulled a sour face as if it tasted unpleasant.

Terrence handed the other glass to me as Lila stood to her feet, slowly turning me to make me sit on the table.

"What's this?" I gestured.

"It's the blue-rose healing tonic. The same thing we put in the epi-pens with the white lilies." She croaked still smiling at me. "And I'm guessing we can't go on our date with a stick in your leg... I think it might get in the way. So lie down on the table, and teach me and Terrence what to do."

Well, I'm certainly not going to argue with the boss, so I laid down on the table and explained, "You're going to need to tie something around my thigh before you remove... whatever it is you grew onto my leg."

Quickly scanning around the room, Lila found nothing useful then started undoing my belt buckle. – She's kind of handy with only one hand, and I'm trying very hard not to comment on that. But I think Lila saw the slight grin on my face when she pulled the belt out of the loops to secure it around my leg, with the other end of my belt in her mouth to pull it tight.

Hmm? – I think I like this one. – She's very intuitive.

"I'm sorry... can someone fill in the blanks here for me?" Terrence asked as Lila prepared fresh stitching supplies and gauze, all while listening to my orders for a change.

"I just asked Lila out on a date," I answered between orders.

Perplexed by my answer, Terrence leaned closer to Lila and whispered, "And you said yes?"

"Yeah... Is that okay?" She whispered back then changed the subject. "Um, I need your help to hold Billy's leg down."

Terrence paused for a moment, and I could see a hint of jealousy in his eyes. – Looks like I'm not the only one who has the hots for Lila. Still, he did as he was asked. But as he pressed down on my leg, I jumped a little from the pain, and Lila sniggered at me.

"Rule 2, Billy... Remember rule 2."

Unfortunately, I had accidentally startled Alex awake as I tried to obey rule 2. Yet Terrence was a little distracted on the whole date issue and continued to puzzlingly question Lila. "I'm sorry, but why did you say yes?"

"It's a thank-you date for stitching her up," I replied for Lila since she was concentrating.

Alex then stood to his feet, starting to stretch, and yawned. "Thank-you date? Lila, what is he talking about?"

Wow. – They both sound like a broken record.

He didn't get his answer because Lila was too busy listening to me as I explained what she needed to do next. All the while I watched in amazement as the vine-bracelet she wears on her wrist grew little tendrils, and acted almost like a second hand for her. – And darn, this girl has skills.

I told Lila everything she would need to do, on the off chance I fainted from the pain. So she quickly pulled everything together before ordering Alex and Terrence to do things.

"Terrence, I need you to hold Billy's leg still. Billy, close your eyes, and Alex, pull the stick out on 3."

Carefully, she leaned down on my chest to keep me from flinching, and whispered, "Rule 2." Then as everyone readied themselves, and I braced myself for the pain, Lila counted, "1... 2."

Sh#! Fudge – That hurt.

Journal entry insert by Keith Connors

I stood amongst the debris of my house and couldn't believe Terrence would do something like this. I mean after the Canadian incident, Mother had stopped in her pursuits to collect them all back and had started taking more of a figurehead role because of her growing condition.

I don't understand. — Lila had asked for peace between our families and that's what my mother gave her. This entire mess is all her fault. — And Lila is going to pay.

When I saw Mother's limo stop in front of the now ash-rotted door, I raced to greet her as she stepped out. And she gasped, looking around at the wreckage, "What happened here?"

"Terrence." I seethed. "He destroyed it."

Mother looked at me, confused and asked, "My dear, who is Terrence?"

With disappointment, I sighed, feeling a wave of helplessness as her mind began to slip, and I explained, "He's one of your sons, Mother... Do you remember?"

She looked back at me with a distant gaze and nodded. "Oh yes, I remember now. Will he be coming to visit us?"

I grinded my teeth, feeling so angry at my brother and his annoying little girlfriend as I helped Mother to get back into the Limo. "No, Mother... But I will be seeing him, very soon."

Before I closed the limo's door, Katty appeared standing next to me, startling Mother, so I calmed her down before I explained, "It's okay, Mother, this is Katty... She's come to help us with your recovery."

I opened the second door and helped Katty to slide into the limo then I stepped in after her, tapping on the driver's window to take off. I told him to take us to our Melbourne

City home where Izzy, Anna, and Rob live. — And they will definitely want to join my cause when I tell them what our brother did.

CHAPTER 6

Jealousy

Journal entry by Lila Winters

After taking a few days to recover, my arm is almost back in good swing. My shoulder, not so much. It's actually been a very slow process. The stitches are holding it together nicely, but the healing rose tonic isn't working as well as I'd hoped. – To the point where I don't think it works for me at all.

I suspect it might be because of the amount of times I've had to use it. I've also noticed a lot of plant ingredients affect guardians differently depending on their element. So I think because I'm a Nature guardian-hybrid the blue-rose isn't working as well for me anymore. And I think over time, I've built up a tolerance, leaving the effects non-existent. – Which means I'm stuck with just the standard guardian speed of healing. – But that's not something I'm planning to tell anyone just yet, not until I've created a new healing tonic.

The downside to that means I'm a little slower at doing things, like getting ready for my date with Billy. I'm also really struggling to find something to wear. I mean it's the middle of autumn almost winter, so my go-to style is usually a thick jumper and some gym pants when I'm not working. But I'm not really sure that's date-worthy.

Instead, I've opted for denim jeans and a long green cable-knit sweater that hangs off my shoulders. And I think I look rather nice. – Or at least I hope I do. – The one thing I'm definitely not doing tonight, is wearing make-up. I want to feel comfortable tonight, and Billy said that the scars don't bother him. – So hopefully that's true.

I looked back in the mirror and took a long, nervous breath as I brushed my still very noticeable white hair with the pretty green and purple streaks. I'm choosing to wear it down tonight, since Billy likes it that way. But the white hair is causing me to wonder if maybe this is too soon. I mean my divorce was finalised last month, but the damage was done months before that. The kids know that Mummy and Daddy aren't married anymore, and they took it better than we expected. Probably because it didn't change anything. – I still live with them, and Matt and I seem to be in a good place with our new friendship. So... I don't know. – Maybe this is just my nerves getting to me.

Right... Nerves. – It's just my nerves.

Once I was ready, I kissed Danny and Ruby goodbye. But Matt asked me to promise to be careful and to come home in one piece this time. I can't blame him for wanting me to promise that. But I know I'm playing with fire if I ever promise something that I know I can't easily keep, so instead I promised that I'd come home.

There was still one thing I wanted to do before I leave on my date, and that is to talk to Alex. We didn't leave things in a good place the last time we spoke, and he hasn't said a word to me since before we left for the Yarra Ranges. I know he's mad at me for pushing him away, but he's supposed to be my friend, and I really don't want our friendship to disappear if and when he wants more from me.

I knocked on Alex's door, begging him to open up for the third time this week, but I still got no response. I couldn't even find Terrence to ask him. So after knocking and calling both their names and still getting no response, I gave up and went down to the lobby to meet Billy.

When I got down to the lobby, Billy was already waiting and talking to Max about the blue-rose healing tonic. I overheard him wishing he had some of the blue-rose serum back when he was working as an actual doctor. – I also heard him say that I was talented, and I kind of liked that. – It made me smile.

I walked up to stand next to them, and blushed a little when Billy looked at me and gasped, "Wow."

Yep. – I am totally nervous.

Max didn't seem too thrilled about the idea of me going out on my own, even with Billy as back-up. – It's understandable, considering my last couple of outings. So I gave him a smile as I lifted my green sweater to show him the new vine-belt that I'd created that has a hidden compartment at the back to hide my dagger. I'm also wearing the vine bracelet that Terrence gave me on my wrist. – And it has actually been pretty handy in a fight.

"Max, I'm pretty well stocked," I boasted. "Plus, I have a doctor here who can stitch me up after I win the fight."

I grinned back at Billy who seemed captivated as he lifted the back of my sweater again to look at the new belt and my favourite dagger. However, I'm still a little distracted with Max.

"Max, have you seen Alex or Terrence today? I just went to their apartment, and they weren't there."

"No, sorry Lila, I haven't seen them... But Adela saw them this morning if that helps."

Great. – That means they're avoiding me.

In not wanting to ruin the night before it begins, I gave up on the negative thoughts, and I pulled my sweater out of Billy's hand as I grabbed hold of his arm.

"Are you ready?"

"Absolutely." He grinned while leading me out onto the street.

We took a tram through the city, and as we sat side by side, I pointed out all of my favourite spots in Melbourne. I then told Billy the story of my first week at the Eden Hotel of how I played cat and mouse with Jessica and the security team. He laughed because he knew the reference. But I choked up a little when I got to the part where I ran into Ben, waiting for me at the top of the Myer Shopping Centre. – Thankfully, Billy understood that too.

We got off the tram just outside Melbourne central, and Billy bought us both hot chocolates to go. And as we strolled around the city, we marvelled at the city nightlife and scenery, and listened to a nearby street busker, singing and playing his guitar.

While we walked, Billy played the Question-game with me, and again I liked that he got the reference. I got to start first, so I asked him about his home town. – It turns out Billy is actually from Canada, and he followed me to the other side of the world to join my crusade against The Board.

I also learned that he too was married before he went missing. Both of them were doctors fresh out of med-school, travelling around Africa to provide treatments and medicines to the villages. But he had been missing for seven years. And on the night that I'd pulled my little rescue op and freed him, the first thing he did was find out where his wife was, only to find out that she had moved on with her life and found someone new. – With children and everything.

I felt really sad for him, and my nose crinkled a little as I pouted. "I'm sorry about that."

"Don't be..." Billy took a deep breath and held onto my hand that I still have hooked around his arm as he explained, "I was kind of expecting it. But I'm glad that she's happy... And right now, I'm pretty happy as well. Because I get to be with you."

He stopped walking and turned to gaze into my eyes, still holding my hand and smiling at me as he spoke, "I'm pretty sure you already know this... but you fascinate me."

"I know." I grinned, biting my bottom lip and feeling incredibly nervous.

He moved closer to me, gently brushing the tips of his fingers along my cheek then across the lip I was still biting. "Well, did you also know that when you bite your lip like that, you look amazingly cute."

Oh my Fracs, he thinks I'm cute. And I think I have butterflies in my chest right now, because he is so close to me that I think he's going to kiss me. – But what if I freak-out again like I did with Alex. – Oh Frac, think, Lila.

Still slightly nervous, I thought quickly, and then decided to just drink more of my hot chocolate as I continued to walk next to him again.

Aw Frac. - Good job Lila. - You really suck at this whole dating thing.

I'm pretty sure Billy picked up on my nerves around the kissing thing, so he very casually went back to the Question-game while still holding my hand as it sat in the crook of his arm. He asked me what it was like growing up as the General's collected daughter and how Richard ended up on my frenemies list.

Again, I choked up a little, telling him about Brody, and how I tried to save his life, but in the end failed. I think after that Billy knew not to ask me anymore questions about my childhood. - Which I think is really sweet of him.

We stopped outside this little Italian restaurant, and I commented amusingly, "I'm going to assume Italian is on the menu tonight."

"And what gave you that idea?" Billy replied with such a cheeky tone. "Wait here."

He slowly pulled my hand off his arm but held it for a few seconds – almost reluctant to let it go. Until he did, and then gradually moved into the restaurant, glancing back at me every couple of seconds.

I watched as he talked to the wait staff and tittered while trying to pull back on my completely obvious smile. I am also slightly confused as to what he's doing, and I feel very tempted to use my super-hearing to listen in. But I also want to let him do the whole human date thing and keep it a surprise.

Suddenly, I got this weird tingling feeling. – The feeling like someone was watching me. I scanned around the street to see so many different people passing me by, and all of them had different emotions and feelings, that it became very hard to get a read.

I wandered down towards the side alley a few doors from the restaurant but stayed where Billy could see me just in case something went wrong. I kept looking around seeing nothing out of the ordinary until Billy appeared next to me, holding a bag of take-out that he had pre-ordered, causing me to jump in fright.

"Is everything okay?" he asked, slightly concerned about my demeanour.

I took a moment to calm my nerves, trying to convince myself that it was just that – nerves. Then eventually I nodded. "It's nothing, just doing a perimeter check... Force of habit I guess."

He chuckled but again understood me as he held his hand out for me to hold. "Come on, I've got the perfect place to eat this."

We took a second tram down Swanston Street then walked through Kings Domain Park, down into the currently empty Sidney Myer music bowl to sit on the front row of seats. Billy left a seat between us as he started setting out the dinner, served in plastic take out containers, and continued to talk to me.

"Now, I know you're not my enemy... but I followed rule 7 and did a little homework on you before our date. So I'm really hoping I got this right... Vegetarian gnocchi with white sauce, no egg... Oven-baked focaccia for our sides, and Coca-Cola for the drink."

He looked at me, nervously hoping for my approval as he held out a fork for me. And I beamed with a smile, nodding as I grabbed a fork, and he handed me one of the bowls.

"What did you get?" I asked.

He shrugged his shoulders as he opened his container. "Same as you... It looked interesting."

"But you're not vegetarian," I rebuked with a slight chuckle.

He peered across at me while getting comfortable in his seat and cheeked, "I'm willing to be convinced... I can't count it out unless I try it."

"Nuh-uh..." I shook my head while giggling. "I'm not even going to try to open that can of worms on our first date"

"First date." He smirked, and it got wider as he looked at me. "So, are you hoping for a second?"

I felt my nose crinkle and my lips peaked to one side, choosing to stay quiet while I ate my gnocchi. But I'm kind of liking this date, so I am secretly hoping for another one.

Oh Frac. – I think I'm blushing. – And I can't stop biting my lip. – And he's totally noticing this.

I peered over to see Billy staring at me with a sassy grin on his face, very much noticing that I'm not answering his question. So instead he handed me a focaccia.

"Okay then, let's get back to our Questions-game... So far, you've told me how you ended up working for Max, and how you... kind of just fell into this super-hot-hero-gig that you've got going on here... You've got two children and a long-lost brother that came with a biological father, that you are still a bit wary about... But I understand your reasons... What about your ex-husband, what happened there?"

I paused for a minute, feeling the swell of emotions rising, and I just knew my eyes had turned black. When suddenly I felt Billy hold my hand and whisper my name. I can now feel a different set of emotions. – I feel his emotions, and it caused my hurt and pain to fall silent.

"Um..." I choked, needing to clear my throat. "Matt... um... when I went missing and taken to the island with Terrence, they had convinced Matt that I was dead, and... he didn't take it well. Then when I came back, both of us were two very different people. And he looks at me differently now... But not in the good way. It's as if I came back broken on the inside and out... And... I didn't think it was fair on him... You know, to ask him to love someone who keeps coming back broken."

Yeah. – I'm really struggling to hold my emotions back, and I definitely have tears welling in my eyes.

I cleared my throat trying to compose myself, but then Billy pulled my hand closer to speak. "Lila, you're not broken... You're the strongest woman I know. I don't think anything can break you."

I felt honoured that he thinks that of me, but I'm not feeling very convinced of it myself as I struggle to open my bottle of Coke, and I got frustrated when my shoulder spasmed from the tension. Billy held his hand out, offering to open the bottle for me then asked if he could take a look at my shoulder to check if it was okay. – Deep down I didn't want him to. But he is the doctor who fixed it, which means he'd know better than anyone if it was getting worse.

"Before I agree to that..." I tentatively spoke. "Since we're on the subject. I was wondering if you would consider, as well as being part of my security team, also being my personal doctor. To be on call whenever I need you... You'd be the one I go to when I have things like this to fix up."

Completely taken by my request, he stared at me a little puzzledly. "I... um... of course. But why are we being so formal about this?"

My fingers twirled around each other as I quietly answered, "I... have over-protective friends, remember?"

He nodded, understanding my real reason before adding, "Lila, I promise you that anything you and I ever talk about or do will be kept between us. But you don't need to be my patient for that to happen."

"I know..." I flirtingly smiled. "But this way, I have an excuse to keep you close to me... I mean what if I get a tummy ache in the middle of the night, or run into hunters that give me a fat lip."

I pointed to where the small cut on my lip used to be, and Billy handed me back my drink before he moved to sit next to me. – I think again, understanding what I was really meaning as he agreed to my request.

"Alright, you officially have your own personal doctor."

"On call whenever I need him?" I cheekily questioned.

With a smile he nodded, "Whenever and wherever."

Feeling a little more comfortable with him now, I turned my back to him, and he gently brushed his hand along the nape of my neck, drawing my long hair forward over my shoulder to get a better look. Then very gently, he peeled back the dressing, and his hand had a fiery glow to it in order to give him better light as he leaned in.

"Huh, it's not infected. But it's not healing as fast as mine is," he mumbled.

I heard the concern in his voice and sensed his worry, so I shrugged my good shoulder, trying to play it down. "It was a pretty deep injury... but I'll get there."

He hmmed softly, still worried about me as he lightly pressed down on the dressing to cover it again. Then I felt the gentle touch of his lips on my shoulder blade just above the wound.

Oh my fracs. – He's kissing it better for me.

Very slowly and softly, Billy kissed every scar he saw on me that led up to my neck, gradually turning me towards him to kiss my lips. And as his lips pressed to mine, I felt amazing with a fluttering feeling in my chest.

He pulled back just a little to study my face and probably make sure I wasn't freaking out or scared off like last time. But I just bit my bottom lip, trying not to smile too much, and stared into his forest green eyes as he whispered, "I've been wanting to do that all night."

Oh Frac. – I can't breathe.

I leaned closer to him, wanting another kiss when my ears twitched, and we both heard the noise of one of the seats creaking in the higher rows. So while continuing to stare into my eyes, Billy slowly reached around my back, pulling out the dagger from my belt. He then placed the dagger in my hand, and the moment we broke eye contact, we both ran at full-speed to the top row of seating, ready to attack – Terrence? – What the frac? Terrence was just standing there, refusing to look at me.

"Terrence?" I grunted then in angered tears looked around to find his partner in crime, and shouted, "Terry, where is he?!"

He peered back, looking so sad when he replied, "He took off just after Billy kissed you."

In seconds, I was running at full-speed after him. – After Alex. – And it didn't take long to catch up to him as my temper fuelled my animal-like super-speed. Then when I was running alongside him, I shoulder tackled him into a tree and slowed to a stop, waving my hands to the tree, commanding it to hold him still. And while Alex struggled to break free, I nursed my shoulder and cringed in a hell of a lot of pain.

"YOU!!!" I shouted, boiling with anger. "Alex, I have been looking for you for days! I've worried about you to the point of not sleeping. I texted you, called you, and stood outside your door, begging you to talk to me... And now I find you here, up to old tricks, spying on me... You're a jerk! You know that... You're a big, lying jerk!"

I was close to tears when he broke free of the branches and landed on his feet. But he didn't move, he just stood there listening to me as I yelled at him with tears filling my eyes.

"You told me that no matter what mood I threw at you that you would never leave. But you bailed on me the moment things got hard. You... you kissed me... and I liked it, and I'm sorry I pulled away but I was scared... Alex, I trusted you and that's rare for me. You are the only good guy in my life who hasn't tried to kill me or hurt me in any way."

"So why then?" he snapped back while moving closer to me. "Why choose him over me? And why did you get scared... of me?"

He stood right in front of me to look down into my teary eyes, and I sniffled, letting the tears fall. "I want to... I think... But what happens if I do choose you... and things go wrong, and I get hurt? You wouldn't be the good guy anymore, Alex... And I'm not ready for that."

The expression on his face changed from anger to sadness as he fell silent and pensive again. He stared at me and caught a tear off my chin, causing me to lean my head in as he cupped my cheek. – I love the caring nature he has for me, and my breath fell short feeling the warmth of his skin against mine.

"You should get back to your date," he whispered, stepping away again.

But I don't want him to leave. – I want him to stay. – I don't want to lose him.

"Alex..." I whimpered, but he disappeared and left me in tears. He left me to walk back to the music bowl on my own.

Alex is supposed to be my best-friend. – He said I was stuck with him. – He said that he wouldn't leave. – But he just did.

I stood at the top of the amphitheatre stairs, trying to pull back the tears while looking around for Billy. But I saw nothing but darkness. I walked down to the front row of seats to see our food still sitting there and has now gone cold.

Great. – That's just great.

"Billy!" I shouted through my sniffles. "Billy, this isn't funny... Terry! Are you here?"

A warm gust of air flowed from behind me as I saw the glow of a fireball, so I cautiously turned to see a dark figure with his skin so dark and brown, but his eyes glowed a fiery red. It didn't take long to realise that it was Stephen, one of Billy's friends from Agronomique's. – But I rescued him. He's supposed to be safe back in Texas with his family.

"Surprise." He hissed through his teeth, and looked angry as he started to circle me. "Do you want to play a game with me, Lila? It's called I take, and you lose."

He didn't wait for my answer and threw a fireball at my head, so I spun around properly with my eyes glowing red to catch it, and then throw it back at him before it got too hot. But I missed as he moved to dodge it, leaning to one side and tsk-ing me.

"Naughty Lila, you've been keeping secrets from us... From the world... You're really racking up the element cards now aren't you, Lila? Hmm... Now if I ask you nicely, would you tell me how many you have?"

The fear in me grew, and I didn't know what to do. I couldn't see Billy anywhere but I could sense others nearby, so I ran for it as fast as I could. I used my vine bracelet to create a shield to deflect the rain of fire as I bolted. But then Stephen raised his hands to create large walls of hot flames around me, and they blocked my escape as they started to close in on me.

Frac!

I was surrounded but I'm not giving up. I raised my hands and used all of my concentration to put the fires out before running up the stairs again, only to be met by Stephen, waiting at the top of the stairs. I really don't know why but I sensed so much anger in him when he grabbed hold of the shield of vines with his fiery hands and burnt it to ash. The vines started to burn me, and I had to pull the bracelet off, dropping it to the ground as it caught on fire.

"Ah... the irony of being a fire guardian." Stephen chortled while circling me again. "We're only immune to the fire we create."

Well frac. – That would have been a handy thing to learn before taking on another fire starter.

Hurriedly pulling the dagger from my belt, I stood ready to fight. Then Stephen moved quickly and without mercy. I dodged what I could, trying desperately to get away. But without the full use of my arm, I was no match for him.

My dagger went flying out of my hands as Stephen struck the back of my shoulder, and I froze in sheer pain, feeling my wound pulsating beneath my skin. His callous laugh echoed through the music bowl before he pushed me back down the stairs, tumbling to a stop on one of the landings. – And I'm pretty sure I broke something because my rib, thigh, and face are all burning.

My green sweater got caught on one of the seats, and I had to rip the sleeve in order to move. But it was a struggle to even get up. All I could do was lay on the cold ground cringing in pain, feeling way too weak to fight.

Oh Frac. – I'm all alone. – Where's Billy? – Where's Terry? – Where's Alex?

I tried to crawl away. I tried to follow rule 2. But Stephen stopped me and picked up my body, holding me up by my hair and the back of my jeans. Only causing me more pain as he turned me towards the stage where I saw Billy being held at gun-point, shouting my name.

He looked like he had copped a beating too, and he was blurry. - Or at least my vision was blurry as Stephen snickered to his team. "Let's see what he's like without his pretty little hero pet around to save him."

My body felt weak and heavy, being dragged up the stairs like a lifeless rag-doll as Billy fearfully screamed my name. I felt the tears seeping into the cut on my cheek, causing that burning pain to spread before everything went dark.
I'm now blindfolded with my hands tied with thick-rope, and I suddenly felt myself being thrown onto the cold metal floor of a truck-bed. But something else was thrown next to me. - Heavier and Bigger than me.

Oh Frac. - It's Billy, and he's not moving.

"Billy..." I clawed at his shirt, and fearfully shook him. "Billy!

CHAPTER 7

The Enemy Of Many

Journal entry by Alex Woods

I didn't sleep at all last night and I'm still fuming this morning. I thought maybe a good workout in the gym would help. But punching and kicking and taking my emotions out on Lila's 'Hector' was not helping.

Terrence is down here too using the bench press, and Katie and Adela are sparring on the mat. A small part of me was hoping Lila was going to join us since she didn't train earlier. She usually trains before sunrise and leaves that damn sexy scent of hers everywhere, but today all I smell is bleach and ammonia. And I know Lila never misses a workout, so I'm surprised she's not here.

The team stopped when Matt walked into the room and asked, "Hey, has any of you guys seen Lila?"

"Nope." I panted, walking over to the bars to start a round of chin-ups.

Terrence hooked up his bar weight, sitting up to question Matt. "Isn't she up in her room, sleeping?"

"No." Matt shook his head, and I could sense his worry. "She didn't come home last night, and she's not answering her mobile either."

"Have you tried Billy's room?" Katie scoffed with a smile.

And Yep. – Just the thought of that made me tense all over.

"Yeah, that was the second place I looked," Matt replied. "And he's not in his room either... Look, I know I might sound really paranoid, but I think something may have happened to them."

He stood in front of me, and I dropped to the floor giving up on the workout, listening to Matt's plea. "Alex, you know this isn't like her. Lila made a promise to me last night that she would come home. And you know she never breaks her promises... Not unless something's gone wrong."

I grinded my teeth, feeling uneasy and reluctant. But Lila is still my friend and I know she would come looking for me. – Even if I was in the arms of another.

"Fine." I sighed. "I'll go look for her."

I grabbed my water bottle and stormed out of the room. But when I stepped into the elevator, Terrence, Adela, and Katie ran at full-speed to stand next to me as we headed to the ground floor.

"So what's the plan, Boss?" Katie asked with way too much glee in her voice.

Something tells me she's hoping to catch Lila in the act. So in not wanting to react, I stayed silent and stared at the elevator door, grinding my teeth trying not to think about that thought. – <u>At all</u>.

Instead, Terrence chimed in with the orders. "You two pair up with Jess and Chase to search the hotel... Keep trying Lila's mobile and ask any of the security team if they saw her come home last night."

The girls both nodded as the elevator doors opened, and I made a beeline for the exit with Terrence right behind me when I heard Adela comment, "Ooh... he looks mad."

"Yeah," Katie added. "I would not want to be Lila today."

Urgh!!! – It's like the whole bloody hotel knows how I feel about Lila. – The problem is, she doesn't feel the same for me.

We headed back to Kings Domain Park, walking toward the Sidney Myer music bowl. And Terrence tried to – I don't know, break the ice or something in an attempt to be nice. "She didn't mean what she said last night... when she called you a jerk... She was just upset. That's all."

I huffed, not overly happy that he was listening in. But it was hard not to with the way she was yelling at me, so I took a breath and grumbled, "Yes, she did... But she's right, and that's what's bugging me."

Wait. – Something's wrong.

The air around us began to smell different. – Smoky and metallic. So I stopped and stood still, with tense shivers running down my spine as I sniffed the different scents scattered around.

"Something doesn't smell right," I mumbled.

Now filled with fear, I ran as fast as humanly possible to the top of the stairs leading down to the stage. And my gut churned, looking around at the melted seats and scorch marks along the walls. Lila's dagger was embedded into one of the nearby seats and Terrence found what was left of her stone-vine bracelet.

I couldn't breathe properly as I walked down the steps to one of the landings, following Lila's scent, and found blood. – Her blood stained on the cement floor and a piece of her sweater caught in the chair.

Damn it. – It feels like I'm living my worst nightmare. – Again.

This is my fault. I shouldn't have distracted her with my stupid feelings. I left her alone and crying in the middle of the park with nobody there to protect her. You're an idiot, Alex.

A Big Stupid Idiot!!!

The rage burned within me when I found the silver ballet flat's Lila was wearing last night, lying at the base of the steps. I needed to vent, so I kicked the nearby row of seats way too hard, ripping them off the hinges then screamed over a dozen curse words.

Then while taking slow breaths to calm myself, I turned to Terrence, holding back the tears and the rage and the swell of fury to speak. "Canvas the area. Find everything that belongs to Lila and any clues as to who took her... I need to call Lila's friend George and figure out if this site has security cameras."

While also filled with fear, Terrence nodded before darting around the music bowl to collect everything. It left me enough time to grunt again, kicking another seat as I looked around at the mess that I left Lila in.

Journal entry insert by Lila Winters

There was a wave of heat coursing through my body, radiating from my shoulder, and I could feel something seeping through the stitches of my wound, and I'm pretty sure that isn't a good sign. My body is still aching from being thrown down the stairs, making it really hard to stand. But what's worse is where I am.

I refused to sleep and have been awake for hours now. But when we first arrived at wherever we are, they kept me blindfolded and needed to force me to unclench my hands from Billy's shirt before carrying me up what I think was stairs, where they chained me in iron shackles.

The chains hung from what I think is a dome or arched-shape roof, given the way it echoes. And the room is dirty with the musty smell of dead rat and crap around me. – I know I'm still in the city because I can hear the sound of the tram signals and trains, and there's people scurrying in the distance. But where in the city is anyone's guess.

All night I wanted to scream for help but the man who put me up here – he said his name was Peter, he claimed that there was a bomb in the room just in front of a laptop with the camera recording me. He also said that the bomb was sensitive to sound and that if I made too much noise it would detonate, killing me and most likely anyone within a two-block radius. And it would all be caught on his live stream recording.

Yeah. – I definitely tested his theory, and I almost blew up the building. But Peter managed to stop it and reset the charge. – But not before he punished me by heating up the iron shackles and burning my wrist until I agreed to stay quiet.

For the rest of the night, Peter sat in the shadows, and I could just barely see him through the cloth of my blindfold. But I could hear him playing with the fire he created to entertain himself when he wasn't watching me try and fail to break free while still remaining silent.

What a frac-head. – It's like he thinks this is a joke or a sick game to him.

More long hours passed when I heard the sound of the scurrying people become more intense. I'm guessing it's almost late-morning, now. Because on a Saturday the city gets really busy with people just exploring the town. – But I can't stay awake forever. I need to know why I'm here.

"What do you want from me?" I tiredly whispered.

He stayed silent, refusing to answer my question even after I repeated it again. Until he finally received a text message on his phone. I heard him move, and I could smell his breath on me. It smelled like cigarettes and whiskey. – Yuck.

The back of his hand slowly ran across the skin on my chest as he pulled at my sweater, and I could feel and smell it being burned off me, leaving me in nothing but my jeans and a bra. Then with arrogancy oozing from him, he gradually ran his fingers down my neck, and along my collar bone as he whispered, "I want... leverage."

Journal entry insert by Billy Jonas

I have now been blindfolded and tied to a cold steel pole for most of the night. My hands are bound with chains being held flat against my chest, making it difficult for me to break free of the chains. And some airhead told me that I was tied to a structural pole, which means if I burnt through it, I would most likely die and bring down the entire building with me.

And I can't do that. – Not without knowing that Lila's safe.

I could feel the warmth of the morning when I heard the sound of a roller door rattle up, and then back down as a car rolled in and squeaked on its breaks. Then the sound of Stephen's voice enraged me as he wished me a good morning while removing my blindfold.

At first it was hard to see, but eventually I could make out the shapes and see his dark skin clearly. I can also see where we are. We're in an old shipping warehouse called Pac-n-send with half of it burned and boarded up.

"Stephen...? What's going on? What are you doing here?" I questioned.

"My job," he retorted.

"Your job?" I scoffed in disbelief, being wise enough to hide my fear. "Please don't tell me your job is to kill friends now... Because you still owe me a Two-four."

He shook his head, laughing at my statement. "Don't worry, Billy, you'll get ya beer... but first I need information."

Still confused and slightly panicked, I'm strongly hoping that Lila is nowhere near us right now as I play the ignorant card. "Information from who? I don't know anything."

I was also discreetly trying to break out of the chains, but my breath fell short when a devilish grin appeared across Stephen's face, and he pulled out a Samsung tablet to show me a live feed of Lila. She hung from chains in nothing but her bra and bloodied jeans with a blindfold across her eyes and bruises all over her body from being thrown down the stairs.

"You don't... But she does," he hissed.

"No! You stay away from her!" I jeered, trying to pull at the chains. "Why? Why are you all targeting her? What has she done to you?"

"Nothing!" he barked back. "And everything... For some reason this girl seems to be in the middle of everything we know. She's known throughout our world and throughout theirs... the enemy's world... Aren't you the least bit curious why such a dainty little girl has managed to turn an entire world of monsters into such chaos? Aren't you curious what her secret is?"

I stayed silent, not giving him any hint of response, slowly contemplating how to hurt him.

"No?" He snickered with that evil grin. "Well, why don't we ask her then... Or better yet, why don't we ask her friends. I have a feeling they'll be a bit more co-operative."

Journal entry insert by Maxwell Eden

This is turning out to be a fairly productive morning for me. I've just finished all my meetings and phone calls, and was about to sit back and start replying to my emails when I saw an urgent email sent by an 'unknown server' marked with the word, 'Lila.'

The email instructed me to click on the link, and I hesitated but eventually did. — Being concerned for Lila. But what it showed me was horrid. It's a recording of Lila with something covering her eyes, standing in almost nothing with her hands hanging from chains. And she looks like she's been beaten. There's also a man standing in front of her, holding up a sign that reads: 'Do we have your attention now?'

In shock, I picked up my phone and called Alex immediately.

"Alex, my office... super-fast," I ordered, clearly indicating to disregard the rules.

As I waited for him, the phone rang again, and I answered it to hear a modulated voice ask, "Do you like the view?"

I felt livid and speechless, unable to find any words to answer such a horrible question. Then within seconds, Alex and Terrence appeared on the other side of my desk, so I quickly turned the computer around to show them the recording while placing the phone-call on speaker for them to hear as well.

"I assume that the rest of Lila's boyfriends have finally joined us for the viewing," the voice asked.

Taking short breaths, Alex and Terrence both glowered at the screen in silent rage then after cursing under his breath, Alex replied, "We're here."

"Good... Now we can get started," the voice stated. "I'm in need of some answers. But first, let's set some ground rules... If you answer my questions truthfully, Lila remains unharmed. But if you lie or even hesitate…"

He paused for a moment for us to watch the man on the screen place his hand on Lila's bare stomach, and as he did, it started to glow beneath him. Lila winced with pain all over what we could see of her face as she tried to pull away from the man, but she couldn't get far because of the chains.

"No! Stop! Please stop!" Alex begged into the phone.

Journal entry insert by Lila Winters

I could hear Alex on the loudspeaker of Peter's mobile as it rested on his laptop. We had been conferenced called in, and I can hear everything. But Peter was smart enough to mute our end, and turned the speaker volume down to a soft rumble. – Almost as if he knew Alex would be loud when he saw me like this. – And Terrence is probably cursing under his breath, trying not to freak out.

Eventually the burning pain in my abdomen stopped when Peter pulled his hand away, and I listened to the fear in Alex's voice as he asked, "What do you want to know?"

It was hard not to miss Stephen's cocky Texan accent shine through that stupid voice-mod he was using on the phone as he replied, "A few nights ago we raided the Connors's mansion looking for something, but it wasn't there. So tell me where to find the island seed."

Seriously? – That is what this whole thing is about? – That damn fraccing island tree-stone.

"I don't know where it is," Alex answered.

To which Stephen tsked. "Wrong answer."

With that response, the burning pain returned as I felt Peter's fiery hands run up the length of my arms, towards the chains where he heated the iron manacles around my wrist.

"No! Please," Terrence begged, sounding so worried. "We told you the truth. We don't know where it is!"

The pain dwindled as Peter let go of the chains, but I felt his breath in my ear as he reminded me to stay quiet while we listened to the phone conversation.

"You did," Stephen replied. "But Maxwell didn't."

Max then blurted out, "Lila took it to Canada. But it was destroyed in the cabin fire."

"Are you sure about that?" Stephen questioned again.

"Yes!" Max barked.

There was a moment of silence until Stephen whispered, "You're lying."

The fear rose in me, knowing what was to come, and in my tears, I started shaking my head trying to move away. Then within seconds, I could feel the heat again as Peter's hand rested on my thigh, burning through to my jeans.

But before the pain got too intense, I fearfully breathed. "No, please stop. I know where it is."

Again, the pain stopped with Peter moving his hand from my leg to my mouth to shush me, burning my lips before his hand stopped glowing. From the phone, I heard Alex scream my name, demanding Peter to get his hands off me. But he didn't listen.

Instead Peter leaned in closer to me and whispered in my ear, "Where?"

Very slowly he removed his hand from my mouth, expecting me to answer him through my now swollen, blistering lips. "I didn't want to leave it at the hotel, so I keep it with me... It's in a secret compartment at the bottom of my handbag."

Peter pulled away from me, and all of a sudden Alex's rambling and yelling was cut off mid-sentence. The last thing I heard was Alex shouting, "I'll find you, Lila... just hold on."

Staying silent, I listened to Peter's movement. But I'm beginning to feel fatigued, and struggled to hold myself up as I fearfully wheezed, "Are you going to kill me?"

"Yes," Peter replied, tapping away at his phone.

"Killing me isn't going to help? My friends will find you." I whimpered, trying to change his mind. But still he said nothing and started tapping his foot impatiently, so I questioned, "Are we on a time limit?"

I heard his feet move towards me as he placed the mobile back down on the laptop and replied, "Well, I do have a concert to get to."

It was then I heard the distant sound of another train blasting its horn and realised where we are.

Journal entry insert by Billy Jonas

I think I'm going to be sick, watching Lila go through all of this pain. I know she's been through this kind of thing before. But to live through it again at the hands of the ones she had saved, it's just horrendous.

Stephen received a text message on his phone and muted his conversation with Mr Eden and Alex's ranting threats to read it. He then stormed over to the back of the large van and brought back Lila's handbag, rummaging through it and tearing it apart to find some large green rock.

"You're sick." I shook my head in disgust, watching him hold the rock like it was the holy grail.

"I'm not sick... I'm angry. Especially at you... for sleeping with our enemy." In his anger, Stephen pointed back to the screen of Lila's recording and glared at me with fire burning in his eyes.

What the hell is he talking about?

"Lila is not your enemy!" I rebuked.

Yet he didn't believe me. He just leered at me, holding the recording of Lila closer to me, ensuring I see her pain as he huffs. "You don't believe me... Well, why don't we ask her that, and see if she tells the truth about what her mission is really about?"

Journal entry insert by Maxwell Eden

It's becoming unbearable, waiting for something to happen, still fearfully watching Lila through the computer screen. I could see Alex and Terrence tense in fear every time the man walked closer to Lila, while we anxiously waited, and waited for the voice on the phone to return.

During our wait, Adela and Katie entered the room, looking for Alex, and they gasped in shock when they saw the video feed. Before I could react, Adela made a phone call, and seconds later, Tyme burst through the door with his father and Matt behind him.

I muted my microphone, so Terrence could fill them all in. And Tyme and Matt's reactions were almost exact as dread fell across their faces. William, however, didn't react as badly. I suspect it's because he's seen this treatment before.

Finally, the voice on the phone returned. "Well, well, Mr Eden, you were wrong. Lila's had the seed with her this entire time. Looks like she's keeping secrets from you as well... Next question... Why was your team at the Connors Mansion?"

I briefly glanced at Terrence, confused as to what I should answer with, eventually replying, "Err... they were doing re-con, looking for information."

Again, there was silence on the phone for way too long and the whole room felt tense.

"I warned you, Mr Eden," the voice replied.

Katie had to look away from the computer screen, knowing what was about to happen. And I cringed as we watched the man in the room with Lila stand behind her, wrapping one arm around her body, resting it on her chest and the other on her back. His hands lit up like hotplates, and Lila's entire body coiled in pain. But as she felt the searing heat, she kept biting her blistered bottom lip to the point where it was swollen and bleeding. — Almost like she's refusing to give in and scream.

As Lila suffered through the pain though, Matt randomly pointed to her chained hand that looked like it was spasming. I stared at Matt, completely baffled but somehow William understood it. Grabbing a pen and paper from my desk, he hurriedly started writing as he watched Lila's hand intently. But when the man pulled away again, Lila relaxed and the spasm in her hand stopped. All William wrote was "Morse code: Train — port — bomb."

With that Adela stepped away, searching for something on her phone as the voice asked his next question, "Riddle me this, Maxwell, who lies about their past and sacrifices others to cover up their mistakes?"

I wasn't sure if I should keep talking or not as the rest of the team huddled around Adela, so I replied, "Eerr... I don't know."

It was the wrong answer, and the voice told me I had one minute to think about it as the man started torturing Lila again.

Adela, Katie, and Tyme then disappeared, following Alex and Terrence out of the office. And I really hope that it's a good sign that maybe they know where Lila's being held.

"Better hurry up, Maxwell." The voice snickered. "It looks like our friend's getting a little bored of this game... We can always speed things up for her."

Matt scrubbed his hands into his hair, unable to look away as the pain on Lila's face intensified, and eventually he pleaded, "Say something!"

"I did!" I admitted, hoping they would stop torturing her if I spoke the truth. "I lied about my past...! I used to be a member of The Board. And I am responsible for the mess you're in."

Journal entry continued by Alex Woods

Lila had given us a clue, and Adela recognised the dome roof in the video and was convinced it was Flinders Street station. So we're now all running at full-speed to save Lila.

We had to slow down when we got closer to Federation Square because the area is packed with people, all enjoying some kind of radio festival with a free concert starting soon and food trucks lining the streets. – This is not good. Especially if William's right, and there's a bomb somewhere around here.

Think, Alex. – What would Lila do? – I got it.

In a hurry, I turned to the group and ordered, "Adela, call George and let him know what's going on. Then get these people to a safe distance. Remember code-C but do what you need to. Katie, Tyme, you're with her... Terrence, you're with me."

All agreeing to my orders, we split up and Terrence followed me through the crowd towards Flinders Street station. And right now, I feel twisted to my core, anxiously hoping and praying that Lila is still alive.

Journal entry insert by Maxwell Eden

There was silence on the phone as I watched Lila become limp again when her torturer stopped burning her. The man then walked toward the camera to grab the phone that sat in front of it, and held the phone up in front of Lila.

We could now hear the whimpering sounds coming from her, and she was whispering Matt's name as she begged, "Matt... Matt please don't watch this... don't watch this... look away... Max, please don't let him watch this."

I looked up at Matt and he shook his head. "I'm not going anywhere, Lila."

We then listened to Lila's cry, but the man with her whispered something into her ear, causing her to stop crying and nod her head. Then the voice on the phone directed his question to Lila this time.

"Lila, you don't seem at all surprised to hear that you've been working for our enemy this whole time... Did you know about Mr Eden's sins when you agreed to work for him?"

She remained silent, so the man in the room with Lila held his glowing hand around her throat as the voice asked again. "Tell the truth now, Lila... did you know?"

The man holding Lila pulled away again, leaving a fresh burn mark on her neck in the shape of his hand as she whimpered, "Yes."

"Hmm... One more question for you, Lila," the voice demanded. "Given that one of your talents is in Nature, do you believe that Mr Eden's intention to save our kind is truly honourable?"

Hearing that question, caused my body to tense, and I held my breath when Lila took a moment and hesitated. I heard her whimpers as I looked at Matt and William both waiting for her answer as well. Then she replied in so much pain, "No."

My heart sank. – How did she know? – Why did she let

me believe that my lies were hidden? – How much does she know about me? – How long has she known?

I exhaled deeply, holding my head in my hands, feeling like a horrible state of a human being. But then I heard the worst words of all when the voice said, "Finish it."

"No! Wait... Lila!" I shouted before the phone disconnected.

I then watched in horror as the man in the room with Lila took off his shirt and pressed his body against Lila's as it glowed a fiery red. We couldn't hear her, but we could see Lila screaming as her face turned red and her skin started to blister.

Oh god. – She's being burned alive.

"Don't watch this!" William demanded to Matt, turning him away from the screen. When suddenly the recording went dark, and Matt wailed, screaming Lila's name while William held him back as he too broke down in tears.

Journal entry continued by Alex Woods

Adela and Katie were smart in forcing the crowd gathered in Fed Square to leave. They ran to the Yarra River and caused it to start raining, creating thick heavy rain clouds that loomed over Melbourne. The downside was most of the people started to run for cover into Flinders Street station, making it difficult for Terrence and me to be discreet in using code-C.

But when I heard the sound of Lila's screams echo throughout the station, I didn't care about code-C and neither did Terrence. We ran at full-speed, breaking down every damn door to get to Lila in the dome roof.

We found her being burned alive by a Fire guardian, and I raced to punch him in his pathetic bare ribs. He screamed in pain, letting go of Lila. And I moved to catch her as she fell limp in my arms while Terrence tackled the guy into a wall.

"Bomb... there's a bomb," Lila kept mumbling through her burnt lips as I tried to break the chains from the cuffs on her wrist.

We knew her fear as Terrence inspected the bomb and yelled, "We've got under two minutes."

"I can't break these. I need the key!" I shouted back.

At full-speed, Terrence darted around the dome but failed to find the key. It wasn't even on the A-hole of a man who held her. I then heard Lila rasp my name, and I held her closer to me to listen to her raspy breath as she pleaded to me.

"Alex... break my hands."

Hoping I had heard her wrong, I pulled the blindfold away from Lila's eyes to see if she was being serious. And she stared into my eyes, trying to hold herself up as she leaned against me and pleaded again. "Break them."

My whole body tensed as I stared at her then looked at her hands, clasping them in mine, and I whispered, "I'm so sorry, Lila."

I didn't want to, but I knew I had to, so I squeezed tightly, crushing her bones and dislocating both of her thumbs. She screamed in agony, and it hurt me knowing I was causing it. But within seconds, I helped her to pull her hands through the shackles and she was free.

Oh Crap Damn. – I'm never leaving her alone again.

Carefully, I scooped Lila's beautiful but fatigued body up into my arms, and my heart ached as she yelped in pain everywhere my hands touched. Her entire body is red and has already started to blister, so I gently held her and whispered, "Hold on, Lila... I'm getting you out of here."

But before I rushed to leave, she tried to pull away and rasped, "No... We have to save the people... I have to stop the bomb."

And while I really love that Lila cares more about the people then herself. – Right now is not the time. – And I am not going to let her die.

"I'll do it," I muttered, hurriedly placing Lila in Terrence's arms.

As Terrence gently held her, he ordered to me. "Throw the bomb towards the river and throw it high."

He then turned to race Lila out of this horrible place, while I grabbed the bomb and ran out onto the roof with less than 10 seconds to spare as I threw it towards the river. The bomb exploded mid-air and the shock wave from the blast forced me backwards, throwing me off the roof, being tossed onto the top of one of the food trucks below. – Breaking a lot of bones, and causing a lot of pain.

OUCH!!!

I heard the screams of a couple of teenagers as my body slowly rolled off the roof of the food-truck and onto the ground in front of them. The seconds felt long and painful. But before everything went dark in my eyes, I saw Adela and George helping the paramedics load me into an ambulance with Lila being loaded into the van next to mine.

CHAPTER 8

The Monsters From Within

Journal entry by Lila Winters

I've created monsters. — I thought by saving the captured guardians with their memory intact, it would be better than no memory at all. But instead, I've left them all with the pain and the guilt, and the craving for vengeance.

This is my fault. — I know it is.

My eyes felt heavy as they pried open and looked around the bleach scented hospital room. Terrence stood at the end of my bed, looking out the window of my private room. He looked worried, and I know he is because his dark-brown hair isn't perfectly combed back like it usually is. — Which means, I don't get to mess it up today.

It might be a little difficult for me anyway. — I seem to have burn dressings on the worst of my wounds, and my skin is dry and blistered with stinging, swollen lips. It also looks like I have the worst sunburn, and my hands and body ache from being broken. — But I think I got lucky this time.

I tried to sit up when Terrence appeared next to me, moving the pillows to help me move and get a little more comfortable. Then he whispered with a gentle and caring smile. "Hey."

"Terry," I rasped with barely a voice to me. "What happened? Where's Alex?"

In my worry, I tried to get out of the bed. But Terrence stopped me, holding his hands up in front of me and shaking his head to give me a firm hint. And I have no plans to argue with him. I know he's just looking after me.

As Terrence watched me concede to his request and lay back down on the bed, he smiled then sat down on the bed next to me to explain, "Alex is here, but he's still in surgery. The bomb exploded over the Yarra River and no humans were hurt... except for a lot of broken windows, and some minor damage to the surrounding buildings. You... are currently recovering from two broken hands, a fractured rib cage, left cheek, and femur. Along with first and second degree burns over all of your body, and a lot of bruises... As for Alex, he was thrown off the roof from the blast, and has broken several bones, including his back..."

Terrence stopped talking when he noticed the tears welling in my eyes then moved at full-speed to grab the tissues, and gently catch the tears before the salty-water hurt my dry skin. "Lila, this isn't your fault... You know Alex would do this a thousand times over to save you... Just like you would do it for us. So please don't blame yourself."

I nodded my head while staring into his blue-green eyes, and started to relax. Then he breathed with a smile, brushing the hair from my face with the gentle touch of his fingers as he explained the cover story George had created for us. Apparently, Alex and I are the heroes who stopped a terrorist attack on

Flinders Street station, and I was caught too close to the explosion like Alex. But thankfully the terrorist was apprehended and is now under heavy guard at the hospital.

"What about Billy?" I rasped as Terrence held up some blue-rose water for me to drink. "I heard him in the background with Stephen."

His brows furrowed and he looked worriedly confused. "Who's Stephen?"

I shuddered at the taste of the blue-rose water but once it had passed, I explained with a gruff voice, "It was Stephen from Agronomique's. I can't remember his last name. But he was one of the guardians we rescued from Canada. So was Nigel, and Peter, and the man who dropped me over the pool... Billy said his name was Andrew. They're all from Agronomique's, Terry... This really is my fault... I let them out into the world with so much hatred and thirst for blood."

"Lila," he whispered, gently holding my braced hands. "Not all the guardians that you rescue are going to be good. But you have always believed that good and evil should be the choice of the individual... You gave them the freedom to choose... It's not your fault if they choose wrong."

Hmm. – I really like that Terrence listens to my crazy ramblings about choices and freedom, and still believes in my cause.

I tried to smile at him but my lips hurt too much, and I winced with a pout. Terrence saw my pain and moved closer to me again, gently applying moisturising cream onto my lips, paying careful attention to the burn of my swollen bottom lip where my teeth had cut through, now leaving me with stitches.

While Terrence was busy fretting over my lips, George knocked on the door of the room to ask if I was up for visitors before he escorted, Matt, Tyme, Adela, and Katie into the room. Maxwell and William entered a few steps behind them, and I could just tell Maxwell felt guilty and scared about all of this.

My worrying little brother stood next to the bed, trying to find the best way to hug me without hurting me. But he's struggling a bit. So instead, I slowly sat up with Terrence's help, and then swung my legs over the side for Tyme to gently wrap his arms around me. And while still fretting over me, Terrence sat on the other side of the bed behind me with his back against mine to keep me upright, and I happily welcomed the support, leaning against him as everyone took turns to greet me.

Tyme was so scared for me. I don't think he's a fan of the danger that comes with being me. And Matt looks like he's been crying, and when he hugged me, he didn't want to let go.

"Lila, I thought you were dead... Again," he cried.

I tried to lighten the mood to cheer him and the others up as I joshed, "Yeah well, I'm stubborn and I don't like dying... Besides, I don't think my team would let me. We still have people to save and an evil organisation to destroy... You know, all that hero stuff we do."

"You definitely are stubborn." Matt laughed as he loosened his hug.

I was starting to feel tired again, and Terrence could sense that I was trying to hide it when I leaned my head back on him. So he moved to try and support me a little more and he stated, "She's getting tired."

George took that cue and ran with it, asking the team to follow him to the café downstairs to finish giving their statements. – Or at least 'a version' of a statement for the police investigation. It's actually really encouraging and good to see George being so cooperative and understanding with our team now.

Adela and Katie were the first to leave, followed by Tyme and his dad as they said their goodbyes again. But before George left, he leaned in to hug me and whispered very softly, "Max showed me the video."

My breath stopped, worried what might happen if that was used as evidence, until he added, "And I promise that video will never see the light of day... ever. It's even been scrubbed from the internet. So the only people who have a copy is Max... now me, and whoever the hell sent it. But you need to promise me that when you find that sick bastard who was on the phone, that you give him hell... Okay?"

Taking a relieving breath, I nodded as George walked out of the room with Matt.

Finally there was just me, Terrence, and Max left in the hospital room. But I'm pretty sure Max and I need to talk. – Alone.

"Terry," I called, still sounding raspy and struggling to move my lips. "I'm hungry... can you find me something to eat?"

Very slowly and carefully, Terrence moved to stand up and helped me to pull my legs back up onto the bed as I rested back on the pillows again. And for a brief moment, Terrence hesitated then kissed my forehead before he left, leaving only me and Max now.

Max stood at the end of the hospital bed with his hands in his pockets, refusing to look at me as he worriedly questioned, "How long have you known?"

"The day after we met," I replied with a slight smile – or the best I could muster. He looked at me confused, asking why I hadn't said anything or why I even agreed to work for him. And I rasped with a chuckle. "Rule 7... I knew your intentions to find your daughter were pure... which was why I helped you. But while your need to make up for the sins of your past is the right thing to do... it's not honourable, especially when you still hold one sin in particular."

I took a few moments to breathe then stood to my feet, slowly moving to stand in front of Max before I continued. "Speaking from experience, Max, it's always better to tell your loved ones the truth, no matter the consequences... And while I know that your actions now will never make up for your past... you should never stop trying. You're a good man, Max... you just got a little lost."

He stared at me with such a long face, and scrubbed his hand through his peppered grey hair before he hesitantly asked, "If I hug you, will it hurt?"

I nodded and chuckled a little. "Yes, but hugs are always worth the pain."

He then slowly and gently wrapped his arms around me to give me a hug, letting out a relaxing sigh. "Thank you... You truly are amazing, you know that?"

Journal entry insert by Keith Connors

The Flinders Street disaster was a nightmare. And the target — Lila Winters, has again failed to be neutralised. I asked for it to be painful, and yes, they didn't sell short on that part. But she still lives, and they failed to take out her stupid team in the process.

Katty is currently at the hospital, dealing with a loose end, Peter Boone. Because she told Stephen that she would spring him from police custody for him. — But I'm finding it increasingly difficult to believe that an entire army of guardians are struggling to dispose of an annoying little Nature girl and her band of merry men.

We've taken up residence in my mother's city apartment in the Eureka towers with my siblings Anna, Robert, and Izzy. So I had a front-row seat of the chaos that ensued after the explosion, and I'm still watching the city workers and police clean up and survey the damage. — All of them still completely oblivious to the war that's brewing around them.

I am, however, happy to receive reports from Stephen that Billy Jonas has agreed to stay with his crew and work as the on-call doctor for them. — They're all stupidly under the assumption that Lila is dead, and Billy believes he has nowhere else to go. But I'm sure over time he will come to agree that our war is worthy of his attention and allegiance.

"Katty." I grinned as she stood at the door looking radiant as ever.

She's an amazing Animal guardian that always keeps her body in good fighting form. And I marvelled at her wonderful body as she walked towards the dining room window wear I stood, handing me a glass of champagne to toast the partial success we had.

"Did you get to her?" I asked before downing my drink.

She disappointingly shook her head, standing next to me on the balcony. "There's a swarm of her loyal security guarding her ward, and several news crew all wanting to speak to the heroes that saved Melbourne. So it might look a little suspicious if she dies in the hospital... Besides, I think I might have better use of her."

Journal entry insert by William Knight

My son has really grown to like his big sister. All night, he sat in her hospital room, looking after her while Terrence waited for any news on Alex's condition. Then as soon as Alex was out of surgery, Terrence and Tyme had absolutely no hope of keeping Lila in her room to rest. So they helped her move a chair into Alex's private room, and all waited for him to wake up.

They've spent two days in that room now, and Terrence has kept making Lila drink the blue-rose water to help her heal while they all try to distract each other by playing board games, sitting next to the window in Alex's room. I, however, am sitting outside in the nearby waiting room, thinking over my life's poor decisions.

I remember the day Lila was born. When I held her in my arms and swore that I would love her forever. Katherine, Lila's mother, had opted for a home birth given the dangers she knew we would be in for breaking the rules and creating a hybrid, which meant I got to deliver my baby girl into this world. And Lila was beautiful and perfect.

Our little angel was born in an old beach house just outside a small town called Karumba at the top end of Queensland, not far from the state border. Katherine and I knew to play it smart, only telling the fewest of family where we lived. Add to that, I grew a forest of trees around the house to give us the privacy and protection we needed.

Katherine's sister Hanna and her husband Richard came to visit us, and see their beautiful little niece on the day of her birth. When Hanna arrived, she complained about the heat and the ridiculous amount of sand, and trees, and the fact that they had to leave their car so far away from the house. But Katherine and I wanted them to see Lila at least once before we said goodbye and go into hiding for Lila's safety.

Hanna was furious and kept trying to convince us to stay. "Look I know she's a hybrid... but she deserves to have at least a glimpse of a normal life. You can stay with us on the farm back in Victoria. It's out of the city, off the main roads. It will be safe for her... And you two are more than capable of protecting her there."

As she said those words, a gas canister was thrown into our front window. Katherine instantly handed Lila to me then morphed into a Bengal tiger – her favourite animal, and jumped through the broken window. Then in a hurry, I turned to Richard and Hanna and demanded them to run as I lifted up the floorboards to reveal a hidden tunnel. And I handed my baby Lila to Hanna, begging both of them to keep her safe, so I could rush to help Katherine.

My memory ended there when I heard the laughter of Tyme and Lila, and saw Terrence walking out of Alex's hospital room looking slightly embarrassed. He walked down the hall and found me waiting at the end.

"Hey... Lila's sent me down to the café to get her some food. Do you want something?"

I politely declined his offer then walked down the hall and stood in the corridor to watch my two children mucking around. Tyme had just accused Lila of cheating at chess. And it was ironic since he was the one who had to move the chess pieces for her, given her broken hands.

Down the hall, the nurse walked into Lila's room carrying meds and fresh dressings, and then stormed towards Alex's room in a huff. She mumbled to herself as she looked for Lila, knowing where she would be, and didn't look happy when she found her.

"Lila, you need to take your meds and you should really be resting in your own room," the nurse demanded. But there is no way Lila would willingly leave Alex's room, and she sat back in her chair shaking her head and refusing to leave. So the nurse ended up negotiating with her. "What if we bring your bed in here, would you be willing to rest then?"

Taking a moment, Lila crinkled her nose as she noticed Tyme nodding to her with pleading eyes. So eventually she agreed. "I'd be more likely too, maybe."

"Fine," the nurse huffed. "I'll need to change your dressings as well. I'll be back in a minute."

The nurse then walked out mumbling to herself again. And I had to hide my smile feeling very proud of the woman Lila grew up to be. Sometimes she can be really stubborn, but I think that's a really good quality in her. – It's kept her alive.

Tyme laughed again while shaking his head at his sister. "You seem to have an issue with doing as your told."

"Sorry..." Lila saddened a little when she saw the slight frustration on Tyme's face, and she stared at the ground. "I just have a thing with hospitals... I don't like them."

"Can I ask why?" Tyme queried, leaning forward and growing concerned at her pout.

But Lila went silent when the nurse returned, wheeling her hospital bed into the room and resting it opposite Alex. The nurse then stood and waited in slight annoyance for Lila to get back on the bed, holding the fresh dressings in her hand as well to give her a not-so-subtle hint.

While trying to be careful, Tyme helped Lila to slowly sit down on the hospital bed and was about to leave when Lila anxiously called out, "Tyme... can you stay? This parts going to really hurt."

He nodded and helped Lila to undo her hospital gown then looked away but still held Lila's hand. – He's such a good brother like that. I followed suit and gave Lila some privacy, stepping to the other side of the hall while looking at the floor. But I felt the frustration and worry rise in me when I heard Lila whimper as the nurse removed some of the old dressings.

Yet something in the nurse's nature gained my attention, and her voice almost sounded suspicious. "Lila... it says in your chart that you were burned in a fire?"

"That's right," Lila replied.

I looked in to try and read the nurse's body language as the nurse questioned again. "Are you sure? Because some of these burns are starting to look a lot like hands."

Lila cleared her throat, most definitely sensing the nature of the nurse as well. Then she straightened her body slightly and pulled Tyme closer as she replied, "It must have happened when the guys pulled me out of the fire."

Oh, my poor baby girl. – I can sense her frustration when she needs to lie.

The nurse stayed suspicious but continued to apply the burn cream onto Lila as she stated, "Well, that's unfortunate... The good news is the blisters on your skin are going down. We should be able to get away with not putting the new dressings on and leave them to air... I'll go check what the doctor suggests, and I'll be back in a little bit... You should also be able to get dressed into your own clothes now, loose-fitting preferably. Was your husband able to bring you any?"

Tyme quickly responded for Lila, grabbing out some of her pyjamas from the bag that he brought with him. "Yes... and I can help her get dressed."

Still suspicious in her nature, the nurse agreed to Tyme's offer yet was quick to leave, carrying the old dressings and hospital gown with her.

Right. – We might need to monitor that one.

Once the room was empty, Tyme began to help Lila put her pyjamas on while being very respectful at the fact that she was naked. He stayed silent as he buttoned up her pyjama shirt but stared at the very prominent hand-shaped burns on Lila's neck and across her lips.

She must have noticed Tyme's stare when she timidly spoke, "Tyme, are you okay? You don't have to do this if it makes you uncomfortable."

Slightly confused, Tyme continued to do up the buttons and shook his head. "No, I'm happy to help. And I want to... It's just I thought you were using the blue-rose thing... I don't understand. It's been two days. Most of this should have healed by now."

"The burns are a little deeper than I thought," Lila replied while turning away from him.

She's lying. – I can see it on her face and sense it from her. – The question is why?

"Lila, your heartrate's rising," Tyme grumbled, and it was clear that he also knew she was lying. "Lila, please, I'm your brother. You shouldn't need to lie to me."

"Alright, fine." Lila sighed and rolled her eyes. "But you have to promise not to tell anyone else... Promise me, Brother."

Tyme seemed reluctant to answer as he helped Lila to put on her pyjama pants, but he also knew Lila was stubborn and wasn't going to say anything until he agreed. So he stood back, slightly disgruntled as he crossed his arms.

"Alright, I promise."

"And I know your dad's listening... so he needs to promise that he won't tell anyone either," she demanded as she looked out and scowled at me still lurking in the hallways.

It hurt to see the hate on her face, but I nodded, agreeing to her terms. She then took a few breaths and quietly whispered, "The blue-rose doesn't work on me anymore... It hasn't for a long time."

"What!!!" Tyme shrieked, and Lila rushed to quiet him with her braced hands, glancing back at Alex still asleep on the bed. But

Tyme grew more upset and questioned, "How long have you known about this?"

Again, Lila looked reluctant to answer, casually stepping away from her brother as she did. "Since New Year's Day. It still kind of worked for a few weeks after. It just took a little longer. But now it doesn't affect me at all."

The look on Tyme's face was of pure frustration while glaring at Lila. "You've known about this for months... You've been on so many life-threatening missions, knowing the rose wouldn't heal you..."

He stopped and grunted, fuelled with anger staring at Lila as he huffed, "You lied to me... after the Agronomique's mission when I took you site seeing in New York... I asked you about your healing and why it was taking so long and... URGH... You gave me the same stupid line. How could you not tell me about this? And don't tell me it's because I didn't need to know."

"No, it's because I didn't want you to know," Lila sniped, standing defensively and crossing her arms. "I knew you would react like this. And I'm certainly not planning on telling Alex or Terrence any of this, because then they'd never let me leave the damn building."

As their volume escalated past a certain level, I walked into the room, closing the door to keep the conversation private. Lila noticed my movement but didn't say anything. She just stayed focused on her brother.

"Look I've been trying to make another tonic. I just haven't had the time."

That definitely made Tyme upset. "Well, if you had told me about this before, I could have made time... That is after all my specialty."

"When?" she bickered. "Between the rescue missions and recon, the training sessions and work. Not to mention the fact that creating healing tonics is really hard to do and requires a lot of my concentration and research. And if you hadn't noticed, my mind's been a little busy lately."

Her voice turned to a growl as Lila held up her white hair, and her eyes turned black. I tried to intervene but Tyme glared at me, so I thought it would be best to give them more privacy and closed the curtains across the room with me on the other side standing guard.

Great. – It's their first sibling fight.

"What about Terrence?" Tyme tried to reason with Lila. "You could have asked him to help you."

"There is no way I would tell him," Lila growled. "He would just react the same way you are now."

"Good!" Tyme yelled back.

"I can help," I interjected from the other side of the curtain.

Finally gaining Tyme's attention, he opened the curtain, seething with anger when he demandingly questioned, "How?"

I glanced over to Lila, who now has pointy ears to go with her black eyes and white hair. Then I explained, "I know a healing tonic that can heal Lila... But she's right. It does require a lot of concentration... I'll need another Nature guardian to help me."

Unfortunately, the only other Nature guardian in the room seems unwilling to help as she crossed her arms and pulled a sour face. "There's no way I'm helping you."

Then still in an angered temper, Tyme looked back at her and pulled the same sour face. "Fine... I'll get Terrence to help him."

In a fury, Lila growled, storming towards him. "Tyme, you promised me you weren't going to tell anyone... That includes Terrence. And there is no way in hell I'm taking anything your dad has to offer... He knows nothing about me."

Ouch. – Those words really hurt.

I was about to chime in but Tyme spoke over me, "He's not just my dad... He's also yours."

"NO!!" Lila shouted. "He is not anything to me. Not a dad, not a mentor, or an elder or even a friend... The man who raised me, the person who claimed that dad title... He kidnapped me, faked my death, lied to me, drugged me, tortured me, and tried to kill me on numerous occasions. He beat me and caused so much of my pain, then had the arrogancy to call it training... And yeah, thanks to him, I know how to hold my own now, and I can cope with pain as if it was just another part of life... But excuse me, if it seems like I have a little daddy trust issues here!"

Tyme stammered, needing to step away again as he stared down at the floor, speechless. - Probably hearing this all for the first time. - In noticing that, Lila gave him a moment as her eyes narrowed on mine yet she still spoke to Tyme. "Your dad gave up his chance to just walk back into my life and help me when he left me in the care of a psychopath... twice."

She scowled at me, and again I felt like a horrible person because it was true. But I'm determined to prove myself to her. "Lila, I'm sorry I abandoned you... I didn't know how to help you on the island. But I do know how to help you now. Please, trust me."

I stared at her pleadingly, hoping she would at least give me a chance when she crossed her arms and appeared standing right in front of me, still with that scowl as she questioned me. "Why? You had 18 years to earn my trust and save me from my hell. But you didn't... And I'm all grown up now with children of my own, so I know what it truly means to be a parent. A good parent. So tell me, why should I trust you now? Why should I even give you that right to be called Dad?"

Again ouch. - I really wish I could tell her the truth and answer her questions. But I don't think she wants to hear it. - She'd probably think it was just another excuse.

Still she continued to scowl at me, waiting for some kind of response. All I could think to do was look back at Tyme, but he looked just as sad as I felt, and sighed while shaking his head.

"Fine, he doesn't have to be your father, and I won't force the issue. But right now, I'm over-ruling you, and I'm breaking my promise. And if you love me and accept me as your brother, you will let me do this."

"Oh, don't you dare pull that brother card crap on me," she growled.

He started to walk out and turned back. "I just did and we're doing this. And so help me, Lila, if you argue, I will wake Alex up myself, and he'll force you to take the tonic... And you know he'll do it... Now stay."

With a very stern scowl, Tyme stayed staring at his sister while holding the door open to escort me out of the room to go find Terrence.

Eerr? – Right, I'm not overly sure this is the best move. Leaving Lila alone in this angered condition. – But I also don't want to argue with Tyme with him wanting to help his sister. – So I'm a bit stuck in what to do.

CHAPTER 9

Want vs Need

Journal entry by Lila Winters

URGH! - I can't believe he did that. And I can't believe I almost turned into a wolf. - Grrrrr!! - Tyme makes me so mad! He made a promise to me, and now he's going to ruin everything. There is no way I would ever trust his father without him first earning it, and he's had years to do that. And months living in the same fraccing building as me. - So like hell I'm going to put my life in his hands.

I paced the room, limping as I walk, too busy contemplating chasing after Tyme and pummelling his arse for breaking a promise than to acknowledge the pain I'm in. But I also have this small issue of looking like a hobbling, heavily burned elf with broken hands, leg and rib that may prevent me from leaving this room. That and Chase and the team were only given permission to guard this hospital floor.

"He's right you know," I heard a voice whisper from the bed.

"Alex." I excitedly gasped, hurriedly limping to the side of his bed and hugging him the best way a could with my broken hands still braced and bandaged.

He too has a broken arm, and both legs are broken, as well as a shoulder brace on both sides. But he didn't flinch when I hugged him even though I knew it hurt him. Eventually, I lifted my head from his chest but refused to let go of him when I saw his eyes open and looking at me with his amazing smile.

"Hi," he whispered.

I cried happy tears, continuing to hug him, and blubbered, "Hi."

"Your hugs won't get you out of taking that tonic," he croaked, moving his one good arm to brush the white hair back to check out my pointy ears before staring into my dark eyes again.

"You were awake for that," I rasped before pulling away from him.

"Yep, I heard every word... And your right. I would have never let you leave that hotel."

I pouted my swollen lips, sitting back down in the chair next to him to cry more. "And people wonder why I don't like talking about this stuff."

"It doesn't mean you should stop," he replied, slowly turning his head to look at me, still with that amazing smile. "Talking or hugging. I like them both. And your hugs are definitely worth the pain, so bring it in."

With a small grin, I slowly climbed up onto the hospital bed to lie next to him, being careful of both his and my injuries. I tucked one of my braced hands between us, resting it against my waist, and the other rested across his torso. Then I rested my head on his chest before relaxing into his cuddle.

He gently ran his fingers along the exposed red skin of my hand then softly around the burns on my arm, and I could feel his body tense up as he looked at the bruises and burns that he could see. But when he relaxed again, he sighed. "I'm sorry for being a jerk."

"I'm sorry too." I snuggled in closer to him, loving the tender touch of his arms around me. I could feel his heart beating, and I felt so happy. But I still cried while holding him close. "Alex... thank you for coming to find me."

He gently kissed the top of my head and whispered, "I would move mountains to find you."

Yeah. – I'm absolutely loving every moment of this because I feel so safe in his arms, and I began to sense all the love Alex feels for me. Then it happened. – All the anger and rage I felt churning away inside me just disappeared, and I started to feel more like myself.

My white hair faded back into that honey-blond colour, unfortunately losing the purple and green streaks that Adela insisted on, and my ears turned back to their ordinary human style. Then as I snuggled in closer, I very happily fell asleep listening to the sound of Alex's heart.

Journal entry insert by Tyme Knight

When Dad and I caught up with Terrence in the hospital café and told him the situation, he was just as furious as I was and agreed to help my dad with the new healing tonic. So we headed back to the hotel to set up in my apartment.

Dad had one of the gas burners on, heating up the juice of several pomegranate fruits. And Terrence stood at the bench, surrounded by pot plants of garlic, sunflowers, moly herb, and even the plant I'm named after, the thyme herb.

Terrence was crushing the herbs that Dad had given him, but he was taking his anger out on them, grinding the pestle into the mortar. Dad quickly looked over Terrence's shoulder and sighed as he tried to explain, "Terrence, the herbs need to be lightly crushed not turned into dust."

"Sorry... I'll start over," Terrence grumbled, angrily throwing the crushed herbs in the bin and picking out fresh herbs again.

"Did you want to talk about it?" Dad asked while watching over the simmering juice.

"No." Terrence pouted then huffed. "Why wouldn't she tell me about this? I've been making those stupid blue-rose tonics for her for months, and she knew they didn't work this whole time."

"That's how she was raised," Dad replied with slight disappointment in his tone. "Remember, Lila was raised by Richard. She was expected to never show any signs of weakness, not even to her friends... And I know I've only been here for a few months, but Lila seems like she carries the weight of the world on her shoulders sometimes... Always expected to be the strongest. Maybe she just didn't want to worry you."

I suspect Terrence was understanding Dad's point of view, and stopped grinding the herbs to hand them to Dad but still looked lost in his thoughts.

"Can I ask you a question?" Terrence asked and waited for my dad to nod while he mixed the herbs in, and then continued, "Why did you give Lila away?"

There was a long pause of silence as Dad turned off the stove and placed the pot of juice on the bench, slightly saddened by the question. "I think Lila needs to hear that story first... If she'll ever speak to me."

The room went silent with Terrence accepting his answer. But eventually Dad snapped out of his gloomy trance. "Right, we need to concentrate... Hold your hand over the juice and focus on the healing properties of all the herbs in it. Then command them to amplify. If we're doing it right, the juice should turn from dark red to a dark purple."

Terrence followed my dad's lead as both their eyes glowed green, and I watched in suspense as the juice changed colours.

"Yes," I quietly cheered getting excited.

Then while Terrence poured the juice into two small jars and tightened the lids, Dad explained, "She'll need to drink this, you can't give it to her by epi-pen. But there's also one more catch... If her body is not a willing participant, it has a lower chance of actually working. She's a Nature guardian remember, and everything I just used is derived from nature."

Yeah. – The penny dropped for me there.

"Wait, you're not coming...? Dad, this is your chance to show Lila how much you care for her."

"She doesn't want to see me. And I am going to respect her wishes... You should too." Dad replied, starting to clean up the mess as if he had given up.

"Dad, she's never going to change her mind if you don't try," I argued, getting frustrated at the fact that I have yelled at both family members today. "Why can't you just try to tell her the truth?"

Dad turned to me and let out a long sigh. "Tyme, I don't think cornering Lila in a hospital is the best place to talk to her, or try to start mending bridges."

"He's right, Tyme," Terrence interrupted. "Lila hates hospitals because of what happened to her as a child. She's always going to be in defence mode when she's there... In saying that, you should stay here too... If it's true that you actually did promise her, and then went against your word, she'll most likely kick the crap out of you and still refuse to take the tonic."

He walked to the door, turning back to me to stop me from following him and added, "Trust me on this, Tyme... just because she's injured does not mean Lila won't put up a fight. Rule 2 is the one rule she'll never break."

He then walked out the door and left us both behind.

"What the hell is rule 2!" I shouted. – Still wondering what the hell happened to Lila as a child that made her hate hospitals.

While holding his head in his hands, Dad sat down at the table and mumbled, "Never let down your defences... Pain can be your friend." Then in a sulk, he looked up at me with so much regret across his face. "Richard taught her that."

I sat down at the table next to Dad, feeling my entire body tense with rage as the next penny dropped, and I realised why Lila hates hospitals. – Remembering what she said about her fake dad. And I really hate Richard for hurting my sister like that. But I also hate the fact that she had to live like that.

Journal entry continued by Lila Winters

My fantastic cuddle session with Alex and the best sleep I've had in months was interrupted by an annoying police officer named Paige, who asked if she could talk to me in private. So I begrudgingly followed her to the empty room a few doors down with my arms crossed and feeling slightly annoyed.

"Have I done something wrong, Officer?" I queried.

She gestured for me to take a seat, but I refused and remained standing.

"No." She sighed, also slightly annoyed at my demeanour. "You haven't done anything wrong. I just need to ask you a few questions."

I remained guarded but sat down on the empty bed and waited as she opened up her notepad to ask her first question. "Okay, it says on your files that you're married, is that correct?"

Yeah. – That's a weird question to start with and she's clearly digging for something.

"Was... I was married," I answered. "We're divorced now"

"So you live on your own?" she questioned again.

I grumbled still trying to understand the suspicious nature she has as I answered, "No, I still live with my husband, but I sleep in a different room... We have two children to look after, and we both agreed it was best for them."

Still suspicious, Paige lifted her head to confirm, "So the relationship is good... you're both happy with the arrangement?"

I nodded and she moved onto her next question, "What about the man you were just with... You looked happy together... Are you in a relationship with him at the moment?"

Yep. – She's definitely fishing, and I think I just realised what she's looking for.

"I think I'm done answering questions." I smiled politely before walking towards the door.

But she brazenly threatened me, "Lila, I need to get these answers from someone. And I'm more than happy to ask your friend next door. Maybe even insist on having you two moved to separate wards... Separate hospitals if need be."

I stopped at the door and leered back at the officer. "Look, Paige, I don't like being interrogated and I certainly don't like being threatened. So if you want me to talk to you, I suggest you start asking the questions you actually want the answers to."

She closed her note-book then matched my stance, crossing her arms. "Fair enough. Then tell me the truth about where you got your injuries."

"As it says in the police report, I was caught in the explosion and burned by the fire."

"Yeah, I remember reading that," Paige snickered with scepticism written all over her. "But you see, for some reason, I don't believe you. And your nurse doesn't either. She believes you're a victim of spousal abuse."

"Well, luckily for me, I'm not in a relationship and I don't have a spouse."

In frustration, she walked towards me and sniped, "Then explain why your burns look like finger and hand marks, or explain the bruises and broken bones that are consistent with falling down the stairs. And why you have a large, stitched wound on your back. And while you're at it, you can explain all the scars that your nurse reported... It states in your medical record that in January this year you were brought into the E.R with an infected knife wound. And the doctor then also sighted fresh laceration scars on your abdomen along with a dozen more... I can even see some of them poking up from beneath your pyjamas and on your face and neck... Now given all that, you can understand how we came to the conclusions of abuse... spousal or not."

I stared at the floor in silence, trying to figure out what to do. - I can't afford another police officer poking around looking for dirt, not after what happened to George.

"Lila, I get it." She softly spoke, bracing herself for a speech. "I get that you love him, and you want to protect him. And I'm sure in your mind he doesn't mean to hurt you... But this relationship is clearly destroying you and your body. And I want to help you, but I can't if you don't talk to me."

Urgh! - This is really frustrating.

Usually, I'm all for women and the community in general looking out for one another, coming alongside the people who look like they need a helping hand. - And yeah, I don't look great at the moment, and my scars are scary and make people uncomfortable. But this woman can't help me.

She's a human, and only understands human issues. If I open up, and tell her all my deep dark secrets, tell her about all the pain I've felt, all the death I've seen, all the horrible things me and many guardians like me are forced to endure, she'll think I'm just making it up. She'll think I'm lying to protect my 'spouse' or whoever she thinks is behind my pain. - It's as if humans deny acknowledging the true injustice their kind and ours are capable of, and view their world with only what they can handle.

I know George struggles with what I am, and with what I do. It's why I haven't told him everything. I'm more concerned about his safety and sanity than his need to know about me and my kind. – But what am I supposed to do with this human?

Human. – Yeah, it gets hard when you see the divide like this.

Still waiting for my response, Paige stared at me until I replied, "I need to make a phone call."

In frustration, she stepped out of the room, pointing to the phone on the bedside table. And I called George, begging him to help me. Thankfully he's still in the building working with Chase to keep the nosey reporters out of the hospital. So he came to my rescue.

Thank-you. – I've never been more excited to see his heavily tanned to light-brown skin, and tightly weaved hair appear in the hallway outside the room I was in. And I watched as Officer Paige got told off for questioning someone in such a fragile state as mine.

George then told the officer to drop the issue, and when she questioned why, he replied with something I would have never thought to say. He told her I worked for ASIS – the Australian Secret Intelligence Service – and that her poking around was going to compromise mine and Alex's cover. He then lowered his voice further and stated, "At the moment the entire world thinks that the terrorist attack on Flinders Street station was a once-off... botched by a couple of security guards out on a date. If you blow her cover now, then she'll miss any opportunity she has to confirm that theory... Now drop it."

Paige looked back at me, scowling through the window then stormed off as George walked into the room I was in and breathed with relief.

"So I'm a secret agent now... a spy." I giggled, failing to hide my amusement through my swollen lips. And my smile tugged at the stitches in my bottom lip.

He chuckled at me while pinching the bridge of his nose. "It's the only thing I could come up with that would stop her investigation. National security trumps spousal abuse... Sorry."

I sat down on the bed again still finding the situation amusing, and he sat down next to me.

"Are you sure you're okay?" he worriedly asked, staring at the burn mark across my lips. "You know I watched the video, and I know that kind of thing would definitely take its toll on a person... human or not."

I nodded but stayed quiet, and he turned to face me with such a curious yet worrying nature. "In the video... when you asked Matt to look away. Did you know that man was going to kill you?" Again, I nodded still staying quiet as he asked, "What did he whisper to you... to make you stop crying?"

I took a moment and honestly didn't want to answer. – I'm still more concerned for his sanity and outlook on the world. But George is trying, and he's been such a good and understanding friend, being super helpful with this entire mess, and I admire his curious nature. – Even if it finds him in the wrong kind of trouble sometimes.

Struggling a little with what to answer, I stared down at the floor and said, "He promised me... that he would turn off the camera before he killed me, as a thank-you for giving him back his freedom."

"Crikey." He gasped in absolute shock. "You rescued him, and this is how he repaid you... That's messed up."

I nodded again, then went back to being silent, and he took that as his cue to lead me out of the room. But before he left, he added, "Take care of yourself... okay, Lila?"

I grinned back and replied, "I'll always try."

Accepting my answer, George walked down the hall as I stepped back into Alex's room, smiling and feeling happy. And I was totally up for more hugs. That is until I saw Terrence standing at the window, looking pissed as ever at me.

Frac. – This is just not my night.

"He really did break his promise, didn't he?" I growled, crossing my arms, thinking about my lying crappy little brother.

Choosing not to say anything, Terrence held up a purple bottle of liquid and sighed, nodding his head before looking at Alex in his hospital bed, also just as upset.

But I remained staring at that purple liquid and shook my head. "Look, I know you guys are mad at me... But I'm not taking that. I'll heal on my own."

I sensed Terrence's frustration as he sighed again, and then darted towards me at full-speed. So I limped at full-speed away from him to the other side of the room, ignoring all the pain in my fractured leg to get away from him.

"Terry don't do this," I pleaded to him.

He stood in front of the door, staring at me, watching each painful move I made when he replied, "I'm sorry, Lila, but in this case, I'm not giving you a choice."

He stepped towards me, and I stepped backwards as I worriedly warned, "Don't... Terry, please... William hasn't earned my trust, you know that... And I don't trust that he knows what he's doing. What if that doesn't work on me? I'm a hybrid remember... What if it makes things worse? Have you thought of that?"

He held up the jar and looked at the fear on my face as he answered, "Yeah, I have thought of that." Then he ran at full-speed towards me again.

Oh Frac. – Run, Lila!

I dodged him and darted towards the door, but he blocked me with every move I made. In the end I had to jump over Alex's bed, and instantly my hair turned white again as Alex sprung up from the bed and grabbed hold of me. Clearly healed of all his wounds.

Damn. – I should have known Alex would want to test it on himself first.

With a firm grip, Alex held me flat on my back against his chest, lying on the bed with one arm around my shoulders and the other locking my hands down against my waist. I screamed at the pain he was causing me, but he still held tight to me.

"I'm sorry, Lila," he whispered then told Terrence, "Do it now."

Through my screams, Terrence poured the ghastly tasting liquid into my mouth. I tried to spit it out, but Alex released my hands and covered my blistered lips to keep the tonic inside. So

I tried to hit his hands away, each time causing more pain to my hands and futilely failing.

They both heard my cries, and I know Alex sensed my pain. But still he persisted and pleaded, "Lila, this will only work if you let it... Please... do this for me."

I listened to his plea and sensed the caring determination from both Alex and Terrence. And because I trust them and care for them, I stopped fighting and relaxed into the hold Alex has on me. The silence filled the room as they both nervously listened to me swallow the liquid, and as Alex felt my tears falling onto his cheek, he slowly pulled his hand away from my mouth.

The room stayed quiet as they both took a breath to calm the room, when suddenly my entire body tensed in Alex's arms from the horrifying pain the liquid was causing me. It was like my senses had kicked into over-drive, and I quickly knew something very bad was going to happen.

ARGH!!! – This hurts. – This really FRACCING hurts!!!

There's so much pain everywhere on me. I can feel every broken bone in my hands resetting into place and my skin tingled as it started to heal the burns and bruises. But that isn't all. Every scar on my body ached and burned as if they were being sliced open again and again. And it won't stop.

A surge of energy raced through my body, and I loudly pleaded, "Terry, turn off the lights!!!"

I pulled away from Alex as fast as I could, keeping a safe distance from both of them as they stood in a fearful awe, not knowing what to do, watching my skin turn to diamond. And while struggling to breathe, I pleaded through the pain for it to stop.

"Terry, turn off the lights!!"

Breaking from his shock, Terrence raced to turn the lights off, locking the door shut with plant vines from his stone-bracelet. Then he pulled the curtains closed as I fell to the ground, feeling the pain of all the wounds and injuries I have ever received in my lifetime repeated to me over and over and over again.

My body caught on fire with electricity orbiting the flames, jolting nearby surfaces with its sparks, and the flames burned through my pyjamas and bandages as I screamed from the agony.

Eventually, after a lot of horrifying seconds and minutes, the pain began to subside, and the flames and electrical current around me disappeared. Then when my screams fell silent, Terrence turned the lights on again to see me standing in the centre of the room, completely naked and exhausted from everything. I was only just able to stand, struggling for breath as my diamond skin slowly faded, leaving completely healed, scar-free skin all over my body.

Every scar I ever had is gone. – Every single one of them.

Trying to steady myself, I took a step forward but stumbled from the residual tingling sensation of everything. At super-speed, Terrence raced to catch me, pulling the blanket from my hospital bed to cover my nakedness as he held me. So now cold and tingling all over, I stared up into Terrence's worrying eyes, and with my last ounce of energy, I wheezed. "You're... both... jerks."

CHAPTER 10

The Unexpected

Journal entry by Matt Winters

The fallout of Lila's date with Billy has finally started to calm. – It's now been two full weeks since she walked out that door looking both nervous and excited for her date. Flinders street station is back up and running, and Lila is out of the hospital. – Although her exit was a little unexpected, leaving Maxwell and George needing to explain Alex and Lila's midnight disappearance and the scorch marks in their hospital room.

Apparently, Lila's brother had planned a coup and went against Lila's wishes, speeding up the healing process for her. But I'm not overly sure she's happy with the results. The new potion Tyme's dad had created healed more than just Lila's current wounds. It healed every injury she ever received. – Right down to the paper cuts and the grazes she received as a child. And I know the type of training Lila had growing up as Richard's prized soldier. – It meant she got a lot of broken bones and cuts and bruises. – Quite a lot.

But the worst part of it, was in the healing process when Lila was forced to relive every single experience of receiving her injuries – multiple times over.

In her words, "It was worse than anything I have ever felt before." And for her to say that after watching the recording of her in chains. — That was saying a hell of a lot.

Tonight is my turn to go out on a date, which leaves Lila home to watch the kids. And because it's Friday, they've decided on a super movie marathon and are currently prepping the lounge-room with sleeping supplies and snacks.

Tyme showed up unexpectedly, holding yet another box of chocolates in his hands with a very guilty look on his face, and I was smart enough to leave that with Lila to deal with. — Since the moment Lila left the hospital, she's been ignoring all of them. — Including Alex. Only dealing with them for work purposes. And I can't blame her for wanting to do that.

Tyme got the cold shoulder from Lila but was invited in the door, possibly because they're both still learning how to be siblings. He was then put in charge of blowing up the inflatable air bed.

Minutes later, while I was helping Danny pop the popcorn, Terrence knocked on the door, holding the third bouquet of flowers this week, to go with the other four he left for her last week. Again, I left that with Lila.

This time he got an icy "Meh" from Lila. But eventually he got to step through the door when he pulled from his pocket the now fixed purple and green tree-stone bracelet that Lila lost during the fight at the Music Bowl.

She held her hand out for Terrence to place the bracelet back onto her wrist, but she curiously asked with slight annoyance, "Are you giving this back to me because you care about my emotions now... Or is it just because you want to know what they are?"

"Can I be honest and say both?" He stared at her with a guilty pout. "Lila, it's been 10 days of you ignoring me, and I can't stand another second of it... I'm sorry... Just tell me what I need to do to make this right, and I'll do it."

She didn't answer him. Instead Lila told him to go and help set up for the movie night, and Terrence took that as a relatively good sign, watching Lila disappear into her room to get into her pyjamas.

I have noticed one benefit to Lila's body being healed. And that is she feels more comfortable and confident to wear her older-style clothes again. — Like singlet tops and shorts, and she doesn't need to wear make up to cover her scars anymore. But I think if she had the choice, she'd rather the scars over having to relive that kind of pain again.

I was just about finished getting ready for my date with Cassandra, one of my work colleagues, when Alex knocked on the door. — And there is no way I'm going to miss this one, eagerly opening the door to see him holding a large TY white wolf teddy with the big sparkly blue eyes. It was a smart move to pick the one animal Lila turns into when she's angry. It looks cute and it definitely looks like her.

I won't lie — I smirked, feeling a little smug as I commented, "So... you're still in the bad books with Lila too?"

"What gave it away?" He shrugged.

I very casually pointed over to the bouquets of flowers around the room and added, "She also got chocolates from Tyme."

He became heavy-hearted, and my grin peaked from ear to ear, feeling slightly better about myself. — Because for once this year it wasn't me that turned Lila's hair white.

"Did either of them work," he nervously asked.

While still struggling to hide my grin, I opened the door further to show both Tyme and Terrence in the apartment, helping to set out the snacks for movie night.

"It got them in the door, but we'll soon learn how your attempt works out... Lila! Alex is here!" I shouted before moving to wait in the kitchen, still silently chuckling at him with a wide grin and my arms crossed.

Now, I know he can sense my current feelings. — But I have no intentions of reigning in my egotism anytime soon.

Very hesitantly, Alex walked in and stood just inside the apartment when Danny ran up to him, trying to tackle him to the ground. Alex playfully fell to the ground as both my kids stacked on top of him, and Ruby may have unintentionally elbowed him in the rib. But he took it well.

"Uncle Alex, we're having a movie marathon," Ruby boasted. "With popcorn and lollies, and Mummy ordered us pizza."

"Yum... I love pizza," Alex replied. "What movie are you going to watch?"

Danny puffed up his chest, showing Alex the Superman cape he was wearing as he answered, "The DC universe with Superman and Batman."

"Cool." Alex happily inspected the cape then instantly jumped to his feet when Lila walked out of her room to greet him.

She stood in front of him, now dressed in her new green pyjama shorts and singlet but stayed very silent with her arms crossed, and again had no hint of a smile. All the while I stood at the kitchen bench, eating the popcorn and thoroughly enjoying this moment.

"Hi..." Alex choked, seeming extremely nervous as he held out the wolf teddy to show Lila. "I got this for you."

Ha! – He looks like he's sweating. – And I'm laughing on the inside.

After a tense moment, Lila accepted the teddy and thanked Alex for the gift but crossed her arms again, giving Alex a dagger-piercing stare. And damn her shoulder is icy. – It went well with that snow-white hair of hers. – She could give the snow queen a run for her money with that look.

Alex was definitely sweating now and struggled to think of something to gain Lila's favour again. But he cheekily grinned before he leaned down to whisper something into Danny's ear then stood up, looking wryly back at Lila.

My curiosity grew as Danny tugged on Lila's green pyjama singlet to beg, "Mummy, can Alex stay for the movie night... Pleeeaase!"

Oh, that's just dirty. – Using my son to get past Lila's icy exterior.

Unfortunately, my phone alarm went off at the worst time and it meant I had to go. So I quickly grabbed my coat and handed the popcorn bowl to Danny, kissing him on the forehead goodbye then moved to kiss Ruby, and told them both to be good. But just for good measure, I kissed Lila on the cheek and whispered, "Bye, Darling." – Just to really rub it in.

Journal entry insert by Lila Winters

Grrr!! – I'm just so incredibly mad at Alex. And Tyme. And Terrence. But Alex especially. He asked me to take the tonic. He asked me to do it for him. And the results were excruciatingly painful.

He's now annoyingly standing at the door of my apartment, and yes, I have let Tyme and Terrence in the door, but I have not forgiven them. I'm only giving them the chance to redeem themselves. – And for some reason, I'm a fraccing pushover.

But Alex, he's different, he said he loved me. But love means showing respect, and he didn't respect me when he tricked me, held me down, and stopped me from spitting out that horrible-tasting liquid.

Ugh!!! – I'm just so angry at him.

When Matt kissed me goodbye and left for his date, I stayed staring at Alex, contemplating what to do or what to say, and I'm pretty pissed that he used my son to invite himself to movie night. But I love Danny enough to respect his wishes, so I nodded to Alex, saying nothing as I walked into the kitchen.

Danny and Ruby shouted, "Hooray," celebrating before they ran into the lounge-room to set up a spot for Alex. But Alex, he didn't. Instead he moved closer to me and might have noticed I had not yet let go of the white wolf teddy he bought for me. – And yeah, alright, I might be hugging it a little. – It does look kind of cute. And I think Alex smiled at that.

"So where's Matt off to?" he questioned.

"He has a date," I casually replied, grabbing some fizzy drink and juice boxes from the fridge.

I turned to Alex and started to pile the drinks into his hands, seeing how one of my hands was still occupied with a wolf, when he asked, "So, are you okay with that?"

"Why shouldn't I be? He didn't have a problem with my date," I griped, and I felt my nose crinkle as I grumbled. "I mean seriously, Alex, the only person who had a problem with me dating was you. And even then, you didn't talk to me about it. Instead you just ruined my date... But what hurt the most about my date was not the fact that I ended up in chains... and yeah, that part really sucked. But what really hurt me was the part when you left me."

With a sad face, Alex stayed silent and just stood there listening to me pour my heart out. – And I can sense all his regret and guilt and his longing to make things right with me. But I want to make sure he knows exactly why I'm mad at him. So I walked closer to him and spoke quieter, making sure Danny and Ruby couldn't hear as I stared into his tear-filled eyes.

"Alex, I thought I was going to die in that tower, knowing that my best friend was mad at me for not loving him enough. Then when we finally got back to a semi-happy relationship... You forced me to relive a life-time of pain a thousand times over."

Alex's jaw clenched as he grinded his teeth. "I didn't know the tonic would do that to you... It didn't for me."

"Yeah well, that's the problem about being a hybrid Nature girl." I huffed while glaring into his eyes. "All the elements affect me differently... Which is why I'm immune to the blue rose... I even asked Terrence if he had considered that while I pleaded with him to not do this. And yet both of you didn't listen."

"I'm sorry." He breathed, staring at me with his pleading eyes, wanting so badly to hold me. – But I strategically placed drinks in his hands for that exact reason.

"I know you are." I sniffled, holding the white wolf teddy even tighter as I placed my free hand up against the warmth of his cheek, and a tear fell from his eye as I whispered, "But the kind of pain you caused me is going to take longer than a few weeks to forget... Now, I'm mad as hell at you... and at Terrence and Tyme because I know they're listening as well. But I care for you all far too much to stay mad... So get comfy, the pizza will be here soon, and we have to watch at least three of these movies in order to call it a marathon."

Yep. – I'm a fraccing pushover.

Alex cleared his throat and did as I asked, moving to the lounge in a bit of a sulk, and I grabbed a bag of crisp chips before I sat down at the end of the couch that Terrence was sitting on.

Ruby had arranged the seating for the night with the inflatable air-bed pushed up against the couch in front of me. Alex was told to sit on the bed with his back up against the couch as Ruby got comfy on his lap, holding a large bowl of lollies and other unhealthy snacks. And Tyme and Danny were getting comfortable on the couch next to mine with an extra-large popcorn bowl to share between them. But just before I pressed play on the first movie, Terrence held my hand to get my attention, looking extremely sad.

"I'm sorry I didn't listen, Lila... I promise from now on I will listen to you. I was just mad at you for not being honest with me. And I thought you were just making up excuses because you didn't trust William... But I swear I will listen from now on... Just please, forgive me."

Aw Frac. – He has the cute worrying puppy-dog eyes on him, and I sense all of his sadness. – Damn it, why can't I stay mad at him? – It's probably because all of their intentions were in the right place when they caused me excruciating pain. – Oh frac damn.

My nose crinkled again as I peered across at Tyme who looked extremely apologetic as well, and I grumbled, knowing that I'm a pushover. So now feeling incredibly irked, I sarcastically huffed as my entire body rolled in frustration, wriggling over to sit behind Alex and let Terrence wrap one arm around me to give me an apology hug. I then snuggled into him and let Alex use my legs as a headrest while we watch the movie.

"You guys are still jerks," I grumbled. "But I forgive you."

Journal entry insert by General Richard Willows

The Board has called an emergency video conference, and that's never a good sign.

I sat at my desk, safe in one of the 'off the books' locations, speaking to a computer screen. Hilary Cole, the CEO of our pharmaceutical's division had called for the meeting and is not happy with the situation we're faced with.

After losing the Canadian site, the loss of personnel in the western division has been difficult to regain. But it's becoming especially difficult to keep up with the war stemming from all sides. We have more than just one enemy to deal with now. Lila had created more enemies with the team she left in New York, sweeping through and hindering every effort we make to recoup our losses. And now there's a new team working in Australia that we have yet to analyse but seems to have no links back to Lila.

Frank Hinds, the CEO of mining, and John Lin, the CEO of our oil industry, as well as a few of our anonymous investors all agreed with Hilary's disapproval and enquiries as to what is being done to handle the situation.

"The situation is being handled," I replied, trying to alleviate the tension.

"The situation is not being handled," Hilary quickly rebuked. "You have lost control, and it has now made its way to our doorsteps."

"Agreed." Frank added, choking back a Cuban cigar. "My soldier count is dwindling every week."

John piped in but English is his second language, and he started speaking in Mandarin but changed to translate. "We too must add that we are also missing yet another Board member."

He's referring to Odele Connors who hasn't been seen in weeks since her home was targeted. Yet still trying to see reason, I barked, "Ms Connors was weak. She became emotionally attached to her subordinates."

"As have you, Mr Jaeger," Frank rebuffed, reminding me of my tentative station on The Board. "And if you were doing your job properly, this situation wouldn't have been an issue."

"That's ridiculous," I snapped back.

"No, Mr Jaeger." Hilary seethed. "Mr Hinds is right, this all started when one of your collections went rogue and was recruited by our old friend Maxwell Eden... We warned you that her kind were difficult to control when you forced our hand to let you keep her in her infant years. And since then you've tried and failed on multiple occasions to keep her under control... and were brazen enough to order the final protocol on her without any of our approval."

"And failed... several times," Frank added.

Our meeting was abruptly cut short as the room Hilary was in burst into flames from an explosion on the other side of the door, and her screen went blank. The others showed no remorse for her situation, and instead Frank barked orders to me. "Mr Jaeger, you have twenty-four hours to get this fixed or you will be given the final protocol. Is that understood?"

"Yes, sir," I replied as the screens all went blank.

Journal entry continued by Matt Winters

Oh crap. – I'm running ridiculously late for my date. – This does not look good.

I raced into the restaurant panting and feeling a little flustered. Cassy, my date, was already seated when I arrived, so I made a beeline straight for her.

"I'm so sorry. There was an issue at home, and I got caught up in traffic."

She stood to greet me, and wow, she looks amazing. – Usually I see her in a lab coat or something more teacher appropriate, but not tonight. Tonight she's wearing her black hair down, which is different from her standard high-top bun, and surprisingly she also has curls that dangle past her shoulders with a slight spring to them as she moves.

"I already ordered. I hope you don't mind?" she asked. Then as we sat down at the table the waiter placed two medium-rare steaks on mashed potato down in front of us.

Oh damn. – This looks nice. – I never eat like this in front of Lila, so I am going to enjoy myself.

Before the waiter left, I ordered both of us some drinks and we got stuck into eating. But there was a bit of tension between us, until Cassy eventually broke and asked the question she was dying to know. "Look, I'm going to be totally honest with you. I have a question, and it's bugging the hell out of me. And you don't have to answer if it makes this weird... but what happened between you and your wife?"

And there it is. – That awkward question that hovers over me wherever I go.

"I'm so sorry," she blurted as she looked at the hesitancy on my face. "You don't have to answer it... I was just curious."

I took a deep breath while playing with my mashed potatoes, pushing it around with my fork. "No, it's a fair question. I just wasn't expecting it this early in the date... Lila and I are divorced."

Cassy stared back at me, definitely wanting more than that. "Yeah, but why? You guys made such a great couple."

Taking another contemplative breath, I continued to eat my steak and slowly answered, "Last year, Lila was reported missing, and soon after, reported dead."

"Yeah, I remember that... turned out to be a mistaken identity, right?" Cassy added.

"Right." I nodded, glad that the cover story still held. Then added, "But it also struck a sour note for me. I suffered for weeks thinking I had lost the love of my life. And when she came back, I was so scared I was going to lose her again that I unintentionally pushed her away."

"That's so sad," Cassy pouted. "Didn't you try to fix it?"

Again, I nodded. "We tried... But in the end, Lila and I both agreed that in order to save what relationship we still have and to protect the kids, it was better if we went back to being just friends. And that seems to have made us both a lot happier."

I looked up to see Cassie staring at me again with pouty lips and her brows pinched together as they rose, making her brown eyes look wider. But that just made me feel uncomfortably weird.

"Anyway... that's my love life, how's yours?" I asked.

She shrugged her shoulders, seeming blasé. "Non-existent, that's mainly why I'm here... my mother was about to set me up on a blind date. And to stop her, I blurted out that I was dating someone at work."

Ah-huh. — Well, that explains the spontaneous date proposal.

Seeming slightly awkward with her answer, she hesitantly smiled. "To be fair, I wasn't expecting you to say yes... But I'm kind of glad you did."

Huh. — I'm not sure if that is a good thing or not.

We could both tell that the other was feeling weird now, so we continued eating but decided to move away from our lacking love life and onto the beauty of science, and that got us talking for hours. We even started debating about how much an animal's behaviour is determined by its environmental factors or its genetic factors. — And that was fun because I have some inside knowledge about that, and she doesn't.

It turns out having an Animal guardian as a friend is actually quite helpful in the science industry.

Journal entry insert by General Richard Willows

I decided to do a little recon, given that the laboratory Hilary was inspecting was only half an hour away by chopper. I landed in the field a few klicks from the lab, and stayed low as I made my way through the dense shrubs and grass. Then I perched myself in one of the trees not far from where a group of people had gathered.

The building was engulfed in flames and a group of our scientists were being held at gunpoint on their knees, and while staying hidden, I managed to ID some of the hostiles. – Stephen Smith, one of Commander Peterson's recruits looks like the ring leader. And Billy Jonas, one of Odele's Fire guardians was taking orders from him.

Billy was looking through our employee profile list, handing the list to Stephen as he reported, "We have seventeen guardians and nine humans here. The rest either burned in the fire or are hiding."

"Are there any Nature guardians?" Stephen asked while scanning through the list.

"No," Billy replied sounding somewhat disappointed at that question.

Losing his temper, Stephen threw the paper in the air and incinerated it. "Damn it! Why are Nature guardians so rare? I need that cure!"

Stephen leered back at Billy when he heard him sniggering, leading him to angrily demand. "Care to share your humour, Billy?"

Continuing to smile, Billy answered with a slightly ironic tone, "I was just thinking about Lila and how easy it was for her to cure an entire facility of Neuritamine droned soldiers... in handcuffs."

"Yeah... well, unfortunately she's DEAD!" Stephen yelled.

Alright. – That's news to me.

Instantly, Billy's attitude changed and in anger, his hands glowed when he turned to Stephen and sniped, "And whose fault is that?"

Noticing the hostility in Billy, Stephen quickly backed down and instead turned away in a huff to address the group of scientists being held at gunpoint. "Brothers and sisters, please do not be frightened. I have come to offer you your freedom."

His speech was suddenly interrupted as one of the younger recruits, Isaac, dragged Hilary towards the group of hostages. She didn't look too good with her usually pressed pantsuit now stained with blood and dirt. And she was letting her fear show.

"Please, please don't hurt me. I'll give you anything," she pleaded.

Stephen marched up to Hilary and sneered, "Information is all I want from you... Where are the other guardians being kept?"

Hilary whimpered as Isaac pulled her up by her hair to answer Stephen. "I don't know. Really, I don't... Ever since the incident in Canada, all the facilities and camps were relocated... Some are still being moved every few weeks."

Damn. – She really is a blabbermouth when her life is on the line.

"That is a real shame," Stephen sighed, shaking his head. "One final question... where are all the Nature guardians being kept?"

With her fear completely obvious, Hilary stuttered, "They're... they're not. There's only two Nature..."

"No..." Stephen interrupted, sounding like he didn't like where the answer was going. "There has to be more than two Nature freaks left on this planet. Now where are you holding the rest of them?"

"I swear, we're not." Hilary insisted. "We don't keep them, we... we eliminate them. Their kind are difficult to control, so The Board follows a strict protocol to ensure order is kept. Every few centuries we eliminate them, only ever allowing two of the oldest Nature tribes to survive to continue a pure bloodline... One of the tribe leaders died over twenty years ago, leaving the heir in the care of the Connors, and we've temporarily lost control of the other tribe... It's Lila, she's the guardian you want."

In hearing that unfortunate amount of information, Stephen lost his temper and threw a flaming dagger into Hilary's chest as he jeered, "That was not the answer I wanted."

He needed to take a calming breath before he went back to completing his speech, stepping over Hilary's dead body as he spoke. "Brothers and sisters, you have your freedom back. But now you have a choice... to join us and fight to free our people, or go and live your lives in the fear of being hunted... The choice is yours."

The guardians of the group all stood to their feet, standing next to the humans as they stayed kneeling. They all fearfully looked at each other and at those holding the guns. Then a dozen of them ran off into the tree line at super-speed, but four walked to stand behind Billy.

All but one remained standing in front of the human hostages. A female guardian, and she looked scared when she asked, "What about them?"

"They're humans," Stephen snickered. "They're of no use to us."

"But we can help them," she refuted.

To which Billy agreed, grabbing Stephen's arm and pleading, "Steve, please... There's been enough death tonight. Remember the choice Lila gave us when we were freed... We're not the monsters here, so don't become one."

Taking a moment to contemplate Billy's words, Stephen glanced back at the young female guardian and then to the scientists cowering behind her.

"They're beyond our help," he scoffed, walking away and nodding to his armed men.

And I couldn't bear to look as I heard the female guardian fearfully shout, "NO!" before being executed along with the other scientists.

CHAPTER 11

Frustration

Journal entry by Lila Winters

Alright, so movie night wasn't that bad. At least we're all on speaking terms again, but my trust in Alex, Terrence, and Tyme is moderate at best, especially with Tyme. – I swear that is the last time I will trust my brother to actually keep a promise. – After all, you should never make a promise that you don't intend on keeping. – Or at least try to keep it.

We had all fallen asleep in the loungeroom partway through a movie, so as I woke up, I found Tyme asleep, sprawled out over the other couch. Danny and Ruby were both snuggled up next to Alex on the blow-up airbed. And I had fallen asleep – more or less on top of Terrence again as we lay on the couch with my arm wrapped around him and his arm wrapped around me.

Oh Frac damn, he is comfy. – And I've really missed this.

I snuggled back down into his warmth, and scanned the room to see all the sleepy heads when I noticed the last movie we watched was on the replay setting, and it was almost at the end of the movie again. But then I heard the sound of someone sipping coffee behind the couch I was sleeping on.

Cautiously, I turned my head to see a woman leaning on the back of the couch, watching the end of the movie while drinking coffee, and naturally I yelped in fright, accidentally waking up the boys.

Tyme immediately jumped into action, appearing next to the woman and pressing her face down on the head of the couch, locking her arms behind her back as she dropped the coffee cup. I felt very proud of my brother for his daring moves. – I've taught him well. – But then I realised who the woman is.

"Cassy?" My jaw dropped as I stared at her, completely confused.

"Oh hey, Lila... I'm sorry I woke you. I was just watching the end of the movie," she muffled her words, casually smiling at me with a slightly scared look on her face.

"What the hell are you doing here?" I asked.

She got cagey but eventually replied, "Um, we kind of had a late night... And Matt said he was going to drive me home."

Cassy squirmed in the hold Tyme had on her, so I nodded to him to let her go just seconds before Matt raced out of the bedroom, buttoning up his pants and apologising. – And I very quickly realised what "late night" was code for.

Fixing her now dishevelled hair, Cassy straightened and adjusted the skimpy blouse she had on then cleared her throat. "I'm sorry if I startled you. I was just getting some coffee, and I kind of got carried away watching the end of the movie... And oh my gosh you guys just looked so cute together."

She eyed Terrence and smiled, silently highlighting the fact that I had pulled myself up to straddle Terrence's hips in order to talk to Cassie, and Terrence seemed content with what I was doing. But I suddenly sensed the jealousy coming from Cassy as she gave Terrence the come-hither look.

What the...?

Okay, now I'm feeling a little bit pissed and judgey at the fact that she's willing to put out on the first date, and then the next morning put moves on what looks like a taken man in the house of the man she just spent the night with. – In front of him.

Wow. – Desperate much.

Yeah, my cat claws came out, and at full-speed, I moved Terrence's hand to rest on my bare thigh with his fingers slightly tucked underneath my short pyjama bottoms. I then side-smirked, eyeing Cassy off and mocked, "Honey, you're way too low for his league... even Matt's."

In shock, Matt's jaw dropped, watching the whole thing. And I think I sensed a little pride coming from him at the fact that I defended him. But it also looked like Cassy was going to bring out her cat claws to fight back. That is until Ruby woke up and asked, "Who's that?"

Instantly Matt jumped in, pulling Cassy out the door, mumbling, "And that's our cue to leave... I'll see you tonight Lila."

Oh Frac Damn. – That was fun.

Now feeling a little cheeky, I looked back at Terrence who has the biggest grin on his face because he knew I was using him as a prop, and we both burst into laughter as I climbed off the couch and him to stand up and stretch. Poor Alex was stuck lying on the bed with Danny still dead to the world on one of his arms, so I thought I'd give him a hand by pulling Ruby off him, and excitedly carried her to the kitchen with me.

"Do you want to help Mummy make some pancakes for these hungry boys?" I happily asked.

It was a definite yes to the breakfast choice, and Ruby had so much fun helping me make pancakes. But we also made a terrible mess in the kitchen, which after breakfast I was busy cleaning. Yet while I was cleaning I grew surprised and curious, and wondered how I managed to get the pancake batter on almost every surface of the kitchen, even the top of the fridge. – But I think I'm just that talented.

While washing the dishes, I let out a very discreet smile as I watched my amazing family. Because while Terrence and Tyme cleared the table of all the toppings to put them away, Alex sat in the loungeroom showing magic tricks to Danny and Ruby. He was hiding his face with his hands then morphing his nose into other animals like a pig's snout, then a dog, and a cat. – My favourite was the bunny nose with the cute little whiskers. I was busy watching Alex when Terrence stood next to me with a smile of his own.

"What?" I asked, eyeing him from the corner of mine.

He picked up a handful of my hair and pulled it around to show me that my white hair was starting to darken to my natural honey-blond again. "I'm glad we still make you happy."

"Me too," I replied as I finished drying the last dish and put it away.

There was a knock at the door and Alex raced to open it, completely forgetting about his duck face. And I had to cover my mouth to hold back the laugh as Max stood at the door and tapped Alex's beak.

"Your bill, sir," he joked.

I couldn't hold it in for long and I laughed in hysterics, and the kids took one look at me and started laughing as well. I was laughing so hard I snorted, watching Alex wiggle his beak as it morphed back into his normal-looking face.

"What's up, Max?" Alex greeted.

And I had to answer through my failed attempt to compose myself. "Saturday is Max's day out with the kids... Danny and Ruby, go put your shoes on."

With excitement, Danny and Ruby raced into their bedrooms and Tyme followed to help them. But I still couldn't stop laughing, and snickered, "So, Max, what's on the menu today? Duck, duck, goose."

I heard Max titter, and I think Alex had had enough of the duck puns because he huffed at me before darting towards me at half-speed. I darted to the other side of the room and kept laughing at him, and he grinned still trying to catch me.

I ended up needing to use Terrence as a shield, backing myself into the kitchen corner with him in front of me as I chuckled. "Okay... okay... I surrender. I promise I'll stop laughing. I'm sorry."

Once my laughter had subsided – slightly, Alex backed down and gave me the cheesiest grin as I slowly moved Terrence forward and gave Alex an apology hug. Max was then greeted by Danny and Ruby who were now both ready to go, and answered my question.

"We're going swimming first and finishing at the all-you-can-eat restaurants downstairs."

"There's no all-you-can-eat restaurants downstairs," I replied, trying to ignore the fact that Alex was poking me in the back while he hugs me.

"It is when I'm there," Max responded with a smile, noticing my terrible attempt to hide my laugh.

To escape Alex, I quickly moved to the other side of Terrence to get his hug instead, poking my tongue out at Alex as he pulled a cheeky face. But I also noticed Terrence had that grin on his face again as I tried to compose myself enough to reply to Max.

"Okay, but don't bring them back on a sugar high."

"No promises," Max grinned as he walked out of the apartment with Danny and Ruby.

The second the apartment door was closed, Alex looked at me with that mischievous glimmer in his eyes. "Now, where were we?"

Oh Fracs. – Even Terrence is in on it as he held me tighter in his arms, stopping me from getting away. I wriggled and giggled, and was eventually able to wriggle free and grinned at them as we started playing shoulder tag at full-speed, using the entire apartment.

We were all having so much fun jumping over furniture and laughing. And by the end of it, I won, throwing both of them onto the inflatable air mattress. Then I climbed up onto the couch and towered over them as they both looked up at me.

"Catch." I cheekily giggled then body slammed onto them, inevitably popping the inflatable airbed.

With our legs and arms all tangled up, we just lay there laughing as we felt the air slowly escaping from the bed. And my wise brother, who had stayed in the kitchen, drinking his coffee where it was safe, was laughing at us as well.

This is just amazing. I just feel so happy, laughing and having fun. And I want this happiness to last. - I want Terrence and Alex to stay with me forever.

Oh Frac. - Oh Frac. Oh Frac. Oh Frac. - I'm in love with both Alex and Terrence. - This is a bad idea. We have to stay friends. - <u>Friends</u>. - Just friends. -You can't ruin this, Lila. - Not this.

I cleared my throat, trying to stay calm as we all stood up and amusingly looked at the deflated air-mattress. Then we started to pack up the loungeroom in a slightly humorous mode. But I was a little distracted by my feelings, and I'm trying very hard not to let it show or look at their kind eyes and caring strong arms.

Frac. - Lila, don't look.

Partway through cleaning, I heard another knock at the door, and when I opened it, my hair turned back to white as I saw William standing in the hallway. I took one look at him and slammed the door closed before turning to Tyme and sneering, "Your dad's here."

And yes, that's one man who owes me a billion apologies. - But right now I'm in a rotten mood, so I stormed into my room, slamming that door shut as well.

Journal entry insert by Matt Winters

This weekend is starting to be pretty jammed packed, and it's only just started.

After dropping Cassy off at her house, I drove out of the city to meet up with my friend and kind of my boss now, Andy Robertson. He was just recently promoted to the head of our research department, and this is our celebratory paintball session.

We enjoyed a couple of rounds shooting everyone and getting shot ourselves. Then when we needed more ammo, we all headed back into the shop. — More like a tin shed, converted into a café for supplies.

"Hey, how'd your date with Cassandra go?" Andy asked while reloading his gun.

"It was... awkward," I cringed, downing my coffee.

Andy angled his head up and looked at me in disbelief. "Really, coz her Facebook page states otherwise."

"Alright fine, the date was great. It was the morning that ended horribly."

Pulling a different OMG face, Andy hissed, "Really? She's that type of girl?"

"No..." I shook my head, thinking how best to explain this. "Lila had her workmates up for a movie night, and well... things got a little weird."

My eyes rolled, not quite sure how to feel. Although I was kind of happy that Lila defended me this morning. — I know I'm not as hot as Terrence, and he's got a lot more muscles and everything than me. But Cassandra eyeing Terrence in front of me was a bit insulting. So no offence to her, but I have no plans to date her again.

Andy looked back at me and saw the unusual, furrowed look on my face which translated exactly what I meant by 'weird' as he finished loading his paintball gun and grinningly replied, "Ah right... now that is awkward... Are you ready?"

"Nah... I'm sitting this one out. I didn't get breakfast this morning." I sighed with annoyance, sitting down to eat my unhealthy breakfast of a bag of chips.

Andy grimaced as his face puzzled. "You're seriously giving up the opportunity to shoot your boss for a bag of chips."

His lack of sympathy irritated me, so I smiled and shot him in the leg while enjoying my delicious breakfast, happily stating, "Now I get the best of both worlds."

"Traitor," he jokingly grimaced while feeling the pain in his leg, but then stood tall. "Okay, I'm willing to accept your defeat, but you're buying lunch today."

As Andy began to walk out with the other paintball players, I yelled back, "Okay, but I just want to add that you're my boss and you earn more money than me!"

I then moved to stand at the viewing window and revelled every time Andy got shot.

Suddenly the room fell eerily quiet, and a familiar voice came from behind me. "I used to love this game as a kid."

The hairs on the back of my neck stood as I jumped in fright, turning to point my paintball gun at Richard as he stood in the middle of the now empty tin shed café.

What the hell did he do with the staff?

"It's okay. I'm unarmed." He raised his hands up in surrender.

Yeah Right. — I'll believe that in a million years.

"What do you want?" I griped, keeping my distance with my paintball gun squared on him.

"I just wanted to talk," he replied.

But you see, I really don't want to talk. I want revenge. So I shot him, several times, covering his pristine shiny uniform with hot-pink paint. And I very much hope it stains. He then fell to the ground feeling the pain, and I smirked at him.

"That was for Lila. Now talk fast or I'll shoot you again."

Journal entry continued by Lila Winters

Adela and Katie asked to join me on my run today instead of me running with Chase, and at first, I didn't object because part of me is needing to exercise... in less of the human way. – To think things through.

Eventually, we had pretty much run all over the inner city of Melbourne – with me secretly still looking for a particular lost person. All this week and what was left of last week, I've been searching for Billy in my spare time, but I'm beginning to fear the worst. – Because if his old friends were callous enough to torture and try to burn me alive, I worry what they might have done to him. But that is just one of my current worries to add to the many others.

In giving up on today's search, I stopped back at the lobby where Adela and Katie looked like they wanted to collapse. I, however, am still in the mood to distract myself and don't feel like I've done enough.

"That had to be at least a month's worth of cardio. How are you still standing?" Adela wheezed, rubbing her aching calves.

"It wasn't that bad," I rolled my eyes, wiping the sweat from my cheek and brows.

Katie looked up at me from the ground where she was resting. "Are you kidding? My legs are throbbing, and my feet are numb. If we were an average human, we'd probably be dead."

It was very funny to watch their interesting recovery poses, sprawled out on the cool marble floor. And I laughed back at them. "So I take it you're going to pass on the gym then?"

They both glowered at me, and I took that as a 'no' then smiled at them before running up the stairs with determination.

I had already started a session with 'Hector' when Adela and Katie finally joined me in the gym after taking the elevator. – The lazy-bones. – As they entered, I briefly glanced at Katie who held her stomach in a bit of discomfort.

"Can we kindly stop moving now?" she achingly begged.

Trying very hard not to laugh at her this time, I continued my session, working up a really good sweat. But then Adela stood between me and 'Hector' and scowled.

"Okay Lila, I'm staging another intervention… You need to slow down."

I stopped and huffed, waiting for her to move, but she didn't. So I rolled my eyes, grabbing a towel to soak more of the sweat off me. "Okay, I'll bite. Why do I need an intervention?"

It seems as though Adela is more than happy to be brutally honest with me <u>again</u> as she pointed to my white hair then lectured, "You're causing physical pain to your body through exercise to mask the strong emotions that you're trying to unsuccessfully hide…You're angry and most likely frustrated at the lack of intimacy you so desperately need… And don't bother denying it. The last date you went on that didn't leave you needing medical attention was before we met."

Well, she has a point there. – Maybe these feelings I have towards Alex and Terrence are just misdirected frustration. – But what the hell is she expecting me to do about it?

"What do you want me to do?" I bickered, throwing my hands in the air, wanting any useful suggestions. "I tried dating and I ended up causing a mass terrorist scare."

"Well, you need to do something about it!" she yelled.

"What would you have me do? Find a random guy and have my way with them," I suggested.

Katie then piped in, agreeing with my idea, so I went for it as a group of male hotel guests that were here on a business trip walked in, ready to do a work-out. Instead, I grabbed one of them by their shirt and gave his mouth a really, really good work-out. I even groaned as he got into the swing of things, wrapping his arms around me and getting very handsy.

When I eventually pulled away for air, I glanced back at Adela and mocked, "You're right. This is a great idea."

But she didn't see it that way and rushed to put her hand between me and the other man's lips, now completely annoyed with me. "No, Lila… they are not a great idea… They are a very bad idea."

She tried to pull me out of the man's very nice embrace, and I cheekily pouted while asking the man, "You don't mind being my bad idea… do you?"

He shook his head and smiled. Then his friend chimed in, "I wouldn't mind it either."

"Ooh seconds." I smiled, happily moving back towards them, ready for another lip workout.

But again, Adela spoiled the fun, standing between me and my new friends as she said to both of them, "Yeah… I'm sure you wouldn't mind. But I know at least two of her other friends that will mind, and they are a lot bigger and stronger than you."

Both of the men looked over Adela's shoulder to me and must have seen my entire body roll with frustration before they backed away, waving goodbye as they walked out of the gym.

"Ugh!!!" I frustratedly yelled, throwing my hands in the air again. "And you wonder why I'm frustrated. I can't have any intimacy or even go out on a date without someone getting hurt."

Katie sat down, massaging her legs and commented, "Why don't you just ask one of your best friends to help you? We all know they'd do anything for you."

Well, isn't she the bright one in the room.

I looked back at her with the sarcasm written all over my body and mocked, "Wow, now why didn't I think of that? Oh right... maybe because they might want to do more than just help." I then turned back to Adela and scoffed, "I think it might be safer if I just stick to exercising."

Luckily, Adela's mobile rang, and she had to answer it, so she couldn't argue back. All she could say was "Fine, but this isn't over."

"Joy," I huffed, returning to punching Hector. But I only got two punches in when Adela interrupted me again, telling me that there was a problem downstairs.

And for the love of all things FRAC – WHY!?!

I groaned, storming out of the gym with Adela and Katie behind me on my way down to the lobby. And just when I thought things couldn't get any worse today, they got worse. In the lobby, I found Matt surrounded by pretty much all of my security guards on duty today, including Chase, Alex, and Terrence. And surprisingly, Tyme was there as well with his dad next to him, scowling and all seeming very protective when they saw me walking from the stairs to stand with them. Because next to Matt was who everyone was focused on. – The good-for-nothing man who claimed to be my father. Richard. And as usual, he greeted me with his cocky, "Hello, Pumpkin."

And I swear I'm 10 seconds away from smashing a pumpkin onto his damn Fraccing head.

"Matt, what the hell is he doing here?" I calmly breathed, scowling at the good-for-nothing piece of Frac standing next to him. "And why are you standing next to him?"

"He needed to talk to you," Matt replied, feeling very uncomfortable, and holding his paintball gun close to him.

I also noticed that Richard's uniform didn't look too crash hot, now stained with pink paint, and my lips peaked just a little as I glanced back at Matt. But my smile disappeared completely when Richard spoke. "I was very persuasive, Pumpkin."

Fuelled with frustration, I glared back at him and jeered, "Call me Pumpkin again, and I will let Alex remove your ability to talk."

"He doesn't get to talk to you... ever." Alex seethed while moving closer to me, standing almost in front of me.

Terrence also moved closer to me, and I sensed his very protective nature as he discreetly held the back of my shirt, holding me close to him. – And I am not going to argue with either of them. But it clearly put Richard in a mood, glancing around at the hotel guests and local shoppers that had stopped to gawk.

"Very well, I'll just talk openly... I hope you don't mind everyone knowing about your extra work activities—"

"What do you want?" I interrupted a lot quieter before he could say anything else. Then I casually eyed back at Chase, hinting to him to move the people along.

"An alliance," Richard replied.

What the Frac. – Is he kidding me? – Even William started to laugh.

"And why do you want an alliance with us?" I sneered in disbelief, folding my arms as my entire body shuddered at the very thought of it.

Richard leaned in closer to me, causing Alex and Terrence to both grab my shirt and pull me backwards, with Tyme, William, Katie, and Adela moving closer as well. – Which seems somewhat overkill. But I'm not going to argue with any of them if they wanted to beat the Frac out of Richard.

Still, Richard was undeterred and continued to answer, "Because we have a common enemy… I'm pretty sure you know that it wasn't my side that tied you in chains and tortured you." He stopped talking for a second as his eyes darted from Alex to Terrence before condescendingly shrugging his shoulders. "Well, this time anyway… And right now they think you're dead. But they're not done with their revenge yet, and a lot of innocent people are in danger because of the war you started… Do you really want their deaths on your hands?"

Out of the blue, Richard got a right hook to the jaw, forcing him to the ground as William towered over him, fuming in protective rage. "Don't ever speak to her like that again. I will not let you use or guilt my daughter into fighting anymore of your wars… you good-for-nothing coward."

"William," I called, crossing my arms, feeling a little happy to see blood dripping from Richard's nose and mouth, but I kept my joy on the inside. William then turned to look at me still seething in his rage, and I looked up at him, seeming rather calm when I asked, "Feel better?"

"Not really," he scowled, turning slightly to keep an eye on Richard.

Richard slowly stood back up to his feet, completely ignoring William as he held a handkerchief to his nose. And with his other hand, he held out a folder for me to grab, and grew frustrated when I didn't budge to take it from him. Instead he handed the folder to Matt then walked out, saying, "Think about it, Pumpkin... That's all I ask."

My security team stayed on high alert as we all watched Richard step into his waiting car just outside the lobby with one of his cadets holding the door open for him. But as his car door closed, it burst into flames with the force of the explosion shattering the glass windows of the lobby floor.

At full-speed, I raced to catch the young cadet when he was sent flying towards the broken glass. And he looked up at me in fear as he broke away from my arms, staring at the flames of the car he was just about to get into before he ran off, just like every other shopper and pedestrian on the street.

Aw Frac and Fruit Cakes. – This is just what I needed. – Yet another suspicious car fire outside my work. – This year is just not turning out well for me.

CHAPTER 12

Cold Hearts

Journal entry by George Nell

I'm not sure I like being Lila's go-to guy when the crap hits the fan, but part of me actually likes what she's doing. – Trying to help others and fighting for people's freedom is very noble of her, even if she has to do it in the shadows.

The car bomb raised a lot of attention in my department because we weren't able to find any of the standard reasons for a car exploding while parked on the street. – No Bomb, no accelerant, and nothing to start the fire either. On the plus side, thanks to Lila's cooperation in going along with my cover story, we were able to link the explosion to the previous attack on Flinders Street station. By spinning the tale that it was a response attack against the Eden Hotel's security for undermining a terrorist attack.

Unfortunately, it's now sparked a special task force being requested from higher up to find the terrorist cell before they do any more damage. – And my week just looks great now. – Not.

As the lead detective on the case, I asked to be the one to go and talk with the victims next of kin, just in case the others asked too many questions. When I got to the hospital, I thought Lila would be there already, but it was just Hanna Willows speaking with the doctor. – Dr James Ellis.

From the report I read last night when they brought Mr Willows in, it took hours to stabilise him and run tests to assess the damage, and several more hours to peel off the burnt clothes from his body.

And they've been monitoring him throughout the night to make sure he doesn't go into shock.

Dr Ellis looked confused shaking his head as he explained, "To be honest, Mrs Willows, I don't understand any of this. That kind of explosion should have killed your husband... At the moment we are looking at second-degree burns to his abdomen and third-degree burns to his face, arms and legs."

Wow. – He's right. That man should be dead. – Maybe Lila did something to save him. – But why isn't she here?

Hanna became distraught, and I tried to comfort her by placing my hand on her shoulder as I asked the doctor, "What can you do to help him?"

He shook his head again to think. "I would probably recommend a skin transplant. He would need several surgeries, and depending on the severity of the arms and legs, we may be looking at amputation."

At that news, Hanna was brought to tears, so I turned to the doctor to ask him to give us a minute, and I waited for him to leave the room before I asked, "Hanna, where's Lila? I thought she'd be here."

She straightened up and riffled through her bag for a hanky, replying, "Oh, she's at work today. She shouldn't have to see her father like this... Why? Do you think she should be here?"

She started to look panicked, but I calmly replied, "No. But I think she can help by using one of those flower-pods."

"What flower-pods?" she questioned, staring at me confusedly and with a hint of worry.

"It's okay, Mrs Willows, I know about Lila."

My subtle hint caused Hanna to step away looking even more confused. "What's wrong with Lila? What has she done? Is she in trouble?"

Suddenly, a burst of pain caused Hanna to hold her head, needing to take a moment. But after a few seconds, she took a few deep breaths then looked back up at me with a completely different and calmer look on her face. "I'm sorry, dear...what were we talking about?"

Hmm? – Something is definitely not right here. – Do Lila's parents seriously not know what she is?

"Nothing," I replied. "I'm sorry, Mrs Willows, but I've got to get back to the station. I'll check in on you later, okay?"

She nodded as I walked out the door, now with a whole lot more questions than I started with. And I know exactly who can answer them.

I went straight to the source and found Lila doing laps of the Eden Hotel swimming pool. She was actually pretty good and was able to swim the entire length of the pool twice before coming up for air. Eventually she surfaced just at the edge of where I stood, slightly out of breath as she looked up at me.

"You should be careful, George, the last person who got caught watching me swim almost got kicked in the head."

"I'll be sure to remember that," I replied, watching her climb out of the pool. "I see the construction workers have already started fixing up the lobby... Maxwell, doesn't waste time around here, does he?"

"Yes... He's unfortunately used to these events." Lila sighed while moving to grab her towel. "We actually have a building crew on our payroll. They're usually renovating bathrooms and shopfronts. But on the occasion, they've been on the clean-up crew as well."

As Lila stood drying herself, I got a little distracted, gazing at the skin of her body. It was hard not to, seeing how her white bikini covered very little of her. But I wasn't looking because of that. There's not even a scratch on her now, and I gasped in amazement. "Wow... it really did heal everything."

She stared at me confusedly before realising what I was talking about, and she looked down at her unscathed bare skin and replied, slightly saddened, "Almost... the scars are gone physically. But mentally they're still there. And now with a very fresh memory of them."

She ran her fingers across her abdomen where the three-animal lacerations used to be, and then held her wrist uncomfortably, probably remembering the many chains that held her and hurt her. Then taking a sharp breath in, Lila changed the subject.

"What's up, George?" she asked.

Oh Right. – I was actually here to ask her questions.

"I wanted to know why you aren't at the hospital with your dad?"

"Err... Next question," she replied, starting to pack up her gym bag and water bottle.

"Alright, why doesn't your mother know about your abilities?"

"Err... Next question," she replied again.

Getting agitated, I huffed. "Okay, why was your dad involved in the car explosion?"

"Next question," she replied again. – And this is getting ridiculous.

"Lila, I've trusted you to be honest with me, and I've jumped through a lot of hoops to stop other people from asking these questions."

"So why are you asking them then?" she rebuked, turning around to glare at me.

"Because I need to know." I seethed, now about to hit boiling point.

"No, you don't."

"Lila, don't make me shoot you," I threatened, glaring back at her. And to be honest I'm just about ready to throw in the towel with this whole thing, especially if she's planning on giving me all this 'next question' crap.

She paused for a moment, probably sizing me up. – I know I've got no chance against her. But I figured if I stood my ground, she'd respect that. Turns out she does, so she answered my questions. "I don't want to see Richard because he's... that guy. He's the bad guy!"

I became focused again, leaning in, and then asked her to define what she meant by 'the bad guy'. And she became agitated, moving closer to speak quieter.

"He's a member of The Board responsible for the disappearance of at least 93,968 guardians, plus scientists and military personnel across the globe... and still counting. Not to mention the many civil wars and terrorist scares that The Board uses as a cover to map their own agenda. Two of my guardian friends told me of the horrors they did while following General Richard's orders... One in particular, was when they slaughtered an entire village in east Africa because one of the children had broken into The Board's facility while playing, and had seen too much."

Wow. – That was a lot to absorb all at once, and she's still going.

"But on a more personal note, he's the one responsible for most of the problems you were sent to investigate when we first started to rekindle this wonderful friendship we have going... And if you actually did your homework and looked back far enough in my medical records, you'd know just how many hospital visits I racked up as a child because of him."

Lila's eyes turned black, and she had to look away to take some breaths and calm down. So I stayed quiet, giving her that time then asked, "Lila, why doesn't your mother know any of this?"

She took a deep breath, almost saddened when she replied, "She does... or she did. A few months ago, I gave Hanna a special tonic that rid her of the Neuritamine in her system, and it worked. She had her freedom back... Unfortunately she began having nightmares of the horrible things she had seen and was responsible for... And no, you should not ask."

Lila stared at me, and I nodded my head, agreeing to that demand before she continued. "Hanna came and asked me for help... so, I helped her. My brother programmed nano-bots to block any negative memories from surfacing. And if she ever tries to recall them, she experiences a mild migraine... To that end because what I am triggers a recall of those memories, she's left not knowing about this part of me."

Now completely saddened, Lila sat down on one of the pool chairs with her head in her hand. And I sat on the chair next to hers, trying to understand all of this, slightly regretting that I pushed the subject. Until I asked, "What are nano-bots?"

"Something that the public is not allowed to know exists." She sighed again.

"Got it." I nodded, staring back at Lila, starting to understand the difficult situation she's been put in. "So what are you planning on doing with your... with... Richard? Your mother's at the hospital right now, trying to cope with the severity of his injuries and his potential surgeries."

While still cradling her head in her hands, I heard Lila quietly growling to herself. And for a moment, I hesitated, but I'm pretty sure it had to be said. "Lila, I know this must be hard... really hard... And yes, I agree, he's definitely a monster. But your mother doesn't need to watch her husband suffer like that... especially if she doesn't know any better."

I thought it wise to leave our conversation there, letting her think about it as I headed back to the station to do my actual job.

Journal entry insert by Alex Woods

Terrence and I have just finished our daily perimeter run, just in time for lunch, when Adela caught us heading into our apartment. She looked completely freaked, and her eyes were puffy as if she had been crying, holding her stomach as she tried to catch her breath.

"Del, what's wrong?" I questioned, opening my apartment to get her a drink of water.

She stood at the kitchen bench and exhaled, "I need one of you... to talk to Lila."

Just as confused as I was, Terrence sat down on the barstool next to her and asked, "Why?"

And while still struggling with her breath, Adela wheezed, "Um... let me rephrase that. I need one of you to seduce her and not expect a relationship from it."

Okay. – Wasn't expecting this conversation from her.

"Again, why?" I asked, slightly put off by the topic we're talking about.

Finally, Adela composed herself and took a deep breath to quickly explain. "Lila is hormonally and emotionally frustrated. And she's destroying her body through exercise instead of giving in to her urges..."

"Del, are you sure you should be telling us this?" I interrupted.

"No," she snapped, slightly annoyed. "And yes, I'm aware that Lila will kill me for this, but it's necessary. Now do what you have to before she kills herself."

I stood to attention at that last part with slight fear in my voice. "What do you mean kills herself?"

Adela then glared at me, getting more annoyed that we weren't getting it. "Right now she's sitting at the bottom of the hotel pool, timing how long she can hold her breath for. And I counted 9 minutes before I ran to get you."

Aw crap.

I looked at Terrence before we both darted towards the door and barked, "Del, next time lead with that!"

At full-speed, we ran through the hotel, damning the consequences of Maxwell's rules. And I dove into the hotel swimming pool fully clothed to see Lila with her flowing white hair moving so gracefully in the water as she sat at the bottom of the pool, and she had her eyes closed while holding weights in each hand.

In a panic, I swam towards her, wrapping my arms around her before pushing up to the surface. Then when our heads broke above the water, we both gasped for air as Terrence hauled Lila from the pool and onto the ledge.

Confused, she looked at both of us then shouted at me. "What the hell's wrong with you? You scared the frac out of me!"

I climbed out of the pool in a fury. "I scared the frac out of you... Lila, you were sitting at the bottom of the pool with weights... I can't even feel my heart right now!"

Terrence wrapped a towel around Lila then pulled her up to sit on the poolside chairs, kneeling in front of her, completely worried about her as he asked, "Lila, why would you want to hurt yourself like that?"

In frustration, Lila sighed while shaking her head at him. "I'm not trying to hurt myself, Terry... I just needed a place to think."

IS SHE OUT OF HER FREAKING MIND? – Damn it, she makes me so angry. – There are so many places in the world, she could go to think, and she chose water. – The one thing I thought she was afraid of.

Terrence eyed me, clearly noticing that I was pissed. But somehow, he managed to keep a slightly level head, helping Lila to dry by using a spare towel as he talked. But I could still tell by the tone in his voice that he was pissed too.

"So why did you choose the bottom of the pool? I thought you hated water."

"I do... and for good reason." She griped, taking a few breaths, occasionally glancing at me. "But it's the only place where I can confront my demons and my fears, along with all the memories that go with it."

I suddenly sensed the heavy dread of emotions flurrying in Lila's heart as she held Terrence's hand. "I'm sorry if I scared you... both of you. It's just when I'm in the water, I'm forced to confront myself and everything else, to think about my life's choices... And in that moment when I'm flooded with so much fear, I feel nothing else... No anger, no sadness, no sense of longing or loss... When I'm down there, it feels like the rest of the world just stops. And I finally get that opportunity to think."

"What the hell could you possibly need to think about for that long?" I grumbled as she started putting her clothes on over her gorgeous white wet bathers.

"George came to see me. He's been assigned to the car explosion involving Richard." She growled while looking back at me, and I sensed her anger just saying that name.

Yep. – That detective has a lot to answer for right now.

Still trying to help Lila, Terrence stood to his feet, carrying her gym bag for her, and while walking to the door he asked, "What did he say?"

Lila stopped walking for a second and refused to look at us. "That's not important... But he's right... So if anyone needs me, I'll be up in Tyme's apartment. I need to ask William a favour." Then she stormed out of the room, still not looking at either of us.

Did she just say William? – What the hell did George say to her?

We followed Lila up to Tyme's apartment and stood behind her, curiously silent as she worked up the courage to knock on the door. She then peered over her shoulder back at me and Terrence, and rolled her eyes, waiting for the apartment door to open. When William opened the door, he stood in shock staring at Lila as she stood there with wet hair, and her wet bathers soaking through her singlet top.

"Lila... is everything okay?" William worriedly queried.

She briefly glanced over his shoulder, looking at Tyme as he stood behind him, and then back to William before she huffed, "I need your help."

We then all watched Tyme as he did his little victory dance in silence. But I could hear Lila growling just slightly in her throat, so my hand gently brushed against the back of hers, and I cautiously whispered, moving closer to her, "Easy girl."

At half-speed, she grabbed hold of my hand, and I could feel her using me as an emotional anchor. – For what? – I have no idea. But I'm not going to argue with her if that was what she needs from me.

William opened the door wider to invite us in, and then Lila explained what she needed from him. She asked him to teach her how to make the purple healing tonic that I forced her to drink. But she's also hoping he'll work with her to make it less painful, and have the ability to be administered via intravenous or epi-pen. – But she won't say why.

With a nervous, yet eager smile, William happily agreed then talked Lila through the process step by step as he showed her each ingredient. Once he had finished, Lila took a moment studying the ingredients, and then walked over to her gym bag, still holding on to my hand as she pulled out her journal. – The journal she got from Agatha after the Canadian rescue mission. – It's almost full now. – With drawings of flowers and plants, and next to the pictures were notes about what kind of properties and abilities each plant has.

Woah.

While walking back with me to the kitchen where the others were waiting, Lila growled again as she read through her notes on the Moly herb.

"I found your mistake, William," she said, placing her journal in front of William to show him her notes, and then highlighted, "The moly herb's healing properties are more potent than anything else on this bench, and is probably what caused the nasty side-effect for me when you amplified it... It's possible the herb only reacted badly for me because I'm a hybrid... But I'm not willing to take that risk and gamble with the potential pain for others."

The room fell tense as Tyme shrunk down in his chair, and William sighed, feeling guilty along with Terrence and me as we continued to listen to Lila.

"Now, there's a few ways we can get around that... You could add the moly herb after the amplification, reducing the overall potency... No that's a stupid idea. And it may not even be effective in reducing the pain... But... If we add a few drops of oil from the stem of a Gerbera before the amplification, it should add to the healing properties and act as a numbing agent. And if we use a snake plant to filter out the impurities, we should be able to use it via the epi-pen."

Holy crap. – This girl is like really smart.

Everyone looked at her in shock and both William and Terrence nodded in agreement.

"That should actually work," William replied. "I don't know why I didn't think of that."

He then looked at the drawings in Lila's journal, amazed at what he saw. "Lila, this book is filled with so much information, and the drawings are incredible... Where did you learn all of this?"

"I learn as I go," she answered, trying to stifle her growl as she snapped the book shut and placed it back in her bag. But I sensed a little sadness when she added, "It's not like I had a teacher for this stuff... Now let's get started."

All three Nature guardians worked as a team to gather or grow the appropriate ingredients. At one point, Lila had to let me go, and instantly Terrence glanced at the vine bracelet Lila was wearing, and then at his before looking over at me, feeling very glad that I was helping her through this. There were only a few moments when she let go of my hand, but I stayed right beside her just in case. – It almost felt like second nature for her to use me as an anchor, and it made me feel really glad.

Once the tonic was finished, William handed Lila the large vial of dark purple liquid and sighed with regret. "Can I ask who this is for?"

"I don't think you'll like the answer," she murmured, continuing to clean the bench.

"It's for your father, isn't it?"

Her ears began to peak, and I could feel more of a drain on my abilities as Lila scorned, "I don't have a father. But yes, this is for Richard."

"I could be..." William nervously stated, walking over to stand in front of Lila, stopping her from cleaning. "I could... be your father... if you wanted that."

I could sense all of Lila's sadness as she picked up her gym bag, and then let go of my hand as she sighed. "From my experience all father's do is disappoint you. So I think I'll pass."

There was so much angered sadness in Lila as she stood at the open door of the apartment, turning back to see and sense William's guilt. And after taking a long breath, she spoke again, "Thank-you for your help today, William... And for defending me yesterday. But I can't be who you want me to be... I'm sorry."

William tried to say something to her but before he could, Lila left.

Journal entry insert by Lila Winters

Terrence and Alex followed me up to my apartment, and they both sat on my bed in silence, watching me as I rummaged to find a change of clothes and raced into the bathroom to dress. – The last thing I want is for Hanna to think that I was mucking around in the pool, instead of taking this seriously.

I felt a bit self-conscious when the only clean bra I found was the red lacy set that Adela picked out to – in her words "spice up the bedroom." And right now I have two men in my bedroom that I don't know how I feel about.

Hmm? – What if she's right, and all I need is a healthy dose of frustration release? – It does make me think.

While staring at myself in the mirror in just my cargo pants and a bra, a sudden spark of fear filled me as images of me hanging from those horrid chains in just my bra and jeans raced through my mind.

"Lila," Terrence's voice startled me as he stood at the bathroom door, worriedly looking me up and down. "Are you okay?"

"Err... yeah." I nodded then hurriedly put my shirt and jumper on, and cleared my throat to apologise. "Sorry, I was just trying to find the courage to do this."

Again he said nothing, and I walked out, grabbing the vial out of Alex's hand. – Who's still staring at it intensely, looking like he wants to destroy it. But something seems to be stopping him.

Instead they both followed me again through the city to the Royal Melbourne Hospital. And I stood outside Richard's hospital room, contemplating everything while Alex and Terrence stood right behind me.

I had thought about using Alex's nifty animal skills to help ground me in my emotional chaos, but I could tell he was getting tired. And even though he would never say no to me, I think this one would be better if I did it on my own.

Alex still didn't like this idea, and he stood in front of me, finally deciding to speak up and try to reason with me. "Lila, this man tried to kill you... You owe him nothing."

Agreeing with his statement, Terrence stood next to him, staring at me, hoping I'd change my mind. So I grinned at Terrence's worrying pout and replied, "Terry, you hunted me and hurt me and almost killed me... But I saved your life and look where we are now."

"Richard is never going to change," Alex argued.

While still trying to hold onto my courage, I hugged Alex and kissed his cheek then did the same for Terrence, and whispered to both of them, "I know... but I'm not doing this for him." Then I walked into the room, leaving them both out in the hall to wait.

You can do this, Lila. - Just one foot in front of the other.

In the room, Hanna sat next to Richard's bed reading from her Bible. "Give us today our daily bread. Forgive us our debts as we also have forgiven our debtors. And lead us not into temptation, but deliver us from the evil one."

Knowing the verse, I stood at the end of the hospital bed, and added, "For if you forgive man when they sin against you, your heavenly Father will also forgive you." I then smiled at Hanna and whispered, "Hi, Mum."

With tears in her eyes, she stood up to hug me. "Oh, Lila, please call me Hanna. Katherine was your mother, and I could never take her place."

I was confused by her words and shook my head. "You remember Katherine?"

"Of course I remember your mother... She had such a beautiful heart, just like you... She was exactly like you, you know. When my mother and father found her wondering the streets of Russia as a child, they knew straight away what to do... Just like Richard and I knew what to do when your parents died."

Wait... I'm not a Willows? – And I'm half Russian too? – Holy Fraccing Fruit Cakes, that's new. – I wonder where William's from? – He does have an American accent. – But that means nothing these days. – Aw Frac. – Focus, Lila.

There wasn't much time before the doctors were due to go on their rounds. So I cleared my throat, trying to concentrate and asked if I could have a minute alone with Richard, and Hanna agreed. "I think I can do that... It's time for me to grab some dinner anyway."

On that note, I asked if she could take Alex and Terrence with her. – For safety. – And I watched as Terrence and Alex escorted Hanna into the elevator before I rushed at full-speed to steal a syringe from a nearby med cart, reappearing next to Richard's bed, ready to inject the tonic in through his IV drip. I hesitated for a split second then just did it. But just as I had finished the injection, I heard his room door open and one of the doctors started to draw back the privacy curtain.

Frac.

The bin was too far away, and I couldn't risk super-speed in front of him. I had to think fast, so I hid the syringe in my hand, putting the half-empty vial of healing tonic in my cargo pant pocket. Then I pulled the blankets up to cover what was left of the purple tonic in Richard's IV line.

The doctor's ID tag read: Dr James Ellis, and for some reason, that name struck a chord for me. But I can't remember how I know him.

"I'm sorry. I didn't know he had visitors," he stated.

While clearing my throat again, I smiled. "That's okay. I'm Lila his... da... daughter."

I choked on that last word. – Eerk. – Just the thought of it makes my stomach churn.

Dr Ellis's eyes lingered on me as he voiced his thoughts. "Hey, I think I remember you... You're one of Maxwell's employees... The one who was in a coma last year."

Frac, he remembers me. – Frac, Frac, Frac.

He could tell that I was nervous, and he glanced down at Richard, eyeing the blanket that was strategically placed, and then pulled it away to see that slight trace of purple liquid in the IV line.

"What have you done?" he sniped, trying to see what was in my hand.

In failing that, he turned back to try and stop the drip line. But I pulled him away, pleading with him, "No! Stop. I'm helping him."

"By poisoning him," he refuted before stepping back and watching me guard Richard.

That's right _I_ am guarding Richard. - My gosh how the tide has turned.

"I'm getting security," he threatened, racing to the door. But just as he was about to open the room door, I appeared in front of him and held it shut.

"How did you do that?" he questioned.

Aw Frac.

I have to make the call, and my entire body tensed as I tried to reason with myself in the attempts to stop me from doing what I'm about to do. But it has to be done, so I showed him the syringe and explained, "It's not poison. Just trust me. I'll show you... Please."

While walking Dr Ellis back to Richard's hospital bed, I pulled the curtains closed again then slowly pulled some of the dressings away from Richard's arm. But Dr Ellis started to freak out again, so I peered up at him and whispered, "Just watch."

He did as I asked and watched Richard's body strain slightly as the third-degree burns on his arms began to heal, leaving what looks like a mild sunburn on his now revived skin tissue. I then scooped out some blue-rose paste from the tub I had brought with me and applied it to Richard's arm, waiting a minute or two before rubbing it off, revealing completely healed skin.

Dr Ellis stared down at Richard's arm then carefully pulled away more of the dressing to look at the rest of his skin, seeing only a mild sunburn as I applied more of the rose paste to it.

"That's not possible... How did you do that?" He stared at me and then at Richard.

I bit my lip, contemplating what to say next, and in the end, I handed him the tub of blue-rose paste and answered, "A little bit of science, mixed with some very old remedies."

Well. – I suppose it is kind of science. – Just not the science he's used to.

"That's amazing," he mumbled while studying the paste. He then walked towards the door, staring at the tub of blue-rose paste still in his hand. "My boss is going to flip when he sees this."

Again, I stopped the doctor by appearing directly in front of him. "No! You can't tell anyone else about this."

He stepped back, a bit freaked out by my sudden movements, now staring at me. "What? This is the find of the century. We could help so many people with this."

"I know." I sighed, feeling a sense of – I've totally-done-this-before moment. "Look, I know you want to share this with the world and I understand your excitement. But you can't... This type of medicine has already been shared with the world once, and it created monsters where greed and power got the best of them... To you, this may save lives, but it can also destroy them. And you can't tell me it won't, Dr Ellis... Greed is a part of the human culture. And it's not going to change anytime soon."

He scowled at me but remained quiet, knowing I spoke the truth, so I continued. "I'm sorry, Dr Ellis, but I can't let you expose me or my medicines... Please."

There was a tense moment as he contemplated my words but then handed the Blue-rose paste back to me before walking out in anger.

A few moments later, George walked in and leaned against the wall. "He said the same thing I did, didn't he?"

"It still doesn't change my mind. The world isn't ready for us." I grumbled, sitting down at the end of the bed, feeling a stronger sense of alienation from the humankind at the decisions I've been forced to make.

George stood in front of me, nodding in agreement. – And that was a shock for me. – But he also seemed somewhat nervous and sad, bracing himself for a speech.

"So I've been doing a little digging and made a few calls. But I wanted to talk to you first before I did anything else... I may have found enough evidence on Richard for him to be charged with the murder of the missing woman that we were led to believe was you. And... if you're willing to testify, we can also apply kidnapping, attempted murder, and multiple assault charges based on the evidence I've gathered on him from your medical records."

Wait. – What? – Did he just say he's arresting Richard?

I stared at George for a moment, and he was close to tears but still hadn't finished as he continued. "Lila, I'm so sorry you had to grow up with that kind of monster... And I really wish you had told me this back in high school. It explains so much about who you are... And I know I probably wouldn't have been able to help you then, but I can help you now... if you let me."

Continuing to gaze into George's teary eyes, I felt a wave of relief. Then I moved at full-speed to hug him, and as he hugged me back, all I could whisper through my tears was, "Thank you."

I asked George if I could be the one to deliver the news, so he waited outside for me. But it wasn't long before Richard stirred awake, and he looked down at his freshly healed skin then felt his chest, realising that he was still alive. – I don't know if this is a downside though, but I can still see all of his old battle scars. – Which means either I made the tonic weaker, or it reacted badly for me just because I'm... me.

Richard eyed me standing at the end of his bed, and then confusedly shook his head. "I don't understand... why wouldn't you just let me die?"

"Because death is the easy way out," I answered. Then with a devious grin, I opened the privacy blinds and walked out, leaving him with George and two police officers, standing outside for him to deal with.

Before I left, I thanked George with a kiss on the cheek and another hug, and then victoriously watched as George went into Richard's room to arrest him.

Okay. – This moment right now is absolutely amazing for me. And I've been waiting far too long for it. – YES!!!!!

In a sense of victory and accomplishment, I was on my way downstairs to tell Alex and Terrence the good news, tossing the tub of Blue-rose paste from one hand to the other when I bumped into a very tall, scruffy man walking up the stairwell.

Oh My Fracs. – It's him.

It's difficult to recognise him with his scruffy black hair, and a two-week-old beard covering that long-chiselled face of his, with his emerald eyes not even looking at me as he moved around me to keep walking.

He was busy riffling through a black backpack, about to pull it up onto his shoulder, completely oblivious to me. – But I know it's him, and I gasped almost breathless. "Billy."

With his back turned to me, he froze at the sound of my voice. I held my breath, watching him slowly turn toward me, and when our eyes met, my heart felt like it had stopped. We stared at each other for a moment then in seconds, Billy darted towards me, and I was in his amazingly strong arms as they enveloped me.

"You can't be real," he doubtingly whispered. "I watched you burn."

He pulled away just enough to study my face with his fingers but still held me tightly with the other arm, refusing to let me go. And I am definitely not going to argue with him. My breath was short as I ran my fingers through his scruffy new beard and along his cheek, also in just that little bit of doubt that it really is him and that I'm not just imagining him. He then tilted his head down and kissed me.

Nope. – Not imagining him.

His lips felt amazing on mine, and I felt so overwhelmed, welcoming every single touch. It was like he was breathing me in.

"I can't believe you're here..." I tearfully moaned between kisses. "I looked all over the city for you... Every day... But I could never find you."

He stopped his kiss yet still held me close, and I gazed up into his amazing green eyes as he stared into mine, brushing his fingers through my long white hair. And with an amazing grin, he whispered, "Well, you found me."

In seconds, I lost all control of my senses, wrapping my arms over his shoulders, running my hands through his wavy black hair and groaning with so much joy as our lips touched again. He lifted me off the ground, and I locked my legs around his waist, refusing to let him go. We got so lost in the moment when he pressed those gorgeously defined muscles in his chest against me, pinning me to the wall as the passion between us rose.

His lips dragged along the skin of my neck then lingered on my chest, and with short breaths, my body tensed and rolled in his arms. Then in hearing my groans of desire, Billy sped off out of the hospital at a ridiculous speed with me still in his arms.

Journal entry insert by Alex Woods

When we escorted Mrs Willows back up to Richard's ward after buying her some dinner, we were greeted by George who very kindly informed Mrs Willows of what was going on and how Richard was being arrested.

I jumped with joy. – But on the inside. This was great news for Lila, but she was nowhere to be found. When I asked George if he had seen her, he said she had left about 10 minutes ago down the stairs, looking for us.

10 Minutes? – She should have found us by now.

In feeling a little worried for her, Terrence and I raced down the stairs but found nothing. I tried to track her by scent, but it only led me into the underground parking lot.

"The bracelet... are you getting anything from her?" I asked looking back at Terrence.

He stared down at his bracelet and answered, "It's mixed emotions. She's angry and at the same time really happy. But she's not scared anymore."

Taking a breath of relief and relaxing a bit, I asked confirmingly, "So she's safe... Can that thing track her?"

With hesitancy, Terrence looked back at me and answered, "Kind of... but I don't think it's a good idea. I think we should just let her vent."

I stood back and thought for a moment, somewhat agreeing with Terrence's plan for Lila to let off steam. But I came up with an idea of my own to help Lila out of the gloomy mess she's in. – Remembering how happy she was yesterday after movie night. – I think all she needs is to have a little fun.

CHAPTER 13

On The Enemy's Side

Journal entry by Lila Winters

I have no idea how to feel at this moment, or if what I'm feeling is even right. – I feel happy and ecstatic and never want this feeling to end.

From the hospital, Billy raced with me firmly in his arms back to I think his apartment. The sun was just setting as he carried me into the room. But I was too distracted with his lips to notice anything else. He placed his hands on my hips and it felt like he was hinting for me to get down, but I didn't want to.

"Uh-huh." I tightened my legs around him, and then lifted my head from his lips to show him how happy I am to be in his arms.

His gaze dropped to my hands as I pulled my top and jumper off, and he let out a pleasurable growl eyeing the lacey red bra I have on as he walked with me to this mattress on the floor, continuing to kiss me as he laid me down. Only then did I let my legs go, and his fingers skilfully unbuttoned my pants to remove them as I worked on removing his.

The room darkened as the sun disappeared with the street lights and the moon washing the room with a soft glow, but I'm still too distracted with Billy's body and arms and other parts. Then when our bodies moved together – Damn, it felt good. And I finally got that emotional release that Adela was pestering me about.

I'm not sure. – But I think I like it when she's right.

Hours have passed now, and we've stayed in this bed, enjoying everything about each other, and not wanting to let go of each other. Eventually, Billy disappeared into the bathroom, taking all of his body warmth with him, leaving me in the darkness and cold air of his apartment. He was taking a little while, and I stared at the door that was left ajar, wondering what was taking so long.

"What are you doing in there?" I curiously leaned off the side of the mattress to peer in. But I couldn't see much of him in the darkness.

"I'm doing... something," he cagily replied. "Don't move, I want to surprise you."

Letting out a giggle, I got comfy again but stayed eyeing the bathroom door, waiting for him to appear. Then the door opened again, and he returned looking completely different but a lot more recognisable.

He laid back down on the bed next to me, and I gently ran my fingers along his freshly shaven cheeks and lips, and I crinkled my nose as I smiled.

"Now there's the Billy I recognise. So handsome... You should surprise me more often."

"Handsome, huh," he cheeked, moving closer to me.

Oh frac. – I can't believe I said that.

I hid my smile, turning my face away from him as I tried to get comfy on his... not-so-comfortable bed. As I did, Billy gently ran his hand along the curve of my bare back, brushing his fingers through my long multi-coloured white and blond hair – that just fascinated him more. All the while I casually scanned our surroundings.

Hmm...

Well, this is worrying. – For the last two weeks, Billy has held himself up in one of the old apartment blocks in the north end of Melbourne. I glanced at a for sale sign on the entrance of the building when we arrived, but it looked like it'd been there for years.

It's a little saddening for me because his living arrangements aren't exactly ideal. I mean, it's dusty with broken walls, no heating, no lights, no furniture, other than a small table, one chair, and this mattress. The kitchen cupboards are all missing doors, and there's only one bowl and spoon on the shelf, next to a box of Cheerios.

It's definitely a major step down from the apartment waiting for him back at the Eden Hotel. – And, yeah, I know he has to share it with Shane. But that boy spends most of his days with Katie, leaving the apartment mostly empty.

It is worrying, yet right now, I really don't care that I'm lying on a mattress on the floor in the dark of the night. – I am with Billy, and I damn well like it.

In the darkness with only the glow of the full moon to light this cold night, Billy gently traced his fingers along the curve of my spine and around the blades of my shoulders. But his gaze became puzzled, and his eyes narrowed as he got up onto his knees, pulling my body into the moonlight to inspect me.

"What are you doing?" I whispered, loving the soft, gentle touch of his hands on my skin.

He studied the skin around my shoulder where not so long ago, he had stitched me back together. "It's gone... there's no scars on you at all. Your skin looks perfect."

I played ignorant, trying to distract his attention, cheekily looking over my shoulder at him, and I bit my lip as I smiled. "Don't you want me to be perfect?"

His eyes darted up to mine as he caressed my shoulder and everything else, breathing me in before whispering in my ear, "I want you to be everything to me... But you know me, I have a doctor's mind... And if I remember correctly, I am the lucky man who you asked to be your personal doctor, which means I want... No... I need to know _everything_ about you."

Mmm. – I like this one.

I leaned over the side of his mattress to find my cargo pants on the floor but quickly glanced at my mobile phone to realise I had several missed phone calls from Alex, Terrence, and Matt.

"Frac." I sighed, crawling off the bed to get dressed. And Billy looked so sad, watching me buttoning up my pants while frantically searching around for my shoes with no success.

"What? You're leaving?" He pouted with a sexy grin. "But I have so many questions in my mind that only you and your gorgeous body can answer."

While still in a curious yet cheeky mood, Billy pulled me back down onto his handsomely naked body before I could finish getting dressed, and I dropped my shirt in the scuffle. Then when he finally let go, I straddled his hips in just my pants and a bra, and his pout grew bigger as he marvelled at the unmarred skin on my torso. So I gave him another kiss and rolled my eyes at his cute but cheeky demeanour as I pulled the half-empty vial of purple healing tonic from my pocket.

"This is a new healing tonic that we perfected today... I, however, had the unlucky treat of having one of its... prototypes, that I originally had no intentions of having. But the Blue-rose water wasn't working to heal my injuries from... the um..."

I couldn't finish that part of the explanation, and Billy's eyes were saddened as he thought about that night as well. I didn't want him to see me cry, so I cleared my throat and moved on in the explanation.

"Anyway... the tonic healed everything. But because I'm a hybrid, the prototype over-reacted, and in the end, healed all my old injuries as well."

"Well, that's good, isn't it?" His eyes puzzled again as his finger traced along my skin.

With my own pout, I shook my head and explained the excruciating pain I was in, and how the process caused me to relive all of my injuries over and over again.

"If you remember, I have experienced quite a number of injuries in my lifetime, that I would much rather forget."

As Billy's hands continued to map my body, I heard his throat rumble in anger. "The General."

I nodded in confirmation, and rage crossed his face as he tensed his hands around me. And I smiled at his protective nature for me then continued. "I'm pretty good at accepting pain with rule 2 and all… But what I felt at the hospital was intense, and I almost burned down the building."

Billy's fingers interlocked with mine, and he held them tight as he sighed. "Well, I don't like that you were in pain… But I love the fact that you're a little firebug. Adding to the natural and animal tendencies you have… It just makes you even more fascinating to me."

"It's not something to love if I have no idea how to control any of… them."

I stopped talking before I said anything else, realising I hadn't yet told Billy about my other abilities. – I contemplated for a second about telling him, but that wouldn't have been fair because I haven't yet told Alex or Terrence everything. So I just sat on his lap, flirtingly annoyed at Billy and my predicaments.

While still smiling at me, Billy pulled his hand away from mine and created a column of fire in the palm of his hand, and then held out it in front of me. "I could teach you… if you'd like."

I watched as the column of fire danced around in his hand, but something caught my eye as the light from the flames glistened off the items hidden in the backpack he was carrying back at the hospital. In curiosity, I leaned forward to grab the bag and cautiously pulled it open, immediately starting to feel this horrid sensation in the pit of my stomach when I pulled out a hunting knife that was surrounded by a stash of hospital supplies and medicines.

Oh My Fracs. – He was stealing from the hospital when I found him. – But why?

Holding onto the knife, I leaned back down onto Billy's lap and glared at him as I realised the truth of the questions I had been ignoring this whole time. – How did he get away from them? Why hadn't he come back to the hotel or come to find me or tell anyone that he was safe? Why is he staying in this apartment? Did he even search for me? Why couldn't I find him when I searched for him?

Oh Frac. – Lila, what have you done?

I struggled to breathe with the pain in my chest, and blinked rapidly, trying not to cry. "It was you... You were the scent that I recognised at the hotel... You blew up Richard's car, didn't you? That's why they couldn't find any explosives."

The fire column in Billy's hand quickly disappeared with the moonlight being the only thing lighting us as he worriedly held onto my hips. "Lila, I can explain."

My breath laboured as the rage filled me, and my hair turned fully white. – <u>Again.</u> – And I really need to get a handle on this hair crap.

"Why were you at the hospital?" I enquired while gripping the knife's handle tighter.

It almost looked like Billy wanted to lie, but something in him urged him to tell the truth. "I was getting medical supplies, and I saw Richard's wife in the cafeteria talking to Alex."

"You saw Hanna..." I interrupted his thought with a realisation of my own. "And you went looking for him... You realised he wasn't dead."

Oh Frac. – This is wrong. – I have to get out of here.

I stood to my feet, fuming with anger as I grabbed my shirt and stormed to the door, mumbling to myself. "How could I've been this stupid? All this time I was worried about you and looking for you... and you were... Urgh!"

My anger stopped me from finishing that sentence, and Billy raced at full-speed to put his pants on, darting to the door to stop me from leaving. "Lila, please just let me explain."

Still furious at him, I stood back, but really I was angrier at myself for being so fraccing blind, and I yelled, just barely holding back my tears. "You're working for them, aren't you? You watched them torture me and try to kill me, yet you still joined their side!"

"Lila, I thought you were dead," he explained, trying to grab my arm.

But I've heard that line before, so I pulled away, refusing to let him touch me as I cried, "Yeah, that happens a lot with me... The problem is I'm stubborn and refuse to die!"

I started pacing, feeling uneasy in my own skin while he continued his explanation, "I'm sorry, Lila... I didn't want to give up on saving our kind. And I didn't think I had anything to lose."

And there it was. – I stopped and stared at him as he scowled at the floor in deep regret.

"Well now you do," I stated, anxiously holding my hand out in front of him. "Come back with me. Your apartment's still waiting as is your job if you want it... Please, Billy, come back with me."

Holding my hand out toward him, I waited for him to take it. But he just looked at me and shook his head. "I can't."

Oh Damn Fracs. – That really hurts.

The pain in my chest felt unbearable, but I held back the tears as I commanded my vine-bracelet to grow, grabbing hold of Billy's legs then tossing him across the room for him to land safely back onto the mattress. The tears fell again as I tried to leave, but again Billy raced to stop me, this time pinning me against the door and lifting my feet off the floor.

"No!" he shouted. "I'm sorry, Lila, but I can't let you go."

I didn't fight him. Instead I glared back at him and spoke with so much disappointment. "I freed you from their prison, and now you want to hold me in yours."

"No..." He pleadingly shook his head, holding me tighter. "I want to protect you... from everyone. From Richard, The Board, even Stephen and his rebels. I want to keep you safe."

I stared into Billy's green eyes, sensing all of his protective nature, and the care that he has for me. Then I calmly whispered , "I don't want your protection, Billy... Now let me go."

Again he didn't, and his hands trembled around me as the anger rose in him. "You think you're safe at that hotel? Max is one of them... He's just using you. I can't just let you go back there... Do you know what he's done to our kind!"

My eyes glowed gold as I continued to gaze into Billy's eyes. Then I held one of my hands on his cheek to calm him, and kissed his lips, causing him to loosen his grip on me before I answered, "Rule 7, Billy... I knew about Max before I accepted the job."

"Then why?" he questioned with so much confusion and anger in him.

My eyes glowed a brighter gold, trying to keep him calm as I replied, "Because Max is the devil I trust."

Suddenly, Billy's eyes widened, staring at me in shock as he let me go, taking a few steps back to look down at the hunting knife that I had driven into the side of his ribs. He struggled to breathe as he fell to his knees, but I caught him, guiding him down to lie on the floor.

In tears, I pulled out what was left of the purple healing tonic and held his head up as I sniffled. "Drink this... It tastes awful and it's going to hurt like hell. But I like you too much to let you die."

His lips parted enough for me to pour the tonic into his mouth, and he grimaced at the taste. I then held his hand as I pulled the knife out of him. But his screams were loud enough to draw the attention of our old friend Stephen, now banging on the door shouting Billy's name, asking if he was alright.

Frac. – Not him.

To buy me more time, I commanded the vines from my bracelet to bar the doors before he could enter. But I knew it wouldn't hold him for long, so to help Billy, I used my shirt, pressing it against his stab wound to slow the bleed as it healed.

"The pain will stop in about a minute, and you'll be back to fighting bad guys in no time," I explained through my sniffles and tears. In seeing my tears, Billy carefully moved his free hand to catch them from my cheek, so I leaned down to kiss him goodbye. "If you ever change your mind, Billy, you know where I'll be... playing with fire and all."

Before I knew it, Stephen had broken the door down to see me kneeling over Billy. So at full-speed, I stood up and grinned. "See ya 'round, Stephen."

Then while still at full-speed, Stephen chased me towards the window, and just narrowly missed me as I dove through the glass and plummeted four stories towards the ground, landing like a cat on my bare feet.

I looked up to see the glass following my fall when suddenly my eyes glowed yellow and a spark of lightning shot from my hand. The shock then shattered the glass into a sprinkle of sparkly sand.

Cool. – I'll have to figure out how to do that one again.

As the sand settled to the ground, I saw Stephen leering at me through the broken window and bellowed, "Argh!!! This woman just won't die."

Knowing his statement was true of me, I wryly waved back at him before I took off at full-speed, running through the streets and eventually stopping in one of the side alleys. – Mainly because I really needed to think things through.

Right now, I'm topless and shoeless, wearing just pants and a bra with bloodstains all over me. And I think I have glass in my hair. – I don't want anyone at the hotel to know that I've been so reckless, and I'm pretty sure I'm lost. – These are definitely not the streets that I usually roam. But luckily, I still have my phone. So I made a call to the one person I know wouldn't freak out. – Much.

"George, I need a ride."

Journal entry insert by George Nell

It was the middle of the night when Lila called, and my wife Anika was pretty peeved when I had to rush out. But when I came back with Lila looking the way she did, my wife kind of calmed down and instead went into a concerned shock.

When I picked Lila up, for some reason she was out near Coburg. She had blood stains all over her, wearing only a bra and pants with no shoes on. I used the cover story of Lila working for ASIS and that her cover had been blown on one of her ops. And Anika knows not to ask questions when it comes to that area of my job. She did, however, offer to help Lila with the glass in her hair. – But... it's now 2am in the morning, and I'm left with a lot of questions, <u>again</u>.

Lila asked if I could cover for her with her work colleagues, and tell them she was at my place the whole night in exchange for answering some of the many questions I have. It seemed like an odd request, given the close relationship she has with her colleagues, but I agreed anyway.

In fearing that the truth would incriminate her, I didn't want to know too much of the details around tonight, just enough to know that, one – the city was not in danger, and two – that she didn't kill anyone. Once those questions were answered, I went upstairs to set up the guest bedroom and fetch some clean towels from the linen press.

By the time morning came, Lila had already disappeared but left a thank-you present for Anika. It was a plant that Anika was talking about last night, the one she used to love back in Japan as a child. – The Asian bleeding heart.

Apparently, Lila had sparked up a conversation while Anika was picking the glass out of her hair last night, telling Anika that she had a gardening hobby and quite a green thumb in the area. So this morning, Lila left the plant on the kitchen floor in a large bamboo pot with instructions on how to care for it and a little note at the bottom reading: "Thank you for being such amazing friends. – See ya soon."

Journal entry insert by Alex Woods

Yep. – I was pretty pissed at the fact that Lila didn't come home last night. But when I got her text just after 2am, explaining how she had lost track of time and was spending the night at George's, my worry eventually disappeared. I suppose she needed someone to talk to and who better than an old high school friend.

It still didn't seem to break Lila out of the gloomy funk she was in, because it's now mid-morning and instead of working, Terrence and I found Lila sitting by the pool with her legs dangling in the water while staring at the ripples. She seemed to be lost in thought, and she still has the long white hair. But I'm determined to fix that.

While Terrence went to gather up the team, I dove into the swimming pool, startling Lila as she shielded herself from the splash. I lifted my head up and grinned at her, gesturing to her to get into the pool. I pleaded and even tried my amazingly cute puppy-dog eyes – which almost worked, but instead she gave me that cute little smile with the wrinkle in her nose as she shook her head.

I was stunned that I'd failed, but still determined, I stood in the middle of the pool and yelled, "Plan B!"

Within seconds, Terrence ran into the pool room at half-speed, grabbing hold of Lila as he dove into the water. And followed behind him came Jess, Matt, Ruby, Danny, Tyme, Adela, Shane, and Katie. They all jumped into the pool along with them, and the smile on Lila's face as she laughed at me, knowing this was all my doing, made me feel successful in my mission.

We had so much fun splashing around and playing water volleyball, and Max, Chase, Roy, and Michael eventually joined us, bringing with them a buffet lunch that Danny and Ruby went for in a heartbeat. And while the others played, I sat at the edge of the pool next to Ruby as she brought over some lunch for me. – All her favourites of course. – I think I'm Ruby's favourite makeshift-uncle.

Ha. – Take that Shane. – And Tyme.

I very happily sat with Ruby and Danny, cheering on their mum as she played double-decker wrestling with Katie, Adela, and Jess. Obviously, Katie was on Shane's shoulders, and Adela was on Tyme's. Jess asked Matt to be her partner, and Lila was on Terrence's shoulders.

They were all very competitive with the one rule of no super moves. And Lila was having so much fun that she didn't even notice her hair had returned to normal.

Game Plan

Journal entry by Billy Jonas

It's been almost three weeks since Lila left my apartment by jumping out the window, and I still can't believe she survived the jump. I also can't believe that she didn't stay with me, or why she continues to live and work with a monster like Maxwell.

I even found out that she saved the monster who had hurt her for so many years, and instead he's now on trial for murder as well as kidnapping and assault charges. – But that kind of justice just isn't enough for me. General Willows deserves much more than that, which is why Lila is clearly a better person than I'll ever be.

I do worry about her though, and I race over to check on her every now and then, just to make sure she's safe. But I'm always sure to keep my distance, because every time I see her beautiful face and that amazing smile, I need to fight the urge to run in and whisk her away from that death trap, running as far away from this city as I can. – And that urge is very strong for me.

Last week, I realised my occasional check-ins were not as discreet as I'd thought. Because when I arrived at the corner alley where I usually hide to see her, I found a large red gift bag with a really nice, warm fleece-lined jumper in it, along with a stack of warm winter clothes and a cute little note that read, "I can't have my doctor catching a cold. – See ya soon."

That's right. – She still calls me her doctor.

Today, I'm on my way back to my usual spot in the alley, hopefully to see Lila doing her usual security loop around the hotel. I made it to the alley just in time to see her standing at the reception desk of the hotel, talking to Chase and looking absolutely radiant with that perfect blond hair. – I know all this is a little stalker-like, but I just want to make sure she's okay. If only to make my day a little less miserable.

As I leant on the brick wall, watching her talk and walk so gracefully, a small smile appeared on me when I noticed something sitting on the ledge of the brick wall just opposite me. It was a little red gift box with my name on it. – That meant she was expecting me.

In feeling a little... happy and curious, I opened the box to find two forest-scented candles in glass jars, and they had a beautiful picture of a white wolf running through the woods etched onto them.

"I was beginning to think you weren't coming." An amazing voice appeared behind me, and I turned to see Lila, looking so radiant. "I like the jumper you're wearing. Whoever bought it must have good taste."

My lips tilted up on one side as I replied, "Well, the amazing woman who bought it for me knows my colour and my style."

Her eyes darted back to the hotel as she softly spoke. "Do you want to come in with me?"

"No." I shook my head and moved closer to her, using my fingers to gently tuck a stray strand of her hair back behind her ear before I whispered, "And you know I don't want you here either. I want you to be somewhere I know you'll be safe."

Letting out a sigh, she looked up at me and handed me a mobile phone. "I am as safe as I'll ever be, anywhere in this world... No matter where I go, Billy, trouble always finds me. But I'm more worried about you. So I thought we could negotiate."

I curiously stared at the phone and then back at her. "Alright, what are your terms."

She took a breath, and then placed her hand on the phone, "I've programmed my number into this phone. And I would like you to use it to check in with me. You don't have to call. You just have to text and say that you're alive. And I'll do the same. This way if at any stage either of us needs the other, we'll know how to find each other... sound fair?"

Thinking the deal through, I'd honestly rather ask her to run away with me. – But I know she won't. She has her family to look after. So I nodded, agreeing to the deal, and she gave me that beautiful smile before she ran off at super-speed.

I was just about to run out of the alley myself, when the phone in my hand received a text message. – The message was a picture of her smiling with the text reading: "Proof that I'm safe. See you soon, Billy."

Aw darn. – Why does she have to be so amazing?

The picture kept me in high-spirits for the rest of the day and most of the week-end. And I stared at it a lot, and did as promised and texted her a lot, smiling every time she replied with the sweetest and most perfect of messages.

All week we continued to text each other to check in, and every night I called to ask how her day was and to say goodnight to her properly. But I still go to the side alley every morning just to see her. — And each time I see her, she looks even more perfect.

The weekend has arrived again, and I unfortunately had to pull my head out of the clouds and get back to reality. Tonight, Stephen has organised a group meeting, and I'm on pizza pickup. It didn't take me long to get them, and when I walked into the old warehouse called Pack-n-Send, I carried with me 23 large pizzas and left them on the table for the group of about 40 guardians to disperse of.

I was a bit annoyed when I walked in because a few days ago, we welcomed back an old friend, Peter Boone, who has apparently been held up in a hospital since the Flinders Street station misfire. — He's the one who hurt Lila and tried to kill her. And I hate him. But unfortunately, we need all the man-power we can get, so I can't kill him. — Not yet anyway.

Isaac and Holy, the youngest of our group — and just barely classed as an adult, were getting comfy on a new couch that seems to have miraculously appeared along with a very nice, large flat-screen TV. They also look like they have no plans in joining the meeting as they sat and watched cartoons, splitting a pizza between them.

"Hey, where'd you get the TV?" I asked.

Isaac giggled at Holly as he replied, "Um... we found it."

Ah-huh. – And that is complete bull.

I placed my hand on Isaac's shoulder and started to burn through his T-shirt, very lightly heating his skin, causing Isaac to stand to his feet, almost dropping his pizza as he grunted, "Argh! Alright, we stole it. What's the big deal?"

"The big deal is that we're supposed to be keeping a low profile," I griped, crossing my arms and glaring at them both. "Don't you think someone's going to notice a missing flat-screen."

While watching our little discussion, Stephen sat at the table, chowing down a pizza slice with his feet up, joking around with a few of the other team members. Then he grumbled, "Billy relax. What are they going to do, arrest us... We'll be gone before they reach the building."

"The police are not the only thing you need to worry about." I huffed, walking over to the table to grab a slice, then leaned against the wall in an angry sulk.

"Ah yes, your little, not so dead girlfriend," Stephen grunted, taking another slice of pizza.

Peter then arrogantly chimed in. "I think you mean the witch who just won't burn."

"Watch your mouth!" I growled, burning my slice of pizza as my hand became engulfed with flames, leering at him.

He stood up creating his own fireball in his hand and bickered, "What's the matter Billy, can't stand the fact that I burned your girl first?"

Yeah, that did it for me. – At full-speed, I let him have it, kicking the crap out of him as we fought each other. Getting a good swing at his face. – And I know that's gonna leave a bruise.

Eventually, Stephen broke up the fight, ordering the rest of the team to pull us apart before condescendingly shouting at us. "Now boys, don't tell me you're fighting over a girl... This is no way to win a war. Now shake hands and get over it."

No. – I don't want to shake hands with either of them, I want to kick both their smug American arses. – And I'm Canadian, so I can say that.

"Billy... Now," Stephen sternly demanded.

I relaxed and huffed out a conceding breath as the team let go of me, and I reluctantly shook Peter's hand. But he was stupid enough to smile and add, "You know what... you might be right. Maybe if I'm nicer to her, I might get a little something on the side too."

At that, I punched him in the face again, really hard, before throwing him to the ground.

Urgh. – Just the thought of him ever touching Lila makes my blood boil.

He readied himself to throw another fireball at me when a ring of flames appeared surrounding us both. – And I really wish I knew how to do that, but only a few of us were trained to that level.

"Both of you need to cool down. Now!" Stephen shouted. "This team is never going to work if you boys don't get along, so play nice... And Peter, if we're ever going to get Lila to join our side, we can't keep calling her a witch."

Finally pulling her attention away from the stolen TV, Holly asked, "You honestly think Lila's going to join our side? How are you going to manage that?"

With a very devious and worrying grin, Stephen smugly strutted over to his table of trinkets and jewels that he had collected during our many raids on The Board's labs and training camps. He picked up the box that had that stupid green rock in it. — The one that he stole from Lila. - And answered Holly's question, "I'm going to win her over by playing the good guy... Lila's need to save people will force her to help us."

"No!" I angered, failing to escape the flames. "I don't want you anywhere near her!"

Suddenly, Stephen appeared in front of my prison of fire, holding that stupid rock and shaking his head. "Oh, Billy, you're still failing to see the bigger picture here... You're the one who hates the death that comes with this war. If your little nature girl agrees to play on our side, then there'll be no more unnecessary deaths... That's what you want isn't it?"

I stayed silent, but he knew my answer. So he continued his little spiel while holding that stupid rock in front of me. "And as an added show of good faith, Billy, if you agree to play nice with this entire team, then you have my word that your little girlfriend will remain safe and unharmed by all of our Rebel factions."

Darn. — I really hate him. But I also want the deaths to stop and want Lila to be safe. So I agreed on the condition that no one hurts Lila.

CHAPTER 15

Nosey Knots

Journal entry by Lila Winters

Tonight is epically amazing because I'm finally doing something that normal parents do. I'm attending Danny's first mid-year school concert. – We're at the Melbourne performing arts centre, and the auditorium is packed, because the school teaches from prep to year 12, which means there are a lot of students and a lot of families. – And I have my family here as well.

Matt's sitting with Hanna at one end of our row of seats, and I'm sitting at the other end. Between us is Tyme and Terrence. Alex has Ruby sitting on his lap, and next to him is Max, Adela, Jess, Katie, and Shane.

Chase really wished he could come, but with me not at the hotel, he has to play the security boss. – Chase and I make a good team like that. – My favourite agreement with him is that he manages the floor and roster, and I train the newbies and do all the paperwork. The paperwork side of things is actually very easy for me, seeing how I'm able to do it at super-speed, and he is humanly slow. – Not bragging or anything, but that's why we make a good team.

The concert was going fantastically, and because Danny's in the Prep-grade, he had two acts, one in the middle and one at the end, and they were both amazing. When Danny's class had finished their last song, everyone applauded, but my row was the loudest as we cheered for Danny.

He waved at me and Matt, and we gleefully waved back while I laughed at our families over the top loudness. The downside from that was I think we caught the attention of someone really important in the school, because she kept staring back at me from the front row for the rest of the concert.

After the show, the school was offering light refreshments for everyone, but my team has no plans on staying. We are going out to celebrate. And Max has booked a table at one of his favourite restaurants, not far from here.

Matt and I were super excited as we waited at the door of the auditorium for Danny to come out, both receiving amazing hugs from him and telling him how amazing he was.

"Danny, I loved every second of it," Matt proudly boasted. "And now we can celebrate... Come on let's round up the others."

Danny happily grabbed Matt's hand, and we split up to go find everyone, but I had only taken two steps when that important lady from the front row walked up behind me.

"Mrs Winters," she called.

"Yes, that's me." I turned excitedly to greet her.

"Hi, my name is Carol Grey. I run the PTA here at the school."

Ah. — So that's why she looks important with her posh pink suit and her very pointy pink shoes, along with that fancy braided hair bun that I've never figured out how to do. — I wonder if she got it done professionally. I mean I know everyone here has that kind of money to throw around. We are after all sending Danny to quite a prestigious school — on Max's recommendations. — Mainly because of the strict security measures. — The school had even asked Chase and me to give their security protocols a check-up at the beginning of the year, so I definitely know they are up to scratch.

Oops. — I got distracted. And she'd stopped talking while I was busy looking at her hair.

"Um... sorry... I'm Lila... Nice to meet you, Carol."
I smiled and shook her hand as she added, "Yes, you're Danny's mother. We were just talking about you the other day."

Oh Frac. — Please be good things. — Lila, shut up and listen to her.

"We were hoping that you would be willing to attend our school Mother's group that runs on Wednesday nights. You know, so we can get to know you a little better... I mean the only thing we know about you is that you work in security, but that's pretty much it."

Right. — A mother's group. Think, Lila, how do you get out of this? — Or should you get out of this? I mean it is Danny's school. — You should be involved, shouldn't you? — Oh, screw it.

While still trying to figure out an answer for Carol, I covered my mouth pretending to scratch my nose and mumbled under my breath, "A little help here please," in the hopes that someone would hear it.
Carol could definitely tell I was unsold by the idea, and went on to tell me how the group first started and what they usually

get up to in the meeting. – Trying to make it sound really fun. But no one was swooping in to pull me away, so while still listening to Carol, I peered over to see Alex standing at the door, holding Ruby in his arms and asking Matt for information about my situation.

"Oh, that's Carol Grey," Matt quietly replied. "She's commonly known as Miss Nosey Knots of the PTA... Looks like Lila's her next victim."

Great, I'm her next victim. – Why isn't anyone coming to rescue me? – Although it does seem a little odd that I can fight an entire army of armed super soldiers, but I can't shake off a nosey PTA woman.

"So can I pencil you in for this Wednesday or next Wednesday?" she asked.

Aw Frac. – I'd stopped listening to her again.

"Umm... this Wednesday," I tentatively answered with a very forced smile.

I can't believe Alex didn't save me. But thankfully, Terrence found me and interrupted us. "Hey, Ruby's looking for you."

Yes!! – Now that is my hero. – Thank-you. Thank-you. Thank-you, Terry.

It didn't work the way I'd hoped though, because before we could make our exit, Carol turned to Terrence and quickly shook his hand. "Oh hi, you must be Lila's husband."

"Eerr... no," I stuttered. "Um... I'm not married. This is my... my friend, Terrence."

Carol's grin got wider, and it was almost creepy looking. "Oh... Well, we also have a great single parents club that meets every Friday. I'm sure they'd just love an extra member."

Frac No. Frac No. Frac No. - Come on, Lila, find an excuse and quick. - Damn it, for some reason my brain is deciding to freeze on me.

"Ah no, I can't make it on Friday. Um... because..."

"She has a date with me on Friday," Terrence interrupted as he held my hand. And I swear I want to kiss him right here and now for saving me like this. - Because there is no way I'd ever want to go to a singles group.

"Ooh, I'd love a friend with benefits like that." Carol grinned again.

Eerr okay. - That was definitely too much information for me. But thankfully Matt called my name from the door and gave us the signal to leave - which was like five minutes too late.

"That's my husband. I mean ex... my ex-husband. Um... goodbye, Mrs Grey." I said, shaking my head as I sighed, trying to understand everything that just happened while rushing out the door still holding Terrence's hand very tightly.

By the time we got out into the car park, Matt and Alex were standing outside the van everyone was packed into, and they both looked very smug and way too happy. They eyed me and Terrence still holding hands, causing Matt to chuckle at Terrence.

"We send you in to rescue her... and you come out holding hands."

"And with a date," Alex added jokingly.

I crinkled my nose at Alex and snapped, "Oh, bite me, Alex."

"Don't tempt me," he joked back in a whisper as we got in the van.

Oh Frac – Wait... what?

On the drive to the restaurant, my phone started buzzing, and when I looked at the ID, it said it was Billy. – Which is weird. – The entire team is in the car with me so I can't answer the phone without needing to answer a whole lot of questions about him. But the timing of his phone call seems odd. For the last few weeks, he's kept his word and texted me every day. But he always does it in the morning to start our day on a less worrying note, then a few times at lunch. Then he calls me and we both wish each other goodnight before bed. – It's only 7.30pm, which is an odd time for him to be calling. But I still can't answer the phone without needing to answer a whole bunch of questions, so instead I sent a text to him.

> Can't Talk. Is everything alright?

Everything's fine. But I went to the hotel, and you weren't there.

> Oh, you silly Billy. It's Danny's concert tonight, remember. And the team's gone out for dinner.

Where?

> It's an all-you-can-eat restaurant. But it's not just around the corner like Maxwell said. I think we just passed the sign towards Flemington.

> Why? Are you planning to finally join us?

I didn't get a response, which isn't that surprising. But I'm really hoping that maybe one day soon, he'll finally come in from the shadows and actually talk to the team. – They do still search for him when we do our daily perimeter runs. But I kind of told everyone, that if he hasn't been found by now, then he's either not in the state, or he doesn't want to be found.

I know I lied, but only a little. – And at least the second part is true.

When we got to the restaurant, it was an actual all-you-can-eat buffet this time, near the Flemington racetracks on the other side of the city. The drive was a bit longer than expected. However, when the kids realised that they could have as much ice-cream as they wanted, Max became the best person in the world to them.

We had to sit at an extra-long table given the number of people in our group. Hanna, Max, Jessica, Matt, Terrence, and Alex sat on one end of the table. And Tyme, Adela, Katie, Shane, and me sat at the other end with Danny and Ruby sitting in the middle.

Apparently, Adela was in desperate need of some girl talk, so she opted to sit next to me. And right now, I really wish Terrence would come to save me again.

"Hey, I heard you were going on a date with Terrence," Adela whispered.

"I knew it." Katie leaned in, excitedly grinning. "I so knew you were into him."

I grew very annoyed at their curiosity as I replied quietly. "No... I'm not going on a date with him, that was just an excuse we used."

Katie wasn't convinced as she stared at me, curiously trying to figure me out. "So you're into Alex then?"

"No..." I shook my head, remembering to keep my voice low. "What is this an interrogation?"

I was clearly not in the mood for it and grumbled as I stood up, walking over to get more food. But unfortunately Adela followed. "Lila, come on... You know they both love you. Why are you pushing them away?"

"I'm not pushing them away," I rebuffed while looking over the food in the buffet. But Adela didn't believe me. Instead she stood in front of me and crossed her arms, obviously not letting the subject drop. So I rolled my eyes and clarified with her. "I'm not pushing Alex or Terry away. I would never do that to them. They're my best friends and you know that... But for your information, the only men, who have actually asked me out on a date in the last 3 years, were Matt and Billy. And everyone knows how both of those dates ended... Urgh... Adela, I'm a date-disaster magnet, and I'm pretty sure both Terry and Alex know that... Look, just drop it, okay?"

I gave up on the food idea, seeming a little too agitated to eat, and decided to take a breather outside for a few minutes. I stayed in the alley and stood at the back door when Stephen appeared in front of me.

He pushed me up against the door with his hand over my mouth to silence me as he warned, "If you fight me, my men have orders to burn this restaurant to the ground... understood."

I didn't fight him. I just nodded, choosing to just listen. And I looked very confused at him, leading him to smirk at me. "Hmm... you're wondering how we found you, aren't you?"

Again, I nodded, still hoping he would remove his hand from my mouth. Then he held in his other hand a phone I recognised.

Billy's phone. – Oh Frac. – My hair turned white, and my eyes became watery when I reached out with my free hand to grab it. But Stephen pulled it away and put it back in his pocket.

"Don't worry, I'll make sure he gets it back... But only if you decide to behave."

Okay, Lila. – You've got a lot riding on this. So don't fight him. – Just Stay.

As requested, I behaved. I didn't struggle to get out of his hold even though the door of the restaurant was freezing cold on my back. I just stayed still, trying very hard not to cry.

"You're a very rare type of guardian. Did you know that, Lila?" He waited for me to nod again before he continued, "Mmm...That's why we need your help. You see, over the past several weeks, we've attacked 12 of the Board's labs and Training grounds, rescuing 89 guardians in total... Unfortunately, they're all still under the influence of Neuritamine... and their loyalty sickens me."

He pushed a note into my hand and sneered. "You remember where we live... don't you?"

Again, I nodded, still trying not to cry at the fact that I'm feeling so helpless, and feared for my family just on the other side of this door. I know there's no way I can save all of them, and I definitely don't want to ruin Danny's special night. – Not tonight.

Glancing around the alley nervously, Stephen whispered again, "I'm going to let you go now." Then he backed away, slowly pulling his hand away from my mouth.

I looked down at the note as he started walking away, and I asked, "What if I say no... what happens to them?"

"They're a security risk." He shrugged his shoulders, looking back at me before he disappeared.

I walked down the alley, very tempted to follow him, but I was startled by Alex who had come out to find me. And in a fright, I accidentally punched him in the face, thinking he was one of them.

"Alex!" I shrieked in shock. "I'm so sorry, are you okay?"

He rubbed the side of his jaw and stood back up, concerningly staring at me. "Yeah... Are you okay? Lila, you're shaking."

No. – I'm not okay. – And there is no denying that. – I feel scared, but I can't tell him why because that might cause him to do something stupid like follow Stephen, which would inevitably lead him back to Billy. – And now I'm stuck in a vicious mess, and I can't stop shaking.

Sensing my fear, and seeing my white hair again, Alex pulled me in close, wrapping his arms around me. "Come here, Lila, I've gotchya... You're safe, okay. I promise."

His words were amazing but I still don't feel safe, and I broke into tears, muffling my sobs into his chest. He asked me what happened, and I told him that I really didn't want to talk about it. And to my surprise, he respected that. He wasn't happy about it, but he respected it. Instead, he just kept holding me, trying to calm me down.

"I'm always here if you need me... okay."

When I'd calmed down enough, we went back inside to join the group, and Terrence appeared in front of me, worried as he sensed my hectic emotions through the stone, and looked even more worried to see my white hair again.

"Lila, are you alright?"

I knew he would sense if I was lying, but I still couldn't tell them, so I held his hand and smiled. "Honestly, Terry, no, I'm not alright. But I'm also not ready to talk about it."

Both Terrence and Alex stared at me worriedly but nodded, accepting my request, then offered for me to sit with them instead. And I was more than happy for that, and ended up finishing the night on a slightly better note.

I took the rest of the weekend to think things through. – And no, my white hair has not returned to normal, because I'm really, really angry. – Furious is a better description, but I need to stay somewhat calm to keep the team from worrying and asking questions that I just can't answer. – Which just makes me feel Fractastic.

Right now I have the fate of 89 guardians hanging over my head. And I have no idea how to help them because I have no idea where they are. To make things really frustrating, I have no idea if these guardians would ever be willing to just walk away and leave the vendetta business to a less destructive team like mine. – Which inevitably leads to me fuelling Stephen's spiteful ways.

But I need to help them. – Not just for them but for Billy. The note that Stephen shoved into my hand was a threat to Billy's safety if I didn't agree to help them. – I did have a brief thought of calling Billy to make sure he's still alive. But part of me is worried that if he doesn't answer or text back, that I'm going to do something stupid and tear this city apart looking for him. – Damning the consequences, I suppose. – But if it's true that Billy will be safe if I do this, then I'm going to trust that his ethical side will convince Stephen that the 89 guardians be given the choice to walk away.

So it's decided. – I'm gonna help them.

There's just one more minor problem. – The blue-rose and lily tonic has a very short lifespan, which means I need to find a way to extend it. So that's what I've spent the rest of the weekend thinking about.

On Monday morning I was still going. So after training and meetings and the general work stuff, I locked myself in my room again, trying to research as much as I could about the plants and the Neuritamine drug. Then I spent the night on the roof-top garden also researching.

Thankfully, I think I've managed to find the missing ingredient. The only problem now is making 89 epi-pens worth. And that is a very hard task for just one Nature guardian. Still, I need to get this done. – I will not let anyone die if I can help it.

I worked through the night on Tuesday, and must have fallen asleep in the garden because I woke up to the jolt of someone shaking me awake. I was in a frightened state and my natural instincts kicked in causing the tree roots around me to spring up from the ground behind who ever had shaken me awake, wrapping around their neck to keep them away from me. I didn't even realise what I was doing as I rubbed the sleep from my eyes, until I heard a voice choking out my name.

"Daddy!" I shrieked in horror as I saw William trying and failing to break free from the plant roots, and I hurriedly pulled the dagger from my boot to cut him free.

William quickly fell to the ground, gasping for air as I apologised, and he wheezed, staring back up at me. "You... you just called me Daddy?"

Whoops.

I stood back, unsure what to say to him. But when he tried to stand, I instantly moved to help him as I apologised again, "I'm sorry, William. I was dreaming. I didn't mean to hurt you."

"I'm okay, just a bit short for air," he wheezed while concernedly looking around at all the crushed blue roses, and the make-shift laboratory bench I had made from the neighbouring plants in the corner of the garden.

I quickly packed up all the vials and epi-pens that I had managed to fill, loading them into my gym bag as I nervously explained, "I must have fallen asleep... I've been a little busy researching how to make the Neuritamine cure last longer."

"And did you get anywhere?" William asked, picking up my journal to hand to me.

I felt a little uncomfortable lying to him or anyone for that matter, so I nervously nodded hoping he would leave it at that. He seemed to accept it and watched as I waved my hand over the make-shift bench, calling it to dismantle itself. So while I walked inside towards the elevator, William was distracted by the plants as they retracted back to their original size.

Oh FRAC!

As I stepped into the hotel's elevator, I realised what the time was. – I had spent all night making those stupid cures that I slept the entire day away in the garden. It's afternoon almost night. – On Wednesday. – I only have an hour to get to that Mother's group at Danny's school, and there isn't enough time to drop the vials in my room, so I unfortunately need to take the vials and epi-pens with me.

Great. – That's just great.

I managed to get my white hair back to blond as I hurriedly drove through the city streets, and made it to Danny's school just in time. But I really needed to concentrate on not getting angry at the world as I raced into the library where the group was supposed to meet. Yet when I enter the room, all I could see was Mrs Grey, sitting at one of the computer tables.

"Lila, I'm so glad you could make it." She smiled, standing to greet me.

I looked around the room with a bit of caution, hearing multiple heart-beats, and in seeing no one visible, I warily asked, "Am I early or something?"

Suddenly, a group of mums jumped out from behind the bookshelves next to me, and yelled, "Surprise!!!!"

And yeah, I am definitely surprised, and again my instincts took over, kicking – who I now know to be Abbie in the chest, forcing her backwards into 2 other mums. – But I can't see their name tags. I then punched Chrissie in the face before pinning Kim and Roxy into the corner wall of a bookshelf, pressing my forearm into the neck of one of them and my knee into the other woman's sternum.

HOLY FRUIT CAKES AND FRAC BISCUITS!
STAY CALM, LILA!

Thankfully my hair stayed blond as I looked around to realise what I had done and screeched, "What the hell is wrong with you people! Why would you do that!"

The one pinned against the wall, Roxy, put her hands up in surrender. "Sorry, it's an initiation ritual we do... for a bit of fun. You know, to break the ice and all."

Very quickly, I released my hold on them and stepped back scowling. "You think scaring people is fun? I'm the head of security and trained in six forms of deadly combat. Scaring me is never a good idea."

I felt confusedly livid at their desperate yet deadly attempt for amusement when Carol perked up, trying to be optimistic. "And now we know something about you. So why don't we all just calm down and have some tea?"

Oh gosh. – Can her grin get any wider, right now?

I helped the mums to their feet, but when Chrissie stood up, she was a bit wobbly and murmured. "I think my nose is bleeding."

Urgh. – These mums are idiots and seemingly desperate for fun. So I grumbled quietly to myself as I pulled out two blue-rose vials from my handbag and handed them to Chrissie and Abbie. "Here drink this."

Kim looked at the vial and grimaced. "Why?"

And still trying to hold back my annoyance, I let out a deep sigh. "They're natural herbs. It will fix your nose, and any other illness you're plagued with today."

They eyed me suspiciously for a moment then skulled down the liquid as I grabbed my handbag and headed to the door.

"Hey, where are you going?" Carol asked while holding a teapot.

And like hell I'm having tea with these people. So I leered back while rolling my eyes. "Home... You wanted to learn something about me, and you did! Goodbye, Mrs Grey."

I walked out the door and didn't look back while racing to my car, hoping to high heavens that none of the mums were following me. – Because my hair has definitely turned back to white.

Holy Fracs. – What did I just do?

CHAPTER 16

I Wasn't Expecting That

Journal entry by Shane Winters

Okay, now I know I'm bragging. But I have the best gig in the world. I get to live and work in a five-star hotel. I have a fire guardian for a sweet hot girlfriend, and my ex-sister-in-law is a freaking super-hero ninja that has a team of super-hero ninjas who work with her.

My life is freaking awesome.

It's Thursday afternoon, and I'm rostered on the concierge desk with Jess. We were both having fun, joshing around when a group of 5 ladies all wandered in from the street. They were looking around at the detailed and finely decorated lobby that was adorned with a butt load of plants and flowers and statues that eventually lead through to the shopping promenade if you follow them.

They all appeared to be nervous as they stepped towards the concierge desk, each silently bickering for one of them to ask the ultimate question that they all seem reluctant to ask, until the lady named Kim introduced herself.

"Hi... um... we're looking for Lila," she asked with a very soft and timid voice.

I politely smiled back. "I'm sorry, but she's not here at the moment. Can I take a message for you?"

She didn't appear to like that answer and took a moment before she again timidly asked, "Do you know when she gets back in?"

Very casually, I glanced over to see Jess also a little confused, and replied thinking that there is no way they'd be willing to stick around for that long. "Lila should be back in about an hour."

Kim backed away from the desk, turning to the other ladies as they chattered and whispered amongst themselves, until another lady, popped her head up, stating, "We'll just sit over in the lounge and wait for her to get back... Thank you."

Ah, okay. — I wasn't expecting that.

They all went over to sit in the lounge area but one of them wandered off into the promenade, eventually bringing back a tray of coffees for all of them as they got comfortable.

I sat back down next to Jess and waited for a while, hoping they'd give up. But they didn't. And knowing full-well Lila would not want to deal with this straight after her perimeter run, I leaned closer and whispered to Jess. "You might want to call Alex."

Jess pulled her lips together, trying not to smile and asked, "Why?"

"Err... because I'm not brave enough to tell five women they need to leave," I replied. — And well, at least I was honest.

Jess had to hold back her laughs, grinning from ear to ear. "Don't tell me you're scared of a couple of ladies. You're dating a fire guardian."

I peered over the counter at the women and half smirked. "Hmmm... a fire guardian or five angry females... I think I'd rather play with the fire."

"Chicken," she scoffed, picking up the phone to call Alex.

About 10 minutes later, Alex walked down the stairs, glancing at us as we covertly pointed to the 5 women still sitting there, chatting away with each other while drinking their second round of coffees. He walked over to introduce himself, and we listened in. — Stealthily of course.

"Hi, I'm told you're looking for Lila," he stated.

Kim excitedly stood to her feet, turning to Alex. "That's right, is she back yet?"

He shook his head, confusedly eyeing the other women as they stood. "No... but I'm Alex. I work with Lila. Is there anything I can help you with?"

One of the women looked Alex up and down then grinned ever so slightly, clearly checking him out. "You don't look like a security guard."

Clearing his throat and trying to ignore the fact that he was currently being ogled, Alex very nicely replied, "I didn't think I needed to wear a uniform to assist one of Lila's friends... You are friends of Lila's, right?"

I was still leaning on the concierge desk, trying to listen when Jess tapped on my arm, pointing outside to Lila as she walked towards the hotel with Adela and Katie. But when she saw the 5 women, Lila stopped in a slight panic then slowly backed away to hide behind one of the advertisement signs, and Adela and Katie confusedly followed.

Very casually, I went out to greet them, pretending to pick up some loose rubbish outside. Then I leaned on the advertisement sign to provide more cover for Lila and talk to her. "I'm sorry, Sissy... We tried calling to warn you, but they just refuse to leave."

"What do they want?" Lila asked, looking up at me from her hiding spot, seeming completely freaked. — Which is not at all what I expected from her.

I shrugged my shoulders. "They want to speak to you."

"Well, tell them I'm busy."

"I did. An hour ago," I snapped, cranky at the fact that she thinks I didn't already try that.

She then ordered Katie to run into the promenade and find a hoodie and baseball cap to hide the white hair that Lila still has and yet won't tell anyone why it's white. Once Lila's hair was sufficiently covered with the hat and hoodie, she gave up the hiding spot and groaned, rolling her eyes as she unenthusiastically dragged her feet into the lobby towards the ladies.

"Good afternoon, Alex." She perked up before turning to the women and smiling at them. "Ladies, I hope you're not here for some more of your harmless fun."

"Actually, we were hoping for your help," Kim replied.

And another added. — More like nervously blurted, "We want you to teach us self-defence."

Eerr? — Right, I wasn't expecting that either. — These women waited an hour for that? — How did they even know Lila taught us self-defence?

The lady then blurted out again, failing to hide her nerves. "We've been thinking about joining a self-defence class for a few months now, but we can't find any good ones."

"We want to learn how to fight like you," Kim added. "We can pay you and everything."

I was actually standing quite close to the group now to listen in, standing next to Adela and Katie who were just as interested. And Alex was still standing next to Lila looking just as baffled as to how the ladies knew Lila and that she could fight.

All the ladies eagerly waited for Lila's response as Lila scanned the group of women, and then briefly glanced at Alex before she apologetically replied, "I don't need your money, and I really don't think it's a good idea."

The ladies looked at each other, all a little saddened, and I noticed something dark on the back of one of the quiet woman's neck while she stood at the back of the group. So I turned to pretend to talk to Katie, wrapping my arm around her waist as I spoke quietly.

"Sissy... the woman at the back of the group has a bruise on the back of her neck, and it looks a lot like a hand."

Katie knew what I was doing, so I gave her a kiss to say thank you before I turned back to see what Lila does. She looked over at the woman I was talking about and took a moment to think.

"Alright, maybe a few lessons. I'll be on the training mat at 7 tonight. You can ask Jessica for the directions."

The women became ecstatic, and all smiled at Lila, thanking her a lot as she waved goodbye to them, directing them back to the concierge desk to talk to Jess again.

As they did, I walked over to Lila and slumped my arm over her shoulder with a grin. "That was very sweet of you, Sissy."

She cocked her head up to look at me and smirked. "I know... and I'll see you at 7 as well, because you're going to be helping me. I think you could use a few more lessons yourself."

I gasped at her in shock as she continued, "You seriously couldn't handle 5 women on your own? And let me guess, you asked Jess to call Alex as well, didn't you?"

I was speechless. — How the hell did she know that? — The worst part about all of this, is that my girlfriend is laughing at me as she rubs her hands together, mischievously grinning as she boasts, "I am so not missing that."

Huh. — My loving girlfriend is revelling in the fact that I'm going to be beaten up by a group of women tonight all because I was a chicken. — That's just not right.

Journal entry insert by Alex Woods

Well, there's never a dull day around here. That was probably the most uncomfortable moment I've been in for a long time and probably ever. I must say, I am definitely not used to being eye candy for a group of middle-aged women, so I'm kind of glad Lila decided to come to my rescue instead of cowering out on the street. — And I know she hid because of her white hair. But the fact that she has white hair at all is a very interesting question, that I'm probably not going to get the answer to.

After saying goodbye to Lila, I headed back up to my apartment to grab some lunch when I found Terrence sitting at the dining table, holding a rainbow-coloured rose in his hand. I started buttering myself a jam sandwich while hesitantly looking at him, and asked, "What's that?"

He took a deep breath with such seriousness to him. "It's a rose for Lila. And you're going to give it to her."

Yep. — I think he's finally gone nuts. First this weird topic comes up with Adela and now Terrence. So I grimaced at him as I ate my sandwich.

"Alright, I'll bite... why?"

Seeming a little frustrated, Terrence stood up, walking over to the kitchen bench to pitch his stupid theory. "Because Adela's partially right, and I think that's why Lila's angry... Lila needs something different. She needs someone to distract her and not be scared of something going horribly wrong while she's having fun. And that's where you come in."

Alright. — It's not that stupid of an idea.

"What exactly do you want me to do?" I asked, getting suspicious of where this was headed.

He then placed the rose on the bench in front of me and stared at it. "You're going to ask her out on a date."

Yep. – That's where the stupidity comes in.

I wolfed down the rest of my sandwich before I highlighted, "I don't know if you've noticed... but both of us have only just started regaining Lila's trust after the whole stalking her on her last date then force-feeding her at the hospital thing... So I really don't think she's going to want to date either of us any time soon."

Terrence crossed his arms and pulled this face that kind of says 'I'm acknowledging that you have some logic but I'm never going to admit it' before he argued, "Alex, you're her best friend. I don't think she'd ever say no to you... I mean it was you who asked her to drink the healing tonic and actually be willing to let it work. Even though you held her down and forced it in her mouth... Think about it. Lila could have easily fought you harder, she could have refused to swallow it or even commanded the plant bases of the liquid to become inert at any stage. But she didn't... she did it for you... Not me. Not Tyme. Not even for herself... She knowingly went through all of that pain all because you asked her to do it."

He let out a long breath then handed me the rose. "She may have only said it accidentally, but she loves you, Alex... And she trusts you... So it's at least worth a try."

Well sure, when you put it that way, it just fills me to the brim with confidence. – Just the thought of Lila willingly putting herself through a lifetime of pain over and over again all because I asked her to, makes me feel just peachy inside.

In knowing Terrence wasn't going to let this drop, I agreed to try. Then after a few hours, I'd finally worked up the courage to head up to Lila's apartment. But that was as far as I got before I froze and just stood there staring at her apartment door, struggling to breathe.

Eventually, the elevator doors opened behind me, and Matt stepped out holding his work briefcase with Danny and Ruby right behind him. He saw me holding the rainbow rose and laughed under his breath. "I take it you drew the short straw?"

"More like thrown in the deep end." I sighed with the look of nervousness written all over me.

He unlocked the apartment door to let Danny and Ruby in before turning back to me, closing the door again. "Okay, here's a little tip to remember... Lila's never been great at voicing her feelings, and she's very careful not to label the relationship. That's something she expects the man to do... She also likes to feel like she still has the choice to say no. So don't do the puppy-dog eyes on her... And I wouldn't approach her with a date. Try phrasing it as a night out with a friend, and see where she takes it."

I nodded to Matt, taking on his advice, feeling a tad bit more confident, then curiously asked, "Why are you so calm... I mean, doesn't this bother you?"

Matt laughed with an obvious sigh at the end, and then replied, "Lila and I have agreed to be just friends, and it's made us a better family for it... I mean, yes, there is a small part of me that hates you and blames you for where Lila is now... If you hadn't have rocked up on our doorstep, asking Lila for help, things might have been a lot different between us. But I've also seen the difference Lila's made in so many lives, and that is because of you. So no, this doesn't bother me."

Wow.

I nodded again, feeling like I'd just received Matt's blessing as he led me into the apartment. And I took a deep breath before I knocked on Lila's bedroom door.

CHAPTER 17

Is Playing On Both Sides Cheating?

Journal entry by Lila Winters

After my perimeter run and dealing with those ladies from the Mother's group, I raced up to the rooftop garden to finish making the last of the blue-rose and lily tonics for the 89 guardians currently being held in God knows where. Once I was done, I ran up to my apartment to shower and get ready to sneak out of the hotel, which now that I think about it, sounds a bit teenage rebellion like. – And for a grown woman, who has most definitely passed that stage, it almost seems a bit silly. – But it's for a good-ish cause, and I definitely do not want anyone else in danger because of this, so sneaking around it has to be.

While in the shower, I focused on getting my hair back to its normal blond. And once successful, I roamed around my bedroom in just my undies and bra, listening to some music to keep myself in a happy mood as I tried to find a clean top to wear. – One that isn't blood stained or mangled.

I was beginning to think I needed to take Adela up on her offer to go shopping again when I heard a knock at the door.

"Who is it?" I queried. And when Alex answered, I freaked out.

Frac. – I need to hide the bag of epi-pens.

At super-speed, I grabbed the gym bag and hid it in my closet under a pile of clothes. But again I still can't find a top that doesn't scream, 'I just beat the crap out of someone.'

Frac. Frac. Frac.

"Err... Come in!" I yelled before running into the bathroom to at least put pants on.
"Lila," Alex called while wandering around my room.

Damn it. – I forgot to close the closet door.

"I... I brought you a present," he stated but he sounded nervous. – And that worries me.
My curiosity was piqued, so I walked out of my bathroom to see why he was nervous, and smiled seeing him standing at the end of my bed, holding a colourful rose.
"It's beautiful." I beamed as he handed it to me. "What's it for?"
I suddenly sensed his nerves increasing, and I looked up at him, noticing his eyes were fixed squarely on a blank part of my bedroom wall. I asked if he was okay, and he started to stutter.
"Um... er... this might be easier for me if you put a top on first."
"Okay..." I mumbled, seeming a little – um well, I'm not quite sure how to put it. "I'm sorry, Alex. I had trouble finding a top

that wasn't mangled when you knocked on the door, and I didn't want to keep you waiting."

He relaxed a little after that explanation, and then very eagerly offered to help me find one, walking over to my closet door.

FRAC!

"Well, I think you still have some of my skivvies in here... If you don't mind baggy clothes still." He reached to the back of my closet, pulling out one of his long-sleeve tops to hand to me, and I stared at him suspiciously. I then looked down at the top, and I could feel my nose crinkling, obviously sending him the wrong message. And he sighed. "If you don't want to wear it, I can run downstairs and see if one of the clothing stores are still open."

"It's not that." I pouted, quickly taking the top from him. "It's just this is the top I wear when I'm mopey and sad... You know, it's comfy and makes me feel better."

Double Frac. – Why did I tell him that?

My eyes peered over to him as I put his skivvy on and saw a little smile peak at his lips. But I was still confused, so I had to ask, "Alex, you've seen and held me naked so many times, and never cared... You've even slept in the bed next to me. So what's changed?"

I heard him clearing his throat as he helped me to pull my long, still honey-blond hair up through the neck opening of the skivvy, and again he sounded nervous. "I was hoping you would accompany me to dinner... and possibly a movie?"

A little surprised by his offer, I grabbed my hairbrush to brush my hair up into a high ponytail while smiling back at him. "Do you mean like a date?"

"Err, no…" he said, sounding very squeamish. "More like a night out with your best friend…s."

"Um… sure… that sounds like fun." I nodded.

I stood in front of him and watched as his demeanour changed from nervous to completely baffled as he stared at me and gasped. "What?"

So speaking clearly, I replied, "Yes, Alex, I'll have dinner with you… We can't do it tonight. But tomorrow, we've got a re-con in the morning and then I'm free. So if we survive, I'd definitely be up for a good unwind. Can you wait until then?"

"Um yeah… tomorrow's great." He nodded, still in a little shock with a hint of excitement in his smile.

Alex then backed out of the room giving me a weird look as he closed the door, and I let out a breath that I didn't even realise I was holding in, glancing over to the closet door and remembering to close it this time.

I won't lie. – The lack of sleep and stress is starting to get to me.

Staying focused, I raced downstairs to run a spontaneous self-defence class with the mums from the mother's group. – I did find it hilarious, watching Shane be the test dummy and the pretend attacker, especially because Katie was cheering from the sidelines for the women, shouting, "WOOO… girl power!"

By the time 9pm came around, the hotel was starting to pack up, and the night cleaning crew were starting their shift. Unfortunately, the fact that I have to sneak out and do something I really don't want to do, made me angry again, which meant I had to wear the baseball cap and jumper to hide my white hair. – Damn it.

I casually smiled at the cleaners as I ducked out, carrying my now very heavy gym bag as well as a little surprise for Billy. – That I'm really hoping he likes. However, this time I used Google maps to find the abandoned apartment building.

To be fair. – I was a bit distracted the last time I was there.

As I stood outside the rundown apartment building that is still for sale, I felt extremely nervous, needing to take some encouraging breaths before I scaled up the side of the building to Billy's apartment along a nifty little beanstalk I grew. The heavy gym bag was straddled tightly to my back, and I have the bow of Billy's surprise gripped in my teeth as I climbed higher and higher.

When I got to the fourth floor, I very nimbly climbed into Billy's now fixed apartment window, only to find the apartment dark and Billy-less. It didn't surprise me, I kind of figured he'd be busy today, but I really hope he's still okay.

I waited for a little bit. But not knowing where Billy is makes me feel really unsettled, and he seems to be taking a while to return from... wherever he is. So I'm trying to stay calm by reminding myself of Stephen's note stating that Billy would only be hurt if I didn't help.

Well, I'm here. – I'm helping. – So where the Frac is Billy?

To distract my thoughts, I wandered through the apartment checking out the things that Billy had acquired since my last visit. He still has a growing stash of medicines in his bag, although these ones look different. He's also managed to find himself a couch. – It looks like he got it from a thrift store because it still has the tag on it.

Next to his mattress sat the two candles I made for him, but I also found a picture of me tucked underneath his pillow. It's actually the picture that I sent him when we started our new deal to always check in with each other. – Wow. – Seeing that he keeps a printed copy of this under his pillow, caused my cheeks to feel all red and hot with my chest all fluttery inside.

It's kind of sweet. – Maybe he really does like me.

An hour has passed and my fatigue is slowly getting to me, and I'm a little worried that I'm going to fall down if I don't sit. So I sat on the very lumpy new couch and continued my wait for Billy to return while trying very hard not to worry or fall asleep.

Journal entry insert by Billy Jonas

Tonight's mission has put me in a bit of a mood. But I've been in a sour mood for most of this week. Mainly because I found out after the fact that Stephen stole my phone and used it to find out where Lila was last Friday night, and Lila has not texted or called me since that very unfortunate encounter outside the restaurant.

The other reason I'm in a mood today is because it's my birthday. And while I'm glad Stephen's holding up on his word and no longer killing anyone, raiding yet another Board warehouse was pretty much the last thing I wanted to do today.

My mind also seems to be distracted these days, and I worry for the team's safety. I know it's probably just me, but I'm beginning to question the motives of our new recruits. Seeing how they spent most of tonight raiding the weapons storage rooms and anything of value, instead of actually rescuing their fellow guardians.

When we got back to the warehouse, Stephen had organised a cake for me and even bought me a Two-four of the good Canadian beer. — Which he has owed me for a while. But since I'm still in a bit of a mood, after the cake, I opted for an early night. Choosing not to celebrate with the others back at the warehouse.

I ran back to my apartment at half-speed, feeling extremely heavy-hearted as I climbed the long winding stairs to my apartment door. Everything in me felt heavy as I let out a long sigh, and I glanced at the time on my phone to see that it was 10 minutes to midnight. – And I still haven't gotten a call from Lila.

Moments passed as I stared at my phone, contemplating calling Lila. – I've been avoiding calling her or checking in on her because I'm worried she'll be mad at me. But I really just want to hear her voice. Even if it's for a moment. – So while standing out in the hallway, ready to run over to the hotel to see her, I made the phone call. But as I waited and listened to the dial tone, I heard a mobile phone silently ringing from inside my apartment.

Curious of the sound, I cautiously opened the door, and found her asleep on my couch with the moon just barely lighting her face.

Holy Darns. – She's here.

She has a baseball cap and a large hooded jumper on, making me smile because she looks so adorable in it. But my smile disappeared, and the sadness crept in when I saw her fearfully clutching her dagger as she slept, and a small strand of her white hair peeked out from the hood of her jumper.

I know why it's white. – Because at the end of the couch sits her white gym bag, the one with the hotel logo on the side. – That stupid water-lily with the three dots hovering above it.

I bet you anything that that's the mark he uses for his collected guardians. He does have a Water guardian as a fake daughter. And that mark is on pretty much everything in the hotel. – Although I've never seen that mark on any of the uniforms. The staff wear either dark blue or purple shirts, and the security all wear black suits, except for Lila and some of her team. I usually see them in gym clothes or clothes that are easy to fight in.

Darn it. – I'm getting distracted and completely disregarding the fact that her gym bag is filled to the brim with epi-pens that have a faint blue glow. And those epi-pens are the reason, the girl of my dreams has white hair. – She always has white hair when she's angry or sad or frustrated.

Okay Billy. – Just breathe.

While staying quiet, I knelt down next to Lila and tried to help her get more comfortable, very gently trying to take her dagger away from her when she woke up. But just barely. She was so exhausted that she struggled to open her eyes as she looked at me.

"Billy... you're okay." She sleepily sniffled.

With my free hand, I cupped her cheek and smiled. "Of course I'm okay. I'm even better now that you're here."

She took another tired breath and rested her head in my hand. "I'm sorry... I must have dozed off... I'll go in a minute."

I moved closer, still supporting her head while holding the hand she was clutching the dagger with, and whispered, "No. Lila, you're too tired... So as your doctor, I'm ordering you to stay... And please don't argue with me this time."

She peered up at me with those sleepy blue eyes and gave me a little smile as she nodded. "Okay."

Wow. – She must be tired. – I honestly thought I'd have to fight her on this one.

She loosened the grip on her dagger for me to put it back in her boot holster. Then I took her boots, baseball cap, and jumper off and put them at the end of the bed for her. She tried to keep her tired eyes on me as I gently scooped her up into my arms to place her on the much comfier mattress. But as I picked her up, she brought with her the thing she was using as a pillow.

I curiously stared at what she held, noticing it was wrapped in red paper with a red bow. Then when I put her down on the bed, she saw me eyeing what I can now see is a present and handed it to me.

"Happy Birthday," she very sleepily whispered with a gorgeous smile at her lips.

Still with her eyes just barely open, she watched me unwrap my present to find a really soft fleece red blanket. I held it close, impressed at how soft and warm it felt then looked up to see her watching me.

"I thought it would help keep you warm at night," she whispered, still looking very tired. "Melbourne gets very cold in winter."

Aw Darn. – She is good and incredibly perfect.

To thank her, I replaced the old blanket on my bed with the nice soft new one to keep her warm tonight. I then gave her a thank-you hug, but I had to hold back my tears, feeling a swell of emotions when she let me actually hug her for the first time in weeks.

After everything I've done. – She has every reason to hate me. – Yet she doesn't.

I was going to opt for the couch until I realised Lila had fallen back to sleep while hugging me, and I really don't want to let her go. So I laid down next to her, hoping she wouldn't mind, and she snuggled in closer to me, letting my arms stay firmly wrapped around her. – And for the first time in a long time, I fell asleep happy.

Journal entry insert by Keith Connors

My patience is running thin, and I'm running out of time to save my mother and her reputation. Some of her fellow Board members have already started to chip away at her industry. The Health and Beauty empire that Mother prides herself on and has spent years nurturing and developing has now gained the attention of Frank Hinds. And he's beginning to send in his sharks to turn on Mother and steal her companies from underneath.

Katty said she was going to pay him a visit and do a little re-con while she was there. So all I have to do is take care of Mother and monitor the situation brewing back in Australia.

I sat in my mother's office, overlooking the night lights of the city when my assistant Mitchel brought in a hand-delivered letter marked — 'For Keith's eyes only'. In seeing that, I waited for Mitchel to leave before I opened it, only to find a group photo of Lila and her team taken at a New York bar. Lila stood in the middle and looked very happy with Terrence and Alex on either side of her. Maxwell, Adela, Jessica, and Katie were on one side. And Shane, Matt, Henry, Jennifer, and Tyme stood on the other while Lila's children stood at the front, holding their mum's hands.

I was enraged and confused, staring at the happy group photo until I looked on the back of it to read Katty's handwriting, stating, "Hit her where it hurts most."

Journal entry continued by Lila Winters

I woke up at the standard time of 4am, in the tight embrace of Billy's arms as he slept next to me in his bed. – Frac damn, this feels really good and somehow calming. – But I can't stay, so very quietly and carefully, I wriggled out of his arms. He seems to be a light sleeper though because he woke up and smiled at me.

"Good morning," he whispered, but was more intrigued at how my hair had changed colour while I slept. He held up my honey-blond hair and smiled more because he knew that it meant that I didn't feel angry when I'm around him. – Even though I should.

"Good morning." I nervously smiled back while biting my bottom lip. "I'm sorry I fell asleep... I've kind of... had trouble sleeping the last couple of nights."

"That's alright... Thank you for staying. And thank-you for the birthday present... Are you feeling better now?"

I nodded while putting my boots back on, and stood up readying to leave when Billy appeared at super-speed in front of me. I jumped, still a little fearful of everything and pleaded with a shaky voice. "Billy, please... I don't want to stab you again."

"And I don't want to be stabbed again," he replied, gently holding my hands while staring into my eyes. "It's just that nod... it didn't look very convincing."

Well, can he blame me? – I'm scared. I'm tired. And I'm worried. And most of all I'm confused about everything. – I'm supposed to be angry right now, but I'm not.

I tried to muster the best smile I could, but Billy saw through that, and in seconds, I was in his arms being held by him again. He didn't say anything. He just cuddled me. And while I like staying in his tight embrace, I stared up at him, feeling a little sad when I gently directed his gaze to the gym bag sitting on the couch. — Which was the actual reason why I'm here and why I fell asleep.

Suddenly, his happy face turned sour while I explained, "You need to tell Stephen that they have a two-week shelf life at best. And if you can, please avoid heating them up."

Very slowly, I pulled away from him again, heading back towards the window when he grabbed hold of my hand and begged, "Stay... please, Lila. Stay with me."

I peered back at him, feeling incredibly torn inside with tears forming in my eyes. "And what would you have me do if I stayed? I don't like being used this way, Billy... I'm not a toy you can play with whenever it suits you or your friends. And I don't like you being used as a threat to make me do as I'm told."

His brows pinched together as he shook his head. "Lila, what are you talking about? I would never hurt you. You know that."

"Huh... You seriously didn't know, did you?" I let out a shocked breath of disbelief, realising why the threat was written on a note. — Because Billy really was there. I wasn't imagining his presence or his protective anger when Stephen had me pinned against that door, waving Billy's phone around in front of my face.

Just the thought of that makes me so angry. But when I stared into Billy's eyes, he looked nervous and worried, so I took a breath to explain, "Stephen threatened to hurt you if I didn't agree to help him. That was the note he shoved into my hand when he pinned me against the door. And I think it's the real reason he showed me your phone... To prove how easily he can get to you."

"What?" He stumbled backwards, struggling to grasp what I had said.

I walked back with him and cupped his cheek with my hand to see his saddened eyes, and insisted, "Billy, they're not your friends. They're using you, just like The Board did... But I am your friend. And I will never give up on you."

I kept a hold of his hand, pulling him towards the window with me, hoping he would just follow me home. But he stopped as he tearfully sighed and shook his head.

"Lila, I can't... They threatened to hurt you if I don't do as I'm told. But they assured me that you would not be harmed by any of the Rebel factions if I stayed... And I'm sorry, Lila, I can't lose you... I can't let them hurt you. Not again."

Sensing his protective nature, I nodded and let my tears fall. "Well, it looks like we're both stuck protecting each other then. So let's make a deal... The next time your Rebel friends wants something from me, you need to be the one to ask. Okay?"

He nodded and gave a very relieved smile as his arms wrapped around me again. Then while in his arms, I let out another breath, trying to pull back the tears before I gave him a kiss goodbye.

My lips lingered on his, loving the way his arms held me tightly, knowing he didn't want to let me go. But he knew he eventually had to, and he was devastatingly sad, watching me climb back out the window to disappear.

CHAPTER 18

Playing the Game

Journal entry by Adela Eden

Okay, so I've been keeping a really big secret, and I can't keep it in any longer. I'm pregnant and it's Tyme's baby. But I've been keeping him at a distance these last few months, insisting that we should just be friends, and now I don't know what to do. – I mean I've only known him for half a year, and I've never had a long-term relationship, so I'm freaking out and I don't know who to go to.

It's just past the 18 week mark, so I know I'm going to start showing a lot more than I am now. Not only that, my physical capabilities these last few weeks have been noticeably terrible, which means this re-con and rescue mission today will be my last one for a while. – I just need to figure out how and when to tell Lila and then her brother.

But before all that, Katie and I have some re-con of our own to do. This morning we got up really early and found Lila doing her laps in the swimming pool at the ridiculous hour of 6am, after apparently going for a jog, instead of her normal work out in the gym. – Which is a shock for me because for the rest of her day, she's literally doing exactly that – training or jogging or working-out.

I mean our supers-plus team is usually the first on the mat at 7am, and Lila's always there making sure we're all *fighting fit. Then she's also volunteered to do self-defence classes with some of the human mums from Danny's school. Add to that our perimeter runs and our rescue ops, and everything she does to be a parent.*

ARGH!!! - What I'm trying to say is how the hell does she do it? - But that's probably a trade secret for her.

Anyway. - We found her in the swimming pool just as she was about to pack up, and Katie and I managed to talk ourselves into all having breakfast together after Lila asked to borrow some of my clothes. - Because all of hers are in her words 'mangled'.

So now we're all sitting up in Lila's loungeroom eating bowls of fruit and drinking breakfast smoothies, all while Lila set herself up on the floor in front of us using the coffee table as a desk, wearing a spare set of my gym clothes. - She's lucky she's the same size as me. - Katie and Jess are both a little shorter than us, which means I'm the only option for her. - Apart from actually going shopping, which we all know Lila would rather fight an army of Board soldiers than agree to.

She was looking over the satellite pics and blueprints of the building we're hitting today, and Katie and I were inspecting the new Neuritamine cure that Lila somehow managed to find time to alter to make it last longer.

Again HOW? - But also again, I'm off-topic.

I glanced over at Katie to see her looking at me, hoping I would start the conversation up because she was chicken. "So, Lila... a little bird told us you have a date tonight."

Pulling her eyes away from the blueprint and her laptop, Lila's eyes darted from me to Katie's before she replied, "I do not have a date. It's just dinner and a movie."

"With Alex." Katie nodded with a complete lack of subtlety to her grin.

"Yes, with Alex." Lila nodded back. "But it is not a date. We're just going as friends."

"Oh come on, Lila." Katie slouched back on the couch, now irked. "Alex asked you out on a date, and he clearly wants to be more than friends with you. And you're totes in need of a love life."

While staying quiet, Lila bit her bottom lip as she tried to hide her face with the laptop - pretending to be busy. And it caused me to think back on these last few weeks. - I did catch her a few weeks ago, buying a whole bunch of men's clothes from the stores downstairs. But I haven't seen Matt, Terrence, or Alex wearing any of them.

"Maybe... she already has a love life," I commented, eyeing her face for more details.

But all she had was a smile and a look of determination, replying, "Look, my friendship with Alex and Terrence is different to your average friendship. I get it... But not a lot of friends have been through, pretty much anything we've been through together. And yes, we hit a rocky patch after the hospital incident... But we got through it. So maybe this is Alex's way of slowly mending that trust issue we have."

I leaned forward, frustratedly glaring at her and snapped. "Lila, they want to be more than friends... Why don't you just let them?"

"Oh, and pushing the more than friends card has really worked out well for either of us..." she growled, glaring back at me. "And you know exactly who I'm talking about. Tyme wanted to be more than friends with you, and look what you did to him... You pushed him away and you hardly see each other now."

"I didn't push him away," I griped and folded my arms. "I just... needed time to think."

"Oh please..." Lila rolled her eyes as she stood to her feet while packing up the fruit bowls. "When was the last time either of you went out on a date? And you can't count just sex as a date or hanging out on a couch watching re-runs."

Umm? - Well, she has a point there.

But I followed her over to the kitchen still intent on pushing the issue. - Because I am determined to win this one.

"Alright, fine. If I go out on a date with Tyme, and Katie goes on an actual date with Shane, will you concede to calling your 'friend's night' a date?"

Lila stayed silent, washing the dishes then placed them on the rack and groaned, "Fine."

Oh my, oh my, oh my. - I do believe I've won this round.

Jumping from the couch, Katie celebrated silently and shrieked, "Yes... This totally calls for a new outfit. We have to go shopping."

"Yeah... No!" Lila chortled. "Today, we are checking out this warehouse in Brisbane and then you can go shopping."

Urgh. - And the win gets taken away. - Work, work, work with this woman. But damn it, I'm going to win this. So I argued, "Fine, we'll do this warehouse thing... only if you agree to go shopping with us and let us pick out an outfit for you tonight, along with the rest of your wardrobe."

She eyed me suspiciously, noticing my glare and silently let out a breath of frustration toward me. "You're not going to let this go, are you?"

With smug determination, I shook my head, trying to hide a devious smile. Eventually causing Lila to reluctantly agree to my deal before we left the apartment to round up the troops.

YES!!! - I won!

Journal entry insert by Lila Winters

So this is actually turning out to be one hell of a jam-packed day, especially after this morning's impromptu run home. – Although the sleep I got while at Billy's... whatever it is he calls his place, was actually not that bad, and having the company also felt nice.

In wanting to keep our mission today short, and because I'm not wanting to leave any paper trails or records of our flight to Brisbane that would definitely coincide with a warehouse attack, I called in a favour and took the team via the tree roots instead. I also learnt how to open the tree portal myself. – So yay for productivity.

We were actually pretty lucky because one of the tree portals is close to the facility we're hitting in the Beerburrum East state forest of Queensland. The building is on an island not far from the port, called Bribie Island, nestled on this huge estate overlooking the beach and neighbouring the islands state forest. So instead of taking a 2-and-a-bit hour flight there and back, plus the extra running time, it only took our team about 30 or so minutes.

The plan today is fairly simple. – Tyme was partnered with me to make use of his time rift, and we were the first to go in while the rest of the team stayed back, waiting for my signal. And because we all have potential plans tonight, I want to avoid a gunfight, so we're going to do this fast and clean.

Tyme and I stayed in the time rift while following one of the workers, who had just finished their smoke-break, back into what looks like a warehouse-laboratory and shipping area. From what I can see, the laboratory is making mineral beauty products. Deriving them from the natural surroundings with Land and Water guardians working in the lab, while the humans stay out in the packing area.

I pulled into a secluded area to phase into real-time, tapping my ear-mic to report to the team. "Okay, my count is 16 Land, and 12 Water in the lab area. 23 humans in the backend and at least 5 guards... one on each exit. Pretty sure all of them are guardians. Count 20 then move in."

Tyme phased me back into the rift, and he looked at me, confusedly asking, "20?"

"20 seconds... Go." I grinned with a slight giggle.

We then worked as a team as he phased me in and out of the rift, each time appearing behind one of the guards to inject them with the Neuritamine cure. Unfortunately, one of the guards fell to the ground earlier than expected, alerting the last two guards. - Oops. - I kind of added a mild sedative to the cure. But I might need to tweak it a bit.

The last guard eyed me when I appeared next to his friend, injecting an epi-pen into his friend's thigh, and he shot at me just as I was phasing back into the rift.

FRAC! - That hurt.

One of the bullets grazed my upper arm, so as I reappeared in front of the last guard, injecting him with the epi-pen, I punched him as well, seething the word, "Ouch." Then held my arm to stop the bleeding.

The rest of the team soon appeared, roaming around at full-speed, injecting everyone else with the cure. Alex and Terrence took the lab area - where the guardians were. While Adela and Katie took the packing area and back dock.

When we were all done, I looked around at the end result of all the humans and guardians on the floor with my team standing over them to check they were all okay. Then I victoriously cheered, "And that's how the games played... Well done, everyone."

Still clutching tightly to the wound on my arm, I walked back out of the warehouse, tapping my ear-mic again to let the others know it was clear. So as I made my way towards the trees in the neighbouring state forest, Jessica, Shane, Chase, and 6 other hotel security members walked into the warehouse to do the analysis and check-ups.

Well, the plan was almost fairly simple.

Still holding my arm to stop the bleeding, I roamed around the forest looking for a particular type of red gum tree. Thankfully, I found one not far from the edge of the tree line, and I looked around to find any weeping bark.

I pulled away one of the pieces, trying to scoop up the sap when Terrence appeared behind me, asking what I was doing, and I jumped in fright.

"Frac! Terry, don't do that."

The grin on his face was so wide as he held back a laugh. But when he noticed me gripping my upper left arm and the blood seeping through my fingers, he instantly turned serious.

"You're hurt," he worriedly noted, moving my hand away to look at the damage.

"It's just a graze... But I think the bullets laced with something, and now my blood feels like acid running through me."

I cringed when his hands touched my skin, and he looked up to see my very frustrated pout. Then with a slight peak at his lips, Terrence instantly knew what to do and started scooping up the tree sap for me, gently rubbing it over the wound. I tried to be brave but it's hurting a lot, and I held onto him for support as I felt the sap drawing the poison out of my blood.

His eyes glowed that pretty green colour, causing the sap to harden. Then as Terrence pulled it away again, we could see crystalized, blackened red shards attached to the sap being pulled out of my arm. It looks like dried lava.

Um? – That's new.

Continuing to fret over me, Terrence tore the bottom of his shirt and used it to bandage my arm when Katie walked up to report, "We're all done in there. And all the guardians have decided to go into hiding."

Adela appeared next to her and grinned. "Right, we've kept up our end of the deal, and we both have dates as well. So let's get a move on."

I groaned, feeling my entire body roll with frustration. "Can you give me a minute... I did just get shot here."

Yet Adela and Katie didn't seem to care, they just started walking back towards the group, and Adela shouted back, "That's not a good enough excuse. Now come on, we have shopping to do!"

"All done," Terrence boasted after patching me up.

I looked up at him, now with a huge and tired pout as I pleaded, "Can you shoot me again." But he shook his head, and his grin returned as he walked back with me. So I sighed. "Well, damn."

Journal entry insert by Alex Woods

I don't think travelling through the tree network agrees with humans, because when the team stepped back through one of the Melbourne ports in the botanic gardens, all the humans of the team threw up. – For the second time.

I helped Chase and Jessica walk up to Maxwell's office to report our success, but the look on their faces when I sat them down was hilarious. They looked green and pale.

Maxwell waited with suspense but asked with slight concern, "How did it go?"

Both Jess and Chase stayed quiet and unsettled as if they were going to hurl again, so I answered for them. "The mission was successful, and we managed to obtain a hard drive of documents and information from the site... But we also found an order request for all sites to relocate. So it looks like the data we retrieved might be useless to us anyway. That and I don't think humans are used to travelling through the trees."

"The trees?" Maxwell questioned confusedly.

I smiled at his confusion. "It's how Lila likes to travel. It's a butt load faster than your plane."

He nodded then started pouring Jess and Chase some water, and I thought it would be best to leave them to recover. So I backed out of the office and headed down to my apartment to shower.

When I got into the apartment, Terrence was already in the kitchen with two very large plates, each topped with a burger and chips from one of the downstairs cafés. – Mmm. – I breathed in that delicious smell and felt my stomach growl.

"You should be careful, Terrence," I commented, grabbing one of the plates from him. "I'm actually starting to like you as a room-mate."

We sat at the table to eat, and it was pretty peaceful in comparison to the last few hours we had. But eventually Terrence asked, "So what's your plan for tonight's date?"

"Dinner and a movie," I mumbled, wolfing down my burger.

"Well, that sounds like fun," he replied back.

I stood up to clear my plate and added, "Good because you're coming with us."

He stared at me as if I had gone crazy, but I very much haven't, so I explained, "You know Lila doesn't want to date either of us... Not like that anyway. So I invited her out as a friend. And this way if I get in trouble, you will too, especially because this was your idea."

Then while mockingly grinning at him for trying to throw me in the deep end, I walked into my room to get a shower.

Journal entry insert by Lila Winters

We've now reached the third hour of shopping out at a large shopping centre called Highpoint. And while Adela and Katie are super pumped about shopping, I'm more super pumped about grabbing an energy booster. So as they went off to do their thing at like the fifteenth clothing store, I went to find a juice stand.

While I was waiting for my order of a super green's smoothie, Peter walked up and stood next to me with a smug grin. "Hello, Lila."

And yep. – I want to slap that grin right off his face, but instead I just looked at him and irked with distaste.

"I'm glad to see you're okay." He smiled with fake pleasantries.

My irked attitude continued as I took calming breaths. "No-thanks to you... Have you come to finish the job? Or are you just looking for your next target to blow up?"

"No. I was hoping we could talk... alone."

He cleared his throat, glancing at me and then at the people passing us by, and I could see that scheming look in his eyes. So when I picked up my juice order, I told Peter to follow me before I walked into one of the large sporting equipment stores. I then wandered up to the back where we had more privacy, but I played it smart and tried to keep some distance between us, using a few treadmills and rowing machine displays as a buffer.

"You surprise me, Lila." He smirked with a slight titter. "I wasn't expecting it to be this easy."

I laughed back and wryly grinned. "You're not going to hurt me."

Grunting at my statement, his eyes darted to mine as if he were challenging the claim. He then stopped walking opposite a treadmill with me on the other side, so I accepted his challenging stare and smiled, ducking under the treadmill controls as I confidently walked towards him.

His hand glowed red as I stood so close to him that our bodies were just barely touching, and I felt his breath on me when he spoke, "What makes you think I won't hurt you?"

My lips peaked at one side as I leered into his eyes. "Because I know... that if you lay so much as a finger on me, Billy will burn your arse to the ground before you even leave this store... Now what do you want?"

A tense silence filled the little space between us. But then I glanced down at his hand to see it return to normal colour before he pulled out a small blue bag from his lower cargo pant-pocket.

"What is that?" I sniped, crossing my arms.

He opened the bag and pulled out the large green seed-stone, and then held it out for me as he explained, "It's a peace offering. A small gesture in exchange for more tonics."

Ah. – That thing. – That stupid little island seed that everyone wants a piece of.

"No," I huffed. "Billy knows what our deal is."

I turned to walk away but Peter foolishly grabbed hold of my wrist with a glowing hand, so I turned back, punching him in the face before side kicking him back into a punching bag. – Clearly he forgot that the last time they took me on, I was badly injured. But now there's nothing stopping me from kicking the frac out of him.

Yet in wanting to keep the peace, instead I warned him, "Peter, I'm not in the mood for this."

I turned to walk away again as I nursed the fresh burn on my wrist. But it caused him to get mad, stupidly racing towards me, again. – Urgh. – This idiot just wouldn't take the hint. So I caught him by his wrist, yanking it behind him, and then grabbed him by his belt to flip him onto one of the treadmill mats. And while he groaned from his pain, I commanded the vines from my bracelet to grow around him to trap him in place. I then pulled the dagger from my boot and leaned over him holding the tip against his crotch, instantly causing him to squirm.

Hmm. – I think he likes this particular part of his body.

"No. Lila, no... I didn't mean that. I'm sorry."

"Feels different being the one tied up, doesn't it?" I jeered with a smirk, threateningly glaring at him as I grabbed the large green tree-stone, placing it between his legs. Then at full-speed, I raised my dagger and stabbed it down.

He closed his eyes in fear, tensing his entire body. But relaxed again, opening his eyes to look down at the shattered seed between his legs all while I laughed at his foolishness.

"Do you honestly think I'd just hand over an ancient-magical tree-stone so easily... Nah-uh. It'll take a lot more than a little heat for me to give that up."

"You're psychotic," he spat, trying to break free of the vines.

"Thank you." I grinned, taking the compliment and stood up to pull an epi-pen from my bag that was hidden in one of the back compartments. I then injected him with a glowing silvery liquid.

"What is that... what did you just give me?" he questioned in fear as he shivered.

I squatted down, half-kneeling next to him to explain, "I was saving that nifty little sucker for Stephen. But it's probably safer if you get it. Seeing how your about to be arrested... What I just gave you is a sweet little mixture I made, with a little help from liquid nitrogen, specifically designed to seek out your body's fiery charge cells and freeze them... But don't worry, the effects only last a few weeks, maybe a couple of months or years... It depends how strong your guardian side is."

Suddenly, two police officers ran up, standing behind me with their guns drawn as they looked at the dagger I was holding. Then one of the officers demanded, "Put the weapon down and step back slowly."

I half-listened, putting the dagger away in my boot holster and groaned as I looked at them. "It's about time you boys showed up. Do me a favour and call Detective George Nell from the Melbourne police department. Let him know Agent Winters has just found his terrorist."

As suspected, they didn't listen, and again the officer repeated, "Miss, I said put the weapon down."

I stood up, observing their behaviour and tried to keep things civil. However, this is not the first time today that I've had a gun pointed at me. So I'm a little pissed.

"I'm sorry, Officer, but I take my orders from Detective Nell... Not you."

Now that my back was turned, Peter tried to break out of the vines, so I kicked him in the head, knocking him unconscious. But I quickly sensed one of the officers about to fire his weapon, leading me to run at full-speed, appearing in front of them to disarm them both. Then while dismantling both guns and emptying the bullets in front of them, I shook my head to show my frustration.

"You know, I'm really starting to hate these things... That's the second time today someone's tried to shoot me." I scowled at the officers then pulled the sleeve of my t-shirt up to show them my rag-bandaged arm, and found amusement from their stunned faces. "As I said. I work for Detective George Nell, and I'm sure he will gladly tell you everything you need to know when you call him."

With a frustrated huff, I handed both officers back their guns and bullets then joshed, "Oh... and if you try to shoot me again, I'll kick you in the head and tie you up with the idiot," briefly pointing back at Peter as I spoke.

"By the way," I added, grabbing my handbag and juice smoothie. "You're currently standing 5 feet away from the man who tried to blow up Flinders Street station several weeks ago... You might want to reload your weapons."

As they started hurriedly re-loading their guns, I casually left the store, completely unbothered at the fact that more police officers were running into the store to aid them.

I started to rummage through my handbag to find a bandage for the burn on my wrist, and probably made it halfway up the corridor before I was whisked away at super speed by Billy, forcing me into a narrow hallway leading to the toilets.

He held me against the wall as I angrily mocked him. "Well this is romantic... Do I get a kiss too?"

"What did you do?" he snapped. – Clearly not in the mood to play.

"I did my job," I snapped back. "That man tried to kill me and hundreds of innocent people. Or did you forget how our last date ended? With my body being dragged up the stairs by your friend before that man tried to..."

"I didn't forget..." he mumbled and looked away for a split second, remembering that horrid time when he was forced to watch me burn. But his fear seems to be driving this conversation. "Lila, you have to undo it... Now! You already know who we're dealing with here, and they're not good like you. These are the kind of guardians who revel in revenge. And you know what they'll do to you... I can't let that happen."

Ah. – We're back on the 'I must protect you spiel'. – Great...

Well, since he isn't in the mood to be nice, I forced Billy to let go of me, pushing him backwards, causing him to pace and breathe through his teeth, brushing his fingers through the dark curls of his hair as he tried to think. And while he was busy freaking out, I had to adjust my now soaked t-shirt and inspect my bandaged arm. – That's now drenched in juice because of him.

"Ugh...You owe Adela a new shirt... Ow..." I grunted as I removed the drenched rag from my arm. "And you owe me another juice cup... Ow, ow, ow."

In hearing my pain, Billy looked up, noticing my injury, and moved closer again to pull the sleeve of my top up to look at it. – Now actually looking concerned for me.

"Lila, what happened to you?" he worriedly asked.

And while completely failing to hide my annoyance, I scowled at him. "I had a mission this morning. But because I was tired, I was slow and got shot."

The frustration rose in Billy as his hands inspected the graze, but he stayed quiet. That is until his eyes moved lower to see my other hand, that he's now realised is covered in ice to cool my left wrist, and he looked at me curiously when he saw my eyes glowing a faint blue.

"You're a Water guardian," he whispered with marvel in his tone.

I felt nervous as I peered up at him and bit my lip as I confirmed it. Then slowly, he pulled my icy fingers away to reveal the fresh, finger-shaped burns on my wrist, and he let out a low growl. "Did Peter do this?"

"Yes... Look, Billy, I promise I did try to be civil with him. But I couldn't risk you racing in when he wouldn't take no for an answer... I'm sorry."

With a long sigh, I pulled out a fresh bandage from my handbag, offering for him to fix it up. And with the saddest pout, Billy gently wrapped the bandage around my wrist, and then very softly kissed the bandage and the still healing bullet-graze further up my arm.

I could see the guilt he held as he stared at the bandage, so I gazed up into his green eyes to negotiate with him again. "You didn't hold up on the deal we made this morning... I would have agreed to help in your team's vendetta if you had been the one to ask."

"I'm sorry. I did try to insist on it being me. But Stephen was convinced that you would help them anyway if he played the stone card."

"Well, he played wrong," I whispered, letting him move a little closer to me. "So new deal... I will agree to help you and your friends with regular deliveries of the cure, and I'll even join you on some of your missions... But only on the condition that Peter goes to jail. Because someone needs to take responsibility for the Flinders Street explosion and the car bomb in order to stop nosey people from sniffing around."

I paused for a second to make sure he was understanding exactly what I was offering him, and then asked, "So, Billy... who would you rather lose in this round... him or me?"

"You know I will always choose you," he breathed, staring back into my eyes as they narrowed onto his.

"Not always," I whispered with a whole lot of sadness in me.

Those words hurt him because deep down we both knew the truth. But he shifted his hands down around my waist, pulling me closer as he leaned his head down, pressing it against my forehead to beg. "Let me prove it to you."

He took a breath then kissed me. But when our lips touched, I pushed him away again, and he looked at me longingly as I stood at a distance from him, shaking my head.

"Kissing me will prove nothing," I explained, almost in tears. "You know my conditions, and I'll still help you if they're met... But right now, I need to go. Adela's buying me a dress for my date tonight... so don't follow me."

He stood and watched as I walked back down the hallway. Then as I peered back, he disappeared. – And Damn Fracs. – Every time he leaves it hurts.

When I finally met back up with Adela and Katie, after quickly buying another t-shirt to change into, they were standing outside a dress store trying to phone me with over a dozen different shopping bags surrounding them.

"Hey, what's up?" I asked while walking up next to them.

"There you are," Adela grumbled, slightly annoyed at my disappearing act. "I thought you ditched us and went home."

"Oh, if I could be that lucky." I chuckled under my breath then picked up some of the shopping bags as we headed into the next dress store, explaining, "I spilt my juice cup and had to get a new shirt… But don't worry, Adela, I'll replace your shirt for you."

"Hey." Katie eyed my bandaged arm. "What happened to your wrist?"

Letting out another chuckle, I lied. "I may have gotten distracted, trying out some of the new sports equipment in Rebel Sports… You know me, I get a bit carried away sometimes."

I know that wasn't the store I'd gone into, but the last thing I need is for them to know where and what I'd really been doing. – I really didn't want to ruin their fun, and the lie was believed, so we continued on shopping like nothing had happened.

CHAPTER 19

The Night Of Dates

Journal entry by Lila Winters

Okay, so the dress that Adela picked out for my 'date' is… well, let just say it's interesting but flattering. She chose a tight, long-sleeved dark-green dress with a round low-cut neckline. The top half hugged my bodice down to my waist then the pleated bottom half flared out so daintily, stopping halfway down my thigh. – And yeah, that's a little short for me.

She was nice enough to buy me boots for the occasion, but they're ankle-high lace-ups with a heel, which means I definitely can't hide my dagger anywhere on me. – But this is what Adela chose and I made a deal with her, so I finished getting dressed and brushed my hair. Tonight, I've decided instead of the standard ponytail, I'd do a messy braid, and I think I look pretty cute.

When Alex knocked on the door, I was super nervous as I opened it. I mean he doesn't usually see me like this. But when he looked at me, he was stunned and gasped, "Wow."

"Is this okay?" I asked, completely freaking out that this was not what he was expecting. I mean this is definitely a date dress, not a friend's dress. So I thought it would be better to explain myself. "It's because of a deal I made with Adela. She goes out on an actual date with Tyme and finally figures out what she's doing with him, in exchange for picking out all of my clothes. I would have opted for pants, but she didn't buy me any... Katie and Adela are taking advantage of the fact that I'm scarless now, and have demanded that I at least try to wear skirts and dresses more often."

Great. – I'm rambling and he's smiling at me.

"You look fantastic..." He grinned then he held out his hand for me as he stood at the door. "Come on, our night of fun awaits."

I took a breath of relief, gladly taking his hand as we walked into the elevator, and we rode the elevator in silence until I asked, "Alex... just one question before we go anywhere... Was this supposed to be an actual date?"

"Yes." He turned his head and nodded. And for a moment I stopped breathing, not sure how to feel. – I think I'm happy. – But then the elevator doors opened and he pointed over to Terrence, standing in the lobby waiting for us and added, "A date with friends."

I beamed with joy, happily resting my hand in the crook of Alex's arm as we walked out towards Terrence who greeted me with the same "wow" that Alex did. Then while walking out of the hotel, I rested my other arm in the crook of Terrence's as well, now feeling happy and relieved and excited. – And pretty confident that this date is not going to go horribly wrong.

Journal entry insert by Adela Eden

Tonight's the night I'm going to tell Tyme the truth. The truth that I'm having his baby. - And I am freaking out to no end. I don't even know if I'm ready for this. I mean, I know Lila's able to do so many things and still have kids, but I'm nowhere near Lila's level of skills when it comes to time management. - And what if Tyme doesn't want this? What do I do then?

Tyme and I were sitting at a table in one of my now favourite restaurants that Lila introduced me to a few months ago. It's a little dumpling restaurant tucked away in China town, and Tyme and I ordered a couple of dumpling plates to share. I think my favourite item on their menu is the little pumpkin cakes. - They are always so delicious.

"You look very nice tonight." Tyme broke the silence we were sitting in while we waited for our food.

I started fiddling with the hem of my blue-lace dress and nervously smiled. "Thank you."

"You have got me wondering something though," he added, leaning forward. So I leaned forward to listen to him. "You made it clear to me that you weren't interested in a relationship. So what made you change your mind?"

Oh Fruits. - Lila was right I was pushing him away. - What if I've spent way too long thinking about this, that I've completely missed my opportunity with him?

"Um... your sister. She made a very convincing argument this morning and made some good points."

He sat back in his chair contemplating my answer. "What were you arguing about?"

I briefly thought of what to answer with, and as the food was being delivered to the table, I answered, "Lila's sex life."

I then got the weirdest and most uncomfortable look from the waiter - who very quickly walked away after he placed our food and drinks down. And Tyme pinched his brows together, trying very hard not to laugh while shaking his head. "I'm not even going to ask."

The conversation died there, and we sat in silence again as we ate dinner, mainly because I'm still trying to work up the confidence to have - that conversation. But Tyme started talking first again.

"I'm sorry, but I really need to know... One day our relationship was great then the next we're just friends. Which I am not happy but okay with. I'd rather be friends than not... But how does my sister's love life end with you asking me out on a date when I don't even think you like me the way I like you?"

My head jerked up when he said those words. "I... like you... I just needed time to think... You know, I thought we were moving a little fast. And I got scared... Before we met, I didn't even know what I wanted in my life. Then you came along and changed everything... I was kind of hoping that this date would help me figure things out... I'm sorry I gave you the cold shoulder."

I don't think he liked my answer because he didn't respond to me. Instead he just went back to eating with his thinking face on.

Alrighty. - Maybe now isn't the time to have... that conversation.

Journal entry insert by Tyme Knight

Right. – I'm totally convinced now that Adela is not on board with this whole date thing. Because all through dinner she seemed distracted and reserved. Then when we walked up into Melbourne Central to go to the cinemas, she disappeared into the women's bathroom for a while and came out holding her stomach.

Huh. – Maybe the food didn't agree with her.

"Are you okay?" I asked.
 She nodded her head and smiled as she held my hand, and I kind of like this part of the date. It's the first time she's wanted to hold my hand in a long time. Maybe she is interested in me, and not just doing this because my sister told her to.

I can't blame my sister for trying though. – She's really cool like that.

We walked up into the cinema complex and glanced at the movies that were screening when Adela found Katie and Shane walking up the elevator behind us.
"Hey, how's your date going?" Adela asked.
"Great, we're waiting for our movie to start...This whole dating thing is super fun," Katie replied, giggling a little as she wrapped her arm around Shane's waist.
"Which movie are you going to see?" I asked.
With excitement, Shane pointed to one of the new super-hero action movies and laughed ironically. "We thought it would be fun to go watch the latest super-hero movie and compare notes... Did you guys want to join us?"
That idea piqued Katie's excitement and she gleefully jumped, trying to convince Adela to go for it. But when Shane looked

over to the ticketing booth, he saw Lila waiting and looking absolutely stunning in an amazing green dress, and gasped, "Wow."

This for some reason caused both Katie and Adela to drag us behind a pillar to hide. They then peered their heads around the pillar to spy on Lila, and naturally I followed, mainly to figure out why we were hiding from my sister.

It was strange watching Adela and Katie both silently squeal in excitement when they saw Alex walk back from the ticketing booth to greet Lila. But Shane's jaw dropped, sounding disappointed.

"Seriously, she chose that guy?"

Katie cheekily looked up at him and giggled. "What, are you jealous?"

"No... I just thought she was interested in..."

Before he could finish his answer, all three of them gasped as they watched Alex and Lila walk up the escalator to greet Terrence, waiting at the candy bar, holding a large box of popcorn and a tray of drinks for all of them.

"Now this just got interesting fast," Shane whispered.

Um...? – Okay.

They kept spying on my sister as she walked into cinema 2 with Alex and Terrence, and I was utterly confused at this whole thing.

"Wait... which one is my sister dating?" I asked, feeling very confused, staring down at Adela who looked just as baffled.

She shook her head at me and sighed. "I really don't know anymore."

Katie worried me though when she looked back at us with a deviously wry grin, and added, "Well I do know something... I want to watch whatever's playing in cinema 2." Then she grabbed Shane's hand and rushed back to the ticket booth to buy more tickets.

It seems like the idea is contagious because Adela looked back at me with those pleading eyes, and I stupidly caved, following her to the ticketing booth. - But only on the condition that if my sister does catch us spying on her that I can blame Adela.

So, instead of watching a jam-packed, super-hero action movie, we all ended up watching a romantically scary yet slightly sadistic vampire movie. And when I say we - it was pretty much just me and Shane. Although at one point Shane was fixated on what Lila was doing as well.

Lila sat in the middle block of seats, closer to the screen. So naturally Adela and Katie wanted to sit off to the side at the back not far from them to get a better view. - The one good part for me is the fact that Adela still wanted to hold my hand. The downside is, she's been so fixated on what Lila's been doing, and not anything to do with us.

Unexpectedly, there was a super scary part in the movie - with a lot of unnecessary screaming and gore. Lila jumped in fright, instantly grabbing both Alex and Terrence's free hands, causing Adela a world of confusion, peering over to Katie who also shook her head in confusion.

Right. - I'm pretty sure I've missed something here.

I did find a slight element of amusement while Adela, Katie, and Shane were busy whispering amongst themselves about Lila's love life. Because while they were distracted, I saw Lila peek back at me with a huge smile on her face.

Oh that is priceless. - She's most likely known about our presence this whole time, and is probably messing with them. And I'm certainly not going to ruin her fun, so I gave her a smile back then returned to watching the movie.

Journal entry continued by Lila Winters

This 'Date with friends' night is turning out to be pretty awesome. Particularly when the guys suggested we mess around with Adela and Katie's heads while we were in the cinemas.

It's fascinating to me that my team just casually forgets the abilities Animal guardians have over Fire and Water. We have a very strong scent-recognition, which meant both Alex and I could smell them the moment they walked into the centre. – And it was incredibly fun to mess with them.

But that's not the only fun we've had. The entire night has been fun. To start the date we went to the Pancake Parlour for dinner, and argued over who ate the most pancakes. We mucked around a bit in the game arcade while waiting for the movie to start. And the movie was... interesting but still fun. Now to top off the night, we're strolling down Swanston Street, enjoying the hustle and bustle while admiring the view of lights and buildings, mixed with the occasional art displays.

Yeah. – This night has been and still is fantastic.

The night was starting to feel a little cold being in the middle of winter and me in a short dress, but both Alex and Terrence stayed close to me with my arms resting around each of theirs. And I just knew they were looking at my smile when I caught them smiling back at me. So I thought I'd break our happy silence and start the conversation.

"Okay, I'm going to admit it, tonight has been epically awesome."

"Yeah," Alex cheekily grinned. "Who knew that the mighty Lila was scared of vampires."

I gasped, crinkling my nose at him. "I just think it's unnatural and weird, that's all... And the fact that they are based on a very real animal, does leave me wondering if maybe they are real. I mean think about it, Animal guardians sometimes take on mild traits of the animals they've bonded with... So vampires are really not that farfetched these days."

Alex and Terrence both looked at me and burst into hysterical laughter as we walked. Then Terrence chortled, "Lila, I think you've put way too much thought into this."

My eyes narrowed on his and my nose crinkled again as I huffed, "Well, why don't you two go off and fight a dragon, then come back and tell me vampires can't possibly be real."

Still trying to compose himself, Alex apologised, "I'm sorry, Lila... If it helps, I promise I will never morph into a vampire bat on the condition that you don't either."

"Deal." I nodded, and then we all broke into laughter because this conversation was hilarious.

After a while of walking through the city, we eventually saw the park trees towering over us instead. We walked along the Yarra River, and it was when I heard the sound of an orchestra playing that I realised they were leading me back to the Sidney Myer Music Bowl.

I hesitated when I saw the tips of the dome, and caught my breath. "Wow, I never expected either of you to bring me back here for our date."

We stood under the cover of the trees not far from the dome but close enough to hear the music as Alex replied, "We remembered how your previous date here didn't end with a very good memory."

"So we want to give you an even better memory to replace it," Terrence added.

Then as Terrence let go of my arm, Alex pulled me close to him and started to dance with me. - And wow. He's actually a pretty good dancer. But he surprised me when he twirled me into Terrence's waiting arms to dance with me as well. They're both pretty good dancers as opposed to me, who isn't at all good. But I followed their lead as they worked together, moving and twirling me between them.

I was having so much fun that my skin began to sparkle and turn slightly diamond-like. Yet they continued to dance with me, both amazed at what I can do. They weren't scared. They weren't worried. They just thought I looked beautiful, which made me sparkle even more. And I think I've found what emotion triggers my land abilities. - Love.

Oh Frac. - No... it's wrong to love them. - I want and love them both. And I shouldn't. It's not fair on them. - And what happens if they ask me to choose, does that mean I lose the other? - And what about Billy? I haven't told them about Billy yet, and what we did, or keep doing. Or even what he and his friends have been doing. - I'm lying to them and again I shouldn't be. - No... This is all wrong.

I began to feel all the wrong emotions, and Terrence noticed the sparkles in my skin start to fade as I pulled away from them in fear. He asked what was wrong, looking down at his vine bracelet and then to mine. He knew I was scared and so did Alex.

"It's nothing." I choked, still struggling to breathe. "I... think I'm just tired from the day."

I turned and hurriedly walked back towards the Yarra River but they caught up with me, and Terrence held my hand, begging me to tell them what was wrong. – But I couldn't. I couldn't even look at them.

"Terry, please don't make me do this... I can't lose you... I can't lose either of you... I don't want to."

They confusedly stared at me, failing to understand what I meant when I pulled my hand away, and I looked at them both through my teary eyes before I ran back to the hotel at full-speed.

Journal entry insert by Tyme Knight

This date night is not going very well for me, and I'm not even sure Adela likes it either. We were walking back to the hotel, hand in hand but we still haven't said much, and again Adela is distant in her thoughts. I mean, it's clear she's trying to avoid looking at me. So I stopped just opposite the hotel because I'd had enough. I pulled my hand away from hers and said just that.

"I'm sorry, but I've had enough."

She stared at me, confused as if she didn't even realise that what she was doing to me was not at all right.

"Look, I get it," I griped, trying to figure out my emotions right now. "You don't like me the way I like you. And I know the only reason we're having this date is because of Lila. But what I don't get is why you're so obsessed with my sisters non-existent or over-active love life."

"Because it's my fault she's alone," Adela blurted out then started crying. "Both Matt and I broke her heart, and I just wanted to fix it. I need to know that she can be happy again."

I stayed staring at her, completely mystified as she kept sobbing through her thoughts and explaining, "Lila had the perfect life before we came along... Before she was roped into looking for me. She had a loving husband, two beautiful children, and a normal job. And when she went to work, she didn't have to worry about being shot or injured or her family being harmed in any way... I just wanted to know if that life is possible for her again... Or at least a shred of it."

Ah-huh. – Well, there is undeniably more to this, and I can tell that she isn't being completely honest with me.

"Okay... no," I answered, crossing my arms in annoyance. "I don't think Lila's life will ever be normal again. And I don't think she'd ever want it to be... But tell me... is it Lila's life you want to be normal or yours?"

She couldn't answer my question and just continued to cry. But before I could say anymore, we both jumped in terror as we heard the sound of a gunshot coming from across the street. We turned to look across at the hotel and saw a man in a ski-mask holding a gun, standing just outside the lobby in front of Maxwell. And Maxwell falling backwards into Chase's arms as he guided him down to the ground.

Holy Crappers!!!

I don't know how she knew, but Lila randomly appeared in front of the man holding the gun, twisting his arm up and taking the gun from him. Then without any hint of reticence in her, Lila shot him in the leg and shoulder. And as the man fell to the ground, Alex and Terrence appeared next to Maxwell and Chase to help call an ambulance.

Everything was happening so fast as I heard Adela scream, "Daddy!!" while stepping out onto the street and getting hit by one of the oncoming cars. – I watched as her body was tossed onto the street as cars screeched to a stop, and my heart <u>stopped</u>.

CHAPTER 20

We Lost One

Journal entry by Alex Woods

We're at the hospital again. Only this time it isn't Lila or me. It was the last person we expected. Maxwell was raced into surgery as soon as we arrived, and so was Adela. And we've been waiting all night for anything.

In the early hours of the morning, around 5am, we were told that Adela was brought back from the surgery, but that was it. – Not even Jess was told what was going on with her. So both Tyme and Jess started pacing in the hallway just outside Adela's room.

Terrence and I have just returned from the café to hand out coffees and breakfast rolls to everyone. But we made sure to pull Lila aside so she could have her hot chocolate and toastie, and at the same take a break from coordinating security around the hospital and hotel. – Which has not been an easy task for her.

While she was eating, Terrence offered Lila his jacket and insisted she wear it until she can get home and change out of her date dress. As beautiful as she looks in that green dress, Terrence and I both knew last night that she was a little cold, and the hospital is not the warmest place for that kind of dress either. – We also wanted to cover the blood-spattered stains on her dress as well. I mean it's understandable, but a few people and nurses were eyeing her concernedly, so the jacket should help.

"Thank-you," she said, and gave us a very tired smile with those puffy and teary eyes.

I wanted to offer her a hug but her emotions seem off at the moment, and I'm not sure why but I think she's avoiding being too close to us. – I think? Or at least I'm noticing that she looks and feels slightly uncomfortable around me and Terrence, and I can't for the life of me figure out why.

I mean sure, she's happy to sit next to us and eat. But once she had eaten, Lila got right back to work. She ordered the team to stay in the sitting area just down the hall from the hospital rooms, and asked Katie and Shane to keep an eye on the morning news. – So we all just sat there waiting for her next orders.

Yep. – Something has definitely gotten to Lila. – And I'm worried it was the date.

More hours have passed now, and Katie and Shane have been watching the news and it's unrelenting need to tell this story over and over again, using amateur phone footage from the nearby pedestrians who were outside the hotel when it all happened.

In knowing that and given the high-profile nature of the Eden family, the media have been barred from the hospital. Instead they've made camp just outside the hospital and the Eden hotel, making security very difficult. So while we've been watching the news, Lila's been working with George not far from us, coordinating with our security and the extra police detail George assigned to assist us.

The footage the media has been displaying is a video of the incident, but it was grainy and shaky. They'd captured Lila's sudden appearance, but it looked like it was just a glitch in the camera, so we had nothing to worry about.

Or at least I thought we didn't until the mid-day news came on, and displayed a news clipping of security footage in a sporting goods store. In the footage, Lila was attacking someone. – And I'm pretty sure it was the man who tried to burn my Lila to death. They didn't show much of the recording, but it was enough to see her defend herself and throw the man onto a running machine. And from the footage, it looked like she had a hand device that shot out a net to trap him.

Aw Crap. – This isn't good.

I quickly called to Lila, and as she walked over, she saw herself disarming two police officers in the footage. Then the clipping stopped there, zooming in on her face before cutting back to the news reporter questioning, "Exactly who is this woman? And is there more to this story?"

"George, I thought you dealt with that incident." Lila turned to George in a huff, oddly rubbing her left arm. – And I sensed her pain as she did.

"I did... or at least I thought I did," George replied, looking just as shocked as the rest of us.

Now slightly upset, I pulled Lila away from the group to demand answers. "Lila, what incident? And why does George know about it? And why did you feel pain when you touched your arm just then?"

She looked angry at me and very nimbly pulled the sleeve of her left arm down further, thinking I didn't notice. – But I did. And she kind of looked as if she wanted to say one thing but stopped to say, "Because he's a police officer, and that's Peter, the man from Flinders Street station that George is looking for."

Ugh! – She is making me so MAD.

"I know that, Lila... but why didn't you tell <u>us</u> about it?"

Her eyes strangely darted from mine to Terrence's as he watched us from the sitting area. But I had reached my limit. I moved to grab her left arm, and pulled back the jacket and sleeve of her dress to find a bandage firmly wrapped around her wrist. She tried to pull her hand from me, but I growled, warning her to keep still as I unwrapped the bandage, feeling my stomach churning as I stared at the finger-shaped burns on her wrist.

"Lila, why didn't you tell us about this."

She stepped back and started twiddling with her fingers, nervously curling one hands fingers around the other. And that's when I knew she was holding back on a whole lot more than just this.

"I... I didn't want to ruin our date," she answered then bit her lip.

Before I could say anything else or even react to that, Dr Ellis interrupted us and insisted on speaking with Lila alone. I instantly objected but got overruled by her as they walked down the stairwell to talk.

Terrence watched me as I stood at the top of the stairs. He knew I was listening to Lila's conversation because he was doing it too, and he didn't look happy either. – He looks pissed.

I stayed quiet, listening in as Dr Ellis talked to Lila, "It's about your friend Adela... I gave her the blue medicine as you asked, and her bones have started to heal, but she's still coughing up blood. I don't think it's working the way it's supposed to... We can run some more tests, but she may need to be booked in for another surgery."

"Have you told her sister yet?" Lila asked.

"No, she requested that you were the only one to be told," he replied, sounding slightly worried.

I could sense Lila's emotion change as she asked the doctor for an hour before he made any decisions. Then I heard her footsteps descending the stairwell. Obviously, Terrence and I followed from a distance as she made her way through the hospital toward the exit. And we watched as Lila tried to leave the hospital and was immediately bombarded by the media, asking her questions as she hurried to the car that Chase had waiting for her.

Terrence and I stayed inside the hospital, watching from one of the windows as Lila's car drove off. But then Terrence pointed to Billy, standing on the opposite side of the street, watching Lila as well, and I got this very bad feeling in the pit of my gut.

"Something isn't right," I whispered. "Where the hell has he been for the last few weeks?"

"I don't know," Terrence grumbled still just as upset. "But something tells me Lila knows and is not planning on telling us."

Yep. - Unfortunately, I think he's right.

With strong determination to find the answers, we went back to the source we knew had more information than us. - Detective George Nell. And we were very convincing when we insisted on George getting us the footage from the sporting store incident. He made a few phone calls for us, then once he received the email of the security footage surrounding the store, he pulled us into one of the hospital tea-rooms to show us.

We watched as Lila talked with the man she called "Peter" and she got close to him. – Way too close for my liking. He also handed her something, but I couldn't tell what it was. That's when the fight broke out, and she ended up disarming two police officers before walking out of the store.

George quickly switched to the camera footage of Lila just outside the store, walking up the hallway and disappearing. But she didn't disappear. She was taken.

"There," I said, pointing to a small corridor in the distance. "Do you have footage of that hallway?"

It took a few minutes, but George eventually showed us footage of Billy standing with Lila. – He was the one who bandaged her arm, and even kissed her wounds better. – It was unclear what they were talking about, but Lila let him get very, very close to her. Then he kissed her, and she pushed him away. – And yep, I lost it. – Storming out of the hospital with Terrence right behind me.

I have no idea how he is staying calm in this instant, because Lila's keeping so much from both of us. – She's lying to us. And now I want the truth.

Journal entry insert by Lila Winters

Frac. – This is not good. Yesterday did not end well and today is not going well either. – And I was right. I am a date-disaster magnet. I just wasn't expecting it to be them.

I had managed to sneak into the hotel via the basement carpark without causing any media frenzy from the news vans parked out front. So I raced up to my apartment to grab my journal and look through the pages. – I just can't understand why the blue-rose isn't working. There's no reason why it shouldn't be. It's worked to heal so many other injuries before this. It should have no problems healing a Water guardian.

I sat down at the dining table, looking at any of the other plants I had researched that had similar healing properties. But none were as potent for these kinds of injuries. – That is except for the moly herb recipe.

Matt sat at the table next to me, placing another tomato and cheese toastie beside me, but just stayed silent. And his presence helped. That is until I saw the news flick on to show the media coverage again. Only this time Danny and Ruby were watching and saw Max's face on the screen.

"Is Uncle Max sick?" Ruby pouted as they both trotted over to the table.

"Yes." I nodded, picking Ruby up to hug her, and Matt helped Danny to climb up onto his knee. Then I added with a determined smile. "But he's going to get better."

In needing a distraction, Matt suggested they make a get-well-soon card for Max and Adela. And while they ran off to grab the craft supplies from my office, I disappeared out of the apartment along with my journal.

I knocked on Tyme's apartment door, knowing that William would be there. And I didn't even have to say anything. He took one look at my sad, tired face, and knew what I needed.

He let me in the door before quickly disappearing into his room, and then came back out holding a journal book as well. It was well used and had leaves shoved between the pages as if they were bookmarks.

"You keep a journal?" I asked in disbelief.

He looked back, a little unsure and explained, "I have to... My memory's terrible when it comes to this stuff. This book stores everything I know... even a recipe for pancakes."

"Eggless pancakes?" I questioned slightly more excited than I expected.

"Um... no..." He shook his head still seeming a little nervous. "But I do have a recipe for that... I researched it when Tyme told me you didn't eat egg... um... On the off chance you ever wanted to have breakfast with us."

Huh. – He likes pancakes and toasties, and he keeps a journal. – I'm more like my real father than I realised. And I may have smiled at him as we started prepping the kitchen bench and finding or growing the plants that we needed.

Journal entry continued by Alex Woods

Terrence and I made our way back to the hotel, using the human method of transportation because of the extra eyes we have nosing around us. But when we got back to the hotel, we saw the ladies from a few days ago. – It's the Mums group that asked Lila to teach them self-defence. They were standing outside the hotel talking to the media. Chrissie, Abbey, Kim, Roxy, and Anita were all there as well as the woman Matt called "Ms Nosey Knots" or in a more polite term, Carol.

Abbey and Chrissie were showing the news reporter some of the defence moves Lila had taught them on Thursday night, and I began to feel really sad for Lila. – I mean she was doing them a favour, and this is how they repay her.

When we walked into the lobby, Carol spotted us and called to Terrence by name. He stopped at the base of the stairs, and groaned with a clenched fist before he turned to greet her.

"Mrs Grey, can I help you with something?"

"Yes," she replied, quite perturbed. "We've been trying to contact Lila all morning, and there's been no answer. We're worried sick about her."

I silently grunted because I could sense that they weren't at all worried. They were just wanting the juicy gossip in order to go blab it to the world.

Urgh. – Keep it together, Alex. – Come on.

Terrence managed to play it smart and used the ignorant card. "I take it you saw the news."

"Who hasn't?" Carol gasped. "Naturally we all came down to offer Lila our support."

Nope. – I was so done, and I snapped, "You call this support? Looks to me like you just wanted to get your 30 seconds of fame."

Scowling back at me, Carol held her hand to her chest as if she were offended. "I would never do that. We only wanted to help."

Ooh damn that made me mad. But as I clenched my fist, Terrence glanced back at me and pleadingly whispered under his breath, "Don't do it, Alex."

He then turned to Carol and calmly explained, "Mrs Grey, Lila is the head of security and is strictly bound by the rules of this hotel... which includes restrictions on talking to the media. And I don't think she'd want you or your friends talking to the media about her either... So if you really want to help, please, go home."

Wow. – Terrence really knows how to keep a level head, and surprisingly it worked. Carol rounded up the Mums group and left.

Once they had left, we went up to Lila's apartment, but Matt told us she had just left with her journal half an hour ago. Terrence quickly guessed that the next place Lila would go was to another Nature guardian, so we raced down to Tyme's apartment. Sure enough, she was there and opened the door smiling at Terrence.

"Good you made it... I was worried you guys got stopped by the media."

Alright. – I didn't think she was expecting us.

"Terry, I need you to come in and help us... We're running out of time."

She didn't really wait for Terrence to respond. She just grabbed his hand and pulled him inside, instantly putting him to work. They were making a large batch of the purple healing tonic for Adela and Max, and whatever they didn't use was going to be given to Dr Ellis for his cooperation and silence in all this. But I kind of felt helpless just watching as they all moved at half-speed to get things done.

Another half hour later when they had finished, Terrence was filling 20 vials with the purple healing tonic while Lila helped William to pack up.

"Hey, William..." Lila called and turned to face him. "We should name this tonic if we're going to let James use it at the hospital."

Surprised at the suggestion, William took a moment to think. "Um, have you got any ideas?"

"Well... it is your recipe. So why don't we call it the Knight serum." She giggled a little, noticing William's face puzzle from the suggestion. So she went on to explain. "I know it seems a little funny, using your last name and all. But it's just a play on words. You know because knights are supposed to be the ones who swoop in and rescue everyone... And that's pretty much what this tonic does."

"Alright." William smiled, liking the idea. "The Knight serum it is... Thanks."

Wow. - Surprisingly this is the first time I've seen Lila actually smile at William and seem completely happy. - It's kind of cute.

As she cleaned, Lila noticed a tattered piece of paper fall out of the book that William was putting away. She picked it up and realised it was a photo of a woman holding a newborn baby. But the photo had been folded so that all you could see was the baby.

Handing the photo back to William, Lila began to struggle with her words. "Here... you... you dropped this."

A little nervous, William took the photo back from Lila and thanked her. And I'm pretty sure Lila picked up on that too, seeing how she started playing with her fingers before she questioned him.

"So do you have a picture of Tyme in there, or is it just me."

Becoming even more nervous at that question, William shook his head. "No, I have an album for Tyme's baby pictures. I think he's shown you that one. This is the only one I have of you... I lost the one I had of you and me."

A strand of Lila's hair turned white as she went back to her journal and pulled out an old photo to hand to William. "Is this the one you lost?"

William looked at the photo and realised it was of him, holding Lila as a baby, and smilingly gasped, "Yes... How did you find it? And why do you have it in your journal."

A little cagey in her reply, Lila shrugged her shoulders as she started to clean again. "Well, my team actually found this picture when they were looking for me last year... And I kept it because it's the only baby picture I have of me not in the arms of a monster."

A small grin appeared on William, and it looked like he was going to say something but stopped and instead went back to cleaning as well.

Journal entry insert by Lila Winters

I got a call from Tyme while we were packing up the last of the Knight serum, and he was panic-stricken and in tears. Apparently, Maxwell had come out of surgery and his vitals did not look promising, and Adela was still refusing to let anyone see her or receive any treatment until she talked to me. – And I had taken a lot longer than an hour, so I told him I was on my way.

When we got back to the hospital, I played as the distraction, walking through the media-circus at the front door all while Dr Ellis greeted Alex and Terrence in through the back door, carrying the Knight serum with them. – Because there is no way I'm going to risk any of them falling into the hands of nosey reporters.

I raced up the stairs as fast as humanly possible to Max and Adela's ward, but I had to stop halfway up the stairs to check my phone as it rang. – It was my mother Hanna, and it's the ninth phone call I've had to ignore, among other phone calls, even Billy's. But I can't talk to Hanna, not yet anyway. There is a definite guarantee that she's seen my little stunt on the news, but I have no time to deal with her fraught familial worry for me. I have enough to deal with coming from Tyme, who was anxiously waiting for me and instantly ran over to hug me the second I stepped onto the ward floor.

He squeezed me so tightly, and he was rambling on about something through his tears. "You have to save her. I can't let it end like this. I have to make it right. Please, promise me you can fix this... Please, Lila."

"Tyme." I hurriedly sighed, pulling back a little bit from his hug to look at his face. "You know I can't promise you anything like that. But I did go to get help... for Adela, and you."

While still in the hug, I shuffled him backwards to look down the stairs as I pointed to William walking up the stairs, carrying the large bag of vials with Alex and Terrence right behind him. And although Tyme looked teary eyed, he had a slight smile on him.

"You went to see my dad?" He sniffled with a trembling lip.

"Tyme, I'll do anything for you... You're my brother."

I smiled as Tyme hugged me tighter, and I thought it would help his emotional state if I pulled William in for a group-family hug as well. And it did. In the comforting familial moment, Tyme felt content and surprisingly so do I.

Hmm? – Maybe there is still a part of me that longs for a father after all.

Once Tyme had calmed down, I walked into Adela's room, following Dr Ellis to talk him through what he had to do with the Knight serum. – Which I will add, Tyme thought was a fantastic name, seeing how it was using his family name for a miracle drug that calmed him down. But he didn't calm down enough. And what Dr Ellis hasn't realised is that I'd snuck someone into the room with me.

Tyme was so desperate to see Adela, but Dr Ellis was insistent on it being family members only. And I was the only exception because Adela had requested me by name. So instead, Tyme stayed partially in the time rift, just enough to be unseen. But he had also pulled my hand – the hand he was still holding onto and refused to let go of – into the partial time rift as well. Just enough to give him the support he needed.

I admit, I am having some difficulties trying to keep Tyme from realising that I'm using my animal abilities to keep him calm, and the gold tinge in my eyes probably doesn't help. But what I sense in Tyme is that deep down he loves Adela. They just never got a chance to explore it.

While standing at the end of the bed, I watched Dr Ellis check to see if the serum was working, and thankfully it is. Adela started to regain the colour in her cheeks, and the deep cuts on her forehead and shoulders were now completely healed. He did a quick exam on her and then nodded to me.

"It worked... that's amazing," he praised. Then as Adela became more alert and awake, he softly explained, "Hello again, I brought Lila, just as you asked... We've just given you another tonic and this one appears to be working. I'll need to run a few more tests, but from the looks of it, your completely healed... Well, almost healed... Again, I'm really sorry... I'll come back when you're ready to... you know..."

For some reason, Adela started to tear up as Dr Ellis walked out of the room, but I quickly stopped him before he left to hand him the bag of Knight serums. "One of them is for Max... William can walk you through the process just in case Max's injuries are too much. But the rest of them you can use as you wish. On the condition that you're careful with them... Oh, and they'll only last for 16 days before they start losing their strength, so use them wisely."

Peering into the bag as I spoke, Dr Ellis let out a long breath, replying, "Thank-you" as he walked out the door to talk to William.

Turning my attention back to Adela, I grew curious to find out why the blue-rose tonic didn't work, so I walked back over to the bed to peek at Adela's medical chart.

"Hey, you had us all worried for a while," I noted while skimming the forms.

It's then I realised what had gone wrong. – She was 18 weeks pregnant, and the baby had died. The blue-rose is designed to seek and mend the most severe injuries, so it most likely spent all its efforts trying to revive the baby, instead of healing Adela.

Damn. – Unfortunately, healing tonics aren't strong enough to revive the dead.

In shock, I quickly closed the med chart so Tyme wouldn't see because I strongly suspect it was his, and I'm pretty sure Adela hasn't told him yet. But she started talking before I could stop her.

"I'm sorry... I should have told you... I should have told Tyme...I... I lost it."

I tried to stop her from talking as I watched her holding her stomach so tenderly. And I felt Tyme's sorrow rising. "Adela, you don't have to tell me anything."

Still, she continued, lost in her own pain. "I lost her... I lost my—"

"Adela, stop!" I snapped with urgency, causing her to look at me confused as if she had done something wrong. But it was me who had done something wrong.

"I'm sorry, but I didn't come in here alone," I admitted then held up an invisible hand.

Suddenly, Tyme's hand appeared in mine as he stepped out of the rift, looking at Adela and where her hands were as he took in sharp breaths. I could feel all of his pain and his regret, and my abilities couldn't help him anymore as he watched Adela burst into tears, apologising to him.

"I'm sorry Tyme, I was going to tell you last night... But I just kept getting scared. And now it's too late."

Instantly, Tyme darted to Adela's side and climbed up onto the bed to hold her in his arms, and as his tears fell, he whispered to her. "It's okay, Adela... I've got you... It's okay."

Yeah. – I'm really proud of my brother right now. Watching him look after Adela like this. – He definitely loves her.

I thought it would be best to give them some space to grieve. And I was just about to walk out when I heard the little footsteps of my children as they wandered up the hall with Matt, each carrying chocolates and two very large cards. I watched them pass Adela's room, excitedly racing into Maxwell's room, so I briefly glanced back at my brother and smiled before I stepped out to go see them.

Max's room was just down the hall, and I watched from the hallway, peering in through the door window as he welcomed Danny and Ruby onto the bed to look at the cards they had made for him, and share the chocolates they had bought from the downstairs shop.

As I got close to the room, I sensed a particular emotion, and it got stronger when William quickly and quietly tried to exit the room. He felt angry and envious and most of all, he felt regret. In sensing that, I thought it would be best to hide myself to not make the regret worse for him. So I hid in the supplies room just around the corner but listened in as Jess followed William out of the room.

"Hey, where are you going?" she asked.

I peered out of the room I was in to see William explain with such a heavy heart. "I don't think Lila wants me to meet her children yet. I don't think she'll ever want me to see her children... And I'm going to respect that."

Jess nodded, understanding his quick exit but suggested, "You never know, Lila can surprise you sometimes... I'm not sure you know this, but almost everyone on the team that Lila works with... the ones she trusts and cares for and considers family has hurt her at least once before. Even me and Max... But she still saved us. Still treats us as family."

"But you never abandoned her when she needed you most," he interrupted her with a sad breath. "That kind of pain sticks."

To that Jess walked closer to him to quietly explain, "Adela told me a few months ago of something Lila said to her. It was really insightful. I think it went something like... just because you've done something bad does not always mean that you can never do anything good or make it right... And I'm sorry to be blunt, Mr Knight, but the fact that you've been allowed to stay in our hotel for months, means that Lila's giving you that chance... So stop wasting it."

The words clearly got to William, and he nodded to her before Jess walked back into Max's hospital room. Then after taking a few seconds lost in his own thoughts of sadness, William began to walk down the hall past the room I was hiding in.

"She's right you know," I stated, gaining his attention as I leaned in the doorway of my hidey-hole. "There aren't many people close to me who haven't hurt me... But I believe everyone should get the chance to redeem themselves. Why do you think I saved Richard?"

He sighed at the sound of that A-holes name, and I walked out to stand in front of him as I added, "I'm not ready for you to be a part of my family. But I do appreciate the fact that you're a part of my life... Um... I would like to hug you now, if that's okay... But if you don't want it just take a step back."

Slowly moving towards him, William didn't move, so I wrapped my arms around him to give him a hug, and then whispered, "I don't know if this helps how you feel, but for the first time in a long time, I don't feel disappointed... so thank you for your help today."

My head rested on his shoulder for a moment, and I don't think he was expecting any of this. But he happily accepted the hug before I explained that Tyme might be needing his dad right about now and that he should go check on him.

CHAPTER 21

When Death Becomes Her

Journal entry by Alex Woods

Lila had disappeared again. And yes, I used my tracking skills to find her, but she hadn't gone far. She was down in the hospital's café, sitting at a table with an untouched hot chocolate in her hands while staring down at the dozen missed phone calls on her phone.

Terrence and I sat down at the table, and then Terrence placed his phone down in front of Lila, showing her a snapshot image of the security footage of her and Billy kissing.

She took one look at the phone and took a deep breath. "I'm not going to win this argument, am I?"

She sounded like she had been crying, but I'm determined to get the truth, so I replied softly, "No."

While twiddling with her fingers again, Lila sniffled, and when she looked up, I saw the tears in her red puffy eyes as she spoke. "Alright, give me your hands... But I need both of you not to get angry... And understand that I did what I had to, and I didn't need permission to do any of this from either of you."

I peered across to Terrence who looked just as hesitant as I did, but both of us agreed then held onto her hand. She closed her eyes, as did we, before she shared her memories with us. The first was of Lila at the Music Bowl being thrown down the steps, and then held up like a trophy in front of Billy who was held at gunpoint.

The next was when Lila was being tortured in the train station tower when she fearfully gasped to Peter, "I have it. I have the seed."

I wanted to pull away at this point, feeling the pain she had attached to the memory. But I held on as she showed us the next memory of George talking to her in the poolroom. "Lila, I know this must be hard... really hard... And yes, I agree he's definitely a monster. But your mother doesn't need to watch her husband suffer like that... especially if she doesn't know any better."

The memory switched to one of Lila meeting Billy in the hospital stairwell and of what it led to. As well as her in his dark apartment, sitting on him half-naked, holding a dagger while asking him questions about the car explosion involving Richard. It led her to yell at him, and then try to leave before Billy stopped her and pinned her against the wall, shouting, "You think you're safe at that hotel. Max is one of them. He's just using you. I can't just let you go back there..."

The memory then skipped to the point where Lila stabbed Billy to get away, but not before she kissed him then jumped out the window to escape Billy's friend, Stephen.

From there Lila showed us the memories of the days and weeks following, of Lila seeing Billy hiding in the alley not far from the hotel, in the end leaving gifts out for him in the hopes to speak to him and ask him to come back. She gave him a phone, and he called her almost every night, and every night she went to sleep feeling both sad and happy at the same time.

My body tensed feeling a surge of jealousy, but my emotions turned to protective frustration. Because the next memory was of the night I checked on Lila in the alley after Danny's concert. Stephen had pinned her against the door, demanding Lila to help him, threatening the lives of so many guardians to make her do it. She had a note shoved into her hand that read, "Do it or Billy dies." – And she felt so scared and helpless in the moments before I found her, and even when I held her.

She showed us all the memories of her working the late nights, researching in her room or in the garden making up the tonic and falling asleep from the exhaustion. Of her sneaking out of the hotel to get to Billy's apartment. And of her sitting on the couch next to a bag of glowing blue epi-pens. Feeling so tired as she fell asleep. Then waking up with Billy kneeling next to her, slowly carrying her to his bed where she gave him a birthday present before falling asleep in his arms.

Yep. – It's getting a little hard to breathe now.

Lila continued, showing us the conversation she had with Billy when they woke up the next morning, where Billy explained that he'd made a deal to work with the Rebels to keep Lila safe. – Which is essentially what Lila was doing for him.

The memory skipped to Lila's meet up with Peter in the sporting store when they asked for more Tonics. And my heart tore a little when she said, "Because I know that if you lay so much as a finger on me, Billy will burn your arse to the ground before you even leave this store."

That part really did hit a nerve for me. But what hurt more was how Billy tenderly cared for Lila's burn wound in the corridor after the incident. – Where he also found out that Lila was a Water guardian.

Ouch. – She told him, and not me.

Her emotions of deep sadness attached to this memory were strong when she re-negotiated the terms of helping him. Then when Billy tried to kiss her and Lila pushed him away, she sneered. "Kissing me will prove nothing... You know my conditions, and I'll still help you if they're met... But right now, I need to go. Adela's buying me a dress for my date tonight... So don't follow me."

Oh god. – She had a date with me. – Lila was attacked yesterday. She woke up in Billy's arms yesterday after she had spent all week exhausting herself, trying to make all those cures. – She had all night to tell us about this, and she didn't. – She had so many opportunities to talk to me, but she didn't. About any of this.

I couldn't take anymore, and I pulled away, standing up from the table, feeling so mad and furious and jealous. Very, very jealous.

"How could you not tell me about this?"

Lila couldn't answer. She just sat in silence, drawing in short sharp breaths, knowing what she had done was wrong. So I stormed out of the cafe towards the back exit.

Feeling so furious and needing to vent, I just kept moving but she chased after me, following me down the streets into the back alleys where I paced, and I lost my temper.

"DON'T, LILA!" I yelled, trying and failing to calm down. "You don't want to be around me, right now!"

Right behind her was Terrence, and he tried to pull Lila away when he saw my rage building. But she wouldn't listen, pulling away from him, trying to get my attention to speak to me.

"No... I get that you're angry at me. Both of you... But tell me what would you have done? This was my mess and I needed to fix it."

I stopped in my raging pace, staring back at her to ask, "Do you love him?"

Desperately needing to know that answer, I stared at her and waited. But she looked at me with her teary eyes and choked on her words. "I... c...care for him, yes."

But that wasn't my question, so I walked towards her, trying so badly to keep myself in check with slow breaths.

"That's not what I asked, Lila... Do. You. Love him?"

She started twiddling with her fingers again as she looked at the ground and cried, "Alex, please don't do this."

My hands held her soft cheeks, gently tilting her head up to see her teary eyes again with me still desperately needing to hear her words. But before I could say anything more, a strong gust of leaves filled the alley, surrounding Lila and Terrence.

I watched in the chaos as Lila and Terrence's eyes glowed green with a hazy white. And when the leaves stopped and dropped to the ground, both Lila and Terrence were freaked.

Lila looked like she was hyperventilating, gasping Hanna's name, and then while struggling with her breath and her heart beating rapidly, Lila pulled away from me, and stared back up at Terrence in fear.

"Lila don't!" he begged. But she disappeared, running off at full-speed.

In a panic, Terrence quickly turned to me and fearfully said, "She's walking into a trap." Then he took off after her.

Journal entry insert by Lila Winters

I have to get to her. I don't care the cost. My legs are aching from running so far at full-speed, and my heart is pounding. But I still don't care. I need to save my mother. I had ignored her the entire day, so consumed in dealing with one mess that I was completely oblivious to hers. And I stupidly put her in this mess just by being what I am.

The leaves gave me a vision of Keith Connors walking into my mother's house after being invited in. – He had lunch with her and then stood outside her house as it went up in flames.

I have to save her. – I'm going to save her.

I ran up the driveway towards the farmhouse and didn't hesitate in racing inside, looking around amongst the smoke and heat, screaming Hanna's name. The house was completely engulfed in flames, and fire billowed out of every room. I tried to control the fire myself, but it had a mind of its own. And I still don't know how to control this element.

The fear filled me when I found Hanna, lying on the floor next to the dining table. She had been hit over the head with a teapot, and the remnants of the ceramic pot were embedded into her chest where she fell.

I screeched her name, rushing to help her and covering my hands with her blood. "Hold on, Mum, I'll get you out of here... I'll fix this... I promise."

Tears fell from my eyes as I struggled to pick her up, feeling so exhausted from everything. I felt the burning pain in my legs and chest from running, and the smoke filled every corner of the house, making it difficult to breathe or even see. So instead I dragged her. – Where? I have no idea because everywhere I turned there was fire. But I'm going to save her. I have to save her.

Journal entry insert by Terrence Connors

Alex and I ran as fast as we could to the Willows farmhouse. And we could see the flames from the road, they were so high. Alex got to the house first and I heard him scream Lila's name as he disappeared into the fires. But I had another target, my brother. — He's the one responsible for this mess. And he stood next to the old willow tree-port, watching his creation with gladness.

Ugh! — He makes me sick with rage.

I tackled him to the ground at full-speed, creating a crater where he lay and jeered the words, "Why? You twisted son of a. . ."

Before I could finish, he tackled me and punched me to the ground. We fought ferociously and fast. But because I was fatigued from the run, I grew tired a lot faster, and it gave him the upper hand.

He picked me up by my shirt and threw me clear across the field, landing in front of the Willows farmhouse. Then he appeared towering over me, standing on my chest and crushing it.

I felt my ribs start to burn with agony and let out a scream before he eased off, hissing at me. "This is for our mother... Our mother is sick and it's her fault... The empire we helped to perfect is being attacked while you dare stand against us and instead stand with her, your little nature girl... After everything Mother has done for you!"

He took his foot off my chest and kneeled down to whisper with so much hate. "And all the pain your little girlfriend feels... from now on, that will be All. On. You."

Standing back up, he kicked me in the chest one more time, and as I writhed in pain, he readied himself to leave with one last threat.

"Oh, and the best part, Brother... Is I'm not done with her yet." He then took off, disappearing as the night fell, and the sound of fire engines were heard in the distance.

I looked back at the farmhouse, hearing Lila screaming, "ALEX, HELP ME!"

In hearing her fear, I fought through my pain to stand, trying to make it inside to help. But there's debris everywhere, and the exits are blocked by fallen roof beams and flames.

"ALEX! LILA!" I screamed from the door but got no response.

Worry and fear consumed me when suddenly, I saw Lila and Alex smash through the kitchen window, holding Hanna's semi-conscious body, landing on the grassy garden bed below. Lila groaned in so much pain as she pulled herself onto her knees, racing back to where her mother lay. But Hanna was barely breathing with her clothes stained with soot and blood, and Lila sobbed, holding her hand and looking at the extent of Hanna's injuries.

"Mum," she whimpered with tears pouring from her eyes. "Just hold on, Mum... I can fix this."

With determination, Lila pulled herself back, digging into her pocket and pulling out a vial of the Knight serum we had made earlier. But it was broken with only a few drops in the bottom tainted with soot and dirt.

"No... no, no, no." She sobbed, looking at the vial then back at her mother before she appeared in the garden, digging around, trying to find anything that would help, and muttering through tears, "I can fix this... I can save you... Just hold on."

Hanna called for Lila, struggling with her words as her chest laboured, and instantly Lila shuffled back to kneel at her side. "I'm here, Mum... I'm right here."

The gaze in Hanna's eyes were teary, and she stared up at Lila with such a proud look on her face, knowing exactly what was to come. She held Lila's cheek and smiled as she shakily reached for the large ruby ring she wore on her right hand and gave it to Lila.

Her hands trembled, holding tightly to Lila's as she rasped her words. "I'm so sorry, Lila... for everything I've done... Please... forgive me."

In that moment, Hanna's eyes became distant and empty as her hand fell from Lila's.

My heart felt heavy as I listened to Lila whimper while looking over her mother, shaking her head with her tears never-ending.

"No... No, I can fix this," she cried, pulling away and racing back to the garden with her bloodied hands clawing into the dirt to find anything. Her hair turned white as Lila kept repeating, "I can fix this... I have to save her... I promised I'd save her."

The agony in Lila's voice was hard to hear. Then with tears in his eyes, Alex gently wrapped his arms around her, pulling Lila away from the garden. She struggled and fought to break free of him, screaming and wailing, begging Alex to let her fix it. But he held tight to her, sitting on the grass not far from Hanna's body as the fire crews started to douse the flames of the house.

Then after a world of screams left poor Lila's heart, she gave up and wept into Alex's arms. And I sat down next to Alex, wrapping my arms around them both as we all wept.

This is devastating. — This should have never happened.

Then after a world of screams left poor Lila's heart, she gave up and wept into Alex's arms. And I sat down next to Alex, wrapping my arms around them both as we all wept.

Journal entry continued by Alex Woods

The death of Hanna has left Lila's heart broken, and she hasn't said a word all week unless it was to deal with the funeral arrangements. Her hair has stayed white, and I never see her smile, not even around her kids.

Hanna had requested a graveside funeral – with the superstition that death should never enter a church. She'd also requested Lila to play her guitar and sing the 'Untitled Hymn' at the funeral. So Lila respected her wishes.

She stood at Hanna's tombstone, playing and singing as the casket was lowered into the ground. At the same time, Hanna's friends came up to pay their respects and leave flowers before slowly making their way back to their cars. Lila's voice was beautiful but shaky and filled with sadness. And once she had finished singing, she said goodbye to the church pastor as he gave her some time to mourn.

The pain filled Lila's beautiful broken heart as she stood, staring at the coffin with tears in her eyes when William and Tyme walked up to stand next to her. With his eyes glowing green, William held his hand out over the coffin, causing all the flowers that were dropped into Hanna's grave to grow larger and brighter to cover the coffin, so that all Lila could see were the flowers.

As he lowered his hand again, Lila held onto it, and he looked at her then down at the hand she held and tearfully smiled glancing at the ruby ring on her finger.

It was painful to watch her cry, but when Lila was ready, she handed her guitar to Danny as he bravely stood next to Ruby to comfort her. Then while still holding William's hand, Lila walked with him and Tyme to stand opposite Matt, Terrence, and me on the other side of the grave.

The soil for Hanna's burial rested on either side of the grave on a cloth base. And we all followed Lila's lead, picking up the edge of the cloth and pulling it up to cover the flowers and the one who lay beneath them.

There was so much sorrow in Lila when she walked back towards the car, and as she passed all the plants and trees surrounding her, they saddened and drooped, losing their colour. And the rain began to fall.

The rain continued to fall throughout the day, and everyone gave Lila the space and time to grieve. But when Matt called us, in a heartbeat Terrence and I were standing outside Lila's apartment. Matt let us in and led us straight to the loungeroom where Lila sat on the couch, looking out the windows at the city, watching the rain as it blanketed the buildings. – The forecast hadn't predicted rain, but we suspect it will be here for a while.

Surrounding Lila were sympathy cards and flowers that were originally once vibrant, and now are colourless and limp. Her hair is still white, and Lila's ears had started to point, with her eyes a saddened black as she cuddled her white wolf teddy while playing with the ruby ring.

I knelt down next to her, resting my hand on hers as she whimpered, "I couldn't save her."

"I know." I whispered before very gently scooping her up into my arms.

While holding her tightly, I kissed her forehead then carried her slowly towards the bedroom as she buried her face into the crook of my neck. And Matt quickly handed Lila's white wolf teddy and blanket to Terrence as he followed me in.

Neither of us said a word, we just sat at the top end of Lila's bed as she nestled in between us, and we just let her cry while she held our hands.

Journal entry insert by Terrence Connors

Alex and I stayed all night with Lila as she cried, and eventually she grew tired and fell asleep. But she still refused to let go of either of us, so we both got comfortable, and as the night grew colder, Alex drifted off to sleep as well.

I watched Lila sleep for a while, haunted by the memories of what my brother said, and I wasn't going to let him hurt her anymore. I'm not going to let anyone hurt her or use her or threaten her ever again. — She doesn't deserve it.

My heart felt torn because I didn't want to leave her, but I know what I have to do. So I gently pulled my hand away, wiping the tears from Lila's cheek before quietly sneaking out of her bedroom, borrowing her phone as I left. I remembered in the memory she shared with us, that she had used Google maps to deliver the tonics. She had also deleted the search, but nothing is truly deleted when it comes to the internet.

While following the phone directions, I ended up standing outside a rundown old apartment block in a town called Coburg. It looked to be empty, but I could hear the sound of people inside. So I silently crept through the halls and found myself in what looks like a common area.

I took a few breaths, reminding myself of why I was doing this before I picked up one of the broken floorboards and thrashed it onto the metal fire hose reel. Within seconds, I was encircled by those I remember to be Stephen and Billy — obviously. As well as Isaac and Holly along with a dozen others that I don't recognise.

Surprisingly, Billy stood back from the group and looked like he had been crying. But Stephen stood in front of me, all arrogant and smug as he curiously stared at me.

"Now this is unexpected... What can we do for you, Mr Connors?"

Yeah, I'm really struggling not to hurt him for what he did to Lila. — Ruining her date and hurting her, making her feel helpless and scared. But I don't want him anywhere near Lila anymore, so while glaring at him, I tossed a bag of freshly made Neuritamine cures on the ground in front of him and sneered. "I hear you're looking for a Nature guardian, and I'm taking Lila off the table."

"Hmmm..." Stephen rubbed his chin and thought for a moment. "I don't know about taking Lila off the table. I like her there... She made a deal, and she needs to—"

"I know what the deal is," I sniped and walked closer to him. "And you'll have my assistance just as she promised. But if you or your rebels go anywhere near her, I'm pretty sure you know what will happen... And I'm positive, you know that it won't be me that holds you down and burns you alive."

I briefly glanced back a Billy, and he quickly realised why I was doing this. So he moved closer to join the group.

"Stephen, I suggest you take the deal... Terrence used to be a hunter. He knows how The Board operates. And... I can vouch for him."

Getting impatient, I stood waiting for an answer as Stephen stared suspiciously at Billy, and then to the bag of Neuritamine cures before he nodded. "Alright, deal... Welcome to the team, Mr Connors."

CHAPTER 22

Phasing

Journal entry by Terrence Connors

It's been four weeks now working with these amateurs that Billy got himself mixed up with. I have tried to be somewhat nice to Billy and talk to him every now and then. But he knows that the only reason why I'm helping this group is because Lila wanted and promised to help him. — And yeah, that only frustrates me more. But I'm doing this for her. — To keep her safe.

Tonight, we're taking on a convoy of trucks that were travelling through the back roads of Victoria with a few assets on board. Stephen and Billy stood in the middle of the road, waiting for three unmarked transport trucks while Isaac and Holy stayed hiding amongst the trees. Then as soon as the trucks were in sight, the road ahead of them started to shatter apart, causing them to screech to an unsteady stop.

The first wave of soldiers was always armed, and they had a shoot first and ask questions later policy. So as they opened fire on us, I raised my hand up creating a shield of branches from the nearby trees to protect us, and then waved my other hand at the trees closest to the soldiers, grabbing them by the legs and pulling them all into the air. The sky began to rumble with the threat of rain, and Stephen grew excited.

"Now the fun really begins," he mocked, creating a fireball in his hand.

We waited in darkness just listening, and then out of the blue, Stephen was attacked by a large black cat and dragged into the bushes.

"I guess he's got that one then." Billy shrugged his shoulders, looking at me.

We soon heard Isaac and Holly yelp as our next target — Kim Santos, a Water guardian, jumped from the trees behind them. At the same time Billy quickly created a flaming shield in his hand as a bolt of lightning came barrelling towards him, seconds before Jarred Robinson tackled him from the side.

I got attacked by Cole Mason, a Land guardian, and his eyes glowed a dark red as his skin turned to metal. The moment I saw his skin, I instantly knew this was going to be easy. He was cocky when he fought, but I was having fun, dodging all his moves.

Yeah. — I'm really beginning to appreciate all the training games Lila likes to play with me. They really do teach you a few tricks. — Like how to wear out your opponent first.

As we fought, Cole only managed to get one actual connecting punch to my chest before it was my turn. I broke off the front bumper of the first transport truck and swung it like a baseball bat, throwing him in the direction of Jarred and Billy, shouting, "Heads up."

In hearing that, Billy dodged out of the way as Cole landed on Jarred, who accidentally let off an electric charge, knocking them both out. And as Cole's skin returned to normal, I shot him with a tranque dart filled with the Neuritamine cure, and then shot Jarred who was pinned beneath him.

The large cat was randomly thrown into the street, and I moved at half-speed shooting her with Billy's tranque gun, causing it to morph back into Tania Black. Stephen then stepped out from the trees and looked around at the target count.

"Where's the fourth?" he asked.

Suddenly, the road beneath him trembled, and Isaac appeared from the ground in a fury, still mid-fight with Kim. But I'm in a bit of a hurry, so when they got closer to me, I shot Kim as well then briefly glanced at my watch realising it was nearly sun up.

"Come on, we need to wrap this up," I demanded.

They all knew why I was in a hurry, so they let me take off without them. And I made it back to the hotel just as the morning shift was starting. Then while still hurrying, I got changed at super-speed before I raced up to Lila's apartment with some fresh flowers.

Alex and I are still trying to get Lila through her grieving process, and the entire hotel is starting to worry about her. — In the apartment, Matt was sitting at the dining table with Danny and Ruby finishing off their breakfast, all just about to head off to work, school, and day care. And I found Alex standing outside Lila's bedroom, holding yet another untouched tray of breakfast.

"She still won't eat?" I asked, looking over at Alex as he shook his head.

"She had the milk but that's it," he grumbled in slight frustration, then asked, looking at me peculiarly. "Where have you been?"

I was a little cagey and looked at him oddly. "Nowhere... Why?"

Matt then walked over to join our conversation, telling me I had dirt on my face.

Yeah Crap. — That is definitely not dirt.

Matt became agitated and he whispered, trying to keep the conversation out of earshot of the little ones. "It's been over a month now. She can't keep doing this to herself. We may need to think of more drastic measures."

"Did you guys try her favourite foods?" I asked, pulling out a bag of Lila's favourite BBQ crisp chips and a box of Turkish delights. Matt glared at me as if that was a stupid idea, so I shrugged my shoulders at him. "What? I know it's not the best thing for breakfast... But it's something."

With a huff, Matt took the tray off Alex and handed it to me. "Can you at least try this first and then the junk food?"

After a long sigh of agreement from me, Alex went off to help Matt get the kids ready to leave and walk them to the elevator while I very cautiously walked into Lila's room.

The blinds were drawn shut, and her bedside lamp was on. Yet all I could see lying on the bed was a fluffy white wolf's ear poking out from the blanket covers. — And yeah, she's been a wolf for over 4 weeks now.

"Lila," I whispered. "Are you awake?"

I sat down at the end of the bed, and the wolf popped her head up then shimmied out of the blankets to rest her head on my lap, and I heard her whimper — just a little.

"Are you hungry?" I queried, holding up the breakfast tray of tomato and cheese toasties.

She growled at me then went back to hiding her head under the pillows.

"I bought you some chips... they're your favourite."

Damn. — I got no response to that either. She just buried herself further under her pillows.

"You know it would be really nice to talk to you properly," I stated, holding out my hand towards her.

Nope, still no response. — Okay, let's try something drastic then.

"Lila, how about we go for a walk today? It's beautiful outside. Spring's just come in and the trees and flowers are starting to blossom in the parks... Come on now... you know natures your favourite element... And mine, and I'd really love to share it with you."

Yeah. — I still got nothing.

Okay then, it's time for Lila's favourite part of an argument. — The negotiation. — Or in my case the ultimatum. "Alright, Lila, you've left me no choice. You can either go for a walk with me on this beautiful day, or I can take you to the hospital for a therapy session and a nutrient drip... And don't test me on this one because there are at least 5 other guardians who will help me drag your butt to the hospital... or the vet... It's your choice."

I don't think Lila's wanting to call my bluff, so she crawled out of the bed to follow me out of the room.

Alex originally thought my idea was terrible, but I did get her out of her room. — I even came prepared with a change of clothes and some food snacks in a backpack for her, on the off chance we get lucky and she morphs back to her beautiful self again.

Journal entry insert by Alex Woods

Terrence has been acting weirder and moodier than usual, and I'm starting to worry if he's getting enough sleep. Most nights he stayed with Lila and me, trying to convince Lila to be happy and morph back into herself. – And seriously, we've tried a lot of things.

We talk to her in the dreamland, and she seems happy enough just to sit and talk to us, and we tell her about what's been happening around the hotel and she just listens. We even tried to get her to come with us on one of the rescue missions that we had targeted in New Zealand. But the best we could get from her was co-ordinating a plan of attack that didn't include her. – And that sucked. – A lot.

I'm starting to worry about her. – And I miss seeing her smile.

I suppose I should be impressed at least, that Terrence managed to get Lila to agree in coming for a walk with us. – Even if she's determined to stay as a wolf. But when we got into the lobby, we started to get a few stares and whispers happening. I mean she is quite large for her size. – Her head is the same height as my shoulder.

Shane ran up to us while freaking out to quietly ask, "What is that?"

"That would be the one you call Sissy." I grinned back.

I think Lila liked that answer because she moved her head closer, brushing up against the side of my arm. I responded in kind giving her a nice scratch behind the ears, and I think she moaned from the enjoyment.

Shane stared at her with his brows arched. "Wow... why is she still a wolf?"

"Well, we're not entirely sure..." Terrence replied. "Maybe you should ask her yourself."

Lila slowly arced her head up to look at Shane, but he seemed reluctant. "Uh, maybe not... But you can't just roam the streets of Melbourne with a large wolf by your side."

Huh. – Now this is a fun turn-around. – Mainly because it was around this time last year that Matt was lecturing me about roaming around the hotel stuck as a large black cat.

Still, we're determined to get Lila back to her happy self, so Terrence patted Shane on the shoulder while leading Lila to the door. "We'll be fine. If anyone asks, I'll say she's a cross-breed."

Shane wanted to argue some more but Katie pulled him aside to "Talk" as we left the hotel.

Yep. – Trying not to laugh right now. – That was just priceless to see.

We took a stroll through the Carlton gardens, and it looked like Lila was actually enjoying it a little. And yes, we did get stopped by a few of the locals, so we told them she was a rare cross-breed. Lila was even happy enough to play along when they asked if they could pat her. – And that was cute. – But there were a few people who weren't so keen on the large wolf-dog walking next to us.

When we got to the grassy fields, we sat down, enjoying the sun as Lila rested between us. She was marvelling at the spring scenery when suddenly she began acting really strange. – And that is a very bad sign. – She was growling and shaking her head as if she were scared.

"Lila... Lila, what's wrong?" I asked, trying to calm her down.

I placed my hand on her head to communicate through the dreamland, but I pulled away in fear – receiving a vision of Lila clawing at her skin, screaming in pain.

Oh, Crapitty Crap. – This is bad.

"Lila... Lila, listen to me! You need to change back, now... Come on, Lila, I need you to do this for me." I begged her, getting down to her level to look at her. Terrence kept asking me to tell him what was wrong, but I had to focus, and I pleaded, feeling so nervous. "Lila, please, do this for me."

She stopped shaking her head and looked into my eyes, and I could feel all of her pain. Then at full-speed, she took off out of the garden, and we took off after her.

Terrence followed me through the streets as I tried to track her. But she's a hell of a lot faster in her wolf form, and I lost her just outside Footscray.

In anger, I stopped in the empty car park and growled with so much frustration. "Damn it, I lost her!!!"

"What? How could you lose her? What the hell happened back there?" Terrence snapped.

"She's phasing," I grunted, and he just looked at me dumbfounded, needing me to explain. "The longer she stays an animal, the harder it gets for her to change back to her human form... It's how the nymphs were first created. The guardians bonded with their element and stayed bonded until the two became one."

"What! Why wouldn't you tell me that sooner?" Terrence yelled, starting to freak out and panic.

While thinking of what we should do, I griped back as I paced, "I didn't tell you because you never asked. And I thought she had more time. But it's hard to tell with her because she's a hybrid. Things affect her differently, remember... And we seem to be learning that the hard way."

He asked me how much time we had, and I really didn't want to tell him, but I knew I had to. "Based on her current phasing stage... about 12 hours... give or take a little."

Completely annoyed at me, Terrence threw his hands up in frustration and grumbled while he thought, "Alright, we need a plan... What do you need me to do?"

I felt a wave of dread, knowing that I've failed Lila yet again. But I'm not giving up on her and we're going to find her. So I turned to Terrence and ordered, "We need everyone out looking for her. Call Adela. Tell her to split the team into groups and search the city. I need you to take the lead to coordinate with them while I try and track her."

I then started running, removing my clothes as I morphed into my grey wolf form, so I could run and track her faster.

Journal entry insert by General Richard Willows

Apparently, my wonderful Pumpkin has decided to pay her dear old dad a visit in prison today. Or at least that was what I'm led to believe. The last person that paid me a visit was that idiot Detective Nell to tell me that my wife was dead, all because Lila didn't have the stomach to face me after she let her mother die, being too busy dealing with that Eden family mess instead of actually taking care of her.

If I wasn't in prison right now, I would have been able to protect Hanna. I always made sure someone was watching her, especially during times of war. And the only reason I'm in prison right now is because I pleaded guilty to avoid it going to trial and drawing unnecessary attention to The Board or their activities. So I am not happy with my Pumpkin at the moment. – She's failed in her duties.

When they escorted me to the visiting room, I originally thought I was sent to the wrong area because my Pumpkin isn't here. Instead it was some nervous woman in her early twenties. She looked like she had just come out of class with her glasses and a messy ponytail. At least she had the decency to wear a business suit, but she miserably failed in the t-shirt department. The smurfs should have never gained traction again. – Little blue things, it's despicable.

I tried to alert the guards, saying that I was in the wrong room, but the woman quickly introduced herself and told me that they made no mistake.

"Hmmm. You told the guards you were Ms Winters... Well, aren't you a clever little one?"

She didn't take kindly to being called a little one, and said smugly, "Would you have agreed to see me if I didn't?"

Remaining quiet, I made my way back to alert the guards, but she caught my attention when she asked, "I want to know more about your daughter... and her abilities?"

I played the innocent card as she showed a video from her computer tablet of my Pumpkin disarming two police officers and emptying their weapons with no remorse, after first apprehending who I think is one of my Fire guardians.

I admit, I might be a little proud of Pumpkin and I grinned a little. But I certainly wasn't going to give this woman anything.

"Oh, and let's not forget about her friends," she added, showing me a video of Alex and Terrence strolling the parks of Melbourne with a white wolf by their side.

Hmm? – Maybe Lila isn't handling Hanna's death so well after all.

"Who has a wolf for a pet?" The woman snickered, pulling out a little recording device before ever so confidently starting her questions. "Tell me about your daughter. Where did she get these abilities? Is she a science experiment? An alien? A mutant?"

Oh, what a silly girl. She thinks I'm going to crack after a few pretty pictures. I tittered under my breath because I knew exactly who could fix this mess. But I also wanted to delay the silly girl from doing anything stupid with this theory of hers, so I gave just a hint of a lead.

"I don't know... Maybe you should ask her father."

She shook her head confused as the guards came in to escort me back. "But you're her father."

I looked back at her from the hallway, grinning. "Only on paper."

Journal entry continued by Terrence Connors

Yeah well, this day is totally screwed. — We've had the entire team out looking for Lila all day with no success. It's now nearly sundown and I'm due to make a delivery to the 'other' team. So I raced over there, hoping my real team wouldn't figure out that I was gone.

Damn. — This is confusing.

Billy and Stephen had successfully managed to convince the targets from this morning's raid — Cole, Jarred, Kim, and Tania to join their cause, and were helping the team unload some newly acquired weapons and explosives into the old warehouse. And no, I don't know where they got them from, but I also don't want to know.

Stephen wasn't happy that I arrived late with the next batch of cures. But I wasn't interested. I just huffed out, "I can't stay, I've got an emergency at home."

Billy guessed that I was freaked and knew it had something to do with Lila. — I've been evasive with him about Lila since I agreed to do this stupid team up weeks ago. And I'm always reluctant to tell him anything when he asks, insisting that if he cared enough about Lila that he would go and visit her himself. — I did notice a few missed phone calls on Lila's phone from him the week after the funeral. But Lila can't answer the phone as a wolf, and I didn't know if she wanted me or Alex talking to him.

However, Lila and him are a... whatever it is they have going, and he should know what's happening. So I sighed before quietly whispering, "She morphed into a wolf the day after the funeral. But now she's missing and she's starting to phase."

He knew exactly what I was talking about. But the others didn't seem to care. They just stood in the background eavesdropping as Billy worriedly questioned, "How long does she have?"

I glanced back at the disappearing sunset and looked at my watch, answering with so much fear in me, "About 2 hours."

Without any hesitation, Billy looked back at his group to state, "Count me out on this round too." Then he followed me, wanting to help. And I wasn't going to argue because we needed all the help we could get right now.

"Seriously!" Stephen cracked in a temper. "What is it about this chick? Why is it whenever she's in trouble, you guys just drop everything and go running after her? I mean, she can't possibly be that good in the sack."

WHAT DID HE JUST SAY!!! — That's it, I'm gonna kill him.

Billy looked like he was about to sock him one as well as he stormed back to Stephen and seized him by the shirt, seething. "Lila is the only reason you're standing here today and not stuck in that Canadian training camp as some mindless drone. She deserves way more than just our help... especially from you!"

Surprisingly, Stephen didn't react to being held almost off the ground, but he did briefly glance at me, noticing that I was just as angry at his words with a clenched fist and a scowl. He then stared back at Billy and rolled his eyes.

"Alright... she's your girlfriend. Go find her."

With that Billy let him go, storming back towards me to follow me at full-speed. I told him to search the blocks around his apartment, and anywhere they may gone together, and then he took off and said that he'll call if he finds her.

Huh. — Maybe he does love her.

Journal entry insert by William Knight

Something was very wrong today. I could tell by the tone in Tyme's voice when he left this morning. But he wouldn't tell me where he was going or why. And now I haven't seen any of the guardians all day, causing me to lose my mind because all I want to do is help and be useful.

I came to Melbourne to find Lila and take her away from this place. But I've come to realise that this is her home and her family. Even Tyme has found a home here. So I want to make sure they're happy and safe in this home. But I have yet to have any luck in that area, knowing that Lila is still grieving the loss of the only mother she ever knew.

As I wandered the halls of the hotel, I bumped into Katie's mother – Jennifer, who had returned from New York today and was also searching the hotel for anyone she knew. I told her she could wait up in my apartment, and she followed me back. But for some reason when I returned, the apartment phone was ringing, which is odd because we never get calls from that phone. Tyme always uses his mobile.

I answered it, and instantly the hairs on my arm stiffened. It was Richard and all he said was, "Your daughter's in danger."

Journal entry continued by Terrence Connors

We've hit a dead-end and we're getting dangerously close to time's up with less than 20 minutes, give or take a little according to Alex. I know I'm panicking. And my hands are wrapped so tightly around the backpack that has Lila's and now Alex's clothes in it. But I'm not giving up. — I refuse to give up on her.

After another search of the city and surrounding suburbs, and any place I knew Lila would have gone, Alex and I planned to meet back at the Footscray parking lot. I held my phone tightly in my hand, reading the text messages as each team reported back their lack of success. Not even Billy had success. But I've got one last lead we haven't tried yet, Lila's friend George. So I made the call while Alex tried very hard not to freak out as a giant grey wolf.

"Terrence, what can I do for you?" George answered. — And damn it. — George sounds happy.

I hesitated just a little but I had to ask, "Hi... have you guys gotten any reports of a large white wolf walking around Melbourne... or anywhere?"

"No... Why would we have a wolf in Melbourne?" he asked worriedly.

Alex stopped pacing and started growling at me as if he were trying to say something, and I think he forgets that I don't speak wolf. And I don't think bonding with him is going to work like it does with Lila and me when she's gone all wolfy. — Plus, I think holding hands and bonding with him is just weird.

Either way, I had to tell George something. "Look, long story short, after Lila's mother died, Lila turned into a wolf and she's kind of stuck that way."

Yeah. — That was a weird explanation to say to a police officer.

George went silent, and the suspense was killing me until he eventually huffed, "Of all the people I know, I was not expecting her to have an identity crisis."

I kind of needed him to elaborate on that, so he talked in simple terms for me. "When someone loses a loved one unexpectedly, they go through a stage of 'what ifs' during the grieving process. Lila's blaming herself for her mother's death. So if she's disappeared, she's probably gone back to the place where everything started to go wrong. You need to pinpoint the exact moment when Lila's world changed, and that's where she'll be... Has Lila witnessed any other deaths that she blames herself for or has she killed anyone... unintentionally... Hello?"

Yeah, I kind of definitely hung up on him. But he was very helpful, and I looked at Alex and took a deep breath, stating, "I know where she is." Then I took off with Alex right beside me.

We ran back to where it all went wrong. Where all of the truths began to unravel. — The National Park, where Lila was collected and presumed dead by the world. Sure enough, she was there, sitting at the edge of the lake with her soft white fur illuminated by the moonlight.

I slowly crouched down next to her, reaching down to hold her paw, and my eyes glowed green as I looked at hers and waited for her to complete the bond.

"Lila, please," I begged as her dark eyes looked into mine. "Lila, Sweetie, it's time to come home."

Her eyes began to glow that beautiful green so she could communicate with me, and her voice sounded amazing, even if it was only in my mind when she thought, "Why? So more people can die."

"No." I shook my head. "Lila, what happened to your mother was not your fault."

With an aching heart, she whimpered, staring into the lake. "No, Terry, it is my fault. Everyone I know either wants to hurt me or dies because of me. You should go... Get as far away from me as you can... You know it's safer that way."

Holding her paw tighter, I leaned closer to her and insisted, "I'm not going anywhere... ever. Lila, I will never hurt you, and I will never leave you... I promise. I care about you far too much to ever let you go."

I heard Alex huff in the background still as a wolf, and I'm assuming it's because he can hear and talk to her in his form as well. But whatever he said helped because she slowly began to morph, and I was finally able to hold her perfectly shaped human hand again, with her soft sun-tanned skin and gorgeous wavy blond hair making her look perfect.

"Now there's the Lila we know and love," I whispered with a relieving smile.

Her beautiful blue eyes peered up at me as she asked nervously, "You love me?"

She smiled, biting her bottom lip as I covered her with my jacket and pulled her in for a hug, very happy to say, "Every day."

Alex cleared his throat, now back in his original form, standing behind a tree to hide his... stuff. And as I rummaged through the back-pack, I chuckled then threw him back his clothes adding, "And so does Alex."

From the bag, I also handed Lila her gym shorts and a singlet top, and then turned around so she could get dressed as well. But from across the lake, I noticed Billy watching us, and he looked sad as I nodded to him to say 'thanks' before he disappeared.

Once everyone was dressed again, we took the scenic route around the park while I made the many phone calls to the team to tell them the good news, since I was the only one who brought a phone. My last phone call was to Jess and then I was done. I then looked back at Lila to see her lips peeked at one side. — I think she's trying not to smile.

"You really had the whole gang out looking for me?" she asked in disbelief.

Alex sheepishly coiled. "Are we in trouble if we say yes?"

She giggled under her breath, shaking her head. "No... I'm just glad that you guys found me."

She held onto both our hands as we continued to walk along the lake, enjoying the surreal peace of it all. But when Lila took a deep breath out, commenting on how hot it was, Alex couldn't help but laugh.

"Um, no... that would be your body's temperature spiking due to the change in species."

Her nose crinkled as she cheekily replied, "Oh, then you won't mind if I do this." Then she jumped backwards into the lake, pulling us along with her. And at the same time one of the nearby trees snatched the backpack from me before I fell.

Damn. — This girl is quick.

As her head broke above water, Lila giggled at us while wading around in the lake enjoying it as it cooled her skin, and she had the biggest, cheekiest smile on her.
"Hmm... I feel much better now." She grinned, biting her bottom lip and swimming toward the centre of the lake. And I'm not going to argue with a late-night swim, especially if it makes her happy.

Journal entry insert by William Knight

After a quick visit to a certain place. – Involving a small favour. It turns out the woman who visited Richard was a journalist. And I may have called in a few more favours to find out exactly where she was to pay her a little visit.

I found her at her office, working late, researching my daughter. She had even managed to track down two amateur videos from the internet of Lila jumping over a side railing in a shopping centre.

Gosh, my little girl is fearless. – But she still needs protection.

I stood at the side of the cubical and grinned when the reporter jumped in fright. – It means I've still got it. "My apologies, I didn't mean to startle you... I heard you were looking for me."

She fearfully pushed away in her office chair while staring at me. "Okay... and who are you?"

"I'm Lila's father," I replied. I also chuckled to try and lighten the mood.

She then spoke as if my answer was so obvious to her. "Right, of course... um... but why are you here?"

I took a long breath, taking a moment to rethink my next actions, but I know what I have to do. So I very seriously stated, "I'm here to protect my daughter."

With those words the reporter tried to run until I caught her and injected her with a syringe, gently placing her back in her office chair as her body relaxed. She began to feel dizzy, asking me what I did to her. And I freaked her out a little as my eyes glowed a hint of green to speed up the tonics effect, and then explained, "That was a little drug called Neuritamine... Now, I'm going to ask you a few questions and you're going to answer with the truth... Have you told anyone else about Lila and her friends?"

She shook her head and I continued, "Good, now I want you to delete all of the photos and recordings you have on Lila Winters, and any other information you've collected on her and her friends."

With reluctance, she nodded, moving back to her computer. But she hesitated, so my eyes glowed stronger, forcing her to begrudgingly delete everything she had – from her computer, phone, and iPad.

I then held a picture of Lila up in front of her and demanded she forget everything she knows about the woman in the picture. Again, she nodded her head, and as she did, I held a white lily on her forehead. Then when it withered, she fell asleep on her desk.

Now with my baby girl safe again, I took off at super-speed. But remembered to turn back on the building security cameras before I left.

Journal entry insert by Billy Jonas

Lila's been found. But to be honest, I still can't stand the reason why she went missing and started to phase in the first place. I know Hanna Willows wasn't her real mother, but to Lila, she was the only family she had growing up.

From the lake, I ran at super-speed back to the warehouse to see if I could make it in time for the next mission. But when I got there, the entire warehouse was on fire. I called out to anyone to see if they were trapped inside, but I got no response.

What I did find was Stephen's dead body just outside the warehouse loading door, clutching a group photo of Lila and her team. Written on the back of the photo was a message in pen saying, "Hit her where it hurts most." And another message below it, but burned onto it, saying, "Thanks for the help."

What? – No. – Please tell me, Stephen had nothing to do with Hanna's death. – He promised me, Lila wouldn't get hurt.

Struggling to breathe, I thought back to the morning after my birthday when Lila had left my apartment, and I went to drop the cures off at the warehouse. Stephen was talking to one of the new recruits, handing him one of the guns we had acquired from the last Board raid, saying, "Pick one, I don't care who."

I didn't think much of it. I was actually more focused on controlling my anger when he didn't go for the deal that Lila and I had agreed to. Instead sending Peter to do the negotiating with her, insisting that he had to make nice with Lila. – Then after that meet at the shopping centre went terribly, Stephen found me moping in my apartment because Lila had a date.

In the attempts to console me, Stephen convinced me to follow her and make sure she stayed safe. – He even suggested that I catch up with Lila after the date and ask her how it went, maybe even invite her back to my place and show how much I really do care for her.

Oh darn. – He wanted me to keep her away from the hotel. – He ordered the hit on the Eden's. – He wanted Lila to be distracted. To be too busy to take Hanna's call. – I watched Lila ignore so many calls that day, even mine. But the other phone calls, they were from her mother.

Damn it!!! – Stephen really did help with Hanna's death.

The rage burned inside of me as I glared at Stephen's dead body, and the photo burnt up in my hand. I then looked back at the flames in the warehouse and screamed. As I did, the flames grew higher, forming a glorious fire ball above me, drawing all of the fire's flames into it.

It grew higher and higher until I stopped screaming. And when I finally breathed, the giant fireball exploded into a ring of flames that spread across the night sky, over the city as it travelled. – And now, with nowhere left to go, I took off again.

CHAPTER 23

Wolf Girl

Journal entry by Lila Winters

Okay, so I think I'm liking being me more than a wolf. – And I mean the normal me with no white hair or dark wolf-eyes or pointy ears. – Just normal me. – And I'm absolutely loving mucking around in the lake with Alex and Terrence.

The sun had set hours ago, and it was a little chilly in the water, but I wasn't really focused on that. I was focused on the smiles on Alex and Terrence's faces as we splashed around and just had fun.

As we waded in the water, I got lost in wonder, staring up at the moon and its vibrancy as the reflection shimmered off the lake. Then I felt Alex's hand brush across mine as he joked, "Go on... howl."

"What?" I giggled in slight disbelief. But I think he's being serious.

"I'll do it if you do it," he dared, cheekily staring at me.

My lips peaked to one side, eagerly wanting to take him up on the dare, and I peered across to Terrence to see him waiting for me to howl as he waded in the water next to me.

"Alright, we'll all do it." I grinned then waited for both of them to nod before my eyes glowed a dark gold, and I let out a loud howl to the moon.

It sounded amazing as Alex and Terrence joined in the howl. It felt like I was letting go of so much built-up emotions and sending it away to the moon.

It felt incredible. – And perfect.

Suddenly, a ring of fire filled the night sky, and I was instantly under the protective arms of both Alex and Terrence as they huddled me between them. Their bodies pressed against mine as we waited for the flames to disappear, and once it had, I peeked over their shoulders and gasped, "What was that?"

"I don't know," Terrence replied, sounding extremely worried. "But I don't think we should stick around to find out."

Agreeing with his thoughts, we all made our way back out of the lake, and stood on the shore, ringing out the water from our clothes. But then my stomach sounded like a wolf's as it growled and grumbled, causing Alex to chuckle.

"Is our wolf girl finally hungry?"

I bit my bottom lip and smiled, remembering how patient both of them were with me, trying to get me to eat my favourite foods for the last month. Then I eyed Terrence as he quickly dug through the back-pack still hanging on the tree, pulling out a bag of my favourite lolly snakes and smiled as he handed them to me.

I gasped with delight looking at them and my grin got wider. "Terry, you're amazing."

"I know," he boasted, pulling the back-pack up onto his back. He then wrapped his arm around my shoulders as he tittered and said, "Just remember to give me the green ones... Come on, we need to give you something a little more substantial than yellow snakes."

Aww. – He remembered my favourite colour.

We slowly made our way back to the city at half-speed and stopped to get some proper-ish food at one of the late-night fast-food diners. But while Terrence and Alex went off to get the food, I noticed the petrol station across the road was being robbed. It was pretty late in the night, so I thought it would be okay if I ran over to help.

I stayed human and didn't use any super abilities, just my sweet arse ninja skills, and the servo attendant thanked me for my help. But when I went back over to find Alex and Terrence, they were furious at me. They stood there with their arms crossed, both fraught with worry, telling me that I shouldn't have gone off on my own.

I kind of got that they were worried about me, and I really appreciated it, so I apologised to them, and they accepted it as we finally sat down to eat. And I ate a ridiculous amount of food and was still hungry. – I guess a month of being a wolf probably does that to a girl. But Alex and Terrence didn't mind. They were just happy to see me eating and not going all wolf girl on them.

The downside is. – I think their worrying for me has gotten a little overboard.

When we got back to the hotel, Max and Chase were thrilled to see me as my normal self again and told me that I could take as long as I needed before getting back to work, which caused

Alex to insist I take more time. But I wasn't interested in more time, I knew Jennifer would need to return to New York soon, and I didn't want to sit in my room and do nothing – except think about everything I didn't want to think about. – So work it shall be.

As the weeks passed, I got back to my 4am work-outs that I very much missed, and Alex even asked to join me. I never minded it, except for the fact that I could always sense this underlying worry in him.

I restarted the mums self-defence classes with the mothers from Danny's school, and the group has actually grown since we restarted the sessions, now including at least two dozen of the mums and some dads. – So I called in Chase, Alex, and Terrence to help with the larger numbers.

I also organised a few re-con missions with the team to check out some possible targets in Perth, Adelaide, and Sydney. – But Alex and Terrence always insisted on being partnered with me. And whenever I got into a fight, there they were making sure I was "safe."

They've become so protective of me that they even tag along with me to get groceries. And I know their hearts are in the right place when they follow me around, so I never get annoyed at them. – Mainly because I really like their company. – Most times. It was more when I got into a fight or a little danger that they would really get on my nerves.

But again, they're my friends – and I love them.

CHAPTER 24

The Undeadly Birthday

Journal entry by Lila Winters

Today is my birthday, and considering my last birthday was – horribly tragic, the team has been organising a big birthday party for me. – And I'm not going to object to it. After the year we've had, the entire team of Security and Supers are willing to take just about any reason to party. So the one thing I know I can count on today is that I'm going to spend it with my friends.

When I walked back into my apartment after my work-out session, that was surprisingly Alex-less, the apartment was empty. – Maybe they were all still sleeping. – With that thought, I crept quietly into my room where I found a large gold box sitting on the bed with a green ribbon wrapped around it. I excitedly opened it to see an entirely new wardrobe of clothes for me.

Ooh. – It looks like Katie and Jess have been busy.

There was a card on the gift reading, "Take your pick but don't be quick." But when I looked through the clothes, I found a little note with Ruby's handwriting on it that said, "Pick me," attached to a stack of clothes tied together. It was a pair of jeans that had sparkling beads sewn onto them, running down the side of one pant leg in a floral-vine design, and the top was a white peasant style with off-the-shoulder sleeves and a mid-length bodice. And if that's what Ruby likes, I am going to wear it.

Once I was dressed, I platted my hair into one long braid and put on my jewellery. I never forget to wear my stone-vine bracelet now. – In order to keep Terrence from worrying about me. – Apparently, the 12 hours I went missing as a wolf was excruciatingly worrying for him. To the point where he couldn't breathe properly. So I never leave my room without it anymore.

My oak tree pendant was clipped around my neck where it always sits. But today, when I put on Hanna's ring, I had to fight back a few tears – just a little. But Hanna wouldn't want me to stay sad forever. – So let the fun begin.

I took a deep breath before I walked out of my bedroom, ready for the day, and I found that the apartment is now filled with 27 bouquets of flowers, all different types and all beautiful. I wandered down the hall into the dining room to see Matt, Danny, and Ruby all waiting for me, and on the table was an enormous stack of rainbow-coloured pancakes with all the topping favourites.

Danny and Ruby rushed to greet me, wishing me happy birthday while carrying two little presents in their hands. Ruby insisted I open her present first. – And I did, to find a gold floral-vine headband that perfectly suited the denim jeans I'm wearing. She very eagerly placed it on my head as I opened Danny's present, which were a pair of green sparkly ballet flats that he said I was supposed to wear today. So I put them on and hugged them both.

"These are beautiful. They make me look very sparkly."

"I like sparkles, Mummy..." Ruby jumped with glee, clapping. "They make you look pretty."

With a cheeky grin and an idea in mind, I leaned down to whisper, "Do you want to see more sparkles?"

Again, Ruby jumped with glee, so I stood back then thought about everyone I love and that warm fluttery feeling I get when I'm around them, instantly causing my skin to sparkle with diamonds.

"Woah" was the only word I heard from them. And I looked over to Matt who was just as impressed as he added, "We have one more present waiting for you outside."

I quickly hugged Danny and Ruby again as they inspected my sparkly skin, but when I hugged Danny, my necklace got caught on his shirt and snapped.

"Huh... I'm so sorry, Mummy," he gasped, worriedly staring at it.

I'm not worried though and I told him it didn't matter, picking it up from the ground as I went to open the door. – But I remembered to turn off my sparkles before I opened the door because I still haven't told the gang about all of my extra abilities, yet. – Except for Alex and Terrence. They know...some. – But again, not all. And Danny and Ruby already know to keep Mummy's cool super-powers a secret.

I know I'm asking a lot of my kids to keep a secret this big. – But it's safer this way. – And they know that.

Waiting outside in the hallway was the whole gang. – Alex, Terrence, Tyme, Adela, Jenny, Katie, Shane, Chase, Max, and

Jess, all holding white roses when they shouted, "Happy Birthday!"

I welcomed them in as they each handed me a rose, and as I closed the door, I looked at all the roses and smiled. "Thank-you, I take it this is the last bouquet of flowers I was missing."

Matt's jaw dropped, gasping, "Wow, I didn't think you would notice it that fast."

I couldn't help but giggle at him for again underestimating my abilities at super-speed. But I became a little more serious because there was one thing I wanted to do before we sat down for breakfast, and I grabbed Tyme's arm, pulling him closer to talk quietly to him.

"Tyme, the entire teams here... did you want to invite your dad, so he doesn't feel left out?"

"Are you serious?" he questioned with an eager grin.

I nodded but then stated, "As long as he knows to keep his distance from my kids."

With a huge smile on his face, Tyme disappeared from the apartment and reappeared with his dad, who looks like he had absolutely no warning of what Tyme was doing. And it caused me to laugh so hard as William stood in front of me, slowly realising where he was.

"Hello William." I chortled, failing to compose myself. "I'm going to assume, based on the confused look on your face, that Tyme didn't give you the heads up before he whisked you out of your apartment."

He shook his head which made me laugh even more before I turned to Tyme and pouted. "Naughty little brother... you should be nicer to your dad."

"Sorry." Tyme cheekily pouted back.

Still failing to stop my giggles, I turned back to William to explain, "I'm sure you already know this, but today's my birthday... And I thought maybe you'd want to join the team to celebrate and also try some of Matt's famous eggless pancakes... He also made the normal kind if you don't like the vegetarian."

Not surprisingly the entire room was staring and waiting for William's answer, and I still couldn't help but giggle as my little brother very quietly demanded his dad to say yes.

"I would love to," William blurted with a nervous smile. "And happy birthday."

"Thank-you." I giggled again, seeing my little brother's huge smile.

I then led them both to the table, quietly reminding my brother of the rules of his dad being here. And again — not surprisingly, William accepted my terms before we sat down to eat the giant stacks of rainbow pancakes.

By the time we had finished the stacks of pancakes, everyone was full, and Max commented, "Matt this breakfast is amazingly creative. I should tell the kitchen staff to start serving rainbow pancakes instead of the normal stack."

Adela and Jess both loved the idea, and Adela grinned. "Yeah, that's a great idea. We should start it today and run it for a month."

"That's brilliant," Jess chimed in. "And we should call it Lila's happy stack."

I peered across to Terrence and Alex, and we started to giggle. But the girls were serious. They even asked Ruby what she thought of the idea, and of course, she liked it. And Max was already in an agreeable mood, so he just sat back in his chair with a smile and said, "Make it so."

Now with great excitement in them, Adela and Jess disappeared out onto the balcony to make the call. – So apparently, I'm going to have a happy stack named after me.

Hmm. – I think their getting a little too carried away with this. – But I'm glad they're happy.

While we waited for them, Shane noticed I had been holding my necklace in my hand this whole time and asked, tapping on my knuckles. "What happened to your necklace?"

I held it up to explain, "The chain broke... I guess it got a little worn out."

"A little worn out..." Katie huffed, staring at it. "That's like your favourite necklace. I don't think I've ever seen you without it."

I bit my bottom lip as I glanced over at Terrence to see him struggling to hide a smile, and Max leaned over to look at it and sighed. "Oh... Well, that's not good at all. If you want, I can have a new chain sent up from the jewellers for you."

I shook my head and declined, "That's okay, I'll pick one up later."

He accepted that then stood up, grabbing an envelope and an old set of keys from the coffee table, handing them to me as he smiled. "Well then, I suppose it's present time."

Curiously, I held the keys in my hand and cautiously opened the envelope to see a photo of an old mansion surrounded by a huge rundown garden estate filled with forest trees. I then looked back at the keys and asked, "Max, are these the keys to that house?"

He nodded as he proudly stated, "And it's all yours now... I noticed my rooftop garden was getting a little too small for you. It's a large estate and it's in dire need of a bit of TLC, but I thought that would be right up your alley... It also makes a very good home away from home if ever it's needed."

I stood up to hug and thank him when Jess and Adela came in, asking if I liked the gift, and they squealed while excitedly hugging me as well. But then they got all serious, telling Max that there were dramas brewing for the party tonight that needed his urgent attention. So they readied themselves to leave but not before Max turned back to me to ask if I could enjoy the day and stay out of trouble.

"I'll try," I chuckled. "But no promises."

With that, the Eden family left, along with Katie and Jennifer as their helpers. Matt also left the table to get the kids ready for school, leaving me at the table with just Shane, Tyme, William, Chase, Alex, and Terrence, all sitting in silence and staring at me.

"Is everything okay?" I asked.

They all nodded with a smile before Chase stated, "Everything's fine, I think we're all just happy."

"O... kay... why?" I questioned further, slightly suspicious.

Alex moved closer to hold my hand still smiling at me as he explained, "Because you're smiling... and you haven't stopped smiling all morning."

Oh gosh. – They've all gone sappy on me. – They're all a bunch of sappy men.

I had to laugh at them and they laughed as well. But then Terrence's mood soured when his mobile rang. "Sorry, Lila, I've got to go."

"Me too... sorry," Alex added, standing up from the table.

WHAT? – They're leaving me on my birthday?

They both kissed my cheek, wishing me happy birthday when I stood in a huff with my smile completely turned to a pout. "Wait, where are you going?"

"I need to run some errands," Alex replied very cagily as he walked towards the door. And my pout grew sadder, so he walked back to explain, "Lila, I know you're confused. I do want to spend the day with you... But I really want to give you the birthday present you missed out on last year. And in order to do that, I need to go get it."

Confused at his words, Shane stupidly asked, "Why didn't she get it last year?"

"Because I was dead," I growled as my hair turned white. Then I stormed into my room to calm down.

I heard Tyme nervously sigh, "Ooh, I think she's mad at you, Alex."

"Nope," Terrence chimed in. "For that she's mad at me. It's my fault she missed her birthday last year."

"And that's a sore subject for all of us," Chase added.

Alex took a second, and frustratingly suggested, "Just give her some time to cool off."

Then they all left and now I'm alone for my birthday.

Journal entry insert by Alex Woods

Yep. – That was not the best ending to Lila's birthday breakfast. But we all knew she might have been a little emotional. I just can't believe it was me and Terrence who made her sad. I mean, she was so happy until we told her we needed to go. – Hopefully she'll cheer-up when I finally get to give her the present I made her.

Terrence and I agreed to head out as a team for safety, but Terrence kept getting these random phone calls that I could tell he was screening and ignoring.

"So, who's been calling you?" I asked as we continued our walk through the park of Carlton gardens, looking for a particular tree that I had hidden Lila's present in.

He shrugged it off, saying, "No one important."

"Terrence don't make me hurt you," I annoyingly grunted.

"It's my brother," he huffed and explained. "He threatened to hurt Lila again if I don't renew my relationship with my mother."

"He's still harking on about your mother. What... is she dying or something?"

"Yeah, she is," he answered. – Which I was not expecting, and kind of seemed unusually shocked at that fact as he continued. "My mother suffers from an illness called Alzheimer's... I had invented a tonic that slows the disease, and it was working for her... Unfortunately, you need to take the tonic on a regular basis in order for it to work."

Then with realisation, I added, "And since you've been with us..."

"She ran out of the tonics a few months ago. And now Keith's desperate," he explained.

I finally found the tree I was looking for, and as I climbed, we continued the conversation as I asked, "So what are you going to do?"

"Nothing."

"What about your brother?"

"What about him?"

"You know he's not going to stop?"

Terrence shrugged his shoulders, getting irritated. "I'm not going to help him... not after what he's done to Lila."

I climbed back down the tree, putting the present in my pocket as we walked back, and questioned, "Your brother's angry, right? But who's he angry at?"

"Me, I guess." He shrugged again still quite irritated.

But I shook my head. "Think about it, Terrence, all of his attacks have been targeted towards Lila. He probably thinks Lila's the one who lured you away... And in a way, she did."

Terrence let out a great sigh of frustration and looked like he had the weight of Lila's pain on his shoulders, and grumbled while holding his head in his hands. "Then what do you think I should do?"

I stopped walking and took a few moments to think, coming up with an idea. "We need to give him another target to hate... Come on, we need to pay a visit to the Willows farmhouse, and then we're going to make a house call."

CHAPTER 25

When Trouble Follows You

Journal entry by Lila Winters

When Matt found out that I was left on my own for my birthday, he offered to spend the day with me and called in sick to the university. – Such a rebel that man.

The first thing on our agenda was to drop Ruby off at her kindergarten. Then we took Danny to school. But on the way back to the car, Matt noticed that I looked sad, and I kept fiddling with the ruby ring on my hand. He asked what was wrong, and he knows me way too well for me to lie and tell him it was nothing, so I caved.

"I can't stop thinking about Hanna... This time last year she was mourning my death. Now it's the other way around."

Matt stopped to dig out his keys from his pocket, explaining, "I'm pretty sure that's the way it's supposed to be... A parent should never have to bury their child, no matter how old they are." He looked at me again and sighed. "But that's not why you're really sad, is it?"

Aw Frac. – He does know me too well.

Before I could respond, Carol Grey called to me while running into the car park. She looked a little shaky, running in heels, so Matt and I made our way back towards her to meet her halfway. – Because running in heels is never a good idea.

"Good morning, Mrs Grey," I said while she caught her breath.

"Good morning," she wheezed. "I just wanted… to wish you… a happy birthday."

Err? – Okay.

"Thank you," I replied while trying not to sound awkward or suspicious of her random rush to say something that could have been done via a text or phone call. – I mean seriously, she ran in heels just to wish me happy birthday.

I waited patiently for her to finally regain her composure before she added, "No… it's me who wants to thank you. Those self-defence classes you've been giving us have made me and the other parent's a lot more confident… And now we feel like we're able to protect ourselves and our families."

"Well, I'm glad I can help." I smiled, but I also watched as her face turned a little sour, and I could sense the gloom in her. "But somethings wrong, isn't it?"

"Is it really that obvious," she said while puffing.

To me, yeah. – But she doesn't know that. So I asked again, "What's wrong?"

Very reluctantly, she answered, "It's one of the mums… Do you remember Anita? We haven't heard from her in a few weeks, and we're getting a little worried. We sent the police round to her house, but they said everything was fine."

"But you don't believe them, do you?" I questioned.

She said nothing, but her emotions of fear said everything for me.

"Give me her address, Matt and I will go check on her."

"What? No, Lila... it's your birthday. I can't ask you to do that."

I moved closer to her, clearing my throat. "Carol, you didn't ask... Now please, give me her address."

Carol knew not to argue with me, so she conceded in giving me the address, and Matt was kind enough to agree to my little detour. He parked opposite Anita's house but looked worried.

"Are you sure you want to do this?"

I stared at the house contemplating my options and considering worst-case scenarios as I explained, "The first time I met Anita, she had a bruise on the back of her neck... Shane thought she might have been being abused, and I agreed with him. Hence the self-defence classes... But she hasn't been to the last two sessions."

"Then let the cops deal with it," he pleaded, knowing what the worst-case scenario might be.

I looked at him from the corner of my eye and answered, "We did. George said the cops can't do anything unless the victims press charges or they have sufficient evidence. But no one's actually seen the abuse and my guess is she's too scared to ask for help."

Matt looked back at the house and grunted, not entirely sold on the idea. "So what are you planning to do?"

With an innocent glimmer in my eye, I replied, "I'm just going to check on her and maybe give her a little confidence boost... Trust me."

I then got out of the car but turned back before I closed the door, and added, "But just in case, call the cops ... And maybe an ambulance."

Now that rule 5 was in play, I walked toward the house, strongly hoping not to use plan B or C.

Journal entry insert by Matt Winters

This is the first day Lila and I have spent together on our own in a long time, but our little house call to Anita's place does have me on edge. I called the police as Lila requested and asked if they would be willing to pop around and do a welfare check on Anita. But just as we were about to finish the phone call, I heard a gunshot from the house.

In a panic, I raced into the house still on the phone to the police, telling them to hurry, but also spotted Carol Grey race out of her car towards the house as well. — So I'm really hoping Lila hasn't used anything unexplainable at this point.

I burst through the front door to find Lila busy pinning Anita's husband to the floor of the loungeroom, pressing her foot down on the hand he was holding the gun with. All the while Anita hid in the corner of the room with a gunshot wound on her arm and covered in a lot of bruises.

Holy... that looks bad.

The police sirens were getting closer, and I worriedly asked Lila if she was okay.

"I'm fine," she answered, still concentrating on the husband. "Just got hit by an idiot who tried to shoot his own wife because she wanted to join us for lunch."

"That's crazy!" the husband rebuked. "She doesn't know what she's talking about!"

Carol kneeled down to check on Anita then snapped back, "Oh right, so how do you want to explain your wife's bleeding arm and the gun in your hand?"

The next thing I saw was the police running in to analyse the situation as the husband shouted while attempting to break free of Lila's hold. "You were trying to take her away from me... I was protecting her"

It caused Lila's grip on him to tighten as she growled, "Yeah, I invited my friend out for coffee on my birthday... Or is it a crime for your wife to leave the house now?"

She held him down and waited for the police officer to remove the gun from the man's hand before letting the other officer arrest him. And as the man was pulled to his feet and placed in police restraints, he barked back at Lila, "You'll regret this! Anita loves me. She needs me. She won't last a week without me."

"And that's where you're wrong..." Lila interrupted, getting intimidatingly close to him to calmly state, "Your wife is a lot stronger than you ever give her credit for. The fact that she put up with your bullshit for so long just proves it... And she may have loved you once, but that was before you turned into a monster."

Angered by her words, Anita's husband had to be dragged by the police out of the house towards the police car as Lila focused her attention back to Anita, who was still cowering in the corner.

Two paramedics had arrived, and Carol stepped away, asking them to give Lila a minute to coax Anita out of the corner as she kneeled down next to her. But when I noticed Lila's eyes tinged with a faint gold colour, I stepped forward to block the paramedics and Carol's view while she talked to Anita.

"It's okay, Anita. He's not going to hurt you anymore... There are people here who are going to help you."

"How... how did you do that thing?" Anita asked still trembling in fear.

Lila leaned in, holding out her hand. "It's like I said, Anita, your husband's no match for me... or you. Just remember that you always have the right to say no, and there will always be someone here to support you. All you have to do is ask... Now, I would really like it if you came out of the corner, so these paramedics can have a look at you. Can you do that for me, Anita?"

It took more of Lila's concentration as her eyes glowed a little brighter, but very slowly, Anita lifted her head to nod to her. "Okay," she rasped as she timidly grabbed Lila's hand, standing up from the corner before making her way over to see the paramedics.

When Lila let go of Anita's hand, she turned back to look at me, and the colour of her eyes returned to normal. But there was one thing that didn't look normal. Lila now has a very noticeable bruise on her cheekbone and a small cut above her eye.

"Lila, your face," I gasped, knowing that I was probably a dead man when Alex sees this. — I wonder if this was how he felt when Lila and I were married, and she ended up hurt.

The fascinating part is that Lila just shook it off. "It's nothing. It'll heal... I'll need to give a quick statement to the police but then we can go."

Um, okay. — She seems to be taking this one pretty well.

After we had finished at Anita's place, we were off again. However, the paramedics were a bit upset that Lila only accepted a steri-strip for the cut above her eye, instead of actually going to the hospital. But she insisted on not going and said, "Don't argue with me. It's my birthday."

So off we went to our next stop, walking down Burke Street mall, looking at all the jewellery stores. There was a long silence for a while until I spoke, "You know Alex is going to hurt me very badly when he sees that bruise."

"No, he won't." Lila smiled but kept walking. "He's just going to huff and puff and act like a silly old ogre."

I chortled. "I think you might be getting your fairy tales confused."

She then looked back at me with a giggle. "I know but it hurts to think... Besides you shouldn't argue with the birthday girl... I told you that."

I put my hands up as a sign of surrender as we continued to walk. "Then an ogre he is... But you know he loves you."

"Does he?" She sighed in deep contemplation. "A man that truly loves me would trust me unconditionally and not treat me like a fragile little doll every time I leave the hotel."

Ah. – So that's why she's been quiet.

As we were talking, the jewellery store we were about to go into was being robbed. Or had been robbed. The alarm in the store started to blare and customers started running out of the store. But when two business men ran past us, Lila grabbed them by the backs of their shirt collars, yanking them backwards and pulling them down to the ground. As the men fell, Lila swerved between them, pulling the guns that they had hidden in the belts of their pants, and aimed them at the men.

"Move and I will shoot," she forcefully demanded. "And yes, I know only one of these is actually loaded. But I can still do a lot of damage with an empty one."

The two men looked up at her and took a second to think before conceding, and the crowd around us started to take video of the incident. A few seconds later, the store security guard had caught up to us, and searched the pockets of the jackets the men were wearing to find the small bags of jewellery that they had stolen. When the crowd realised what had happened they started to applaud, just seconds before four police officers ran through the crowd to arrest the men.

Lila very happily handed the weapons to the police officer, and asked if the security guard was okay before she walked back to me to continue her little rant, saying, "Look, I know Alex means well, but I am anything but a fragile doll."

Well, she definitely has a point there. — She barely broke a sweat taking on those two men.

Unfortunately, one of the police officers recognised Lila, and asked, "Hey, weren't you guys just at a domestic dispute out in Melbourne south."

Whoops.

"Are we in trouble if we say yes?" Lila asked with a wry grin. But the police officer didn't look like he was in a cooperative mood, so Lila innocently added, "Look, I didn't mean any harm here. I was going to the jewellery store to get a new necklace and they just came running out."

The officer's face puzzled as he questioned, "But how did you..."

"Army brat," she interrupted.

"Oh... Well, try not to make a habit of getting into trouble like this," the officer ordered, accepting Lila's weak explanation.

Lila politely smiled then replied, "No promises officer... but I will try."

He huffed at her non-committal before adding, "Stick around, we'll need another statement from you." Then he walked into the jewellery store to talk to his partner.

Now feeling slightly thankful that we got away with it, I pulled Lila off to the side and took a huge sigh of relief. "Phew, that was close... So much for a fun birthday."

"Are you kidding?" She stared back at me with a massive smile, and her nose all crinkled up. "This day has been amazing... And the best part is we're only halfway through it."

Alrighty. – So birthday fun not ruined.

Lila sat on a nearby bench and waited for the police to be ready while I popped into one of the cafés to bring her back some lunch. And as I handed her a veggie burger, I suggested, "Maybe you should think about wearing a mask or a disguise, so you're not recognised while saving the day and all... You know, like a superhero."

She dug out her lunch from the bag, and tittered. "I would... but the best thing I can do is turn into an elf with white hair. And a cape and mask is really impractical... and stupid."

I shrugged my shoulders, taking a large mouthful from my burger and mumbled, "An elf is better than nothing."

Hmm? – She's definitely right though. – I can just imagine her doing high-kicks in a cape. – Very impractical.

Once Lila finished giving her second statement, we didn't have much time left to get a necklace chain for her because we were due to pick up the kids from school and kinder. But after the school pick up on our way back to the hotel, we paid a visit to the cemetery to leave flowers at Hanna's tombstone.

When we arrived, there was an old lady kneeling next to Hanna's grave.

"Excuse me... can I help you?" I asked.

The old lady got up on to her feet, a little shaky as she stood to face us, looking at Danny and Ruby, and then back to me to reply, "My apologies. I was simply visiting an old friend."

Lila curiously stepped forward. "Really, how did you know Hanna?"

"Oh, it's a little hard to remember these days... But don't worry, I was just leaving," the old lady answered, shaking her head a little. She started to walk away but turned back to Lila and said, "Oh, and happy birthday."

Lila thanked her then moved to stop her from leaving, grabbing her arm as she passed us. "Wait you don't have to..."

In a panic, Lila quickly pulled her hand away from the old lady and stood protectively in front of us, demanding, "Matt, stay behind me."

The old lady smirked back at Lila with an odd grin, and rasped, "Don't worry, dear, you're not on my list today." Then she disappeared from the cemetery.

I'm going to assume now that she was a guardian, so I asked, "Who was that?"

"I don't know," Lila replied with worried uncertainty. "But I just felt a whole lot of evil coming from her."

Since we had the kids with us, I tried to lighten the mood. "Well, she's gone now... So chop, chop. We still have lots to do today."

I then put on a brave face and directed the children to place the flowers on Hanna's grave all while Lila stood guard.

Journal entry continued by Lila Winters

Today is going really well, and I've been having so much fun laughing and mucking around with my family, especially on the way back to the hotel. Matt and I were chasing Danny and Ruby into the lobby of the hotel, playing tickle tag, and I was chasing Ruby which meant she was too focused on me to realise she was barrelling right into Uncle Tyme's legs.

He was also not watching where he was going, carrying a large bouquet of balloons while talking to Adela and his dad. So I moved at a slight super-speed to catch Ruby just in the nick of time, spinning her around with me and holding her in my arms as I chortled.

"Woah... sorry, Uncle Tyme."

He stopped and tried to move the balloons to actually talk to us, saying, "That's okay little Ruby... What happened to your face?"

Yeah – that last bit was directed at me as he stopped to gawk. In his shock, he accidentally let go of the helium balloons, so again I moved at a slight super-speed to catch them before they flew off. I then handed the balloons to William, seeing how Tyme was a little busy gawking at the bruised cheek and cut above my eye while waiting for me to reply.

"Nothing much, just had to run a few errands today."

His jaw dropped at that answer. "Lila... Alex and Terrence will be furious when they find out you've been running errands on your birthday."

"And you know what..." I retorted, still smiling. "I don't care. They could have prevented me from getting shot at today if they had actually wanted to spend the day with me."

As I cheekily grinned, I carried Ruby into the elevator where Matt and Danny were waiting while Tyme freaked out more. "Wait, you got shot at? Lila, that's not okay…"

Thankfully the elevator doors closed before I got my little brother lecture, and as we rode the elevator up, Danny, Ruby, and Matt burst into hysterical laughter with me.

I know my Brother can be a little over-protective sometimes. – But I still love him.

When we got up to the apartment, Danny and Matt were the first in the door and were too busy laughing with me to notice Izzy Connors – one of Terrence's sisters, hiding behind the door. She punched Matt in the face then pushed him, sending him sliding into the kitchen before she seized Danny by the collar, holding a gun against his neck, causing Ruby to rush and hide behind me.

"Move and I will shoot him!" Izzy claimed while glaring at me. – And I suspect she may have been following me today.

I stood still and took calm breaths, keeping a smile on my face as Danny looked at me. But I also took a super-speed moment to analyse the scene.

– Right now, Izzy is standing in my apartment. I sense the stress and fear in her, and can see her dishevelled and not brushed long brown hair. Her blond highlights have re-growth as well. And what she's wearing does not match the description Terrence gave me of her, now wearing tracksuit pants and an oversized jumper as opposed to the designer clothes that she apparently is never seen without. – Oh, if Terry could see her now.

But no matter what she's wearing, she seems slightly desperate and clearly wants something, and I think I know how to handle this now, so I snapped out of super-speed to talk. -

"Okay, I'm not moving," I replied then calmly addressed my daughter. "Ruby... I need you to go check if Daddy's okay. Maybe give him a hug for me."

Unfortunately, Ruby was too scared to move, but I was pretty sure Izzy wouldn't notice my eyes turn a little gold to charm Ruby. So I slowly moved my hand onto Ruby's, and spoke calmly. "Ruby, everything is okay... But Daddy might have a booboo, and I need you to check on him for me."

It took a little more of my concentration, but I got Ruby to move towards Matt in the kitchen. And Matt stayed seated on the floor at. the far end of the kitchen bench, giving Ruby a hug while I stood and waited for Izzy to do something, remembering to stay smiling.

"You're Lila Winters, right?" she asked.

I could really sense the desperation coming from her now as I confirmed, "That's right... and you're Izzy Connors."

While I spoke, I discreetly signalled Matt with my hand to brace himself and duck for cover, using my fingers as a countdown. Then at the count of one, my eyes glowed a ferocious green and all the flower bouquets scattered around the room created plumes of pollen, filling the air.

Izzy tried to cover her face from the pollen, and I used the distraction, moving at full-speed to pull Izzy out of the way for Matt to race and grab Danny before hiding back in the kitchen. Then suddenly a strong gust of wind filled the room, forcing the pollen out through our balcony door. – That is for some fraccing reason left open.

Damn it. – There better be a fraccing good reason for that.

While Izzy was trying to regain her bearings, she looked around the room to see me standing behind her, dismantling her gun. I then moved at full-speed towards her, and as she moved to defend herself, I grabbed her arms and flipped her in the air. Then while she was in mid-air, I used all the force I had to push her down into the floor, creating a small crack in the floor tiles.

She groaned as she hit the floor and I stood over her, commanding the vines in my bracelet to bind her wrists before I moved closer to her. "You know, I really don't like it when people threaten my family."

"Oh, like you threatened mine," she barked back.

I leaned down and pressed my letter opener against her neck as I explained, "I have been nothing but patient with your family, even after everything the Connors have done to me. And it's only because of the love I hold for your brother, Terrence, that you are currently still able to breathe... Now, what do you want?"

She glared up at me to answer, "I want your help."

Well no fraccing der.

"Just a helpful tip..." I leaned closer to state, "Next time, you should try asking for help without the gun. It might be less painful for you."

I pulled away and loosened the vines binding Izzy's hands as I nicely ordered, "Now let's try this again, shall we... Hello, my name is Lila Winters, and welcome to my home." Then while calmly smiling at her, I helped her to stand before I asked, "What can I do for you, Ms Connors?"

She stared at me for a few seconds, trying to figure out why I was being so calm before asking if I could help save her mother from her Alzheimer's disease. – She even said please.

"Alright," I answered.

To which both Matt and Izzy replied, "What?" in unison and slight confusion.

Urgh. – Again with the unison crap.

I held my hand up, briefly glancing at Matt with my eyes glowing gold to calm the room, yet still stayed focused on Izzy. "But first you will apologise to my son... You threatened him in the safety of his own home. So I will not help you without Danny's permission."

Slowly and cautiously, I led her back to where Danny and Ruby were hiding with Matt, and watched carefully as she kneeled down to their level to speak.

"Danny... um, hi. My name is Izzy, and... I'm very sorry if I scared you or hurt you. I didn't mean to."

Danny stepped closer to Izzy, scowling at her and showing no ounce of fear when he griped, "You hurt my daddy."

"I know." Izzy nodded. "And I'm sorry. But my mother is very sick, and she'll die soon if I don't get your mummy's help."

Danny took a moment then looked back at me and asked while pointing to Izzy. "Do you know how to fix her mummy?"

Off the top of my head, I could think of a few tonics that may work, so I leaned on the kitchen bench and replied, "I know how to do a lot of things, Danny. But I won't do anything without your permission... Izzy's mum can find help from someone else."

He then glared back at Izzy and questioned her. "Do you promise not to hurt any more people?" Izzy nodded, so Danny continued, "Then yes, my mummy can help yours."

To that Izzy smiled and her body relaxed as she thanked Danny and stood up, looking back at me.

Well, Frac-damn. – I'm proud of my son.

Danny and Ruby came over to hug me, and I kneeled down to whisper, "You two were very brave, and I'm very proud of you... Look after Daddy for me, and I'll be back before the party."

I briefly looked back at Matt and winked with a smile, standing up to follow Izzy as she walked out onto the balcony and asked if I could fly.

"Only when I have to," I replied then realised why the door was open. "Right, that explains how you got in."

I turned back to Danny and Ruby, and insisted, "Danny... Ruby, don't ever do this next part without me with you... Okay? This next trick is very hard to do, and it's just for Mummy... got that?"

I waited for them to nod then asked them to close their eyes before I jumped off the balcony. And as I peered back, I saw them all watching from the balcony as Izzy flew in a vortex of wind, and I flew on a vortex of leaves over the city.

Journal entry insert by Alex Woods

It turns out the Willows farm didn't completely burn down, and luckily we managed to find some of Richard's military uniforms. So I morphed into Richard just before we strolled into the Eureka towers, in the hopes to go up to the Connors apartment.

Robert Connors met me down in the lobby, looking rather puzzled at me as he stepped out of the elevator. "Richard...? I thought you were in prison."

I struggled a little in trying to mimic Richard's behavioural pattern. - Mainly because I didn't really like the man, which meant I never paid much attention to him. And morphing into a human is actually pretty hard to master. So all I could think to do was snicker.

"You should know better than anyone that you can't imprison a man who doesn't exist. I'm here to visit your mother. I hear she's ill, so I brought flowers... And a visitor."

I directed my gaze towards the main doors where Terrence was waiting and looking rather disgruntled. - Playing his part fabulously. - He wasn't overly convinced of this plan. Because I'm planning on using him as a Trojan horse to divert the attention away from Lila while also coaxing around for information. - And the plan is working perfectly.

With eager excitement, Robert rushed to greet Terrence with a hug. "Terrence, it's good to see you, brother."

"You too," Terrence replied, kind of returning the hug. But I think he's more shocked that he got that kind of welcome from his brother.

Huh? - Maybe it's just Keith who hates him.

Once the pleasantries were out of the way, Robert led us into the elevator and up to – not quite the penthouse apartment but pretty close to it, and the apartment took up the entire floor.

Woah.

We followed him into one of the sitting areas of the apartment, and he offered us a drink. But before we could answer, one of his sisters walked out of a bedroom, greeting us with a smile, saying, "Terrence, you're home."

However, the smile did not get returned when we both saw Lila standing behind her with a cut and bruise on her face. And I gasped in shock. "Lila."

Instantly, Terrence punched Robert in the face, knocking him to the ground as I grabbed the sister and threw her across the room. But Lila moved at full-speed to attack me.

AW CRAP! – I'M STILL RICHARD!

She twisted my arm behind my back and tripped me forward, slamming me into the ground, causing me to lose all my concentration and morph back into myself.

"Alex?" she confusedly yelped, letting me go and standing back.

In seconds, Terrence appeared in front of her to inspect her face and worriedly asked, "Lila, what are you doing here? What happened to you?"

She brushed his hands away and scowled at both of us, rushing to help Izzy to her feet, explaining, "Nothing happened to me. Your sister asked for my help... so here I am."

HAS SHE LOST HER FREAKING MIND?

Terrence was just as shocked as I was, asking, "And what, you just came here willingly?"

She stared back at us a little cagey, biting her lip. "There may have been one... or four guns involved with today's escapades... But your mother's dying. So I helped her... It's only temporary though. I will need to do more research if I'm going to cure her."

Yep. – I really don't think Terrence liked that idea, and he pulled Lila away from his sister to talk. "You're actually going to help my mother... after everything that's happened?"

She nodded her head – and I think I lost mine. "Lila, you shouldn't be here. It's way too dangerous."

"Oh, so your allowed to be here but I'm not?" She irked back at me with a snide huff.

AND DAMN-IT. – I'M SO MAD AT HER.

Suddenly, we heard a gunshot coming from the bedroom that Lila just came from, and within seconds, an old woman stormed out of the room and shot Izzy in the stomach and Robert in the leg.

"Urgh Frac... I'm so sick of guns!" Lila shouted before angrily running at full-speed to disarm the woman.

For some reason, the old woman didn't fight back. She just stepped backwards, stating, "I told you, Lila... You're not on my list today." She then jumped out the window, smashing through the glass and morphing into a huge eagle.

And just to really push our luck, Keith walked into the apartment. He eyed Robert and Izzy writhing in pain, and then spotted Terrence trying to pull Lila closer to him while standing in front of her protectively.

"Keith, it's not what you think. We were just trying to help," Terrence explained.

As expected Keith didn't listen, taking one look at the gun Lila was holding before throwing a fireball at both of them. At full-speed, Lila pulled Terrence out of the way, getting hit in the arm instead. But she ignored the pain and kept moving, grabbing both our hands before jumping out of the broken window as well. And as we fell, she created a leaf vortex and flew us back down to where her car was parked. – The one we had borrowed for the day without necessarily asking her.

Journal entry continued by Lila Winters

I cannot believe this. – It's my birthday and my two best friends that supposedly love me, left me on my own to go play dress up as my good-for-nothing fake father. And they're angry at me right now.

The nerve of them both.

We all stayed quiet as Alex drove <u>my car</u> back to the hotel after unintentionally ticking off Terrence's crazy arse brother, Keith. I wanted to walk home, seeing how I was angry at both of them, but I didn't have much of a choice because Terrence wouldn't let go of my hand, and Alex looked like he was going to pop a vein in his neck. – So I opted for silence instead.

When we got back to my apartment, I was still giving them the silent treatment as I sat on my couch, late for my own birthday party. With Terrence sitting on the coffee table in front of me, applying red gum tree-sap to the burn on my arm and the cut on my face. All the while Alex paced and grunted like a silly old ogre behind him, being useful by holding my floral headband.

As Terrence started wiping away the tree sap from my eye, I winced in a little bit of pain and kind of broke the silent standoff we were all in. Terrence spoke first but had such kindness and worry in his voice.

"So... did you want to explain the bruise?" Terrence asked, pulling off the butterfly stitch from the now scabbed-over cut on my eye.

I huffed and glared at Terrence, but the look he gave back to me was so annoyingly cute. You could just tell that deep down he was more concerned than mad.

Frac. – I hate the fact that I can't stay mad at him.

My entire body rolled with frustration, looking at his concerned blue-green eyes. Then he held my hand and pouted. "Please, Lila."

I tightened my hand around his, sensing his worry and let out a breath. "I was helping out one of the mothers from school this morning. Her husband got a little violent and tried to shoot me but shot his wife instead... ALEX, you're going to wear out the floor, and it already needs repairs."

Finally, Alex stopped pacing to snap back, "You shouldn't have been there in the first place. None of this should have happened to you." In frustration, he pointed to the arm Terrence was now bandaging and added, "Lila, you were supposed to stay out of trouble today and enjoy your birthday."

Yep – I lost it, pulling away from Terrence to yell back. "I did! I actually did enjoy my birthday... I spent the whole day helping people, and I even had fun too. But I would have had a lot more fun if either of you bothered to spend it with me... Now I don't want to know why you were at the Connors apartment tonight because I'm going to assume you had a damn good reason. But I do want to know why both of you skipped out on my birthday... All I wanted was to spend the day with my friends. And for some fraccing reason, neither of you wanted to spend it with me. So the only sucky thing about my birthday... is you two!"

Now that I got that off my chest, I sat back down on the couch, crossing my arms and tried so hard not to cry. Alex went back to being silent, and Terrence stayed sitting on the coffee table, pouting and feeling incredibly guilty.

Very slowly, Alex walked towards me and knelt down in front of me, whispering my name, all sad and pouty faced as well. I didn't look at him, I just kept angrily staring at my knees. So instead he placed a small yellow gift bag on my knees and said, "Open it."

I glowered for a second at the bag, and then opened it, pulling out a small wooden pendant carved into the shape of a large black-cat's paw print with blunted claws.

I was close to tears when Alex rested his hand on my knee, and said, "Lila, I'm sorry I wasn't there today... I made this for you last year. Only, I forgot where I hid it until this morning. That's the first animal you helped me to morph into... a large black cat. I wanted it to be a symbol of our friendship, but I also wanted to change it a little because of this year."

He then turned the pendant over for me to see the carving on the inside of the cat paw. It's of a smaller wolf's paw print with a beautiful diamond that was cut perfectly to fill the print.

Oh wow. – This looks gorgeous .

I'm trying really hard not to cry right now. But I might have let out a small sniffle as he held my hand in his and explained, "And that's your first animal, the wolf... And now it truly represents our friendship... I really am sorry about not being there today. After I finished with the present, we really should have come back to you. But I was thinking more about your safety than your happiness, and that's my bad. But—"

I interrupted his speech when I wrapped my arms around him and hugged him so tightly as I cried, "Alex, this is beautiful... and amazing...Thank you."

"Your welcome." He pulled me up onto my feet to hug me back and held me just as tight.

I stared down at Terrence to see him looking incredibly sad and playing with his fingers. So I pulled out of Alex's hug to sit on Terrence's knee, forcing his attention to me. Then I whispered, "This is the part where you hug me and make everything better again."

With a tiny hint of a smile, Terrence snaked his hands around my waist and whispered, "I'm sorry... I promise I will make this up to you."

Oh Frac.

I looked at the kitchen clock and gasped, grabbing Alex and Terrence by their arms as I pulled them with me out into the elevator to get down to the party in time. But I was a bit nervous, so just before we got to the function room doors, I stopped and asked, "Do I look okay?"

And yeah – I'm feeling incredibly nervous about the way I look. I mean, the bruised face and the bandaged arm may be a bit of a party downer for everyone.

"Well..." Alex thought aloud. "You have got a few things missing."

I silently panicked, but then he brushed the hair off my face, placing the floral headband back on my head before he stared back at Terrence with a smile. Terrence chuckled a little when he saw me biting my lip and playing with my fingers, and then he pulled out of his pocket my white oak-tree pendant, now attached to a new necklace chain. He took Alex's wooden paw charm from my hand and placed it on the necklace next to his oak-tree pendant, and then clipped the necklace back where it belongs. – Around my neck.

"Now you look perfect," he whispered.

I was over the moon to hear those words from him, and they both held their hands out toward me to escort me into the party. So now my birthday is absolutely perfect.

CHAPTER 26

The Package

Journal entry by Alex Woods

After a few weeks of recon, we decided the best target to hit was the Adelaide branch of a company called Austral Pharmatech. My group consisted of Terrence, Lila, and myself. We were waiting for mid-morning so that the headcount would be at its highest, and while we waited, we met up with Jennifer who was perched on the rooftop opposite Pharmatech, keeping a lookout and doing head checks.

I think Terrence and I had a few qualms about hitting a high-rise target in the middle of the city. Leading him to ask, "Jenny, are you sure about this company? I haven't heard of its name before."

"Positive," she replied. "Our team in New York got the information from a highly reliable source... This company has recently been sold and renamed. But the CEO and owners name never changed in the transfer... Hilary Cole."

Terrence looked at Jennifer suspiciously and doubted. "Hilary Cole? The head of The Board's pharmaceuticals division, just willingly gave you the address?"

"Actually, it was Hilary Cole's personal secretary. And it wasn't quite willingly."

With realisation, I accused Jennifer of drugging people, and to my surprise, she willingly admitted that her New York team uses a diluted dose of Neuritamine to make the targets more co-operative. But what surprised me more was Lila's reaction. It was not at all what I expected. She just continued to look out over the building, doing headcounts.

What the...?

"I've got confirmation," Lila stated. And I crept over to hide next to Lila as she explained, "So far I've counted at least 9 Water guardians in a lab on the twenty-sixth floor... But what gave them away is the number of armed guards they have on each floor. It's way too many for a company that does research."

I was still annoyed at one situation and now confused at the other, and grumbled with frustration. "I don't get it... This lab is operating in the middle of the CBD. Why hasn't the government shut it down?"

Lila looked at me and smiled at my ignorance. "Alex, it's researching pharmaceuticals. It doesn't really scream evil corporation... That, and the General always said the best way to hide a bad deed is to mask it with a good one and do it for all to see... Which is probably how The Board's managed to stay hidden for so long."

She glanced at my watch then tapped on her ear-mic, ordering the team to get into position as we started walking down the stairwell. But Lila raced ahead to catch up with Jennifer, and when we heard the heated nature in Lila's voice, Terrence and I hung back a bit.

"Jenny, I understand your determination to find these people, but the way you secured this information is unacceptable."

"We only used a small dose... it won't harm anyone," Jennifer rebuked.

"I read your report, Jenny, and I know the risks of Neuritamine," Lila sternly rebuffed. "But if we use drugs to get the information we need against the subjects will... then we're no better than The Board. From now on, any leftover Neuritamine is to be destroyed. Understood?"

Jennifer's voice became agitated, arguing, "But we can use the Neuritamine to our advantage."

"No," Lila insisted. "I will not sacrifice on our ethical standards just to gain an advantage... And if this is the method you insist on using, we will no longer help you."

Jennifer looked like she wanted to say more but stopped and stormed down the stairwell in a huff. Then Lila looked back at both Terrence and me to see us smiling at her. – And I am definitely proud of her right now.

"Thank you," I said while walking down the stairwell to greet her.

"You're welcome... Now move it. We have a job to do."

Journal entry insert by Katie Hooper

Today is my day to shine. Lila has put me in charge of Data retrieval and all the interior ops stuff that I'm supposed to do. – And I've written a step-by-step list on my hand and keep repeating it in my head, so I don't stuff it up.

My team consists of Adela, Tyme and me. And because of Tyme's time rift, we're able to walk right into the building, following a Water guardian named Kelly White. – Or at least we think she's a Water guardian.

We followed her into the elevator, and waited until she was alone to pull her into the time rift with us. But Kelly instantly flipped out and created an ice arrow in her hand, using it to attack Tyme.

He kept dodging her attacks until Adela was able to inject her with the epi-pen. Then when Kelly finally fell to the ground feeling dizzy, Tyme vented his frustration.

"Why did she have to go after me?"

Brimming with sarcasm, Adela tried to comfort him with a cute but condescending smile, "It's okay buddy... I gotchya."

She even gave him a little kiss on the cheek.

Aw that's just so cute. – I really wish they would just kiss and make up, instead of this 'just friends' stuff. – I mean they are totes made for each other.

I let out a slight giggle as I leaned down to grab Kelly's ID badge and lab coat, and then picked up the ice arrow to get a better look at it. And Adela gazed at it, so entranced at the design.

"I really need to learn how to do that," she mumbled.

But we had no time for that as the elevator doors reached the level we needed to be on. So Tyme quickly picked the unconscious Kelly up as Adela looked at me and said, "We'll be right behind you. Good Luck."

Before my eyes they all disappeared with me fading out of the time rift. Then as the elevator doors opened, I was ready to go, with my first stop being the security room.

Journal entry continued by Alex Woods

Lila's in teaching mode today, trying to coach Terrence on how to create that leaf platform thing that she so confidently uses. Our team was needing to land on the roof top from high above, so Terrence needs to carry all three of us from one high-rise building to the other. Using the low-lying rain cloud, that Adela created this morning to blanket the city as cover for us. – He essentially has to fly up over the clouds and then straight down on the Pharmatech building, but he is nervous as hell.

Lila tried to encourage him, placing her hand on his shoulder, and then smiled as we stood on the helipad of the high-rise building next door to the target. "You got this, Terry... And don't worry, if we fall, you've got about a 240-metre drop to catch us again."

Terrence glared at Lila and then stupidly looked down and trembled. "That's not funny."

It caused Lila to laugh so hard before she said, "Terry, you'll be fine. If we start to drop at all, I'll be right here next to you."

That seemed to give Terrence just that little bit more confidence. Then after a lot of deep breaths, Terrence was finally ready, and successfully created a leaf platform, carrying all three of us up above the clouds.

Lila was so excited and cheered for Terrence, and only had to step in once to save us. – And that was because we nearly ran into a flock of birds. But we landed on the Pharmatech roof all in one piece and silently celebrated before getting back to work.

We helped Lila to break the filter cages off two of the main air-conditioning vents, and then emptied out two little bamboo gift bags full of seeds into the air vent.

"How long do we need to wait?" I asked as Lila looked at my watch for a time check.

She looked back at Terrence as they both stood at individual vents on opposite sides of the rooftop, and answered, "Katie will give us a signal in 5... 4... 3... 2..."

As she finished counting, the building's fire alarms blared, and large plumes of fire and smoke burst out of the third and fourth floor. Then Lila screamed, "Now!"

With that, both Terrence and Lila's eyes glowed green, causing the seeds in the air vents to blossom and excrete clouds of a blue sweaty pollen being drawn in and dispersed through all the floors of the building.

I leaned my head over the side of the building to get a better look at the fire billowing out of the lower floors, and commented, "That's one hell of a signal."

To make our escape, we evacuated down the emergency exits, along with all the staff of the Pharmatech building, and noticed the pollen was working. People were becoming dizzy and confused, so we helped them and reminded others to keep evacuating the building.

Our team quickly met up at the evacuation point with the others, where we could keep an eye on Chase, Jess, and their team as they did their standard announcement to the group offering the usual 'come with us if you want your freedom' speech, before they analyse and debrief with the cured guardians.

While Jess was talking, surrounded by a large group of our security team, Tyme pulled us into the rift to disappear. But they had a slight problem. – Part of their mission task was to seize as many of the weapons from the Pharmatech guards as they can, and knock out anyone causing a problem to avoid a gunfight and to keep the humans of our team as safe as possible. But the guardian they were tailing is currently unconscious in Tyme's arms, instead of standing with the rest of her group.

"What's wrong with her?" I asked.

Tyme grew irked, rolling his eyes. "She woke up and panicked when one of her co-workers walked straight through her."

I heard Lila hold back yet another giggle as she looked around at the well-manicured gardens and native trees. Then she nodded to Tyme before stepping out of the rift to grab a small waratah flower bud that began to fully blossom in her hand.

She stood back next to me and waited for Tyme to pull her back into the rift before she asked, "Katie, I need you to make a very small flame in the centre of the flower."

Katie smiled as her eyes glowed red and carefully created a tiny column of fire, placing it in the centre as directed. We all watched as the flower began to smoke a little, and then Lila waved the flower under the guardian woman's nose, causing her to slowly wake.

She stared up at Tyme, completely freaked, so he tried to calm her. "It's okay, Kelly, you're among friends here."

It was very strange. Kelly took one look at Lila, and the fear in her doubled. Lila and I both sensed it, and we glanced at each other, confused as to what was going on with her. Then out of the blue, Kelly broke away from Tyme, slowly inching away from Lila and the team.

"It's okay. You're safe," Lila said with a slight gold tinge in her eyes. "We're not going to hurt you."

"It's... it's you," Kelly stuttered, still staring at Lila in fear. "It's really you... you're..."

"Lila Winters," Lila answered for her.

"No." Kelly shook her head with her fear increasing. "I know your mother."

"You knew Hanna?" Lila questioned, now with white streaks appearing in her hair at the very mention of her name.

But Kelly shook her head again. "No. I know your real mother, Katherine. You look just like her. You work for them, don't you? Just like she does... That woman is evil and cold-hearted... You... you stay away from me."

Okay? – And here I thought Katherine was dead. – Apparently not.

Both Terrence and Lila briefly stared at Tyme who instantly became cagey for some reason, and I'm guessing they sensed his nature change. But Lila turned her attention back to Kelly and apologised for scaring her before she said, "Tyme, let me out of the rift."

He did as Lila asked with his eyes glowing silver to let her out of the rift. And with Lila's hair now turned completely white, she took off at full-speed.

Terrence then let out a long breath, turning to Adela. "Will you guys be right here?"

"Yeah." Adela nodded. "Jess and Chase look like they're almost done. So we'll meet you at the next meet point."

We were just about to follow after Lila when Katie piped up, pulling a small parcel out of her jacket pocket. "Oh hey... I found this in Hilary's office. It's addressed to Lila... It says it's from Billy."

I glared at the small parcel, thinking back on those horrid memories Lila shared with me. – The ones where she chose him over me, and I really hate those memories. – I admit I'm still slightly jealous and maybe a bit territorial, so I grabbed the box before we stepped out of the rift to find Lila.

Journal entry insert by Terrence Connors

Yeah. — Alex is about to do something stupid. — Really, really stupid.

We stopped two blocks away from the team, and Alex was eyeing the parcel in his hand that is clearly addressed to Lila. I wanted to keep looking for Lila, but Alex had already started opening the box when suddenly, Tyme ran up at full-speed to knock the box out of Alex's hands seconds before it exploded, releasing a cloud of black gas, beginning to fill the alley.

I moved quickly before it reached me, calling to the leaves from the nearby trees to enclose on the gas and absorb its toxins. The leaves then fell to the ground, all black and charred with the gas inside them, disintegrating in the wind. But I wasn't fast enough because both Tyme and Alex were lying in the alley, unconscious.

I screamed Alex's name when Lila appeared next to me, after jumping from the roof of the building, and then she stared down at my stone-vine bracelet as she sensed my fear.

"What happened?" she asked, leaning down to check if they were both still breathing.

"There was a package addressed to you. Alex was holding it when it exploded with gas."

Lila peered across at me and then at the chard box and leaves as she injected them both with the Neuritamine cure before waking them up with the waratah flower. After a few seconds, Tyme and Alex slowly woke but seemed somewhat delirious, laughing at each other — which is very strange. But then Alex called out for Lila and stood up, looking around for her.

Um...? — Okay.

Lila stood right in front of him to hold him steady and answered, "I'm here, Alex... I'm right in front of you."

He smiled then held Lila's face with both his hands, clearly struggling for balance as he pulled her close and kissed her, quite passionately. — With tongue and a lot of groaning. — It was uncomfortable to watch, and Lila glanced at me from the corner of her eye just as confused as I was.

"Alex!" I shouted, noticing Lila was not returning the kiss. "Alex, she needs air."

He pulled back on the kiss, still holding Lila's face and garbled, "I L...ove you, so... very... much."

"That's nice," Lila replied, watching Alex sway all drunk-like. "Alex, can you tell me how many fingers you see."

She held both hands out straight and made it easy with the answer being ten. But his answer was "Woah, Lila, how many hands do you have."

Yeah. — He's clearly not okay.

Tyme started giggling as if he was a small child who had done something wrong. So I held Tyme steady while Lila tried to convince Alex to follow us. — Which shouldn't be too hard for her, considering he loves her so very much.

Back on Maxwell's plane, after the team had finished the relocation process for the rescued guardians – via flights or the use of the tree port, Jessica and Jennifer were wanting to debrief. I tried to explain what I could to them while Lila kept Alex and Tyme comfortable at the back end of the plane where Chase and the rest of the security team were sitting. And Tyme and Alex both seem to be drowsier and less giggly now, so that's a good sign. – I think.

Katie looked back at Lila, and then back at our group to question, "I don't understand... why would Billy send a bomb to Lila? Weren't they... you know?"

I cleared my throat, feeling uneasy with the topic. "How do you know about that?"

Katie struggled to answer, looking to Adela for assistance who cagily chimed in, "We had our suspicions."

I didn't respond to them because I didn't want to add to the hotel gossip about Lila's sex life, knowing others in the security team were listening in. But when I said nothing, Katie got too eager and grinned. "But they are, aren't they? That must totes suck... I mean, I thought you or Alex had dibs on her?"

"Lila is not something you can just lay dibs on." I scowled at her, trying not to let my feelings show. "And we're getting off-topic."

Katie frustratedly rolled her eyes, but pulled back on the attitude when Jennifer agreed with me and added, "We need to find out why Billy sent that bomb."

Then Adela interrupted, "And why it was in Hilary's office."

"Are we sure it was Billy who sent it?" Katie questioned, leaning forward again as she explained, "The office secretary I spoke to said it was left in the office by Keith."

"I think you're right." Jennifer nodded. "What if Lila wasn't the target? Think about it. How would Keith know Lila or even any of us would be there to find the package?"

"We could have a spy at the hotel," Katie speculated.

But Adela disagreed, "Unlikely. Our staff are regularly screened, and the hotel is swept for bugs every month."

Jennifer then questioned if Hilary was the target, and I answered quite definitively, "No, that doesn't make sense. Hilary died a few months ago in a lab raid. Keith would have known that."

"What lab raid?" Adela asked, eyeing me suspiciously.

And yeah, I lied. "It was just something I read in the news."

Damn. — I thought I would never have to lie like this again.

Adela stared back at Lila who was still focused on Alex and Tyme, and then grew quieter. "What about the people who attacked Lila... the ones who tortured her. Do we know who they are yet?"

"What do you mean tortured?" Jennifer gasped in shock. "Have I missed something?"

At that, Katie became uncomfortable, apologising for not filling Jennifer in on some of the more difficult dramas we've faced over the last few months. Then Lila appeared next to her, stating, "And you never will. That is something no one needs to relive or know about... Ever. Now, you need to take your seats, we're just about to land."

As they sat back in their seats, Adela stood and grabbed hold of Lila's arm, annoyed at her calm attitude. "Lila, doesn't any of this concern you?"

"It does," Lila answered, staring down at Adela's hand, waiting for her to remove it before she continued. "It does concern me... But my main concern right now is Alex and Tyme. There's no point speculating until we have all of the facts... Katie, did you manage to get the files we needed?"

Lila glanced over to Katie as she nodded, and then ordered them all to buckle in before she went back to Alex. But I followed after Lila, walking to the back of the plane with her.

"Lila... Lila, stop!" I demanded, and she turned back to me, seeming irritated as I quietly asked, "You're planning on seeing him, aren't you?"

I worriedly waited for Lila to respond, and after a long thought time, she nodded. — But I think she might have been contemplating lying to me again, and I'm really glad she didn't.

"Lila, it's way too dangerous," I whispered, hoping to change her mind.

She moved closer to me, staring up into my eyes and spoke so quietly to ensure no one around us heard. "Terry, there's only one way to get these answers, and I know he won't hurt me... So I'm asking you to trust me."

Damn. — I hate it when she asks that. — I'd trust her with my damn heart if she ever asked for it. — But I know she never will. She doesn't see me that way.

I took a long breath and nodded, not showing any ounce of happiness as I sat down next to her, buckling up. "Fine... but I'm going with you. And there's no argument about that."

She said nothing as the plane started to land, so I assumed that to be a yes.

CHAPTER 27

A Living Nightmare

Journal entry by Terrence Connors

We got back into the hotel just as Shane was closing off the promenade section for the night, and he rushed over to Katie to give her a giddy hello kiss and asked, "Hey, how'd it go?"

"Another successful mission," Katie boasted. "We just hit a few bumps on the way home."

She casually pointed back to Tyme and Alex as they walked in with Lila, and they both seemed to have recovered well, now able to hold themselves up and all. But Lila became worried when she noticed Tyme starting to sweat with his heartrate increasing, and asked if he was okay.

He looked up over her shoulder at Maxwell who had just walked in from the streets, carrying takeout dinner for all of us, when Tyme randomly grabbed Lila's arm, screaming, "Lila... look out!" Then he threw her across the room.

Thankfully, Alex raced to catch her, and both landed softly on the lobby couches. But Tyme was going nuts and ran at full-speed, kicking Maxwell to the ground with our dinner going everywhere.

I raced to pull Tyme into a headlock, yelling at him, "Tyme, what are you doing? You just threw your sister!"

He tried to break free, glaring at Maxwell and freaked out again when Adela rushed to help Maxwell stand.

"No! Adela, get away from him!" he shouted trying to lunge at him with a murderous stare in his eyes.

I yelled at him again, tightening my hold on him. "Tyme, what's wrong with you? It's Maxwell... It's Adela's father!"

He suddenly started to feel dizzy and relaxed a little, looking at Maxwell as he confusedly shook his head. "I'm sorry... I don't know what just happened."

Mere seconds passed before Tyme freaked out again, realising he just threw his sister, so we looked back to see if Lila was okay, only to see Alex swatting at her skin as if she were covered in something.

He sounded frightened when he pleaded, "Lila, move! You got to move now! They're all over you!"

Alex then grabbed hold of Lila and threw her across the room again. This time towards the reception desk. So I let go of Tyme and raced to catch Lila before she hit the desk while Shane stood in front of Alex, shouting to get his attention.

"Alex! There's nothing there!" he insisted.

I focused on Lila, holding onto her, and asked if she was okay before placing her down gently. She was a little shaky but nodded and thanked me, holding onto me for support. But Alex lost it again.

He started screaming and calling me Keith, demanding I get away from her. Then he moved at super-speed and punched me in the face. Lila tried to help me, but Alex grabbed hold of her and sped off up the stairs at full-speed.

And just to add to one chaotic mess — Tyme started shouting, "Fire! She's on fire!" as he stared at Adela. He then ran to grab the fire extinguisher and was about to let it loose on her when William appeared, holding a frying pan and hit him in the head.

Well, that's one down. — Now I need to find Alex.

I took off up the stairs and found them out on the roof-top garden where Alex had bent the railings around Lila's wrist to stop her from leaving. Lila was demanding Alex to let her go, but Alex was convinced he was protecting her. Then when he saw me, he stood in front of Lila, demanding I stay away from her with his protective nature for Lila dramatically increased.

While keeping an eye on him, I looked over to Lila and asked, "Lila, are you hurt?"

"No," she fearfully answered. "But I can't move my hands without slicing them open."

I took a worrying breath and pleaded, "Promise me you won't move then... I'll get you."

She nodded, and I took a step closer while talking calmly. "Alex, it's me... Terrence... I need to get to Lila."

The very moment I said her name, Alex tackled me to the ground. But he only got in a few punches before I was able to call the roots from the garden to pull him away from me and keep him still. I then rushed to free Lila from the railing, but as I did, Alex morphed into a grey wolf, breaking free of the tree roots and charging towards us.

Holy Damn it!

With more panic in me now, I moved even faster to help Lila. And the second I got Lila's hands free, she morphed into a white wolf, fighting Alex to protect me.

They fought ferociously. — Well, Alex did. — He bit Lila, digging his teeth into her shoulder and neck, causing Lila so much pain. She yelped as Alex tossed her across the garden. Then he made a beeline for me when I shouted Lila's name.

I quickly broke off the already broken railing, holding it like a baseball bat. And as he charged, I swung at him, throwing him into the side of the building. He struggled to get up and eventually fainted. But I was more worried about Lila and rushed over to cover her with my jumper as she slowly morphed back into her human form, naked and unconscious.

I gently held her to check the wound. — And yeah, it's bad. Her skin looks like it's been torn open where Alex's wolf teeth had dug in.

"Come on, Lila... wake up for me, Sweetie." I worriedly stared at her while applying pressure to stop the bleed. And thankfully she woke up, reacting to the pressure.

She groaned in pain trying to move and slowly realised I was holding her as she opened her eyes and winced. "Did you win?"

"Kind of," I answered, brushing the blond hair out of her face and feeling a wave of relief to see her amazing blue eyes. Then I gently showed Lila her fresh wounds.

Katie and Shane hurriedly ran out onto the garden, looking for us and shouted, "What the hell just happened?"

They were shocked as they surveyed the damage, staring at both Alex and Lila's torn clothes on the ground and the state of the garden. — The garden that's now torn apart with roots and plants scattered everywhere, as well as sculptures and the water feature in pieces on the ground or embedded in the wall.

I carefully pulled Lila up onto her feet and held her upright, looking over at Alex who had now morphed into his naked human self. But when he started to stir, Katie shot him with Jessica's tranque gun.

Journal entry insert by Lila Winters

I have no idea what just happened down in the lobby or why. But I do know that when Alex wakes up, he is going to be in so much trouble for biting me.

Terrence walked me — more like carried me, up into the conference room, and I'm currently sitting on the table, naked with a hotel blanket wrapped around me as I watch Chase and a few of our security team carry Tyme and Alex into the room. They handcuffed them to the chair, and were ordered by Jess that if either of them tries to break the cuffs to not hesitate in tranque-ing them again.

William was helping to carry Tyme in and gasped when he saw me sitting on the table, covered in blood, with Terrence busy trying to clean my wounds. Max was also sporting a few bruises, and was being escorted up with Adela and Jenny helping him.

Jenny asked if he was okay, but Max was more concerned about me. So Terrence explained, "The wounds are deeper than I'd like... On the bright side, they're clean. But on the down-side, your garden is in dire need of a make-over now."

"Sorry," I piped in. "I will fix it... first thing tomorrow."

"You'll do no such thing." Max glared at me, shaking his head. "I will arrange for the maintenance crew to design a new garden... You need to focus on healing."

William eagerly offered to help Terrence make the Knight serum for me, and I butted in, "No... I'll call Dr Ellis in the morning so he can have a look at it."

Saddened by my words, William stared at my wounds before pleading with me. "Lila, I can help you. Please, let me do this."

I winced, getting distracted by the pain Terrence was causing while slowly stitching up each of the many teeth wounds on me, and I gave him the death stare. But he just grinned back at me — inevitably making me smile again. So I turned my focus back on William who's now sad, and I held his hand as I talked to him.

"William, that's not what I meant. I know you want to help… and I appreciate it. But I'm already immune to the blue-rose tonic, what are we going to do if I become immune to the Knight serum as well… I don't know about you two, but at the moment, I'm fresh out of recipes. So from now on, the three of us…" — Referring to Terrence, William, and myself. "Should only use the healing tonic if we're dying… Okay?"

William nodded in agreement with a hint of a smile. — Probably at my genuine concern for his well-being. Then I peered over my shoulder at Terrence and waited for him to nod as well.

Suddenly, the room fell eerily tense as we all heard Alex slowly begin to wake up. He confusedly stared at his bindings and then at Shane, Katie, and Adela all aiming weapons at him as he scanned the room.

Alex eyed my wound before Terrence applied the dressing. Then he called my name, trying to break out of the cuffs when Adela stopped him, snapping with such seriousness. "Move and I will shoot you."

"Shoot me?" Alex puzzled. "Why? What happened to Lila?"

"You happened to Lila." Shane scowled at him. "You went all psycho wolf-man on her and bit her."

Alex stared back at me, struggling to believe he would ever do that to me, and I gloomily nodded to him. "You also threw me across the lobby and the garden and tied me to the rooftop railing, trying to protect me from Terrence who you thought was Keith."

I curiously stared at Alex realising he was in shock then asked, "You don't remember any of this, do you?"

"No." He sadly shook his head. "I don't remember any of that?"

Tyme was next to wake, and again looked confused that his 'kind-of' girlfriend was pointing a tranque gun at his chest. – And that is an awkward moment. – He looked over at me then asked, "Lila, what's going on?"

"Well, you also threw me across the lobby… But from what I'm told… you went psycho on Maxwell then thought Adela was on fire before your dad came to the rescue, and hit you in the head with a frying pan… And I'm assuming you also don't remember any of it?"

Their jaws dropped and they both stayed in a slight moment of shock, staring at me and the tense crowd in the room. But I suddenly felt a hint of pain, and I let out a small whimper as Terrence finished bandaging my shoulder and helped me off the table. And I'm pretty sure the sound of my pain was what triggered Alex to go all tropo again, pleading for me to run. He then stared at Terrence and begged him not to hurt me, bargaining for my life. To make things worse, Tyme stared at Adela and started crying, begging someone to save her as well.

I definitely didn't want Adela seeing Tyme like this, so I raced to grab Adela's tranquiliser and said, "Sorry, Little Brother," before I shot him. And Shane helped me out by shooting Alex.

I handed Adela back her tranque-gun and demanded, "Keep them restrained and sedated… I'll be back when I can." Then while adjusting the blanket around me, Maxwell asked what I was planning to do, and I replied as I left, "To see a doctor. Terry, you're with me."

We decided to take my car out to Coburg, mainly because I have a change of clothes in the boot of my car for this kind of occasion. So Terrence drove while I got dressed in the back seat. – And it didn't surprise me at all that he knew the directions towards Billy's apartment block. But I don't think Terrence has cottoned on yet.

When we got to the abandoned apartment building, we took the stairs up into Billy's apartment, cautiously looking around the room, but found no one. I did, however, find a smashed melted phone on the floor next to his bed.

Well, at least I know why he stopped checking in.

"I don't think he's here." Terrence stated while looking at the mouldy food in the sink, and then asked, "Lila, are you sure this is a good idea?"

"No," I griped, getting frustrated. "But Alex is in trouble, and I don't know how to help him or Tyme. And right now, Billy seems to be our only safe lead. But I would really appreciate if people stopped doubting me all the time... It's not like anyone else is coming up with a better plan."

I felt more pain coming from my shoulder, realising it had started to bleed through the bandage. So Terrence gently pulled the singlet strap off my shoulder to apply pressure and wait for the bleeding to stop.

He stood close to me, and I clutched onto his shirt as I tried to deal with the pain. Then he whispered, "Well, here's my plan...

First, I need you to take some slow breaths. And then I'll need to redress your wounds... But there is one other place we can try if you'd like."

"He's not there," I answered with a slight pout. "The warehouse burned down weeks ago. I don't know why."

In shock, Terrence worriedly stared at me. "How do you know that?"

"The question is why didn't you know that?" I cheekily smirked back at him. "You're the one who's supposedly helping them... right?" He glared down at the floor, remaining silent when I whispered. "Now who's hiding the secrets."

In his worry, Terrence tried to explain himself but struggled, and I couldn't help but smile at him. "Terry, it's okay... I've known for a while... During my grieving time when I was stuck as a wolf, you always came back smelling like them... But I never stopped you or dobbed you in."

He still looked sad, so I shuffled to stand in front of him and held both of his hands. "Terry, I knew you were doing it to protect me. And as long as you came back home after it all, I was... kind of alright with what you were doing... But the next time you try and guilt me for keeping secrets from you. I am so bringing this up."

I giggled at his pout, and his eyes darted from the floor to my smile when he heard me laugh. Then within seconds, he was kissing me. I pulled in closer to him, enjoying the soft touch of his lips on mine. When at random, he pulled away, looking at me confused as he held me in his arms.

"I'm sorry... I... I don't understand... I just kissed you... And you kissed me back."

While gazing into his blue-green eyes with my brows pinched together, I felt a little confused as I held onto his arms. "Um... did you not want me to?"

Before he could answer me, his brother Keith stood at the door.

"Aww, how romantic." He sighed, glaring at Terrence and feigning sincerity. "Oh, I'm so sorry, Brother, was I interrupting something here?"

Terrence held me tighter, pulling me around so I was behind him and griped, "Yeah, actually you are."

I didn't argue with him holding me, but then Keith glanced back at me, noticing my bandaged shoulder and grinned. "Oh, I get it... That's supposed to be her kiss goodbye before she bleeds to death... I heard Alex got a little too kinky with your girlfriend tonight. I don't blame him... She does look tasty."

He looked at me as if I was his next snack, and Terrence lost it and tackled Keith to the ground. Keith tried to create a fireball, but I crushed it – stepping on his hand and causing him a lot of pain. I then looked down at him and scoffed, "Damn straight I'm tasty... But you'll never get to know."

"You sent the package to Lila, didn't you?" Terrence questioned rather intimidatingly. "Tell me how to cure Alex."

Keith looked at my foot crushing his hand and then back up at me, and I reluctantly relieved the pressure for him to answer. "Your tasty girlfriend here needs to die."

Frac damn it. – Why? – Why does he hate me so much?

In complete disbelief, Terrence let Keith go and moved back closer to me with a shaky breath. "What?"

In a huff, Keith stood to his feet, dusting off his designer shirt and snickered. "In order to save Lila's other lover, Alex's worst nightmare needs to become a reality in front of him... My guess is, his worst fear is losing his favourite girly chew toy... Sorry, Brother, but there are no winners in this round."

Keith's eyes darted to mine as he deviously grinned, causing Terrence to lose it again and punch him in the face, knocking him back down to the ground as he shouted at him, "You're sick, you know that?"

He then grabbed my hand, hurrying me out of the apartment with him. Keeping me very close as we rushed back out to my car.

CHAPTER 28

A Tale Of Two Lovers

Journal entry by Terrence Connors

Lila stayed quiet as I drove back home, but right now I feel really nervous and confused. — I mean, I still can't believe I kissed her and that she kissed me back. She didn't pull away or tell me to stop. — It was almost as if she was enjoying it.

Oh damn it. — I'm so confused.

There's one thing I do know for certainty, and that is there is no way I'm going to let Lila die. But I also know she will never forgive herself if she doesn't try absolutely everything to save Alex.

"I'm sorry." I sighed while taking slow breaths. "I'm sorry my brother's doing this to you."

She placed her hand on my knee in an attempt to comfort me, and smiled at me as she spoke, "It's not your fault, Terry."

"Yes, it is," I grunted, feeling so incredibly helpless and angry. "Keith blames me for Odele's illness getting worse because I left. And he's taking it out on you because... you're the reason I left."

She reached up and held my hand. — And damn, I love her caring nature.

"Do you regret leaving the island with me?" she asked.

"No," I replied without a shadow of a doubt. But then hesitantly asked, "Do... you regret me leaving with you?"

As I asked that, I pulled into the basement car park, nervously waiting for her answer. She still held my hand, using the other to unbuckle herself. Then she leaned over to kiss my cheek and said with that sweet smile, "Never," before getting out of the car.

Yeah okay. — She doesn't regret it, and she kissed me again. — But it was on the cheek. — What does that mean? — Aw damn, focus, Terrence. — Save Alex then figure out Lila.

I got out of the car, racing around to help her. And as we were about to step into the elevator, William appeared next to us, slightly out of breath. "Lila... I have an idea on how to cure Tyme and Alex... But it's very dangerous, and it's going to hurt."

As we rode the elevator up to William's apartment, he explained his idea, and Lila agreed to it. I wasn't overly sold on it though, so Lila pulled me out into the hallway, still holding my hand and asked me to trust her again. And I instantly caved the moment she said, "Terry."

Damn. — I just love it when she calls me that.

Now both in agreement, we went up to the rooftop garden after first explaining what the plan was to Adela. But we all thought it might be best to keep the whole excruciating pain part and potential death, out of our explanation to the rest of the team. So all Shane and Katie had to do was let Alex and Tyme go, and tell them that Lila and Adela were on the rooftop garden, cleaning up.

William and I stayed hidden around the corner side of the garden while Lila and Adela pretended to clean. Lila had made up a tonic to help stop her heart and made one for Adela as well. Adela knew the entire plan and the fact that it was dangerous, and cringed with unsettling feelings at the orangey-coloured liquid that Lila handed her. But she still drank it, pulling a sour face at the taste.

"This is going to hurt, isn't it?" Adela asked, turning to Lila.

She already knew the answer, and Lila half grinned at her as she explained, "Dying always hurts... it's the staying alive part that's hard... Just... whatever you do, don't walk into the light. Otherwise you won't come back."

In shock, Adela stared at Lila and gasped, "You make it sound like you've been there before."

And yeah — Lila has. — Which again makes me mad because that was also my fault. But Lila then said something that I was not expecting when she returned to her pretend cleaning. "I've seen that light a few times. And it probably won't be my last... But I made a promise to Terry... And you know I don't break my promises. Not willingly anyway."

Oh my gosh. — She did. — She promised me she wouldn't die.

My shock matched Adela's but hers turned to horror, and she looked like she wanted to say more. But before she could, Alex and Tyme walked out into the garden looking for them. William and I remained hidden in the side corner of the garden, wearing ski-masks, and waited until Alex and Tyme were close enough to witness. Then we took a deep breath in and worked up the nerve to run at super-speed towards the girls.

As William stabbed his knife into Adela's stomach, I looked into Lila's blue eyes, and she rested her hand on mine as I drove Lila's dagger into her stomach. But I was nervous, and I might have done it harder than she expected because she clutched my sleeve, and the pain I saw in her was unbearable for me as I let go of her.

In that horrid moment, Alex and Tyme both screamed their names and raced to help them while William and I escaped, jumping off the side of the balcony and landing on a waiting leaf platform.

I was very distracted, but I successfully controlled the platform, guiding us down to the ground. I couldn't breathe the entire time as my thoughts remained on Lila. So as soon as we landed, we took off our ski masks and raced at super-speed back up to the garden.

We found Alex holding Lila's body in his arms, and Tyme held onto Adela's limp hand, sobbing and begging her to come back. Keeping up the act, we ran out to see them, and I asked what happened before I leaned down to check Lila's pulse and found nothing.

"She's dead," I fearfully gasped.

William leaned down next to Tyme, trying to comfort him and noticed a black liquid seeping from his eyes as he cried.

"Terrence," he called, pointing to the black tears.

I felt a bit of joy and looked back at Alex to see his eyes weeping black as well. — It's working. — The plan's working. Yet still, I'm struggling to breathe properly as I scoop Lila's lifeless body up into my arms. And so help me, this is horrifyingly painful having to do this again. It was so bad that I needed to block the memories from my mind as I held her and cleared my throat.

"Alex, we need to move her... Lila wouldn't want her children to see her like this."

He agreed with me but wanted to carry Lila himself, so I handed her over. Tyme then tearfully pulled Adela up into his arms as well and followed us down to his apartment.

They placed the girls on Tyme's bed and sat next to them, holding their hands and crying thick black tears all while William and I watched, waiting through the night, hoping to the high heavens that we didn't really kill them.

And yeah. — That is a worrying thought.

The morning has come, and the black tears turned clear for both Alex and Tyme, but Adela and Lila still haven't revived. I sat at the end of the bed, nervously staring at Lila's peaceful and beautiful face as I fiddled with my fingers the way she usually does. — I also kept reminding myself of the promise she made to me, and that she's going to come back to me.

Eventually, William noticed Adela's foot twitch and our nerves were slowly disappearing when we sighted her now heavily bleeding wound. It meant her heart was getting stronger.

Slowly, her hand tightened around Tyme's hand, and he lifted his sad face to see Adela wake up gasping for air and quickly moving her hand to stop the bleeding. Then with gleeful relief, Tyme breathed and embraced her so tightly.

"Adela... Oh, thank God. I thought you were dead."

Alex watched Adela come to life, and then stared at Lila's still lifeless body and leaned his head on her chest to check for a heartbeat, or any breathing or blood moving. But there was nothing.

I stood at the end of the bed breathless, fearing I had killed my best friend as Alex shouted her name, trying to shake her awake. I could feel my heart ripping from my chest as I silently pleaded. "Come back, Lila... Please, come back to me."

The moments passed and now everyone including Adela was waiting in such tense uncertainty. Until finally Lila woke up gasping for air, and everyone took that breath of relief as Alex wrapped her up in his arms, so thankful to hear her breathe.

"She's alive!" he tearfully praised. "I can't believe it. You're alive... Lila, you scared me to death."

Lila felt her now bleeding stab wound and groaned from the pain. "Yeah, Alex, that was kind of the point... ugh... ouch."

Now able to breathe, I moved to quickly grab the first aid kit and appeared on the bed, straddling Lila's legs as I applied pressure to her wound. But she grabbed the sleeve of my shirt again, reacting to the pain.

"Sorry," I whispered, and she took it well, trying to smile through the pain.

Tyme shook his head though, still failing to understand. "Lila...what are you talking about?"

She couldn't answer. She was a bit preoccupied, staring up at me while clawing her fingers into my leg, trying to cope with her pain. And William was also a little preoccupied, moving past Tyme to start cleaning and patching up Adela's bleeding wound before injecting her with the Knight serum.

But eventually he explained, "You and Alex were poisoned with a very strong hallucinogen, which caused you to relive your greatest fear over and over again... The best way to counteract it was to make you actually live through your fears."

"You stabbed Lila?!" Alex shouted angrily at William.

Fearing for my life — just a tad, I stayed focused on Lila, cleaning the wound before pulling out the sewing needle and thread to start stitching her up. — <u>Again.</u> — I then very tentatively glanced over to see Alex scowling, and answered, "Actually... I did."

As suspected, Alex gave me a death stare. But then Lila jokingly added, "Yeah... but, Terry, do me a favour and be more gentle next time."

"Next time!" Alex shrieked. "Lila there's not going to be a next time. You don't even know if your idiotic stunt worked."

Lila winced as I pierced the sewing needle into her skin again, but she just kept clutching at my leg for comfort as I asked, "Well, tell us, Alex... who am I?"

He scowled at me this time and snickered, "Your name is Terrence and you're an idiot."

"Yep, he's back." Lila grinned, staring up at me.

I grinned back, finishing the last stitch, and then placed yet another fresh dressing on her as she chuckled but kept holding my leg for comfort.

"Whose stupid idea was this?" Tyme asked, watching his dad clean the last of the blood off Adela's now fully healed wound. But when

William looked back and admitted it was his idea, Tyme looked like he was going to kill him.

"Dad, how could you? They could have died."

"We did die...in a way," Adela chimed in, standing up and stretching out the stiffness in her body as she yawned. "But it isn't your dad's fault. It was our decision to make."

"It was a stupid decision," Alex grumbled, crossing his arms.

"And so was opening the package in the first place," Lila snapped back, failing to hide her cheeky smile behind that judgemental stare.

He went silent from her comment, clearing his throat, unsure what to say. — I did tell him it was a stupid idea. And yeah, I'm definitely smiling, knowing that this time I'm not in Lila's bad books.

Slowly and carefully, I helped Lila to stand so I could wrap a support bandage around her stomach. And while she held her singlet up for me, she added, "Alex, I will do anything to save your life, even die for you... But if you haven't noticed, I kind of have a habit of just not dying. I'm stubborn like that."

She winked at me, biting her bottom lip while ignoring Alex's annoyed grunts at her. — And I knew what she was talking about, and I'm really happy that she's keeping that promise for me.

Eventually, Alex calmed and wrapped his arms around her again. "Damn straight you're stubborn... And let's keep it that way."

But the tender moment was hilariously interrupted when we heard Lila's stomach growl, causing Alex to pull away with the biggest grin on his face. And Lila shyly shrugged her shoulders with a cute pout.

"What? Death really makes me hungry."

I held back a laugh, watching Alex cave and ask what she wanted for breakfast, and of course, it had to be pancakes.

Journal entry insert by Lila Winters

Alright, I'll admit it. – What we just did was painful and reckless and stupid. But I would do it all over again for any of them.

Tyme suggested we all go downstairs to one of the restaurants, and have the now popular 'Lila's happy stack' rainbow pancakes. So we all cleaned up and changed our blood-stained clothes to less scary ones, and it surprised both Alex and Tyme when they realised that we had a change of clothes for all of us, sitting on Tyme's dining table this whole time. – It may have been a stupidly dangerous plan, but I wanted to show William and Terrence that I had confidence in them by planning a head before they faked our deaths.

Plan C was to rush us to the hospital. – So either way we had a change of clothes ready for us.

Once we were ready to go, we followed Tyme out of the apartment. – All except for William.

"Hey," I said while hobbling over to him – trying desperately not to ruin Terrence's sewing masterpiece. I held onto William's arm for support and may have struggled to hide a bit of the pain, but I eventually found the strength to ask, "Are you coming?"

He smiled back at me, and then let me hold his arm to help me walk as we followed the rest of the group down to the promenade. But Alex and Terrence weren't far away, occasionally looking back, feeling a little hesitant to let me out of their sights. – And it was no guess as to why.

I was a little slower than the rest of them as I nursed my tightly bandaged stomach. But William was patient with me, and we walked through the promenade at what felt like a snail's pace.

"Thank you, William," I quietly spoke, and waited until our group was at a distance before I continued. "What you did last night must have been really difficult for you... I admit, I was surprised when the prison called to inform me of your second visit to... him."

Tensing the muscle in his arm, William peered over to me and worriedly cleared his throat. "Nothing gets past you these days... does it?"

I shook my head and stated, "Rule 3."

With a sigh, he nodded, "Never turn your back on the enemy... It pains me to see that you adhere to those rules so strictly."

Ouch...

Feeling slightly frustrated and sad, I took a moment then grumbled, "I'm sorry... They're what keep me alive most days. The General may be a monster, but he was smart enough to teach his little Pumpkin how to survive while she was studied... I can't really help it now."

William stopped us from walking and his face grew sadder as he turned to me. "Lila, you never have to apologise or even explain yourself to me... I am very proud of you. And everything you are... Because even though you've been raised by a monster, you grew up to be a blessing and a hero. And you inspire others around you to be better—"

I interrupted his speech, causing him to tense up as I reached my arms around him and hugged him. I'm not sure if he wanted the hug, and I felt a little nervous. But when he relaxed and folded his arms around me as well, I whispered, "I'm sorry... I just rarely ever hear those words. So... thank you."

He knew which words I was referring to, so he held me tighter and whispered, "I am very proud of you. I have been for a long time."

It was a beautiful moment, that was abruptly ruined when Tyme walked out of the restaurant and celebrated with his victory dance before running up to join in the cuddle. And in being a push-over, I pulled my arms around Tyme to include him.

"This doesn't change anything... I'm still not going to call him Dad."

"You will, just give it time." Tyme grinned back cheekily.

In hearing the brazen attitude he has for his big sister, I punched him in the arm – gently. But it did cause William to laugh, having to break us apart, saying, "Tyme, stop annoying your sister."

"But it's fun," Tyme joshed back.

While pulling a sour face at him, I teased, "Yeah well... I'm going to eat all your pancakes then."

I poked him in the shoulder one last time before I called Terrence's name and in seconds, he appeared next to me – sweeping me off my feet. And I happily sat in his arms, sticking my tongue out at Tyme as Terrence carried me into the restaurant. Then when we all sat down at the table, everyone burst into laughter as I ate the top pancake off Tyme's stack.

I think I'm beginning to like being an older sister. – It's fun.

CHAPTER 29

Even Secrets Lie

Journal entry by Lila Winters

It's only been a week, and the teeth marks are healing nicely. – But the guilt Alex feels every time he sees them has stuck around. The knife wound, however, was a little deeper and is taking longer than expected to heal, which Terrence does not like at all. – And he worriedly frets over me to no end. – Every day, Terrence would be waiting at my bedroom door at the early hours of 4am, wanting to help me get ready and check or change the dressings before making breakfast for me. – I did ask him if he wanted to stay with me over the nights, so he didn't have to get up so early. But he said no. – Which surprised me. – But I figured out why.

It's Sunday night, and Alex and Terrence have invited me on another date night to make up for how the last one ended. It was also Alex's way of apologising for opening something that was addressed to me, which in the end I had to pay for.
I didn't mind their reasons because I'm having so much fun on this date night, enjoying the warmer air of late spring while taking advantage of the longer days. So to finish the night, we're now walking through Fitzroy Garden, eating ice-creams.

"You know... I'm really starting to like these date nights. I almost feel normal again." I smiled, briefly glancing at both of them.

"And what would you be doing right now if you were normal?" Alex chuckled.

I had to think about that one. I mean, it's been almost two years since I met Alex. – But those two years have felt like a lifetime for me. I think I was stuck for an answer, so Terrence chimed in, trying to help.

"Well, for starters, she would have never met you or probably me again."

Oh Frac, he's right. – And that would be a horrible thought.

"I changed my mind." I pouted. "I don't like these date nights at all."

Alex laughed at me again and cheekily joked, "What's the matter, miss me already?"

"Maybe." I huffed as I felt my nose crinkle, moving closer to hold on to Terrence's arm. "Or maybe I just miss Terrence."

I bit my bottom lip, trying not to smile too much as he gasped, "Ouch." Then he smudged his ice-cream onto my cheek as we all laughed.

Suddenly, we heard the sound of screeching tyres and what sounded like a nasty car accident at the end of the park. Alex and Terrence, both handed me their ice-creams, then Alex told me to "wait here" as they went to investigate.

"What? No, I can help you," I rebuked.

But Alex turned back to me and demanded, "You still haven't healed properly... Now stay."

Argh!!! – He makes me so mad sometimes. – Gone are the days when he actually trusted me to leap off balconies and run into burning buildings with him. – Grrr!!!

Since I didn't want to have an argument with them and ruin the night, I stayed put. And I watched as they helped the people in the car accident get out of their cars to see if they were okay.

The problem is, neither Alex or Terrence noticed the melted tar on the road behind the cars, which probably caused the accident. And melted tar in the last few days of spring meant only one thing. – And it isn't good.

I looked around for any signs of Keith and I was going to call to Alex and Terrence to warn them. But before I could say anything, Keith whisked me away, causing me to drop the ice-creams.

He held on to me tightly while he ran at super-speed. – All the while I was trying to think. – I couldn't risk a fight in the middle of the streets like this. There's just too many people. So I need to think of a disguise, and quick.

Off the top of my head, all I could remember was what Matt said, and I acted quickly, turning my hair white and making my ears point to their elfy-appearance to disguise myself. Then when I was ready and saw an opportunity, I commanded one of the nearest trees to reach out and grab me.

The tree then yanked me from Keith's arms, and I somersaulted back down to the ground, unfortunately landing in the middle of La Trobe Street, next to the state library.

Aw Frac buckets. – That hurt.

As I held my bandaged torso, a few of the oncoming cars slammed on the brakes, swerving to avoid hitting me. I nodded to them as I stepped off the street, ignoring my pain as I broke the branch off the tree that saved me. – But apologised to it as I did.

My eyes glowed a light shade of green to make the branch into a long sparring stick. Then I waited for Keith to appear back in front of me, seeming a little upset.

"You couldn't just come quietly, could you?"

I stood ready to fight and grinned. "You'll have to kill me first."

He circled me, and his eyes darted to my stomach and could see the support bandage sticking out from beneath my singlet, and the almost healed teeth marks on my shoulder.

I swivelled to follow his steps, and he took a sharp breath, shaking his head at me as he spoke. "Damn... that is such a shame... because I'm not allowed to kill you. Make your life a living hell, yes. But kill you, no."

Keith grinned at me before grabbing hold of one of the humans who was cowering on the steps leading to the state library, and grasped his neck tightly. Then as Keith's eyes glowed a fiery red, the cars that had stopped on the street burst into flames, trapping the people inside. And still with that evil grin, he glowered back at me with a threatening tone. "So how about we settle for everyone else then?"

Instantly, I held my hands up in surrender, placing the sparring stick on the ground at my feet. "Okay, I won't fight you. Please, just let him go."

Keith's grin grew wider because he had no intention of letting the human go. Not until the nearby tree gave him no choice, reaching out again to snatch the human away. Then a millisecond later, Keith was attacked by a large, very angry grey wolf that dragged him out into the street.

Terrence soon appeared next to me, wearing a black masquerade mask and a baseball cap. And with his dark ruffled hair, he definitely reminded me of one of the cartoons I used to watch as a child.

"Nice save, Tuxedo Mask," I joked, failing to hide my smile.

He looked back at me and tittered. "Thanks, Serena."

I gasped with glee that he knew the reference, and he leaned down to whisper, "Who do you think watched those silly cartoons with you when you were little?"

He looked at my lips as they failed to hide my joy, but then saw me nursing my stomach, and asked, "Are you okay?"

Oh Frac Damn. – I'm more than okay. – I have the awesomest friends in the world.

"Yeah." I nodded. "I'm just trying not to tear the stitches and cause you to fret over me... Not that I don't want you to. It's just there are people stuck in those cars."

"You know I can multi-task, right?" he replied with a grin, running off to help the humans and ushering them to safety all while I tried to focus on controlling the flames.

I managed to put out one of the fires in the cars. But when I turned to the other, I was distracted as the grey wolf was thrown past my head with Keith turning his attention towards me again.

Moving quickly, I kicked the sparring stick up into my hand and went – as Alex would put it "all ninja girl on him," finishing it off with a swift smack in the side of Keith's arrogant face before kicking him backwards into a car door.

And *FRAC!!!* – I tore a stitch.

Keith stood to his feet, nursing his pride and injuries as I held my stomach again and warned, "Back off, Keith, you're out-numbered in this round."

The large grey wolf stood next to me, growling at Keith. Then as Keith listened to the sound of sirens in the distance, he disappeared. Alex-the wolf whimpered, sniffing at the blood seeping through my top, and I knew he was worried, so I looked into his big eyes and smiled, scratching him behind the ears.

"I'm okay... I'll let you look after me when you're you again... And I promise I'll stay with Terry until you're ready."

He huffed as he ran off at full-speed, and while I waited for him to return, I helped the last two people that were still trapped in the fiery car.

The door was jammed on the back-passenger side where a little boy was stuck, and his... well I think it's his grandfather had climbed in from the other side, trying to unbuckle him from his booster seat. But the buckles were stuck together as they melted from the heat.

I ripped the passenger door off its hinges, placing it next to me, and asked, "Can I help, please?"

The old man stared at my elfy appearance then hurriedly explained that the boy was stuck. So I nodded then looked at the little boy and said, "Brace yourself," before grabbing hold of the seat buckle and ripping it from the booster seat.

Moving carefully, I pulled the boy into my arms while I helped the old man to climb out, and then led them to sit on the steps leading to the library. Once seated, I inspected the little boy's arm which was burned and weeping then ran across the street, returning with a small white rose in my hand.

"What's your name?" I asked him.

"Chris," he whimpered.

"Well, Chris, do you want to see a magic trick?"

He nodded, and as my eyes glowed green, I held up the rose and turned it blue in front of him. He gasped in amazement, looking up at the old man who seemed to be in shock, still staring at me.

"Now, I need you to be a brave boy and hold very still. Can you do that for me, Chris?" I asked. And as he nodded, I broke the rose petals off and placed them on his burn.

Chris seemed to be a very curious little boy as he tugged at my pointy elf ears with his other hand, so I peeked up at him and joshed, "Ouch... they're attached to me you know."

His face filled with wonder as I looked up at the old man to explain, "This is going to hurt, you might want to hold his hand."

The old man did as he was told in holding Chris's hand, and my eyes glowed a brighter green as the blister burn healed on Chris's arm.

Once it was all healed, Terrence appeared next to me to report, "Everyone's out and safe. But we need to go... now."

I stood up to see Alex – who was now dressed but with no disguise, waiting in the distance. So I nodded to him before I followed Terrence, running off at half-speed. – He wanted to pick me up, but I wouldn't let either of them do that.

Yeah – I am still a little peeved that they told me to stay.

We ran into the hotel through the basement and up the stairs, finally stopping on the loungeroom floor of my apartment. All panting and gasping for air. My white hair and pointy ears then returned to normal as I wheezed and took in more breaths.

"Well, that was a fun date night... We should do this every week."

Alex disappeared into the kitchen and brought back the first aid kit to change the bloodied dressing on my stomach and tittered. "You should really look up the definition of fun."

I stared up at him and took off my top so he could see the wound better. Then I happily stated, "I got to play super-ninja girl with my two best friends... And I will say, we make an awesome trio."

With joy, I beamed at both of them as Alex helped me to my feet to wrap my stomach with the fresh support bandage again.

But my smile slowly drooped to a frown, and Terrence could sense my emotions change through the bracelet, and sat up to ask, "What's wrong?"

I may have hesitated in answering him, knowing he wasn't going to like it. "Your brother, Keith. He said something before, and I don't understand it."

"You shouldn't listen to my brother. He's an idiot," Terrence grumbled.

Still, I continued to voice my thoughts. "He said, he wasn't allowed to kill me. What's changed his mind?"

I stared back at Terrence, waiting for some kind of revelation or something, but he was busy looking at Alex as if they were speaking telepathically to each other. Alex then attached the bandage clip to my dressing and started putting the first aid kit away in a somewhat hurry.

"It's getting late," he replied. "We should let you get some sleep."

"But I'm not tired..." I puzzled with a pout. "Can't you guys stay a little longer?"

Terrence shook his head to reply, "Nah, Lila, we don't want to wake up the kids." Then he headed towards the door as well.

I knew they weren't being honest with me, so I followed them and suggested, "We can head down to your apartment if you want. I don't mind. I just need to grab a clean top."

Still, they were determined to leave with Alex walking out of the kitchen to follow Terrence, and he kissed my cheek before he opened the door. "Sorry, Lila, but I'm pretty tired after tonight. We'll catch up in the morning."

"When?" I greasied him and pouted. "After you finish steaking out Keith's apartment for the night... or before your daily perimeter run to check that no one's lurking in the shadows waiting to kill me?"

Huh. – I thought so...

They both looked at me and sighed with sadness, realising they had been caught out in yet another lie. And I crossed my arms, knowing they weren't planning on changing their minds.

"And you dare lecture me about keeping secrets... only to do it yourselves."

With sadness, Alex held onto my hand and whispered, "We're only doing it to protect you."

But I know better than that, and my teary yet angry eyes peered up to meet his to reply, "Lying protects no one you love... I learnt that the hard way."

I then pulled my hand away from him to slowly close the door as I disappointingly looked at Terrence and said, "Since you've already changed my dressing, I think we'll skip the morning wake-up call... See you tomorrow."

Watching me take off my stone bracelet to stop him from knowing how I feel, Terrence moved back towards me, almost in regret. But I closed the apartment door on him, not wanting either of them to see me cry. – Still I know they can hear me.

I want them to knock on the door. – I want them to stay. – Not because they have to protect me but because they want to be with me. – But they didn't. – They left.

Feeling really upset that again they left me and are still treating me like a fragile doll, I walked back to my bedroom and sobbed while throwing away yet another blood-stained, dishevelled shirt.

I peered up and saw Matt coming out from his room, wanting to check out the noises that he had heard. He was only in his pyjama boxers and his hair was all scuffled, and I froze, wondering if I should hide the wound dressing from him. But I decided against it.

"Sorry, did I wake you?" I asked quietly.

"No, I was just reading" he answered. "How was your night?"

"It was... fun, I guess."

My statement wasn't convincing for him, and he looked at me confused while following me into my room. "Then why are you crying? Did something happen between you and the guys."

I walked into the bathroom to get changed into my pyjamas at half-speed. Then while walking back out, I answered, "Kind of... maybe... I had a run-in with Keith again tonight, and he said something that scared me... And I know I'm supposed to be the brave one around here, but right now I'm scared as hell."

I sat down on the bed and began to cry again, feeling a little abandoned by Alex and Terrence. These days they spend all their time and effort trying to protect me, that now I feel like maybe they've lost confidence in me.

Frac Damn It. - I'm not fragile and I really wish they would see that.

Matt sat at the head of my bed, and then pulled me backwards into his arms and just hugged me tightly as I whimpered and sniffled.

"Matt," I said softly.

"Yeah," he whispered, pulling the bedsheets up to keep us warm.

I got comfortable, snuggling into his hug and mumbled, "Thank you."

Journal entry insert by Matt Winters

Lila fell asleep in my arms last night, and I got the feeling she really needed that sense of security that a hug can give people, so I kept on holding her. It did have me wondering why Alex or Terrence hadn't volunteered for this job, but I wasn't going to object. — I love the fact that Lila is able to rely on me like this again.

As the sun rose, we were woken abruptly by my wonderful little brother, storming into Lila's room, shouting, "Lila... Sissy, wake up. You need to see this!"

Naturally, because Lila went to sleep scared, she woke up scared when Shane leaned on her bed to wake her. So while still half asleep, Lila pulled the dagger that she hides under her pillow out of its sheath and pressed it against Shane's chest.

"Woah...Sissy, it's me," he croaked then glanced back at me, who is topless, before he stupidly asked, "Are you guys back together now?"

I groaned becoming annoyed at him when he asked, watching Lila put her dagger away. "Wait... why do you sleep with a dagger under your pillow?"

"For protection," Lila sniped as if it were supposed to be obvious.

And again, he stupidly asked, "Why would you need protection in your own room."

I groaned again, louder this time. "Shane... just tell us why you're here before I make her use the dagger on you."

Lila grinned back at me while carefully stretching out and adjusting her bandages, slowly waking up when Shane said, "Lila's on the news."

With that, she disappeared from her bed and the sound of the television appeared from the loungeroom. Then with a smirk on his face, Shane eyed me. "So... are you guys back together now?"

And no — I did not hide any of my annoyance as I scowled at him, getting up from the bed and whacking him over the back of the head as I left Lila's room.

I went into mine to grab some clothes, and dressed before I wandered out into the loungeroom where Shane was nervously standing next to Lila as she channel-surfed, checking all the stations.

On the screen was a news clipping of a phone-video that captured a car accident and fire, as well as Keith being attacked by a wolf — which I assume was Alex. And when the wolf got thrown, there was a recording that showed elf-Lila kicking Keith's butt.

"Woo... go Lila," I cheered with a happy smile.

Shane didn't share my enthusiasm though. And Lila was too angry to smile.

"Argh! Stupid humans with their stupid camera phones." She growled, throwing a couch cushion at the TV, and then started pacing. "Why is it whenever something dangerous happens you humans have a sudden urge to record it?"

"Money." Shane piped in before looking at me confused. "Did she just call us humans?"

Lila's hair turned white as she yelled at Shane's response. "Who does that? I mean if you're in the middle of a crisis, you should be doing something useful like helping or running, anything but recording."

Well, yeah okay. — She has a point there.

Silently screaming out her frustration, Lila threw another pillow then grunted with annoyance as a knock at the door echoed through the apartment. She stormed to the door, and her hair turned to her natural blond before she opened the door to see Tyme and William standing there, both panic-stricken.

Tyme wrapped his arms around Lila and let out a relieved breath. "Thank God you're alright. Why didn't you tell me you were attacked? Are you okay? How's your wounds? I saw blood in the video... Did Alex or Terrence check the dressing?"

Without even asking, Tyme lifted Lila's pyjama top to make sure her bandages were okay. And I heard Lila growling very quietly as she — kind of patiently waited for Tyme to calm down when he saw no blood. But he was still waiting for an answer from her.

"Tyme, I didn't tell you because it only happened last night... And Alex and Terrence changed the dressing before they left." Lila replied with a slight growl as she pulled away from him, glancing back at William. "But why is your dad here? Danny and Ruby will be awake soon, and they'll start asking questions."

Tyme pushed into the apartment, pulling his dad in with him, and huffed, "The kids will be fine. Your dad was worried about you, and so am I... Lila, I think you should stay in the hotel until you're better."

Woah...

Lila's death stare got icy as she scowled at Tyme. "I told you to stop pushing that whole dad crap with me. Just because we share the same blood does not make us family... William said he was fine with this current... bridged void we have. You should just be glad we're at least on speaking terms and stop forcing the fraccing issue."

Tyme looked like he wanted to argue more, but Shane interrupted. – Which is rather bold for us humankind.

"Um hello... we're kind of getting off-topic here. Lila, are you going to explain what happened or should we just keep watching the news?"

"Shane, chill," Lila grumbled. "I was disguised. No one will recognise me."

Shane pointed back to the TV screen and shouted, "How is white hair and pointy ears a disguise?"

I had to put my hand up here, and admitted, "Actually, that was my idea."

But Lila shushed us all to listen to a little boy on the news give a statement to the reporter. The little boy was so excited, explaining, "There was a big car accident, and a huge wolf and the car was on fire. And an elf lady, she ripped the door off the car and saved me. She fixed my arm and..."

Lila muted the TV, looking back at Shane and grinned, "See, they all think I'm an elf."

"Lila..." Shane grunted, moving his hands to his hips as he frowned. "Elves aren't supposed to exist. They live in fairy tales and stories."

Now exasperated by the issue, Lila was on the verge of losing it, so she threw her hands up and shrugged her shoulders. "Well, what did you want me to do then? Let Keith take off with me to God knows where and do God knows what with me? And I suppose you want me to just let the people burn in their cars as well."

"Yes... I mean, no! Urgh! I just wish you'd be more careful," Shane pleaded, and then turned back to me who was just leaning on the back of the chair, watching this all unfold. And in confusion Shane asked, "Why aren't you getting upset at this... she's your wife?"

"Ex-wife," I corrected. "I can't play the husband card on these situations anymore. And besides, at the moment I'm on her side... If she has the ability to save someone, I expect her to save them. It's just what she does. And she's not gonna hide in this tower either. She has a world to protect."

I glanced over at Lila to see her lips peak to one side as her nose crinkled. But it disappeared again when William stood in front of Lila to explain, "Lila, the last time one of our kind was exposed to the public, it didn't end well. The humankind... they don't understand who or what you are. We're different, Lila, and that scares them."

As she heard those words, Lila stared back at the muted news footage with a sudden revelation. "That's why he couldn't kill me... He did this on purpose."

She then looked back at me to explain, "Keith planned this whole thing. He wanted to cause a scene and expose us... or at least expose me."

Shane got more frustratedly confused at that and asked, "Why would he want to expose you? He's a guardian... he'd be exposing himself too."

She shook her head and answered, "Because he's trying to force us into hiding... Our existence in this world has been kept secret by the world's governments. And though they will never admit it, governments always operate on a need-to-know basis... They have secrets to cover up other secrets. If the public risks finding out that the government has been hiding our existence, then they'll have no choice but to sweep us and our entire team under the rug."

I huffed, slightly irked at Keith's play. "So what your saying is... Keith doesn't have the manpower anymore to take you on alone, so he's getting the government to do his dirty work?"

"Exactly," Lila confirmed as she started think-pacing across the loungeroom, causing Tyme to worriedly ask what she was planning to do. Then after a few laps of the loungeroom, Lila stopped pacing, stared back at the TV and answered with a wry smirk on her face. "I'm going to let Keith play his game, and I think I might even give him a helping hand."

Oh dear. – I know that look.

For a few seconds, Lila disappeared into her room then walked back out in her favourite mission boots, leggings, and a singlet top, placing her dagger in her hidden boot holster and her stone-bracelet on to her wrist. And now extremely nervous at what Lila was doing, Shane moved towards her, trying to get her attention.

"What is that for?" he questioned. "Sissy, why do you need your dagger? Where are you going?"

Lila didn't answer and completely ignored both my brother and hers as they stated the obvious. – That she was injured and still healing. She walked straight passed them to talk to me, whispering to me the plan, using movie reference's we both knew. And I formed a wry grin as I nodded, actually really impressed with her plan.

She pulled her head back to look at me, waiting for me to agree, and then grinned, kissing my cheek to say thank-you. But before she left, she went over to whisper something to William, and he too nodded but looked very worried.

Now ready and with a plan, Lila went for the door when Tyme pleaded with her to stop or to take him with her. But she was on a mission, and I bravely stood in front of the apartment door to stop him. And surprisingly — although I suspect it was out of request, William stood next to me to back me up as I confronted someone who is clearly a lot stronger than me.

"Tyme, this is something she needs to do on her own... Besides, Lila needs you here for her plan to work."

Not surprisingly, Shane frustratedly stood next to Tyme with his arms folded, and grumbled, "What plan?"

Journal entry continued by Lila Winters

Well, this plan can either go two ways. – Very good or horribly wrong. But I'm pretty confident I know the players on this board game, and they are very predictable. If you goad them in just the right way, they'll strike. So now it's time to have a little fun and play super-elf-ninja mum.

Before I left the hotel, I turned my long hair white and wore it down to really play up the elfy-look with my pointy ears poking through the hair. – And the fresh wolf bite scar really added to the whole warrior elf-vibe I was going for. So after taking a breath for confidence, I took off, running at super-speed.

My first super-hero moment was a three-car pile-up. The man in the front car was trying to help the middle car that had been sandwiched and crumpled. I appeared next to the man and asked in such a surreal, echoing voice, "Are you injured?"

He jumped and cursed in fright, replying, "No," then explained that the girls in the car were stuck.

I asked him to step aside before I ripped the car door away from the middle car, and then asked the two women, "Are you injured?"

They both shook their heads to say no, and sure enough, the passenger was filming me. I ignored the phone and played up my echoey voice. "Are you able to exit the vehicle or do you need assistance?"

Both females nodded and climbed out the driver's side as I walked to the back car and found a man unconscious with his head resting on the steering wheel.

I opened the car door and stared at him for a moment then explained to the man from the first car. "His heart rate is fine, but his breathing is shallow."

The man from the first car was still cursing and staring at my appearance, and asked, "What? How do you know that? Who...? What are you?"

I looked back at him and answered, "A friend... Refrain from moving him until the ambulance arrives. He may still be injured." Then I disappeared, running off at super-speed.

Well, that's one down, time to find another one. And it didn't take long. – This one I suspect is actually going to be a fun one. – At one of the nearby schools, there was a fight brewing with a crowd of teenage students circling a fellow student. They were cheering and recording with their many mobile phones as a student was being beaten up – by I'm assuming the school bully on the back of the school oval.

The young student being beaten was strong and kept getting back up, but the bully kept swinging. So before he threw his next punch, I awesomely somersaulted over the students, landing in front of the bully to protect the beaten student – who I now know is Oliver, based on the name on his school book. Then as the bully started to swing, I raised my hand to block his punch, causing him to step back, holding his hand while grunting in pain.

"Don't you know it's rude to hit a woman." I smiled, echoing my voice again.

The other students stopped and gawked as the bully stared at me and asked, "How the hell did you do that?"

My grin grew wry as my eyes glowed green, and I replied, "It's a secret."

The bully huffed as the other students gawked at him and chuckled, so I sarcastically gasped. "Oh, was I interrupting? Because it looks like Oliver here was just about to win against your pretentious need of an ego boost."

The group of teenagers laughed at my statement as the school bully stood taller and boasted, "Your freaky little elf mind must have lost a few brain cells to think he was winning... I'm twice his size and stronger than he'll ever be. Not even you stand a chance against me."

Well, aren't we the bold one.

I turned to help Oliver stand, and he asked how I knew his name. So I pointed to his school books before I suggested, "Follow my instructions if you want to win the fight."

He looked at me and tentatively nodded, but his body was drenched in fear. So my eyes glowed a dark golden to give him a little confidence boost before I told him what to do.

While listening to my instructions, Oliver dodged and ducked and weaved then finally karate chopped the backs of the school bully's knees, causing him to fall.

Oliver looked like he was going to pull a more crushing blow when I called him to stop. Then all the students looked at me as I stood tall, still speaking with the echoing voice, "A true warrior knows when to stop fighting. Only a coward will strike when the opponent is down."

Accepting my advice, Oliver nodded again as I handed him his books, and he said Thank-you before walking off towards the classrooms. I then very, very cheekily smiled back at the circling teenagers before I disappeared again.

Well, so far so good. – And I have not yet torn my stitches. Which means Terry can't grumble at me. – Alex can, but he grumbles at everything.

I did quite a lot more things after that. – I stopped a dog from getting run over and returned him to his owner. I stopped a woman from being hit by a tram because she was too busy on her phone. There was a lady getting pick-pocketed but was too busy to notice at the time, but I handed her stuff back anyway and scared the living daylights out of the thief.

There was one incident that didn't have any cameras or phones, yet I couldn't just stand by and let it happen. – I heard the screams of a woman in the distance, and followed the sounds towards a house where I found a young child, screaming and running from the house out onto the street, about to be hit by a delivery truck.

The truck slammed on his breaks just as I appeared, pulling the little girl off the road and into my arms. The child was frantically screaming for her mummy, so my eyes glowed golden again, resting my hand on her cheek to calm her down.

As she calmed, I heard a struggle coming from inside the house and handed the little girl to the truck driver as he raced from his vehicle. I rushed inside to see two men pinning a young woman to the ground, so with one hand, I pulled both of them off the woman, throwing them onto the couch, and then commanded the vines from my bracelet to tie them up.

The truck driver came running in with the little girl and helped the woman to stand as I disappeared again. – Thinking I had done enough good deeds for the day.

Journal entry insert by Alex Woods

I can't find Lila anywhere. I couldn't even follow her scent after waking up to the worst news report I could ever imagine. After spending hours looking all over the city for her, I came back to the hotel to see almost the entire guardian team, including William, in Lila's apartment, talking to Matt and watching yet another news report of Lila going all crazy.

SHE'S GOING TO GET HERSELF KILLED.

I stormed into her apartment, calling her name when Matt stood to his feet to talk to me. "She's not here, Alex."

"What the hell is she doing? Why would any of you let her do this?" I seethed, trying not to strangle anyone.

"It's part of her plan," Matt huffed back. "You have to trust her."

Before I could react or say anything more, Terrence appeared next to me, hurryingly stating to Matt, "They're here."

Shane then disappeared into Danny's room, bringing out Danny and Ruby, all while Matt grabbed hold of my arm and explained, "Alex, you need to let them take you in... Terrence will fill you in when you get there."

"Like Hell I will... Lila's still out there!" I barked back, fuelled with anger.

"Alex, you need to trust her," he pleaded, walking with me towards the panic room. "She may be injured, but she knows what she's doing."

Terrence opened the door of the hidden panic room then ushered Matt, Shane, and the two children inside, closing it on them as we all heard the footsteps of several soldiers storming in through the door. But amongst all the commotion and yelling, I jumped out of the balcony window, morphing into a small barn owl.

I watched from a distance as the team surrendered and was placed in ridiculously thick handcuffs. Then one of the soldiers whispered to the man – who looked like he was in charge with a fancy suit and all.

"Sir, the area is secure. There's no sign of her."

The man in charge deviously grinned, looking down at Terrence lying on the floor, seeming as if he had just caught a major prize or finished his first hunt, and arrogantly stated, "She won't be far. If she's anything like her father, she'll find us."

CHAPTER 30

Rule 6

Journal entry by Lila Winters

Before I left to track down Terrence and the others, I had to leave a plan B, on the off-chance that plan A doesn't work. I left an envelope on George's office desk with all the information he needed to finish what I started. And on the envelope, I wrote: "Plan B," with a USB and note on the inside reading: "If I don't return," along with my signed name.

I tracked Terrence's scent most of the way. But I was having difficulty finding Alex's scent. It kept sending me in the opposite direction, so I stayed with Terrence's and used our tree-stone bracelets as a marker. – The emotions of the stone-wearers are a lot stronger to read the closer they are to each other, and Terrence was supposedly told by Matt to think about the strongest emotion he had to help me find him. The emotion Terrence chose was passion. – And that is a very strong emotion.

Eventually, I caught up with their convoy and followed it from the cover of the trees. But I need to wait until they're inside the facility for my plan to work, so I stopped to hide and rest, feeling incredibly tired after running at almost a half-speed for... I've actually lost count of the hours. – All I know is that I've done enough cardio for at least a week, maybe two, and I'm really hungry.

While taking my much-needed moment, I took the time to very carefully adjust and tighten the bandage around my stomach. And yeah – my stab wound is aching right now. – But it's not bleeding. So Terry still can't get mad at me.

I stayed hidden and watched as a convoy of black 4-wheel drives escorted the large black delivery van with my team locked inside it into a high-gated facility. From what I could see of the facility, it was a very large modern-style building in the middle of a well-manicured estate with a grass field surrounding it. Attached to the building was what looks like underground car parking. – Most likely leading to several underground levels that would not be on any blueprints or public records.

"Joy, it's Canada all over again." I chuckled to myself before climbing down from the tree I was perched in.

When I landed on the ground, I felt someone grab my shoulder. And in fearing I was busted, I elbowed the man in the face then turned, kneeing him in the stomach and pushing him to the ground, only to realise it was Alex.

FRAC.

"Alex," I quietly shrieked, watching him spit blood from his mouth. "What are you doing here?"

He stood to his feet, spitting out more blood and replied, "I was looking for you."

And frac, I want to hit him again. – He's completely ruined the plan. And I irked, making claw-like hands towards him, struggling so badly with my frustration.

"Argh! Alex, you're supposed to be on the base with Terrence and the others. Didn't Matt tell you the plan?"

"Yes... well, kind of. But I needed to know you were safe."

Urgh! – Frac and Fruit Cakes. – Plan C, Lila, and think of it quick.

I paced back and forth, trying to think. My whole plan was reliant on Alex being on the base with everyone else. But once again, he didn't listen. And now wanting to know my thoughts, Alex very stupidly tried to stop me from pacing and cursing under my breath to talk to me.

"Lila... I just wanted to help you."

And yeah – I lost it, quietly screaming at him, "No, Alex!!! You listening to Matt would have helped me... You don't want to help me... You want to protect me!"

"Of course, I want to protect you."

"I DON'T NEED YOUR PROTECTION!" I yelled. "I needed you to stick to the fraccing plan! And if you had any ounce of respect or trust for me, you would have done so!"

My emotions got the best of me, and the tears pooled in my eyes as I started pacing again. And again, Alex tried to stop me from pacing, grabbing hold of my hand to beg, "Lila, stop... please!"

"NO YOU STOP!" I shouted at him, and I felt his pain when I let out my frustration. "Stop loving me and start trusting me again... I don't want this, Alex. I want the Alex from two years ago. The one who trusted me and listened to me and treated me as his partner. His equal! That Alex was someone I knew would always have my back, facing the danger with me and not trying to hide me from it... And he definitely wouldn't tell me to stay! I want my friend back... I want the Alex I loved back! And if you can't be him... then leave!"

I stared at him, waiting for his response when he let go of my hand, taking a moment to compose himself. I knew he wanted to cry. Probably because it was the first time, I told him that I loved him. – But it was in the middle of a fight, and it was used in the past tense.

"I... I can be that Alex," he replied, taking slow breaths. "What do you want me to do?"

I started pacing again and thought of a new plan. – A plan C that should hopefully lead back to plan A.

"I have an idea," I said, grabbing hold of his hands and holding them close to me. "But this plan requires you to trust me... Can you do that?"

I stared into his eyes and sensed the truth from him, and part of him did trust me when he nodded. So I told him the plan. It hasn't changed by much, all I had to do was sneak him into the building by creating a large enough distraction. And the way to do that is to make them see double.

Alex morphed into me. – And yeah, it looked and felt weird.

Together, we raced at full-speed towards the two guards at the gates checkpoint, and knocked them out cold before pulling them into the nearby bushes for us to steal their uniforms. So now Alex and I are identical.

We ran at half-speed towards the building, each from different directions, and both ran through the doors of the main reception area where we broke off to make as much damage as we can. – I'm actually really glad that they were expecting me because most of the soldiers were waiting in the reception area, guarding the front door, which meant I didn't have to go looking for them.

And yes – they really are that predictable to think that I was predictable. I just don't think they were expecting two of me, and it caused a heck of a lot of confusion. But while I continued to fight, Lila 2 – Alex – disappeared. Then once he was safe, I eventually let the soldiers win and surrendered to them.

I knelt on the ground, letting the guards pull at my arms to keep me still, and as I did, a man named Agent Phillip Green. – And I'm serious that's his name. – It so has to be fake. – Either way, he walked up to me and grinned as he ordered the soldiers to cuff me and lead me to an interrogation room.

The idiot thinks these cuffs can hold me. These are the same cuffs The Board uses. The one with an electrical trigger in the centre that goes off if you pull too hard. – And I've broken out of these before.

Way down, in possibly the lowest part of the building in a white-cement-covered room, Phillip sat down on the opposite side of the interrogation table, and opened up a file all about me. – Almost. – It stated that I was a Nature guardian cross hybrid Animal guardian, but that was pretty much it.

Huh. – Looks like Odele really does believe in keeping secrets.

With arrogance, he placed surveillance photos down in front of me. One of Alex and Terrence, then of Adela, Tyme, Jennifer, Henry, William, and Katie.

"You've collected quite an army, Ms Winters."

I leaned back in my chair and grinned. "You remind me of someone on The Board... so... arrogant and smug."

He tittered, leaning forward as he grinned. "And you, Ms Winters, remind me of your father... General Willows."

Pausing for a moment, he waited for me to react. But I didn't. So he continued, "Look, we're on the same side here, Ms Winters... But I'm sure you already knew that before you busted in here hurting a lot of my soldiers."

I leaned closer to him as my grin disappeared, and I hissed, "General Willows is not my father... And I'm positive you already knew that before you broke into my apartment and kidnapped all my friends."

"You're right. I do know a lot about you and your team," he said smugly.

"I doubt that," I mocked as he placed a stack of files on the table with all their names on it. – Except for one.

He pointed to the photo of Tyme and stated, "Yet, I don't know him?"

Oh Joy. – Now my interrogation has really begun.

Richard actually did teach me quite a few tricks of his trade when I was training to be the perfect little soldier girl. One being the best way to get information. – Make the target feel so smug and victorious, that they feel confident to ask you the questions they don't know by telling you what they do know, all while under the assumption that you will never have the opportunity to repeat or act on the information you get. And Agent Phillip Green fell for it. – Hook, line and sinker. – What an idiot.

Journal entry insert by Alex Woods

I think Lila was right. Even though her words hurt when she said it. – My love for her clearly endangered the entire team. And if I had listened to Matt, most of Lila's plan would be done by now.

Her original plan also included her not fighting because she was being mindful of her still healing knife wound, and didn't want to worry me or Terrence if it re-opened. – Yet me not following her plan meant she had to fight and be a big enough distraction for me to get in. – And I definitely sensed her pain when she was fighting the soldiers.

Yep. – Terrence is going to be really ticked off with me.

I hid in the cleaning closet while Lila was taken into custody. Then using the ID picture attached to the uniform I stole, I morphed from Lila's form into a man named Archer. – And yes, it is really nice to be back in a man's body. – No offence to Lila's body of course. – It's just I prefer to look at it. Not be it.

In saying that, Lila's plan is partially back on track. I just need to go and free the others. And it was fairly easy since most of the people on this base are humans. I knocked the soldiers that were guarding the base-cells out in a second.

Gosh. – What was I worrying about? – Lila could have done this with one hand behind her back.

When I walked into the cells to find the rest of the team, they didn't recognise me. But when I opened the cell door, Tyme looked at me suspiciously and asked, "Lila?"

I kind of didn't want to tell them it was me. But I didn't want to lie, so I answered with such a sad sigh, "Not quite."

With cheek, Katie grinned at me. "You're in trouble, aren't you, Alex?"

I huffed at her begrudgingly but stayed focused. "Do you all remember the plan?"

They all nodded as I un-cuffed their hands, and then disappeared in pairs to carry out their mission. Katie, Jennifer, Adela, and Tyme were on data recovery. William and Terrence were on guardian recovery, and I was on Lila recovery.

It kind of feels good that she still expects me to rescue her. But she wants me to do it in style. – To send a really clear message that the government are in way over their heads.

Journal entry continued by Lila Winters

This interrogation is going rather well. So far, I've learnt from Phillip that they are only newbies to the project, recently assigned to oversee our kind because Mission Control had been dismantled. They know what we are but not the full extent, and they know about The Board but only based on mission controls reports. – Which are of course corrupted.

He also has no idea what kind of operation we're running at the hotel or the fact that we have a New York based team, and pretty soon if all goes to plan for the NY's – a London based team as well. All Agent Green knew was his job. – Analyse and protect our secret at all cost, and deal with any threats that arise or threaten the security of this nation.

Yada yada yada. – Same old spiel wherever you go.

As the interrogation went on, he kept asking me questions, and I kept eluding him by giving him vague answers. He was determined to find out who Tyme was and what his abilities were. And I just kept saying he's a friend, causing him to lose his patience with me, realising I was being difficult.

Pfft... No der.

"Ms Winters, I suggest you co-operate with us. I will get the information I want one way or the other."

Now more than happy to move from interrogation to negotiation, I leaned back and tapped my fingers on the table. "And what's in it for me? What have you got planned for me and my friends when you finally get what you want?"

"We relocate you. And if you actually tell me what I want to know, I'll ensure your living arrangements are comfortable," he answered, assuming it was his only offer.

"Yeah, but you see... that's just not going to work for me." I grinned, shaking my head.

He leaned back all smug, crossing his arms. "I'm afraid you don't have a choice."

I was laughing to myself – but on the inside – because this guy has nothing on me, and I could take him in a second. But I needed him to realise that he wants me and my team to be his allies and not his enemies, so I have to keep playing this game while I wait for Alex.

"There's always plan C," I said while twiddling with the photos of Alex and Terrence on the table.

Phillip then placed an envelope down on the table. – One I recognised. – And then questioned, "What happened to plan B?"

The envelope was the one I'd sent to George – on the off chance I didn't return. The problem is the USB inside the envelope doesn't have anything of value on it. It's actually a Trojan horse to 1 – weed out the leak in our hotel's team, and 2 – deliver a tiny little computer virus that Matt had created to disable a facilities intranet and security systems.

Clever man that Matt is.

With such perfect timing, Alex barged into the room disguised as one of the soldiers we had tied up at the front gate. "Sir, there's been a security breach. The prisoners are gone."

Phillip stood in a fury, asking how, when Alex punched him in the face. He then pinned Phillip against the wall as he morphed from the soldier back into me, and grinned with such cheeky attitude just like mine as he said, "Because I let them go."

Frac damn. – I look feisty.

Phillip shook his head in disbelief, gasping, "No. That's not possible."

"Oh, but it is," the other me boasted. "And I've had so much fun roaming these halls. But it's time for us to go."

Plan A was back on track, but neither of us realised just how desperate Phillip was when he drew his gun and shot me. – The real me in the arm.

Naturally, Alex reacted to me getting hurt, shouting my name and giving the game away, leading Phillip to shoot the other me in the stomach, now knowing I wasn't her.

Alex fell to the ground and morphed back into himself, holding his stomach in pain as Phillip stood over Alex's body, readying to execute him. But before he did, Phillip looked back at me, still sitting in the chair leering at him as he mocked me. "Yep, just like your father."

In seconds, I sped from the chair, breaking the handcuffs and absorbing the electricity that hit me, sending the spark flying up towards the light, shattering one of the bulbs and causing the other to flicker. Then while using my night vision and the semi-darkness, I pulled Alex to safety before snatching the gun from Phillip's hand and crushing the barrel.

As Phillip scanned the dark room looking for me, he barked into his radio, ordering for the emergency lights to be turned on. – Which was helpful to me because it gave me the heads up to turn my night-vision off before they came on. And as the back-up lights lit the room, I appeared behind Phillip, looking angry as ever when I kicked his feet from beneath him, and then pinned him to the ground as I held his throat.

"General Willows is a manipulative liar and a murderer. Push me far enough and I can be much worse," I growled as my hair faded white and my eyes turned black.

I peered across to Alex to see if he was okay, but what I saw in him felt so much worse than the bullet in my arm. – He looked scared. – Of me.

Suddenly my eyes felt like they were on fire as the hand around Phillip's throat started to glow and burn his skin. I pulled away as soon as I could and punched Phillip before I stood to my feet, still trying to maintain that act of intimidation. Then while taking slow breaths, I shook my hand, forcing the glow to disappear as I spoke.

"You invade my home, kidnap my friends, and dare threaten me. And you say we're on the same side... But I've heard that shit before. So if you really want to be allies with me, then prove it. Sit down in the chair and we'll talk terms."

Phillip stood to his feet, nursing the burn on his neck and taking a moment, eyeing me and sizing me up. As he did, I kept a general eye on him while I pulled Alex to his feet and absorbed his pain so he could stand. – But I didn't let his pain affect me.

Carefully, I tore open the uniform Alex has on to check the wound, and from the looks of it, the bullet went straight through his torso which means I can heal him without issue. So I pulled out the two blue-rose epi-pens that I had hidden in the bandage around my torso, and then injected one into Alex's stomach.

Alex very kindly tore part of his shirt up and used it to bandage my arm and slow the bleed while I addressed Phillip again. "Tic-toc, Mr Green... I'm not one to offer alliances a second time around."

Phillip watched in amazement as Alex's bullet wound healed completely, leaving a minor scar. Then he made the wise decision to sit down in the chair opposite me.

When he was close enough, I injected the second epi-pen into Phillip's leg, causing him to wince a little as he felt the burn on his neck and the bruises on his back start to heal.

He seemed fairly cooperative after that, and by the end of the discussion, we had made an alliance between our – let's say organisations.

The agreement is for both parties to share information with each other and meet every few weeks for a general debrief. He also requested the healing tonic I just gave him, as well as the Neuritamine cure. – Not knowing that they're the same thing.

I agreed to it because having the government on my side feels good for a change, and it also means Phillip has to regularly screen his men as I do mine to avoid infiltration again. So I like this plan. – I like it a lot.

Once we had agreed on all terms, Phillip escorted Alex and me up out of this awful, plant-deprived building to the front driveway, where my team appeared waiting for me – with a few extra guardians that Terrence and William had found along the way.

Phillip confusedly stared at them and was going to ask how, but I interrupted him by politely shaking his hand. "It was nice meeting you, Mr Green."

"Likewise," he tentatively replied. "My men will be here shortly to return you to the hotel."

I smiled at his gracious yet suspicious offer then politely declined, "Thanks, but we have our own ways of getting home... See you in a few days, Mr Green."

"It's Phil," he piped in. So I nodded, conceding to call him Phil. But he also implored, "Just do me a favour and stay out of trouble."

I grinned back at the team, especially at Alex, and chuckled under my breath as I looked at Phil and shook my head, "No promises."

The team plus extras then took off at full-speed into the tree-line, except for Alex and Terrence, who waited for me as I walked closer to Phil.

"Oh, and if you ever abduct my friends again..." I leaned closer, handing Phil a black rose while whispering into his ear a not-so-subtle threat, and his eyes widened as I stood back and innocently smiled. "It's a pleasure doing business with you, Phil. See you soon."

With those words, I took off at full-speed with Alex and Terrence right next to me.

CHAPTER 31

Diamond In The Rough

Journal entry by Lila Winters

Alright, I think Alex is avoiding me. We haven't really said anything to each other since our fight at the government facility heist on Monday. It's now Friday, and last Sunday during our friends-date, Terrence and Alex said that they wanted to do it again with me, and we had settled to go on a date every week on Friday with each of us taking turns planning the activity. But tonight Alex and Terrence have opted for a guy's night, inviting Matt and Tyme to go with them. – Shane was invited to join them as well, but he's working on the desk tonight. And since all the boys are busy, the girls have roped me into doing a girls night.

Chase offered to babysit Danny and Ruby for me because he wanted an excuse to watch one of the new releases from Disney. – Which is technically a children's movie, and he wants to protect his image. He's already taken over my loungeroom, and set it up for a night of Disney classics with popcorn, pizza, and lots of sugary lollies.

Hmm. – Sugar. – This night may end hilariously bad for him.

With no real excuse left for me, I reluctantly agreed to the girls-night on the condition that there was no shopping involved. But my mind seems to be on other things at the moment.

I really want to talk to Alex and find out why he was so scared when he looked at me. – Did he think I was a monster or something? – I was being a little intimidating when I was pinning Phillip to the ground. And I know I was angry, but Phillip had compared me to the General several times and shot me, and Alex. – I was just barely keeping my emotions in check.

Maybe that's why Alex is scared. – Because I'm a hybrid who can't control her abilities.

The girls-night was not really my scene, and I lost interest pretty quickly after dinner. I claimed I didn't feel well, rambling on about a head cold and needing to sleep it off, and then headed back up to my apartment with them wishing me to feel better soon.

When I got back, Matt was already home as well, but he was in his room, researching something that he had a thought about while he was halfway through dinner at the guys night. – He apparently just got up and left, which now explains the random text message I got from Terrence, asking if Matt was okay.

I'm actually really glad that Terrence is still happy to talk to me, and he still comes up to my apartment every morning to have breakfast with me. – And to check and change the dressing on my stomach and the bullet wound dressing on my arm.

He's just texted again, asking if I'm enjoying girls night. So I texted Terrence back.

> The dinner was good, but I've opted for a research night instead.

> It looks like Matt has the same idea. He's in his room, reading. And I'm headed to my office.

Research?

Lila it's Friday. You should be having fun.

> Research can be fun…

> Besides, I'm trying to find a cure for your mother.

You know I don't want you doing that.

> I promised Izzy. And you know I don't break my promises.

I know. And I love that about you.

Do you want me to come back and help?

> No. Just have some fun and keep Tyme out of trouble.

> I'll see you in the morning.

Okay. See you then.

I got set up in my office to do some research to fulfil the promise I'd made to Izzy Connors. And after a few hours of reading through quite a number of the old journals in my office, I think I've finally come across something that just might work. I found a journal that talks about the "blood of the Rare" with a drawing of all the guardian elements surrounding a young male, who was bleeding from a knife wound and holding a dagger in his hand. And at the bottom of the page is a list of ingredients with the list labelled: "The drop of life."

Well, it does have me wondering if I had all of the elements in me. I mean I have displayed quite a number of them already, so maybe this could work. But I'd need to test out my theory of having all the element abilities. – The question is how?

I thought since Alex and Terrence wanted me to be honest with them more often, that this might be a good opening to finally get to talk to Alex. I texted Terrence to tell him that I may have found something. But I got no response from him.

Still wanting to talk to them, I went down to their apartment to wait. But just as I was about to knock on the door, I remembered Alex's face and the fear he had, which made me scared and sad. – What did he think of me in that moment of fear, and what would he think of me if I really do have the ability to control all the elements? – He was scared when he found out I was an Animal guardian. – And I know he freaked out when I told him I could create fire. – So what will this do?

Oh Frac. – I can feel the fire in my eyes again and my hands beginning to glow. I had to pull away from Alex's door, making sure I didn't touch anything as I took deep breaths, trying to calm down.

Damn Fracs. – I really need to get a handle on this fire thing. And the best person to help me with this is Billy. – I just hope he's still there.

I crept down into the basement, not wanting anyone to see me leave, when I heard a car pull into the basement car park. It was Adela's car, the one Tyme had asked to borrow.

I quickly hid behind some parked cars, and my eyes glowed gold as I used my animal abilities to mask my scent from Alex. But my heart aches at the fact that I need to hide from him.

Alex, Terrence, and Tyme were in the middle of a conversation as they got out of the car, and they were talking about me.

"So what, you're just going to pretend like nothing's happened between you two?" Tyme asked Alex.

"Yep." He nodded. "She told me to stop loving her, and I have to at least try to respect that."

Tyme pulled a sour face and sighed. "Ouch, that's really gotta sting."

But Terrence jumped to my defence. "I'm sure she didn't mean it in that way. She was probably just angry that you didn't trust her."

"Do either of you?" Tyme asked. Then both Alex and Terrence looked at Tyme confused as he repeated, "Do either of you really trust her?"

Well, that's an easy answer. – It should be an instant yes. – But it wasn't. – Not even from Terrence. – What???

In deep thought, they stood waiting for the elevator when Alex replied, "I trust Lila with the world. It's the world I don't trust... Lila's rare. She's a guardian with more than one ability, and to The Board and the rest of the world, she's like a rare painting or a blood diamond... People have died to get their hands on her."

"Well, she can't be the only one of her kind, surely there are others like her?" Tyme questioned.

"No, there isn't." Alex shook his head. "It's been forbidden for our people to breed amongst other types for centuries... That law was made in order to control the balance of power amongst governments and tribes."

"Well, I guess my dad didn't get the memo," Tyme suggested, shrugging his shoulders.

"I'm not so sure about that..." Terrence sighed before he explained, "Alex, do you remember the story I told you and Lila, about the German soldier... For years the governments on both sides hunted and tracked that soldier's family and his children."

"Yeah." Alex nodded, and then asked, "What happened to them?"

It was then I could sense Terrence's fear as he looked around the basement cautiously. I crouched down further behind the car, trying to stay hidden as Terrence whispered, "After what we've seen Lila do, it made me curious, and I've been doing a little digging... 40 years ago the American government had captured the soldier's last known surviving family member... It was a 9-year-old girl... They found her in Russia, hiding in a small town. The report I found said that she had a family, but the only one they managed to find was the girl... Her name was Katerina Dunst."

"Katherine?" Alex croaked. "You think Lila's mother was that little girl... How do you know all this?"

"I may have swiped my mother's computer tablet during our last visit. It has quite a lot of reports about Lila... But I also found out that Odele was the one charged to retrieve Katerina when she fell off the radar 30 years ago. It took a few years to track her, but when she was retrieved and brought back to The Board, the report stated Katerina had recently given birth."

I could sense Alex's fear heighten, stepping back, scrubbing his hands through his hair, and gasping, "Hang on... Are you trying to tell us that Lila's the descendant of a Mega guardian, who destroyed 9 villages and is responsible for the deaths of thousands of innocent people?"

Again, Terrence shook his head. "He wasn't a Mega. He was missing a few elements, Time, Electricity, and Nature... Yet according to Odele's notes, the only element Katerina was missing was nature, and I'm pretty certain that's where William fits in... Katerina was trying to finish what her family started. She was trying to create a Mega..."

Well, it looks like I wasn't the only one curious about what I am. And all this time, Terrence already knew.

Yeah. – That really does hurt.

Suddenly, I sensed Tyme's fear as he struggled to speak, "My sisters a Mega... Does... does she know?"

I peered up to see the shock across Tyme's face, and it really hurt to sense his fear. But then Terrence looked at Tyme, taking a moment to answer, "I don't think so... I wasn't sure how to tell anyone, especially because you're trying so hard to get Lila and your dad on speaking terms... If Lila found out, that the only reason she was born was to complete the elemental puzzle, it would crush her heart... So I don't think any of us should tell her."

What?!?

"Terrence is right... This will only upset her more," Alex added. – And I tried so hard not to let my anger push through and give away my position as he stepped into the elevator.

Those lying pieces of Fracs. – Lecturing me about telling the truth and being honest with them, yet they have no hesitation in keeping this from me. The whole thing just made me feel so frustrated, and I may have let out a sniffle, struggling to hold back my tears.

Frac.

I think Tyme heard me, because he was slowly walking back towards the car I'm hiding behind. But thankfully, Alex called to him, causing Tyme to give up and race back into the elevator.

While staying silent, I waited until the door had closed before I disappeared, running out into the streets, feeling betrayed and hurt.

I was so blinded by my tears that I accidentally ran into William way too hard as he was heading back to the hotel. He was drinking a coffee and I stupidly spilt it all over him.

"I'm so sorry." I sniffled with tears streaming down my cheeks.

He looked up at me to see my sadness, asking, "Lila, what's wrong?"

"It's nothing, I..." I cleared my throat and tried to pull it together. "I just have something in my eye. I'm sorry but I need to go." Then before he could say anything else, I raced off into the night.

I kept running until I got to Billy's apartment out in Coburg. I was still crying but also trying to stay quiet as I cautiously crept into his apartment.

The room was dark as I whimpered, "Hello."

Without warning, I was pinned to the wall as I felt Billy's hand clutching my throat and dragging my back up against the plaster. He growled and told me I'd picked the wrong man to mess with, and then yelled, "I will not go back!"

Oh Frac. – He thinks I'm a hunter.

I struggled to breathe because he was grasping my neck so tight, and I choked. "Billy... please... Billy."

In my fear, I grabbed the hand that was crushing my windpipe, and the fire burned in my eyes again as my hand glowed, accidentally burning Billy's arm. He let me go, pulling away in pain, and I fell to the ground drawing as much air into my lungs as I could, nursing the pain in my neck with the back of my forearm, avoiding the glow of my hands.

He heard my scared breaths and whimpers then created a small flame stem in the centre of his hand, moving it closer to me to light my face.

"Lila?" he gasped. "I'm sorry, I didn't see who you were. I thought that..."

"It's okay." I barely wheezed, keeping my glowing hands up and away from everything. "It's my fault... I'm sorry."

"Lila, your hands," Billy interrupted, staring at them.

I whimpered again, watching my hands slowly return to normal as I struggled to speak. "I know... but I can't control it... I need your help."

Journal entry insert by Billy Jonas

Aw Darn. – This is the first time I've seen Lila in months, and I stupidly crushed her windpipe. – I'm such an idiot.

Moving quickly, I pulled her up onto her feet and raced to light the nearby candles at super-speed, appearing back in front of her and apologising again. I then walked her to the kitchen and lifted her up to sit on the bench.

"Lila, have you been crying?" I asked, caressing her cheek to wipe the tears away.

"No." She quietly sniffled, tucking some of the loose strands of her hair back into her braid. "I mean, kind of... it's complicated. I'm sorry... This was a mistake. I... I shouldn't have come."

At super-speed, I placed my hands on her hips to stop her from moving and pressed my forehead to hers as I whispered, "This will never be a mistake."

She did that cute thing she does with her nose and bit her bottom lip as her fingers danced around each other. Then she drew closer to me as my arms enveloped her body, and she whimpered, "Thank you."

I soaked in every moment of her before I asked, "Now, what is it that you need my help with?"

While staying in my arms, Lila explained how she accidentally burned the neck of a government official and nearly burnt down Alex's apartment door, leading her to ask if I could help her control her fire element. But she also talked to me about her, who she really is, and that she's a hybrid Mega with all the elements.

She even showed me a few of them, turning on my apartment lights by sending electricity into them. And I'm very impressed because now I can see her properly. Sadly, I noticed the darkening hand-shaped bruise on her neck, making me feel very mad at myself. But I was also able to see what she was wearing. – A tight-fitting singlet top and the yellow cardigan that I had left in a yellow gift box at the hotel desk for her on her birthday.

I felt my lips tilt up just a bit, very happy to see that she liked her birthday present. Then Lila nervously stared up at me with those beautiful, teary blue eyes of hers, moving back into my arms as she cried with a raspy voice, "I can do a lot more than that, but again I can't control them. And I don't know what to do."

I could see the fear all over Lila's body as she trembled in my arms, so I agreed to help her. Not just with her fire element but with the others as well.

I led her out onto the rooftop for more space and less flammable objects, and then showed her how easy it is to create the fire before explaining, "Our powers are amplified by an emotion. So to control the fire, you need to harness and understand the emotion it's linked to."

A little confused, Lila rasped, still trying to regain her voice. "But I'm not entirely sure what the emotions are."

Part of me ached at the fact that I caused her that pain, but I continued and asked, "What was the emotion you felt when you first turned into a wolf?"

She walked around and paced a little while playing with her fingers. "That one's difficult. I mean, my white hair first appeared on the island when Richard shot my friend and blamed my disobedience for it. But when I turned into an actual wolf, it was New Year's Eve. I had just found out Matt had cheated on me, and I took off, running into a group of hunters... I was fuelled with so many emotions that all of the elements came through at once. But rage seems to be a common factor. I mean, every time my white hair appeared after that... it's usually when I'm angry."

Darn. — This girl's been through a lot.

"Okay... What did you feel before when I had you pinned against the wall?" I asked.

"Um... I couldn't breathe and I thought you were going to kill me. So, I was scared," she answered while rubbing the bruise on her neck.

"Scared... good. Okay, we can work with that." I said, a little puzzled while staring at her. "Alright, I need you to think about what you're most afraid of."

She looked around for a moment and got lost in thought, staring over the city towards the bay, and then rasped, "Okay, I've got it."

"Now focus on that fear and push that emotion from your mind and into your hands."

She closed her eyes for a second, trying to concentrate when suddenly a burst of flames shot out of Lila's hands towards the wall. The strength of the flames was so strong that she was thrown backwards from the force of the blast. And when the flames disappeared, so had she.

I called her name, looking around the rooftop, only to hear her raspy voice try to scream mine. I followed the sound of her voice, looking over the side of the building to see her hanging onto the top floor window ledge with her hands glowing bright red, scorching the window sill as she gripped to it.

"Don't move. I'll come down and get you, just hold on!"

I raced as fast as I could down to the top floor apartment, kicking open the door, and caught Lila's hands just seconds before she fell. The blistering heat from her hands, seared mine as I held tight, pulling her in through the window. She then landed on me, trying to pull her hands away from me as she started to panic more.

Standing to her feet, Lila kept her distance from me. – I think she's scared that she's going to hurt me. – Her feet started to glow as she burned through her sparkly green shoes, and then began to burn through the carpet.

"Billy!" she fearfully rasped. "What do I do? How do I stop it?"

"You need to change your emotions... Think of something other than your fear," I answered, trying to mask my panic and ignore the thought of her burning straight down into the apartment below and setting the building on fire.

I think Lila had that same thought when she replied, "How? I'm freaking out and burning everything, which makes me freak out more... BILLY!!!"

Thinking on my feet, I thought the best thing to do was to make her feel my emotions. She said she could do that as an Animal guardian. So I thought of how I feel about her and amplified it as I stood behind Lila, wrapping my arms around her and lifting her off the floor to cradle her in my arms.

She struggled to break free from me, trying to keep her glowing hands and feet away from my skin. But I held her tighter, keeping her close to my chest as I thought about everything I felt for her.

I admire her. Respect her. Adore her. And love her. – And I want her to sense that in me.

Seconds passed, and Lila slowly started to calm, relaxing in my arms. So I leaned against the wall and slid down to the floor, still holding tight to her as she nestled into my lap and her glowing hands and feet returned to normal. I then saw something amazing. Her skin shone like diamonds, twinkling in the moonlight.

"Lila... are you okay?" I whispered, brushing the fringe of her blond hair back.

She clenched my shirt, trying to slow her breath, and cried, "No... just... don't let me go."

I have no plans to. – And I don't ever want to.

While holding onto her gently, I waited, listening to Lila's heartbeat slow as she rested her head on my chest. – I think she's enjoying the emotions I'm giving her. – Until my emotion changed, realising she had a massive gash in her thigh, and it was bleeding badly. I think she was still in shock though or ignoring the pain. – Rule 2 and all.

I brushed my hand across the blood to show her. But she was more concerned about the weeping burn blisters on my hands and wrists in the shape of her dainty ones.

"I burnt you..." she gasped. "I'm sorry, I didn't mean to hurt you."

With the uninjured part of my hand, I caressed her cheek and smiled. "I know... but you're bleeding and you need stitches."

I pulled my hand away, realising I had just rubbed Lila's blood all over her face and in her hair. Then her eyes peeked up at me as she cheekily grinned. "I'll fix you if you fix me."

Well, that sounds like a fair deal.

She had to fix my hands before I could stitch her up, and I watched her in absolute amazement. The way she creates those flowers is just so elegant and her face beamed with joy as those beautiful blue eyes of hers glowed green. It was so natural for her. – The relationship she has with nature is like she had bonded with it and it was a part of her. And that's what she needs to do with the other elements.

Journal entry insert by Tyme Knight

When I had finished guys night and left Alex's apartment, I was a bit bewildered at everything I had just learned. – Lila is... well, she's super powerful. And that makes me scared. Not of her but of what people will do to control her. She's probably the first of her kind. And Terrence said the only element Lila needed was Nature to be complete. – That means she has the ability to control Time. – She's like me, only different.

And what about her children? – Danny might be like her as well. He's going to be in constant danger if he develops any abilities. I know it's not always a guarantee for the offspring if the guardian mates with a human, but it's happened before.

When I got to the door of my apartment, I hesitated, wondering what I should do if Lila was still in there. I mean, Adela had offered the use of her car in exchange for my Xbox and TV for the night, which means she might still be there.

I had to brave it at some point, so I opened the door to see only Adela and Katie, sitting on the couch, playing a car racing demo.

"Hey." Adela greeted. "You look like you're going to be sick. Are you sick like Lila?"

Fear raced into me as I questioned. "Wait... Lila's sick?"

"Yeah, she came down for dinner but called for an early night due to some head-cold or something, and Jess left 10 minutes ago."

That's strange, guardians don't usually get sick.

In knowing that, I walked into my room to call Lila and see if she was okay, but it went straight to voice mail. I tried calling her again as Adela nervously leant on the frame of my bedroom door with Katie egging her on about something.

"So, are you sick?" Adela asked.

I shook my head. "No, guardians don't get sick. You know that."

She nodded, slowly realising she'd been partially stood up by my sister but quickly brushed it off, looking slightly anxious. "So, are you busy tonight?"

I was distracted because Lila wasn't answering her phone, so I opted to send her a text when Adela asked if she could stay the night.

"Um... Yeah sure, I'll set up the couch," I mumbled.

Katie then stormed into the room, pulling the mobile from my hand and snapped, "Hello... she didn't mean like that. What she meant was that she wants to sleep with you in your bed."

Adela quickly got agitated, snatching the phone back off Katie, and then handed it back to me. And I stood up, completely confused about what was going on.

"I'm sorry... I don't understand. Last time we talked, you wanted to be friends... And I was happy to do that."

"I did," Adela replied, still looking extremely nervous. "But it was because I was scared, and... and needed time to process everything. And I'm glad you stayed with me, and gave me that time. But... I was hoping now, after everything... to maybe reach that next step with you again."

Oh...

Not knowing what to say, I paced the room as the thought of Danny being taken away by hunters because he might be a hybrid raced through my mind. It made my stomach churn. I then thought of the baby Adela and I almost had, realising that it too would have been a hybrid. Something that was rare and forbidden.

"Um... I'm sorry, but... no." I sighed. – In complete shock that I said no.

"What?" Katie shrieked in disbelief. "This woman is madly in love with you, and you're just going to say no when she asks for something more... Have you lost your mind? Just a few weeks ago, you were in tears at the thought of losing her."

Trying to calm the room, Adela pulled Katie back to stop her from yelling. "Katie, it's okay. There was no harm in trying."

I quickly stopped pacing and tried to explain, "No, it's not like that. I want to... I do. And Katie's right, I can't bear the thought of losing you."

In hearing that, Adela stared back at me, wanting more, waiting for more. And I shook my head, still trying to understand my own thoughts. "I'm sorry, but I just found out some information tonight that I don't know what to do with... And I'm going to need some time to think it through."

I sat back down on the bed lost in a world of worry, and Adela must have given Katie a look that clearly said, 'You need to leave' because Katie came up with a lame excuse and left.

Journal entry continued by Lila Winters

After I patched up Billy and his hands were all healed, he started gathering the supplies he needed to fix me from his stash of stolen medical supplies, and he emptied out his backpack to get a better look at what he had. – He's still very impressed that his apartment lights are still on, still drawing energy from me, and he commented that I'm even more fascinating to him now.

I sat down on his mattress when he appeared kneeling on the floor next to me, helping me to straighten my leg out so that he could remove the make-shift tourniquet of his belt from above my thigh. He then very carefully pulled off my bloodied, torn jeans to get a better look at the wound.

I took my yellow cardigan off as well because I didn't want to get any more bloodstains on it than it already has.

It only has a few blood smears on the sleeve and one on the shoulder. – So it's totally fixable.

It's my favourite cardigan, and Billy smiled when I raspingly told him that. – I also told him that a very nice man left it at the hotel for me on my birthday, but he didn't have the decency to stick around like I did for his birthday.

With a curious grin on him, Billy cheeked, "Would you have let the nice man stay in your bed on your birthday, like he did for you?"

"If it convinced him to come home and stay with me, then yeah, I would have." I very confidently croaked, still struggling with my voice.

Yeah – I don't think Billy was expecting that answer, and he went very quiet when he saw me quickly opting to not look directly at him.

Instead I focused on what he was doing. His hands felt so soft and gentle. But when he cleaned the wound, I yelped and instinctually glared at him. He then held up a small metal sliver that he'd just pulled out of my leg, and he pouted as his brows furrowed. "Sorry... that was stuck in there pretty deep."

I could hear myself growling at him as he continued to pull out more of the metal slivers, and occasionally he would glance up at me with a little peak at his lips. But a small pout had formed on mine, and I had to ask, "Billy... why didn't you come back... when the warehouse burnt down?"

His eyes peered to mine, and then he shook his head, unable to look at me anymore. "I... I couldn't face you... after... um... after I learned..."

Struggling with his words, I placed my hand on his. But he pulled away, and I grew more confused and nervous. "Billy, please... Please be honest with me."

"Stephen helped in killing your mother," he blurted out, now filled with regret, and very hesitantly kept his distance from me as my eyes flickered black. "You were right. He was just using me. And I was blinded by my mistrust towards Maxwell because of his past that I didn't see the real monsters until it was too late, and... I'm sorry."

The sting in my chest felt like it was rising and growing, but I managed to breathe through it and not let my hair turn white. Instead I played with my fingers and stared up at him to ask, "So where is Stephen now?"

"He's dead... He was killed when the warehouse burnt down."

"Okay... Good." I nodded, not sure how to feel at this moment. – But I had started this conversation for a reason, and I'm not giving up, even if I have to lose what's left of my voice in the process. "So... that... that means there's no reason why you can't come back with me. He can't keep you from leaving or threaten to hurt me anymore."

His eyes darted to mine again and looked baffled as he stayed staring at me. And now feeling a little nervous, I cleared my throat as I glanced down at the open gash on my leg and realised it was still seeping blood with metal things sticking out of it. – And I've stupidly distracted the man, who's supposed to be fixing it.

Oops.

With a casual smile, I grabbed the cloth from his hand to apply some pressure to the gash before I spoke, "I told you, Billy, I'll never give up on you... Plus... if it's alright with you, I'm still hoping you'll be my go-to doctor when stuff like this happens. If so, it will be a lot easier for you to fix me if I don't have to travel out here all the time..."

I paused for a moment and realised something that I might not have accounted for, and then added, "Unless... you... you really don't want to."

Oh frac. – I hadn't thought of that reason. – What if it's true and he really doesn't want to come back? – What if he doesn't actually like me as a friend or a boss or even a person? – I honestly thought that when he was sharing those feelings with me before, that the love he felt was for me. But I can't be certain. – It has been a few months. And I am a lot to handle.

And we didn't really leave things on a good note. – Oh Frac, Billy, please say something.

He stayed staring at me, watching me almost chewing on my lip, and he struggled not to smile as he went back to cleaning and fixing my leg. – And yeah, I'm trying really hard not to growl at him from the pain I'm in. But then he peered up at me and asked, "You would seriously let me come back? You're not mad at me, at all."

"Oh, I am mad at you... for a number of reasons." I crossed my arms and sighed, looking around the apartment as I spoke with a gravelly sound. "But mad or not you're still my friend... And I do not want you staying in this cold, dark apartment. Not when there's a perfectly good apartment waiting for you back at the hotel... It has a comfy bed and lights and hot water, and a TV. And... and me... it has me... You'd be able to train with me in the morning again. And you can join me and Terry to have breakfast... Or I can do something else to make you more comfortable... Just... please, please don't say no."

Pulling the cutest puppy-dog eyes I could muster, I stared at him. But he stayed focused on pulling the many slivers from my leg. Then eventually, with a tiny tilt in his lips, he nodded. "Okay."

"Really?" My shocked smile beamed with eager joy.

"Yeah." He nodded again, finally looking up to show me his cheeky grin. "You had me sold when you offered the comfy bed. But to throw you and breakfast in the mix, how could I ever turn that down."

My smile grew even bigger as I giggled and shook my head at his overconfidence. He went back to fixing me again, and when he finally pulled the last metal shard out of my leg, I relaxingly breathed, and he started stitching me closed instead.

Finally...!

It's getting late now, and I'm starting to feel very tired, so I stretched out, relaxing back onto his pillows and that awesome plush blanket I'd bought for him. – Mmmm. – This is definitely coming home with us tonight.

My top had ridden up when I stretched out, and Billy stopped stitching for a second, glancing at the new scars that I've acquired since the last time we met. – The stab wound Terrence gave me is fully healed now, just like the wolf bite. But the bullet wound in my arm is still a little tender and red. Billy didn't look very happy to see any of them, but then he smirked at me again with a little twinkle in his eyes.

"What?" I rasped with curiousness.

He went back to his sewing and answered, "I was just remembering before when you were all sparkly... Your skin was like diamonds. It was beautiful... I'm just really glad that you're so trusting of me."

I smiled a little at his answer, but it quickly disappeared as I became lost in that thought.

"What's wrong?" he asked still focusing on his sewing.

"Well, you're the only one who hasn't lied to me now... And at the moment isn't afraid of me."

His brows furrowed, but he stayed concentrating on the last few stitches and asked, "How could anyone possibly be afraid of you? You're beautiful... inside and out."

My sadness grew, and Billy looked up to see my pout as I answered, "Alex, and Terrence, and now Tyme... there all scared of me because of what I am."

"That's crazy," he replied. "I'm positive both Alex and Terrence love you. And your brother definitely loves you."

He finished the last of his stitching and bandaged his handiwork. Then scooted up to sit next to me, leaning across my chest to meet my eyes.

"What happened?" he asked while wiping the blood off my cheek with a cloth.

I choked back the tears, looking away from him, answering with a shaky voice. "Terry keeps lying to me, thinking that he's protecting me. And Alex and I had a fight, and we haven't spoken since. And after the incident with Agent Green, all I sense from Alex now is fear... They're all afraid of me, Billy, and of what people will do to control me... That's why I need you to come home with me. I need you to teach me and help me and most importantly, be honest with me."

Suddenly, my ears perked as I heard the bottom floor staircase creak, and I smelled Keith's scent and whispered his name. Before I knew it, Billy moved me to stand behind the apartment's front door to hide, handing me my jeans before racing to get rid of any evidence of me being here.

Very quietly, he asked me to turn the lights off again. And I did, leaving just the street lights outside to light the room. Then with amazement, Billy stared at my golden teary eyes as I focused on masking my presence, and my heartbeat slowed with my breathing becoming shallow.

The scent of Keith's – I'm going to assume body wash became stronger. And it was only a few seconds before I heard Keith's voice no more than a few feet next to me with nothing but a door between us. – And unfortunately he brought friends with him. – I can hear them, hiding out in the stairwell.

Frac. – Terry's gonna be so pissed at me.

"Hello Billy," he murmured.

"Keith Connors... what brings you to my neck of the woods?" Billy asked, standing tall to intimidate him.

Keith tittered, completely undeterred, leaning on the wall while glaring at Billy. "I've just received word that a few months back, your crew raided 3 transport trucks and took something that's very important to me."

Billy shrugged his shoulders and shook his head. "We took a lot of stuff that day. You're gonna need to be more specific."

"The stones," Keith sniped, not wanting to waste time. "Holly tells me you know where they are."

Hearing the name Holly caused Billy to tense and question if she was still alive.

"She is... for now," Keith answered. "As is the rest of your team... Well, except for Stephen. Sorry about that... Now tell me, where are the stones?"

As Billy tried to negotiate for the release of his friends, he signalled to me then moved his foot onto a creaky floorboard. And as usual, Keith lost his patience, clearly in no mood to negotiate when he snickered. "Yeah... but you know, it just doesn't work that way anymore. My boss doesn't like to compromise... or negotiate."

The next thing I saw was Billy getting hit with two tranque darts to the chest before falling to the ground. Trying not to react, I stayed hidden while Keith's friends dragged Billy out of the apartment. Then I waited and watched in the shadows of the room as Keith loaded Billy into his waiting car and drove off.

I wanted to fight, but I wasn't sure how confident I'd be about not causing public chaos and a social media frenzy again. – That, and Billy had just finished stitching me up. So I stayed in the shadows of the apartment, then once Keith's car lights were out of view, I raced to the creaky floorboard, trying to pull it up and failed. – But now I'm determined, so I tried to burn a hole through it, focusing on my fear but keeping the feelings Billy shared with me close to the surface. And it worked.

I did it! – Billy is going to be so proud of me when I tell him.

There was a hidden compartment under the floorboards, hiding a large wooden, locked box with engraved leaves and branches twisted around it. It looked Celtic in its style, but it had The Board's marking. – The so-called "birthmark" burned into the bottom of it.

Journal entry insert by Tyme Knight

Adela wasn't taking too kindly to my vague answers, so I told her the truth – almost. But she didn't like the truth either, and griped, "So you don't want to make our relationship official and move forward because of the risk of making another baby that's like Lila... a hybrid?" She looked at me as if I was crazy then she questioned, "But you're a Time guardian right, and William's your father and he's a Nature guardian. That makes you like Lila as well, doesn't it?"

"No." I shook my head. "I've never been able to control nature."

"Have you ever tried?" she rebuffed. And I looked at her dumbfounded. – She of all people should know that the guardian ability is given to the firstborn. But she asked again, "Have you ever tried to control nature. Did William ever teach you?"

I shook my head again as I explained, "My mother taught me everything I know. Dad wasn't around much because he didn't want to bring unwanted attention around our kind."

Before she could ask her next question, my dad walked into the apartment. He had a dried coffee stain down the front of his shirt and pants, and he looked befuddled and distracted, carrying a rather large pot plant with him.

"Dad, you're back. How was your walk? And what happened to your clothes?"

"It was good." He grunted, placing the plant up onto the dining table. "I ran into Lila on my way back, and she was crying, so I thought I'd make her a present." He then pointed to the plant and explained, "It's a heliconia lobster claw... I adapted its growth slightly so it would survive in the colder climates... Do you think she'll like it?"

"Dad, it's amazing. She's going to love it... But what do you mean she was crying? Why was she crying?"

"I don't know." He shrugged his shoulders. "She just ran out of the basement really upset. I asked her what was wrong, but she ran off."

My fear and worry came back to me. – I knew I'd heard something in the basement before, and damn it, I should have checked it out.

"Dad... how long ago was this?" I asked as my face got real serious.

I stood in front of him, desperately waiting for his answer of "A few hours ago." And now freaking out, I raced to grab my phone to call Lila again.

"Crap... she was there. She heard everything," I mumbled.

Adela looked at me funny, watching me pacing the room, freaking out more when Lila didn't pick up, again.

"Tyme," Dad grunted, standing in front of me to stop me from going bonkers. "What's going on, Son? What did she hear?"

I glanced back at Adela then looked at Dad, knowing I had to be vague. "Alex and I were in the basement with Terrence. We were talking about... Katerina Dunst."

Dad's eyes widened at the name and fear shot across his face.

"We need to find her, come on," he demanded, dragging me out of the apartment with him. – Probably leaving Adela with a whole lot of questions.

We raced down the hotel stairs and into the lobby, about to run at super-speed when Lila appeared, limping through the lobby door, barefoot and in chard, bloodied pants.

WHAT THE HELL HAPPENED TO HER!!

I could see a fresh bandage through the blood-soaked hole in her jeans, and she looked rattled with a heavy bag hanging from her shoulder, and a red blanket tucked under one arm as the other hand firmly held an old wooden box.

"Lila!" I shrieked, failing to mask my worry. "Are you okay? What happened to you?"

She looked up at me and William, but before she could say anything, I appeared standing inches from her, boiling with anger, lifting her chin to look at the dark bruise on her neck in the shape of a hand.

"Lila, what the hell happened to you?"

"Err... I fell off a roof," she rasped with barely a voice to her. She then limped her way to the reception desk where Shane was on duty and Katie was 'helping.'

Shane stood up and gawked at Lila's state. But all she did was look at him, and he just knew not to ask.

"Katie, those files that we obtained from our last excursion. Did it have anything about the Connors in them?" Lila croaked rather demandingly.

"Yeah, a whole heap," Katie nodded.

I stood right next to Lila, still waiting for my answers. And she grunted a little, rubbing her injured leg in pain before she walked to the elevator with her hands full, ignoring me while still addressing Katie. "Good, I need you to grab the files and meet me in the conference room in 5 minutes. Don't be late."

Again Katie nodded, and then disappeared as Dad and I followed Lila into the elevator. But as soon as the doors had closed, Dad started questioning her with so much fear in him. "Lila, where did you get that box?"

Seriously? – He's worried about the box?!?

Lila didn't take well to the interrogation and stayed silent. But he asked again with his 'dad' voice. "Lila, where did you get that box... And is it from the same person who did this to you?" He then pointed to the hand-shaped bruise on her throat, looking very concerned.

That's better. – Get your priorities right, Dad.

She looked up and greasied Dad then rasped, "You know what they are, don't you?"

It was Dad that stayed silent this time, still waiting for the answer he wanted. He stared at her, so she rolled her eyes at him, moving her head away from his hand before she answered, "Billy had them hidden at his apartment... Keith showed up wanting to know where they were and took Billy instead."

"What the hell were you doing at Billy's place?" I angrily grumbled, realising the stuff she was holding is probably his.

"I can't tell you that," she sniped back.

"Lila, I'm your brother... you should be able to tell me anything."

"Really..." She turned to me and scowled. "You seriously want to lecture me about honesty tonight? You really want to go there, Little Brother?"

I backed down and slouched a little in my guilt. "You heard, didn't you?"

The doors opened as she turned to walk out and so casually griped, "Heard what?"

Dad followed Lila into the conference room with me a few steps behind him. We then watched Lila trying to pick the lock with one of her hairpins, and she let out a growl when Dad pulled the box away from her.

"I'm sorry, Lila. I can't let you do this," he claimed with a shaky voice.

"William, give me the stones," she threateningly ordered as her eyes glowed green, and the office plants started to grow around us.

Dad was undeterred though, and instead he asked, "How do you know what's in the box?"

"William," she rasped still struggling to speak. "I am asking you as the man who supposedly wants to be my father to trust me and give me the fraccing stones."

Damn. – She played the dad card.

Dad conceded pretty quickly and handed Lila the box, looking away as she indelicately ripped the lock off the box and opened it, only to find 9 of those tree stone things similar to the green one she asked me to help her hide. She then looked on the lid of the box to find the same photo Dad carries around with him of Lila as a baby in the arms of Katherine.

Silence filled the room but Dad couldn't stand it, and he turned back to see Lila holding the photo, looking silently angry. And he nervously breathed, "I can explain."

Before he could, Katie appeared next to Lila, holding a USB in her hand. So Lila croaked with her raspy voice to address Dad, "No. Now is not the time for that... Right now, I have a friend to save and a promise to keep. So either sit down and help me or get out."

He didn't hesitate to follow Lila's orders, sitting down at the table next to her, to help her find the information she needed. And I followed suit. – Still silently grumbling at the current state of her.

CHAPTER 32

Trust

Journal entry by Alex Woods

Terrence seems a bit distracted tonight. I know he wanted to spend the night with Lila, and I know they've been texting each other for most of the night. – But I think he was trying to be a good friend and keep me company while I try not to dwell on the current rift that Lila and I are in.

A few hours ago, when we were on our way home, he got a text from her that said she had found something to help cure his mother. So when we got back to the hotel, he went straight up to see her. But 10 minutes later, he came back down to our apartment, reading a text message that said, "I think we should skip breakfast tomorrow. I need some time to think."

I asked, "Why the sudden change?" and "What did you do?" But Terrence shrugged his shoulders, talking to me while trying to call Lila's mobile.

"I don't know. I went up to her apartment and knocked on her bedroom door, but she's locked it and won't come out. And now she won't even answer me."

He tried to call Lila's mobile again but still got no answer. So he sat down on the couch and texted her, asking to talk. – And he's been waiting for her response ever since.

It's almost 1 in the morning now, and he's spent hours staring at his phone, contemplating going back up to see her. I was just about to turn off the TV for the night and tell him to just try again in the morning when a loud continuous knock rang through the apartment. I opened the door to have Adela grunt at me for the annoyed look I was giving her.

"We've got a new mission. Get dressed," she ordered, and then barged into my apartment.

"Seriously, it's the middle of the night," I snapped while glaring at her.

With no ounce of patience, Adela looked back at me with a furious stare. "Lila was at Billy's tonight. Keith showed up and attacked them and took Billy... so Lila's just formed a rescue plan, and wants us to go after him and whoever else Keith's holding captive while she runs distraction for us."

"What?!" Terrence shouted in shock. "Why was she at Billy's on her own?"

Adela shrugged her shoulders and grumbled, "I don't know. Probably doing something you two don't want her to do... I didn't ask... But just so you know, she didn't come back looking too crash hot. And she's really pissed at Tyme for something she heard you all talking about down in the basement."

Aw Crap.

Terrence looked at me in a panic, now knowing why Lila doesn't want to talk to him, all while Adela continued, "Now I don't know what you idiots said, and I don't want to know. But I'm pretty sure the reason Lila was at Billy's place tonight, and now looks like crap, is your fault... So get your arse dressed and get in the car."

We both did as she ordered and followed Adela down into the basement carpark. Katie was already at the van, prepped and ready to go, and Jessica and Matt stepped out of the adjacent elevator to us, with Matt holding a box of blue-rose epi-pens and Jess holding 4 mini ear-mics.

They had everything planned out and was just about ready to go with most of the work already done. Jessica and Matt had even been working on this virtual city map so they could monitor our movement, and has also acquired a heat-seeking drone to follow us and track potential hostiles. – Which is really epic and cool.

Apparently, Tyme and William have already gone ahead to scout the building, and are going to meet us at the meet-point. And William has been asked to step in for Lila, and help Terrence dispense and grow the seeds through the air vents.

"Wait, where's Lila?" I asked, interrupting the plan brief.

Katie and Jess stayed silent, looking at Adela. Even Matt stayed quiet, and Adela hesitated for a second, looking at Terrence and me before she answered, "She's gone to the Eureka Towers."

Yep. – I am just about to lose it. – I know she asked me to be "that guy" the one who doesn't worry about her constantly. – But this is a whole different level of dangerous idiocy.

Before I could react, Matt grabbed my arm as well as Terrence's, and pulled us away from the group. "I know what you guys are thinking. But don't do it... I talked to Lila before she left for the towers, and she was really mad. But she wanted me to give you this."

With the look of dread all over him, Matt handed Terrence a crumpled-up note, along with Lila's stone-bracelet and the necklace that holds my black-cat paw pendant with the diamond wolf print in the middle and Terrence's tree pendant with the ruby stone in the middle.

Matt then gave us some space as he walked back to join the group. But Terrence didn't look overly happy to be holding Lila's necklace and took a deep breath as he straightened out the note.

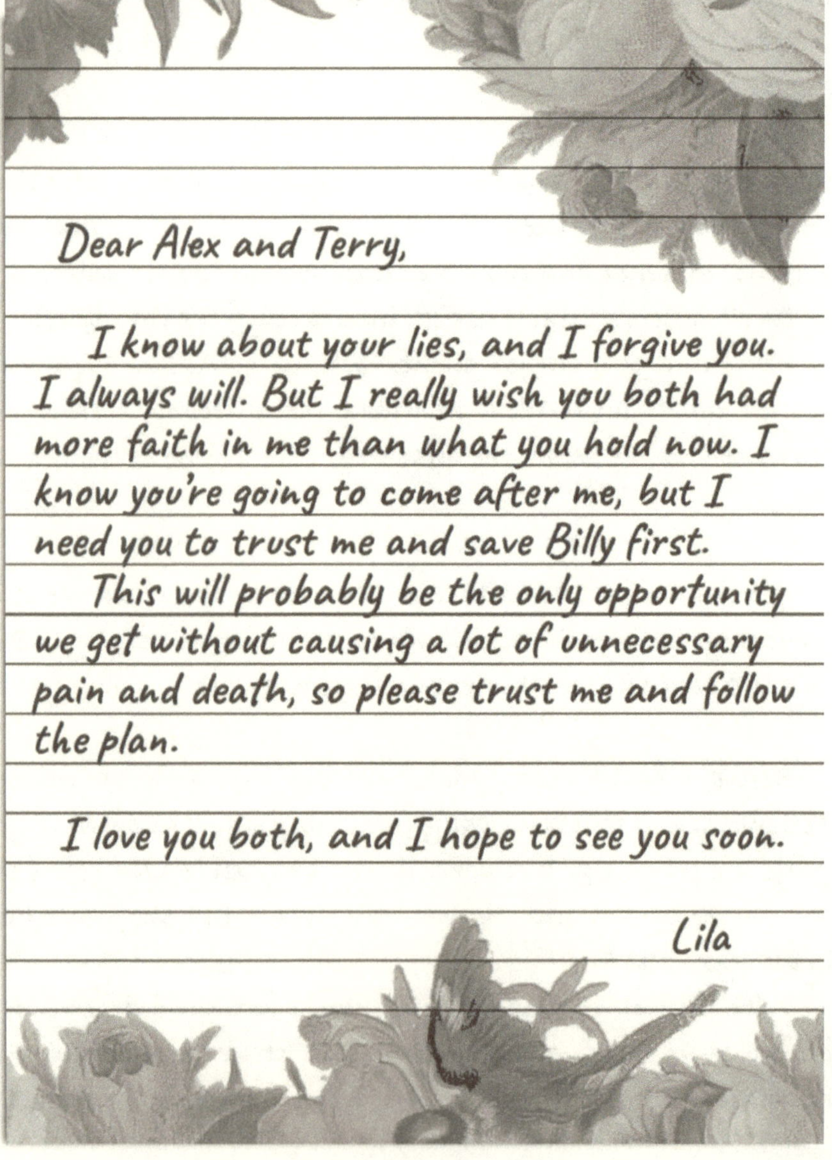

Dear Alex and Terry,

I know about your lies, and I forgive you. I always will. But I really wish you both had more faith in me than what you hold now. I know you're going to come after me, but I need you to trust me and save Billy first.

This will probably be the only opportunity we get without causing a lot of unnecessary pain and death, so please trust me and follow the plan.

I love you both, and I hope to see you soon.

Lila

Terrence's breathing became very slow, and I could sense the anger in him as he folded the note back up, and then kicked the door of the car in a fit of rage while walking back towards the group.

"Aw shit." I sighed then agreed to Lila's request and followed Terrence.

Journal entry insert by Lila Winters

Well, this is a long-shot plan at best. And because Izzy hadn't invited me here, I couldn't just use the elevator, and I needed to get into the very high Eureka Tower apartment through other means.

Yeah. – No problem. – Should be easy. – Right?

Now standing at an extremely high altitude, in the dark of the way too early hours of the morning. – I'm guessing 2am-ish? – I'm currently using the leaf platform and being very, very careful to force open the dining room window of their penthouse apartment. – Which I am just now learning is incredibly difficult to squeeze through, because it's just a long narrow sliding glass at the very top of the viewing window. – No doubt it was to prevent people from jumping to their deaths, which is a wise idea. I just don't think they expected someone like me would one day need to climb in through it.

I fell to the ground of their dining room floor, holding in my grunts of pain while clutching my leg, and I quickly hid under the table for a few moments, hoping no one heard my commotion. Luckily, no one came, and it looks like no one's home. – Almost.

Izzy was sitting with her mother when I crept into the room. She was crying at the state of Odele's condition, which has deteriorated significantly since my last visit, but when she saw me, Izzy freaked and pulled a gun on me.

I put my hands up in surrender and spoke quietly to mask my croaky throat. "Izzy, it's okay. I came back to help, like I promised."

"You did this," she cried.

Disputing her claim, I shook my head. "I didn't shoot her, you know that."

Izzy watched as I walked further into the room, closing the door, and she angrily sniped, "I saw what you did in Adelaide. That lab was the only hope we had of saving her."

"I can help her," I explained, moving closer. "I found a cure that might work."

"NO!" Izzy shouted, holding the gun higher. "Keith told me what he did to your mother. I'm sorry but I can't trust you."

I could sense the anger rising in me from the thought of Hanna, but I buried it again and kept Izzy's eyes on me. I was distracting her from the bouquet of flowers growing in the vase behind her as it grew larger. Then one of the leaves tapped on Izzy's shoulder, and when she turned toward it, it sprayed a pink mist and made her fall asleep.

As she fell, I raced to catch her and gently placed her back down in the chair, covering her with a blanket. Then I thanked the gardenias for their assistance before I got to work.

I brought most of the ingredients with me in my satchel-bag, already mixed. The only thing it needed now was the blood of the rare. – My blood. – I also brought my journal, with the torn-out old journal paper shoved in amongst the pages, because I wanted to double-check that I got the instructions right. – And I have.

Still, the last ingredient made me a bit squeamish, and I pulled a sour face when I grabbed the dagger from my boot, slicing a small cut into the tender tissue at the base of my thumb. I then clenched my hand into a fist, forcing the blood to drip into the fresh tonic. Then while focusing on all the elements around me, my eyes glowed green then gold, then bright red to dark red to blue, and yellow, white, and silver – the same colour Tyme's eyes glow when he steps in and out of the time rift.

Oh, wow. – I really do control all the elements.

"Please let this work," I whispered as I helped lift Odele's head and tipped the shiny white liquid of the tonic into her mouth, cringing at the fact that I'm helping a dying woman drink my blood.

Yuck.

I rested Odele's head back down, and she opened her eyes to look at me and smiled. I don't think she remembers who I am, so I kindly whispered, "Go back to sleep."
She did as I asked. Then as I held Odele's hand, her skin slowly began to change colour and look a hell of a lot healthier.

Holy Frac! – It's working. – She's getting better.

"Huh… that was easy." I smiled, standing back and taking a relaxing breath.
But I spoke too soon, hearing the sound of the elevator doors opening onto their floor level, and Keith shouting, "Izzy… I'm home."

DOUBLE FRAC. – Time for phase 3.

Keith wandered into Odele's bedroom to see Izzy asleep in the armchair next to his mother. He looked around, and was just about to walk back out when he stopped and walked further into the room to pick up my leafy, vine-covered side-satchel, sitting at the end of the bed. – And I'm pretty sure the vines gave it away for me, so I gave up with the whole hiding in the closet thing and stood behind him, whispering, "Hi there."

I dodged as he tried to hit me, and I cheekily smirked in the mood to play some games with him.

"Now that's no way to treat your brother's best friend," I raspingly spoke, and then pouted and elbowed Keith in the chest. "Bad Keith...very bad, Keith."

Moving at super-speed, I winded him then pushed him backwards, out of the bedroom and into the small sitting room. He was about to get up but looked at me, confused as I walked towards him with electricity sparking from my fingers.

"Now, Keith, you know I don't like it when you hurt my friends," I grumbled, still struggling with my voice as I threw a lightning bolt at the floor next to him.

But I was suddenly interrupted by a woman who looked like Keith's secretary as she side-tackled me at full-speed, sending me flying onto the couch. I stared back at her to see her eyes turn gold before she morphed into the woman in William's picture. – The woman who's supposed to be my real mother with long dark-blond hair and striking blue eyes, now staring at me.

"No..." I breathed in confusion and shock. Then I blacked out, feeling a strong hit to the back of my head.

Journal entry insert by Matt Winters

Jessica and I have been working on this cool new tech idea that I had. – I may have gotten the idea from an Xbox game, but it's still really awesome. – Nerds like me dream about having this kind of tech. So it's super handy having a billionaire as a friend.

We've now converted the conference room into an operation's centre with holographic projectors creating a 3D display of sections of the city, including blueprint outlines of the buildings. – All thanks to the information Lila's team acquired on their last visit to the government.

Tonight, Jessica's running comms and I'm working the new drone to monitor the team's heat signatures. We've also installed GPS trackers in their ear-mics to discern who's who. And while I know this mission is super dangerous, I am having so much fun, finally being able to contribute something to the team.

The Board building where Lila believes Billy has been taken is a large office building in the industrial park out near Scoresby. – Which is about a half-hour drive out of the city. The building has 6 floors, so the team split into groups of two to search each of the levels, after the regular air dispersal, with Alex, Terrence, William, and Tyme, starting from the top floor down because somehow Lila taught Terrence how to fly.

"Alex, you've got nine heat signatures on your level," Jessica stated.

"Friend or foe?" Alex asked.

Jessica tried to zoom in on that level, but it was difficult to tell, so to help her out, my eyes narrowed, looking at the building outline to try and guess the answer. "The rooms are too small to be an office or a lab... They might be holding cells."

"And you've got two moving in the hallway... possibly armed," Jessica added.

We listened as we heard the scuffles through the mics of Alex and Terrence taking down the armed men — or women. — We can't tell from here. But it kind of feels like we're watching a video game at the moment as we watch their movements on the projector.

A few floors below, Katie and Adela were on data retrieval, and Tyme and William were assisting any of the strays and helping them out of the building. But as suspected, not everyone was under the influence of Neuritamine.

That's right. — They're willingly working for an evil organisation that essentially enslaves people for money and power.

The good thing about doing a mission in the middle of the night though is there's less people and hostiles around. So the teams orders are that if any guardian or human tries to attack them, they get knocked out and left behind.

Again, Jessica and I watched Alex and Terrence's heat signatures in a bit of suspense as they searched the cells near them and reported back that they found Billy.

We then heard Billy sounding confused and panicked, asking, "Alex, where's Lila? Is she okay?"

All he got was a grunt from Alex then he stayed quiet, walking back with him to the other group of rescued guardians before making their way down the emergency exit.

"Guys," I reported, "Del and Katie are back at the meet point... and Tyme and William just appeared on screen again. So they're good to go when you are."

"Thanks, Matt. Any word on Lila," Alex asked.

I cleared my throat, glancing at Jessica because neither of us wanted to tell them the bad news.

"Matt!" Alex griped louder.

"Lila was on separate comms... But we lost contact with her about a half-hour ago," I replied, and I honestly thought Alex was going to freak out. But he didn't. "Alex? You there?"

"Yeah... I think Lila knew we needed all the help we could get on this one," he replied and then ordered, "Katie and Del... I need you to regroup with the rescued guardians. Take them and the cars back to the hotel... Billy, are you up for a rescue op?"

"Hell yeah," he eagerly answered.

"Good... William, Tyme, run ahead to the Eureka Towers, check out the area. Try and find a back door. We'll meet you there."

The comms went silent after that with most of the team's heat signatures disappearing off-screen, including Billy and two others he was with. I then stood back and jumped in celebration for another almost successful rescue.

"Yes!!! This is working perfectly," I commented while admiring the 3D display.

Yet not in a celebratory mood, Jessica turned to me with a puzzled look, and asked, "How do you do it?"

I had to look back at her for clarification on that one.

"How are you so calm, knowing that Lila is always the one willing to run distraction. And every time she does, there's that risk that something's gone wrong, and you're just so... I don't know... used to it."

I stared back at Jessica with a little grin, thinking of how Lila operates this team. — She always encourages team-work and the building blocks of friendships. So I answered, "Lila told me once when this whole thing started, that if a leader has lost faith in their team then there's no point going out onto the battlefield... She's pretty smart that way... Lila trusts each and every one of you. And she goes into the fight, knowing that she has the best people ready to back her up."

It was then I realised I still had my mic on and Katie replied, "That chick should write a book or something... The amount of smart crap she's says like that."

Whoops. — I'm not sure if Lila wanted them to know that.

Journal entry insert by Lila Winters

My head feels like it's throbbing as I slowly wake up. I'm still a bit groggy. But I can hear Keith talking and poking at my bandaged leg. "She's bleeding... do you want me to fix her?"

The woman's voice, or should I say Katherine's voice, sighed with disappointment. "No, we can fix her later. Right now, we need to talk... Wakey, wakey, Pumpkin."

Oh Frac. – She called me Pumpkin.

I opened my eyes to realise both of my hands were cuffed to each arm of a dining chair, sitting in the middle of their apartment loungeroom. These are the same cuffs The Board like to use for their prisoners. – Which means my biological mother is not dead and not one of the good guys either.

Yep. – I'm really striking out with the nice parents in my life thing. – At least William's trying, I suppose.

I took slow breaths, analysing the room as I came to. Keith was standing over me, and Katherine was sitting on the couch playing with my dagger. The other Connors brother – Robert was standing behind her with I think Anna, his sister. And they had friends with them, but they don't look very friendly, all wearing intimidating black suits and no smiles.

Keith was getting impatient with me, and he pressed down on the stitches in my leg as he deviously grinned, "Come on, Lila, don't keep us waiting."

The pain grew intense but I tried to hold back my screams, glaring at him with eyes fully awake now.

"Gently Keith, we still need her in one piece," Katherine requested, leaning forward and smiling at me. "Well hello, Pumpkin... Are you okay?"

Alright, that was weird. – And nice. – I think she's trying to be motherly.

I growled from the pain I felt, now slightly ticked off. "Who are you? And why are you calling me Pumpkin?"

"Seriously?" Keith snickered. "You don't know who your own mother is."

I scowled back at him, giving him the death stare as my eyes turned black. "My mother is dead... You killed her, remember."

He kneeled down and held my hand, looking regrettably sad. "Yes, and I am so sorry for your loss... I was angry at my brother, and I couldn't control myself. But she was also expendable for the little test we were conducting... A necessary loss."

"A test?" I shook my head in confusion.

"Yes... We were wanting to see how you respond to the death of your human captor..."

"Hanna was not my captor," I growled with the anger in me growing. "She was kind and loving and—"

"She was whatever Richard brainwashed her to be." Katherine interrupted. "And before that, she was whatever James and Henrietta Willows brainwashed her to be."

I glared at her with tears forming in my eyes. But Katherine showed no ounce of care as she inspected her finely manicured nails, and spoke with disdain. "I'm sure you know by now that I am not a Willows. They were one of the many who hunted our family... But little did they know that the Dunstians are not ones to be hunted. We are the hunters... And as for Hanna, she was such a sad case. No life or mind of her own. She was married off for strategic gain, and again used as nothing more than a puppet."

"Stop it." I shook my head, not wanting to listen.

But Keith tried to comfort me and shush me while gently catching one of the tears as it rolled down my cheek. "Shhh... Lila... It was for the best. She's at peace now... I think... But... now that you know the truth, I am really hoping that one day you'll forgive me, like you did for my brother."

Yeah. – No.

With a disgustingly arrogant grin, Keith kissed my cheek but lingered way too long, so I pulled away then snapped my head back at half-speed towards him, head-butting him and breaking his nose. The swift hit forced him backwards, cupping his face as he grunted in pain. And I muffled my laugh, watching the blood fall from his nose as his sister ran to his aid.

"Pumpkin..." Katherine tsked, shaking her head at me. "The young man just offered you an apology and his friendship... That is no way to behave."

I irked at the pet name but stayed focused. "That was a crap apology... And here I thought all he wanted was the stones."

That caught her attention. "What do you know about the stones?"

"I know that they're not really stones." I deviously smiled back at her.

She appeared in front of me, holding <u>my</u> dagger against my cheek, and seethed, "Where are they?"

But you know – I'm just not that scared of her, and I giggled as I stared into her cold, icy blue eyes and answered, "Somewhere you will never find them."

With that response, she drove the dagger down into my bandaged thigh, slicing through the stitches and digging further down. I held back my screams as she pulled the dagger out. Then I grinned at her because I can sense Alex and Terrence nearby.

About Fraccing Time.

My skin became covered in sparkles, hardening like diamonds, and my hands glowed, burning through the handcuffs in seconds. I then stood to my feet, ignoring the pain as I grabbed Katherine by the neck and threw her across the room, smashing her into a wall.

As she landed, I turned to Keith, glaring at him as my elf-like white hair and ears appeared to go with my ridiculously scary black eyes. In reaction, Keith raised his fiery glowing hand towards me, so I raised mine and sent a burst of lightning from my hand, barrelling towards the stream of fire that hurtled towards me.

The force met in the middle, and it was a struggle to maintain a constant electrical stream until I threw an oversized ice-ball at him with my other hand, hitting him in the face again.

He broke away and griped, "Damn it! What is it with you and my face?"

I towered over him and sarcastically pouted. "Aw, what's wrong little Keith... You trying to look good for my wannabe Mummy. Because seriously, you can do better."

While mocking her, Katherine stood to her feet with her skin covered in steel, holding an electric fireball, now with anger raging through her. And she sneered, looking around at her – whatever they are – friends. "I suggest you do as you're told, little girl. You're no match for us all."

"You're right, I'm not..." I grinned, standing in the middle of the room. "But I brought friends too."

As I said that – Alex, Terrence, Billy, Tyme, William, Isaac, and Holly all appeared in the room, after kicking in the stairwell door. I held my hand out towards Terrence, calling my vine bracelet to me, and as it wrapped around my hand, the vines of the bracelet grew into a long sparring stick as I stood ready to fight.

Journal entry continued by Alex Woods

Lila looks like a serious Mega-bad-arse ninja, standing in the middle of Keith's apartment. She looked so confident, like she knew we were coming this whole time. Terrence was a bit shocked when he felt Lila's bracelet ripped from his hand. – But damn we weren't expecting that.

William gasped Katherine's name in disbelief, and Katherine tried to escape, disappearing into thin air. But when Lila called Tyme's name, he appeared next to her, pulling her into the time rift with him, leaving us to deal with who was left.

I scanned the room to find Keith on the floor, looking like he had already taken a beating, and I am delightfully proud of Lila for that.

With a chuckle, I tapped Terrence's shoulder to point him out, and he too smiled, whispering under his breath, "Nice."

The team then worked together as we took down the other guardians, injecting them with the last of the Blue-rose tonics, causing them to become dizzy and fall unconscious.

I think it was very wise of Lila to add that sedative factor to the epi-pen cure. – Although I'm still not happy as to why she adapted the cure in the first place.

Every now and then, Katherine and Lila appeared, moving in and out of the rift, mid-way through their heated and violent fight, so we all tried desperately to stay out of their way. And it seems like Katherine's team had the same idea. – Dodging them while fighting us.

By the time my team was done, we gawked as Katherine was thrown out of the time rift by a strong gust of wind, smashing into the wall next to Keith, holding the handle of Lila's favourite dagger in her hand. – But the blade was missing.

She lay on the ground, too weak to stand as Tyme and Lila stepped back out of the time rift with Lila looking mad and shiny with her skin covered with diamond sparkles. – But damn it. – I found the other half of Lila's dagger embedded into her shoulder. Yet the pain she felt was being silenced by her anger and strong determination, with her hands glowing a fiery red, and electricity streaming around her body and through her white braided hair.

Holy Crap. – She looks like a freaking Mega-elf-ninja goddess.

With glowing blue eyes, Lila raised her hand to create ice shards floating and encircling Katherine, slowly encroaching on her as she lay so still and weak on the floor.

"Lila, no!" William shouted, and Lila stopped to look back at William as he spoke. "You're better than her, you know that."

Hearing his words, Lila lowered her hand while still staring at William. But Keith took advantage of Lila's distraction, scooping Katherine up into his arms before he disappeared, running off at full-speed. It looked like Lila wanted to chase after them, but she didn't. She just stood back and took a relaxing breath out.

I took a breath of relief as well, feeling a slight sense of victory but then sensed an odd emotion come from Lila as she peered around at us and then at all the unconscious guardians, and the destruction we had created in the apartment. With broken furniture, artwork, walls, windows, and a few minor injuries on us and the others, the apartment didn't look too great. But the look on Lila's face was of sheer terror as she glanced at herself in the now broken mirror. – She didn't look too great either, and she began to glow brighter with her whole body turning a fiery diamond red.

"BILLY... HELP ME!" she shrieked, looking at us and stepping away as the clothes on her body caught fire and burned.

Billy raced to try and hold her hands but pulled away from the heat. And she cried as her skin burned brighter.

"Billy," she fearfully whimpered, stepping away from him.

He kept his distance while trying to help her. "Lila, tell me what you're scared about."

What? – What the hell does she have to be scared about?

I stepped towards her, wanting to help, but she looked at me in fear again. Her feet began to burn through the carpet, so Billy moved at full-speed with his arms and body glowing red as well to try and match her heat. Then he picked her up and wrapped her legs around him to stop her from burning anything else.

It was painful for him, and his clothes began to burn. But as he held her, I sensed his emotions change. – He was amplifying his emotions of happiness and love, and giving them to Lila. And it was working. Her glow began to fade. – Almost.

"ALEX!" Billy yelled. "It's you! Last night Lila said you and Terrence were scared of her!"

"What?" I gasped, shaking my head. "I'm not scared of her!"

Billy looked at Lila, holding his hands around her torso. But as he did, Lila shook her head at him. "No... I don't want to hurt them."

With determination, Billy stared back at me and shouted, "Prove it!!!" Then he pushed Lila away from him, throwing her shiny, glowing body in the air towards me.

I didn't hesitate, racing to catch her. And as I landed to the ground with her in my arms, her fiery glow disappeared, leaving her with just beautiful diamond skin. She curled into a ball in my arms, trembling, and kept whispering to herself, "Don't hurt him. Don't hurt him. Don't hurt him."

I held her tight and leaned down to whisper in her ear. "You could never hurt me... You love me too much for that."

Her trembling body slowly calmed as I let her sense everything I felt for her. As I did, I watched her diamond skin sparkle brighter, and she started to cry, looking up at me with her tears turning to diamonds as they rolled down her cheek and onto my shirt.

Woah. – Now that's cool.

While I hugged her, Terrence raced to find a throw rug to cover her as the ash from her clothes fell away, leaving just her and her beautiful, yet slightly discoloured diamond skin still curled in a ball on my lap. Then as the sun began to rise, Terrence's sister, Izzy, walked out of one of the bedrooms, holding Odele's hand to aid her.

"Terrence," she cheered happily. "She did it... Look, Lila did it... Mother's all better."

Odele looked around at the mess and frowned. "Well, good morning, Terrence... What happened out here? Did you have another party?"

Terrence pulled the 'I don't know' face and answered, "Um... we ran into a bit of trouble, and I'm gonna throw Keith under the bus here and say it's his fault."

He peered back at Lila still curled up in my arms. When Izzy appeared in front of us, holding Lila's shiny hand, causing Terrence to tense up and move closer. But Izzy stayed focused on Lila and was smiling at her with so much joy.

"Lila, I don't know what you did... but thank you. For the first time in years, Mother is actually happy and looks healthy... I'm so sorry for everything my family's done to you, but I really hope you can forgive us."

Robert and Anna were the next to wake up and looked at Odele oddly as she smiled at them. "Good morning, my dears."

She greeted them both with a hug, and they confusedly smiled and welcomed the hug. Robert then stood up, looking at Izzy as she continued to stare at Lila, who still hasn't moved from my arms. And he became puzzled, shaking his head at the whole scene.

"I don't understand... Does this mean we're friends now?"

With excitement written all over her, Izzy looked up at Terrence then back at Odele who agreeably nodded. "If that's what you want, dear."

Um...? – I think I'm in shock, hearing Odele being strangely nice. – And happy. – What the hell did Lila do to her?

Still with a burst of too much excited energy, Izzy appeared in front of Terrence and looked as if she was begging her older brother. "Is that okay... can we be a family again? Please, Terrence, please?"

He didn't answer her. Instead he looked down at Lila and appeared next to us, holding her still-sparkly hands as he whispered, "Lila?"

Suddenly his eyes glowed green and mine glowed gold when I heard Lila's voice in my head. "I'm not sure if you boys have noticed, but I'm currently naked, and have half a dagger melted in my chest and a bleeding leg... So whatever the frac you decide, Terry, do it quick then take me home."

We both relievingly chuckled at her before Terrence stood up and nodded to Izzy, who then gleefully leapt into Terrence's arms, celebrating and squealing, "Yes!"

CHAPTER 33

Rule 5

Journal entry by Lila Winters

We're starting to make good traction with our fight against The Board. – The Connors family have called for a truce, and were very nice in letting me keep the blanket that was covering me for our trip home. Billy still agreed to come back to the hotel and join the team, and even asked if his young friends Isaac and Holly could join my team as well. – Both of them seemed very excited when I agreed to their request, and became even more excited when the team led them into the lobby of the Eden Hotel where Adela, Max, and Jess were waiting to greet them and get them settled in their own rooms.

Alex stayed focused on me, carrying me straight into the elevator with Terrence, Tyme, William and Billy following us. Then the second I was back in my apartment and Alex had placed me down on the bed, Billy got straight to work to start stitching me back together. – Yet again.

When Billy asked for everyone to clear out, I don't think any of them were planning to listen to him. – But I'm still pretty ticked off at all of them, and in significant amount of pain, so when I growled the words "get out" I think they all got the message. And instead they waited out in the loungeroom, listening to the sounds of my pain through the closed bedroom door.

The melted knife in my chest was the hardest and most painful thing for Billy to fix. – And I was left sweating and crying when he finally got it out of me.

Damn fracs. – That was my favourite dagger.

Once I was all patched up, Billy very kindly ordered me to be on bed rest for the remainder of the day, and asked to push it to at least three days. – He even negotiated by offering to bring me breakfast, lunch, and dinner and whatever else I desired to keep me from getting up.

Yeah. – I am so going to milk this for everything it's worth. And I plan on calling him in the middle of the night, asking for pancakes. – This is going to be fun.

His first mission was to get me some breakfast, and while Billy went on the hunt for some food, Alex, Terrence, and Tyme took turns to apologise to me for keeping secrets, and not trusting me like a true friend should.

Terrence was especially worried as he held tight to the white-oak tree pendant that I'd given back to him. Alex's paw pendant is still attached as well, but it was the tree pendant that almost brought him to tears. – It means a lot to Terry when I wear it because he gave it to me when I was little. When we were childhood besties. And in his eyes, when I wear the necklace, it's acknowledging our lasting friendship. – Even though I still have no memory from that long ago.

I let him put it back on me once he had promised to always trust me. And while he gave me a sorry hug, he also added that no matter what, he will never be scared of me. So with that, I gave him a kiss on the cheek to say thank you.

Wow. – To have Terrence promise that to me. – It really means a lot.

It's been three days now of resting and taking it easy and calling Billy in the middle of the night, requesting the oddest of things. And sure enough, he brought it up to my apartment each time. – Be it pancakes, Skittles, something to read, or just a piece of fruit or someone to talk to.

Now finally released from bed rest, I'm beginning to feel a lot more like myself, starting the day with a smile, knowing that today is going to be perfect. And I'm extra-super excited because this morning I get to set up the Christmas tree with my kids. – I'm even wearing Christmas colours, wearing the dark-red tennis skirt that Adela bought for me and has been dying to see me wear, along with a green and white crop-top.

I think I wear the ensemble quite well. – Now that I don't look all scary with a whole bunch of scars covering every inch of me. I mean I do have some scars, but it's not as bad as I used to be. The hand-shape bruise on my neck and a few of the others I acquired from fighting Katherine and headbutting Keith are slowly fading with a hint of yellow left in them. The bandage around my stitched-up thigh is completely visible because of the short length of the red skirt, and the stitch dressing for my shoulder stab wound – the one just below my collar bone is also visible with the crop-top's collar being a wide U-shape.

But I've been very strategic in my wardrobe choices over the last few days. – I've noticed that when Billy, Alex, Terrence, and Tyme are able to see that there's no blood seeping through the bandages, they tend to relax a little and hover less.

Not that I mind their company. I just don't want them to worry. – More than their usual worry, that is.

Once the Christmas tree was set up and the apartment was decked out with all the Christmas decorations, I made my way down to the gym. Today I'm working on my sisterly love with Tyme, down in the training gym, teaching him how to disarm a hostile as he requested.

I don't think he was expecting me to be ready to train him so soon, but I really just want to spend some time with him today, and have some fun as well. – Plus, I am absolutely positive he's going to try and take it easy on me, because he's just so sweet like that.

He's following my instructions perfectly, so when he finally managed to secure my weapon, which was actually one of Danny's Nerf guns, I was overjoyed and wanted to go that extra step. "Good job… Now punch me."

He looked back at me in shock, shaking his head. So I had to insist, "Come on, Tyme, I'm a big girl. I can take it."

"Lila, it's only been three days. You're still healing."

I irked – just a little. "Tyme, it's taken you 16 tries just to get the weapon from me. I promise you're not going to hurt me… Now hit me."

He grumbled and then moved to punch me in the face, and I caught his hand mid-swing then twisted it down, moving my free hand to almost punch him instead. Expecting to feel pain,

Tyme closed his eyes, but I stopped and patted his cheek condescendingly before I let him go.

"That was good. But next time use the core of your body to swing into the movement," I explained then demonstrated the movement using my old Hector. And Tyme watched me throw a punch into it, making Hector rock backwards and wobble as I turned to continue the lesson. "Also, until you build up your hand strength, use more of your wrist. The bone in your forearm is a lot stronger than the ones in your hand and is less likely to break upon impact"

I stood back in front of him, ordering him to punch me again and not hold back this time. He tried and I dodged his movements while goading him to keep trying. And again, Tyme was following my instructions perfectly. Each time I blocked or dodged his hand, he'd try another movement that I had taught him. And I tried to hit him, leading him to block my movements as well.

Yes. – This is perfect. – He's learning as we fight.

Eventually, he managed to punch me in the face, knocking me to the ground. But he suddenly pulled away, holding his arm in pain. "Argh! Why? Why do people do this?"

I got up and laughed, rubbing the soon-to-be bruise on my jaw, and chortled. "Tyme, if you assumed that self-defence was going to be painless, you might want to consider an alternative means of winning a fight."

Still laughing at him, I walked him over to my gym bag and pulled out some blue-rose paste for his hand, and he grumbled at the pain as I healed it for him.

"No. I'm going to need to learn this eventually." He pouted, looking up at my jaw, and could see it starting to swell when he noted, "It's just hard to think that you do this every day?"

While I focused on his healing hand, Tyme not-so-discreetly checked my bandages to see no blood seeping through them. – For like the umpteenth time. – And I shrugged my shoulders to reply, "I practice almost every day with Alex, and sometimes Terry, but I still think they're holding back with me... Don't worry. You do get used to the pain eventually."

He leaned back against the wall as I handed him a drink bottle, and he sighed. "Well, I think I've had enough pain for the day... Is there something less painful I could learn?"

My brow arched at his vague request. "You'll need to be more specific. I'm able to teach you a great number of things... because I am just that awesome."

With a huge grin, Tyme stared at me then we both burst into laughter at my giant ego. But eventually he replied, "Well, tell me a few of the things you know how to do, and I'll see if I like them."

I could sense Tyme was seeking something in particular but was being cagey about it, so I pushed for the point. "Tyme, what is it that you want me to teach you?"

For some reason, he needed to take a minute to work up the courage. "Um... I was wondering... if you could teach me how to control nature."

Alright. – Wasn't expecting that one.

"Seriously?" I questioned, and my brows pinched together so hard that I think I created a wrinkle.

"Well, it's something Adela said about our... I mean my dad, being a Nature guardian and all. It's a long shot I know... But—"

"Okay," I nodded, interrupting him. And he looked at me, shocked that I agreed, so I added, "There's no harm in trying. Come on, let's start now."

Tyme followed me up to the newly renovated rooftop garden that now has a huge round fountain in the middle, where you can sit and look out over the city and enjoy the garden scenery, which looks amazingly colourful with all the flowers in bloom.

I showed Tyme a few of the basics, like making a flower bud blossom, all while I explained that my strength with nature comes from the bond I have with it.

"It's almost like you're asking nicely for it to do what you need and giving it the instructions step by step."

Now it was his turn, and he stared at the flower for ages, becoming increasingly frustrated. He even tried meditating with me to try and find that bond. But when that failed, he gave up, and we just sat on the edge of the fountain ledge, enjoying the sun instead.

"Hey, Tyme... Why didn't you ask your dad to help you with this?" I asked while totally winning at the thumb-war we're playing.

I sensed him getting cagey again as he explained, "Yeah... he's kind of gone into panic mode since he saw the whole Mega guardian warrior side of you. I mean, you were super awesome. And powerful. And seriously, you didn't even need my help going in and out of the time rift at all. Plus, that whole part about your real mother being on the same continent as you has caused him to go all freakily quiet."

"So what, you both knew Katherine was alive?"

He went quiet, staring at my face – probably trying to gauge if my smile was fake. – It isn't. But his nervous emotions gave him away when he failed to answer. So as we started the next thumb war round, I let out a sigh.

"Tyme, I think we've both figured out that keeping secrets from each other isn't healthy for us... The stab wound in my chest and thigh are a big enough hint for me... So why don't we make the same promise that I have with Terrence and Alex?"

"And what's that?" he asked, in a bit of frustration because he lost the round.

We started the next thumb war round as I explained, "I promise to always be honest with you, and you do the same... The only exception is when it's someone else's secret, because that's their own prison not yours... And I get that me having an evil biological mother alive and kicking everyone she meets is something your dad should have told me. So no stress, I'm not peeved at you."

"Thanks." He chuckled, still struggling to win against me. "I think that's a fair promise, so I agree."

I let him win the thumb war round, so we could shake on the deal. Then he pulled me in for a hug, still being careful of my stitched shoulder and leg. And I smiled, sensing the love he felt for me, and hugged him tighter.

"I love you, Little Brother. You know that, right?"

He didn't say anything, but I did hear him take little breaths while hugging me tighter as well. Unfortunately, he had to let go when Matt ran into the garden all excited.

"Lila! I think I've done it... and you are going to love it." Matt puffed, slightly out of breath as he looked at us and grinned. "And now it's my turn to call a team meeting."

I stood up and chuckled while helping Tyme to his feet. Then I replied with a wry grin, "You should be careful, Matt... Someone might think you actually like working on the team."

The team was called to the conference room via text, so Matt, Tyme, and I made our way up to the conference room and waited for everyone to arrive. – I admit I may still be in too much of a playful mood with Tyme because while we waited, we kept moving in and out of the time rift, trying to catch each other. And I am loving this whole brother-sister relationship we've got now. – It's perfect.

I'm definitely having way too much fun for someone who's supposed to be taking it easy, and Tyme and I thought it would be hilarious to play a little prank on the team. So both of us stayed in the time rift as Adela, Max, Jess, Chase, Michael, Roy, Isaac, Holly, Katie, Shane, Billy, William, Alex, and Terrence all walked into the room and took their seats.

Wow, this team is getting big. – And this doesn't count the NY's or the London team.

When Alex sat down at the conference table, he scanned the room, asking where I was. Then with the biggest and cheekiest giggle, I appeared sitting on his lap with my arms wrapped around him, and Tyme appeared standing next to Matt, using him as a leaning post.

"So, take it away boss," I said to Matt with a grin from ear to ear.

Everyone jumped in fright at our sudden appearance, and Matt and Tyme both cackled to themselves as they watched.

Even Alex jolted a bit, but then relaxed when he realised it was me.

I really struggled to pull my grin back or hold my giggles as I glanced sideways at Alex, and he poked me in my uninjured leg as revenge for scaring him. But I got comfy on his lap, wriggling closer to him as Terrence handed me the protein shake that I'd begged him to bring up for me in lieu of the breakfast I didn't have with him this morning. – He didn't want to have breakfast with me this morning because he wanted to let Danny and Ruby have the morning with me to set the Christmas tree up. But he and Alex asked for my help to set up their Christmas tree, so I'm having dinner with them tonight, and we're going to have a Christmas movie night while setting up their tree.

See. – My day has started perfect and is going to end perfect.

"You're in a playful mood," Alex commented.

"Yeah, just mucking around with Tyme." I smiled while gleefully biting my bottom lip. "I can stop if I'm annoying you."

He sat back and got comfy, pulling the 'I'm happy' face, and replied, "I'm just glad to see you smiling... I think we all are."

I peered around the room to see everyone smiling at me, and joshed, "Aw... you guys have gone all sappy on me." I then turned to Billy and sarcastically sighed. "Billy, you shock me with your sappiness."

With a slight chuckle, he shrugged his shoulders. "What can I say, Christmas makes me all warm and fuzzy inside."

My grin could not be contained anymore, but I also need to be a responsible leader and bring us back on topic. So while failing to not laugh, I said, "Anyways... Matt, I believe you have a new mission for us, so please intrigue us with your wisdom."

Matt chuckled and looked at me, shaking his head as he turned on the holographic projectors that displayed a 3D version of the Eden Hotel. Tyme then switched places with Jessica, so she and Matt could present their hard work. All the while Alex became entranced with the new tech and leaned in, wrapping his arms around my waist to keep me balanced as he commented, "Wow... You guys have been busy."

I cheekily shushed him as Jessica held up a basketball size machine filled with a whole bunch of finicky tech stuff and explained, "We need these devices to be placed in four positions on level 20, here." She pointed to the required corner of the holographic hotel then continued, "We also need another 4 on the roof... They all need to be perfectly aligned in order for each to receive the right frequency. Then once we turn them on, they should act as a force field around the upper levels of the hotel."

Alex's brows furrowed and he got all serious. "What do you mean by a force field?"

To demonstrate, Matt opened the conference room door and set four smaller devices up around the frame of the door, using a laser to make sure they were perfectly aligned, and then turned them on.

There was a faint glow to the door for a second, but then it disappeared as he enlightened us. "It's kind of like an electric fence. It transmits an energy wave from one device to the others, and if you speed up the process fast enough, it creates a makeshift wall."

Adela and Chase both leaned in, really interested now.

"Cool." Adela grinned, inspecting all the tech stuff. "Did you make this yourself?"

Matt excitedly nodded, replying, "With Jessica's help, yeah."

He then walked over to me and pulled me up to follow him because I was the guinea pig for this demonstration. And while I followed him, Jessica held up a small lapel pin and kept explaining things to the group.

"Each of you will be given a device that creates a small magnetic field. Sort of like a bubble which allows you to pass through the field unharmed."

"Observe," Matt said while handing me a pin before I happily skipped through the force field.

I noticed Terrence and Alex quickly swivel their chairs around, still smiling at me. Even Billy's smiling. – And yeah, I'm in a ridiculously happy mood because today has been pretty awesome.

"So what happens if you don't have the device?" Alex asked while cheekily drinking my protein shake.

Ohh. – The nerve of him.

I greasily eyed him then raised my hand to ask one of the office plants in the room to snatch the shake back from him, and slap him on the wrist for me. He grunted at the plant, and I heard Billy and Terrence stifle their chuckles as Matt asked Alex to be the next guinea pig.

"Alex, why don't you try to hold Lila's hand."

I held out my hand to Alex and tried very hard not to smile and give away Matt's subtle attempt at revenge. Then as Alex's hand reached the force field it hummed, sending a small current through him, causing him to pull away, rubbing his now numb arm. And I laughed hysterically on the other side.

"You cheeky sod..." he growled at me with his own smile. "You knew that was going to happen."

I kept laughing at him as I walked back into the room, grabbing what was left of my protein shake and sitting on Terrence's lap instead. Alex then sat down next to us and poked me in the ribs, and just for the fun of it, so did Terrence.

Ha! - Yeah, that was really fun to watch.

Getting back to the actual meeting, Max cleared his throat with a slight chuckle and seemed overjoyed at Jess and Matt's creation. "Well, at least this will make the hotel a lot safer for us, and prevent any more unwanted guests from snooping around."

"Err, not quite." Jess pulled a sour face as she spoke, "There's one minor problem... It's about the devices the government and The Board implanted in all of you in order to brand you with the tribal marks on your necks... We've been studying Lila's old one, the stone Alex brought back from the village. And we've discovered that they're giving off a low-level frequency that not-surprisingly cell towers are able to pick up. It's most likely to keep tabs on you in the field or on the off chance you all escape... Which you all have... The good thing is the frequency isn't that strong and it's difficult to get a specific location read, so it isn't able to pinpoint exactly where you are at any given moment. But it does give at best a 200-metre radius of your position... That said, with so many guardians in one place right now, you're all kind of acting like one giant beacon for everyone to see."

Alrighty. - That's not a good part of my day.

Jess looked over to me and pulled the 'sorry face,' hoping I had any ideas, and I had to think about this one.

"Okay." I sighed while twiddling with my fingers. "So we just need to figure out a way to turn them off."

"Well, you managed to do it, how hard could it be?" Alex added.

Remembering exactly how hard it was, I glared at him, and then casually reminded him. "I also lost the ability to use any of my powers for a week."

Terrence swivelled in his chair to say something, and I had to wrap my arm around his neck for balance and saw his lips peak at one side as he suggested to Alex and myself, "What if they do it in stages, and wait until we activate the force field… That way everyone will be safe if they do lose their powers."

"You want us to hide in the hotel," Billy grumbled, unhappy with the idea. "What if something happens outside the hotel?"

I turned to Billy and answered, "Well, Terrence and I don't have devices, and I don't think Tyme does either. So we should be able to handle things."

"Actually…" Matt interrupted with mild hesitation. "We think Terrence has a tracker in him as well."

I gasped at this revelation and watched as Matt pulled out a little UV torch that he 'borrowed' from his work. Then he explained that last Friday when Terrence, Alex, Tyme, and him went out for their guy's night, Matt noticed a glowing mark on Terrence's neck, which is why he just up and left so randomly.

Oooh intrigue.

Slowly, Matt walked around to shine the UV torchlight on the back of Terrence's neck to display an invisible tattoo. The marking was two letters, C and V, overlapping each other with a diamond border circling it.

"C... V? Isn't that your real father's initials?" I mumbled while getting absurdly close to Terrence's neck.

His hand clenched on my leg, and I could sense his frustration, so I jokingly teased him a little. "Well, now you can join me in my club of evil parents-ville. It was getting kind of lonely here."

His lips peaked again as he joked back, "Do I get a flag?"

"No." I giggled. "But we have matching bracelets."

I cheekily grinned as I rested my stone-vine bracelet next to his, and he grinned back, relaxing his hand again. But Tyme pouted which was clearly fake.

"Aw... now I want a bracelet."

"Sorry, Little Brother," I chuckled with a just as fake pout. "Club privileges... And your dad's just not evil."

William smiled and swivelled in his chair, acting over-dramatic, playing along with me as he pretended to comfort Tyme. "My apologies, Son... I have failed you in my evil-less-ness."

Ha! – Yep. – That did it for me.

I laughed so hard at him, struggling to stop. And I had to hold the stitches in my chest because I couldn't stop laughing. But the pain was totally worth it.

Eventually, I pulled my composure back together to give out some directions. But it was still with a slight chuckle. "Okay... so I like the force field idea, and if Max is all good with it, we'll install them today."

I got a general okay nod from Max before I continued, but I was really struggling not to laugh because Alex and Terrence kept poking me in the ribs. "With regards to the tracking devices, Jess, are you able to work with Katie and search through the new data... ha... for any information on turning them off... eh-huh.... That is if Matt's able to make do without you for the installation."

Jess looked over to Matt and they both nodded, so again I continued, quickly glancing at Alex's watch. "Okay then... as for the rest of us, suit up, we've got a building to climb."

Journal entry insert by Matt Winters

I can't believe we're actually doing this, and that Lila put me in charge with everyone taking my orders to set up this really cool tech. – And seriously, my nerd-brain is going nuts. – I mean if this works, then me and Jess are freaking geniuses.

Alex, Terrence, Billy, and Lila all agreed to do the lower installation of the devices, which meant that they all had to abseil down the outside of the building simultaneously to ensure correct alignment.

Each of them were in their respective corners getting suited up, and I decided to help Lila in getting ready. I hesitated for a moment, thinking about what I was asking Lila to do, glancing at the very recent, still-healing injuries in her shoulder and thigh. Then I stupidly looked over the side of the building.

"Wow, that's a long way down. Are you sure you want to do this? You are still healing."

She peered up at me with a huge smirk on her face. "Are you volunteering?"

I hesitantly looked over the side of the building again and she giggled. "I didn't think so."

We were all ready now, and Tyme was paired with Lila to be her anchor. William was paired with Terrence, and the new guys Isaac and Holly had Billy and Alex, while Adela played my assistant.

"We're ready when you are." Tyme nodded while looking back at me.

But I am nervous as hell and not at all ready. Lila grinned at me, and her eyes had a golden glow as my nerves disappeared, and I randomly signalled, "Lead the way, Lila."

Oh My Damn. – She just charmed me before climbing off the side of a building. – That woman's got nerves of steel.

I watched in amazement and listened to my ear-mic as they all reached the base floor of level twenty, and then I walked them through the attachment process. They all needed to drill and prep a base plate into the side of the building, using laser beams and building markers to ensure correct alignment, and they were all doing perfectly.

"Phase 1 complete," Lila said, giving me the thumbs up as she just hung there, waiting for the others to confirm as well.

Now it was my turn, and I worked with Adela to get the top four devices in place as well, aligning them perfectly with their lower counterparts. It took a bit of time, but then I gave Lila the thumbs up, giving them all the order to climb back up.

Everything was going so well until I heard Tyme shout Lila's name in a panic. I looked over the side of the building to see Lila being attacked by a large bird that looked like an eagle. She tried to scare it away, but it wasn't until Billy threw a fireball at it from his corner of the building, that it flew off. But in the process, the bird partially severed the rope attached to Lila's harness.

Instantly, Lila grabbed the good part of the rope before she fell, but then screamed from the pain she was causing to the still-healing injury in her shoulder. And just to make things worse, her hands began to glow a fiery red.

Not Good.

Panic strewed across her face as she cursed, racing back to the top as fast as she could. But her shoulder injury was slowing her down. Alex, Billy, and Terrence all reached the top and knew she wasn't going to make it. So Billy handed the end of his rope to Alex and Terrence, and yelled, "Anchor me!" before running at full-speed towards the adjacent corner and jumping off the side of the building.

The momentum as he fell caused him to swing back towards Lila at a ridiculous speed, and he caught her when he shouted the words "Drop!" Then the jolt of catching Lila caused them both to swing back the other way and sent them flying up into the air above us.

I looked back to see Alex and Terrence's arms moving so fast to reel the rope back towards us. Then in seconds, Billy and Lila landed on them, tossing them all into the back of one of the rooftop's air conditioner vents.

Holy Damns. – That was close.

Lila's hands were still glowing when Tyme rushed to aid her, shouting her name. But in a hurry Billy appeared in front of him and demanded, "Don't touch her yet!"

He then turned to Lila, trying to help her stand, being careful of her glowing hands while Lila gazed into his eyes, trying to focus on her breathing as she worriedly mumbled, "That was close...That was very, very close."

"I know... but try to focus on me, okay," Billy spoke calmly, staring into Lila's eyes. "We all had you down there... It's all good."

"LOOK OUT!!!" Lila screamed as she raised her hands to throw a fireball at the large bird as it tried for round two.

The fireball scorched the wing of the bird, causing it to stagger in its flight away from us. And I turned back to Lila to see her beam with excitement as her hands returned to normal, and she jumped into Billy's arms, celebrating.

"I did it," she squealed. "I hit the target, and I didn't burn anything else in the process."

Billy held her up, just as excited for her and congratulated her. "You are a ridiculously fast learner. A plus, Lila."

Now with her excitement back, Billy put Lila back down on the ground for Tyme's turn to hug her. And while Tyme held her, Lila looked at me and asked, "What's next, boss man?"

Oh wow. – She almost fell to her death and she's still excited.

I took a moment for my own heartrate to go down before I explained that all I needed to do now was turn them all on remotely, and it was done. So Lila nodded and watched as I typed the code into my computer to activate them, and then heard the gentle hum start in each of the devices.

"And that's lunch!" Lila shouted. "Who's in? Coz Matt's paying."

She grinned as she gave me a celebratory high-five before leading everyone back into the building. And because it was my idea to do a potentially and inevitably dangerous mission, I have no dramas in buying the team lunch from the downstairs promenade.

We all decided on having Italian for lunch and invited Katie and Jess to join us and take a break from their research. Max was already downstairs, part way through a business lunch when he caught us heading into the restaurant, and when Lila reported our success, he was very excited and offered to pay for our lunch, instead of me. — Which I'm not going to argue with.

The range of food on the table was a lot, and the team dynamics were very loud and excitable as we ate lunch together. But Lila randomly had to step away when Chase came into the restaurant, wanting to talk to her.

They stood outside, and you could tell that everyone at the table was watching them through the window, but neither Lila or Chase was talking. Instead they were sharing a phone between them, each taking turns to type something.

Sneaky.

When they had finished, Lila hugged Chase then dragged him in to the restaurant to talk to us, but Lila was more focused on Isaac and Holly. — Strange? — Peering across, I noticed Billy become nervous and tense, watching Lila's actions while glancing at Isaac and Holly as well.

"Okay." Lila braced herself with excitement. "So do you want the good news or do you want the kind of bad news."

"The good news," Isaac and Holly said in unison.

"Alrighty... so I made some calls and spoke to Jordan and Zera, and they would love to have you join their team."

"In London?" Holly beamed with eager excitement.

"In London." Lila nodded with a little chuckle.

Letting out an excited squeal, Holly raced from the table to hug Lila, and Isaac followed, both hugging her and almost knocking her over. We could see from the brief pain that crossed Lila's face followed by the doting smile, that the pain was worth it for her. But Billy stood up, now confused and acting all parental on them.

"Hang on, I thought you both wanted to join Lila's team here."

"We did," Isaac replied, looking a little nervous. "But when Max and Jess were talking about everything that you guys do, and that there's a team based in London. We thought it was a good opportunity."

Billy wasn't sold and suspiciously stared at them with his hands on his hips in a bit of a huff, leading Lila to laugh at him. "Oh, come on, Billy. They just want a chance to see the world. And Zera and Jordan will take excellent care of both of them... and keep them out of trouble."

Still with a grumble, Billy eyed the odd but cheeky smile Lila had, and questioned, "Okay, but neither of them have asked what your 'kind of bad news' is. And I'm curious if they're even going to bother asking."

Ah. – He used logic on them. – Clever.

Slowly, Holly and Isaac released Lila from the hug, looking up at her, nervously waiting for Lila to deliver the bad news. But Lila still had her chuckling grin, staring back at Chase as he stepped out of the restaurant and then led both Jordan and Zera into the restaurant to say hello to everyone.

Adela and Katie greeted them with a smile and a hug before Lila introduced Isaac and Holly to them. But then she spoke with such seriousness, "The bad news is that you two will need to say goodbye to Billy, and he's going to be all sad and sappy."

At that accusation, Billy crossed his arms and rolled his eyes as Lila explained that Jordan and Zera had stopped in to stock up on the Neuritamine cures, and were hoping for Lila to open the tree port to send them back home, which meant Isaac and Holly have less than an hour to pack and go. – That is if they're still interested in going.

With nervousness all over them, Isaac and Holy turned back to Billy, almost as if they were asking for Billy's permission. They waited and waited. Then Lila decided to join the waiting group, and stared at Billy with the puppy-dog eyes.

Oh, that's just too cute. — And Sassy.

"Ugh... Fine." Billy relaxed his stance. "But you two better stay out of trouble and keep your darn heads down."

Now excited again, Isaac and Holly gave Billy a jumping hug, acting like typical, overexcited teenagers. And it caused Lila to laugh at Billy so hard as she sat back down at the table and invited Jordan, Zera, and Chase to join us as well.

"Aw," Lila cheeked. "See, the tall man does have a heart... A sappy, sappy one"

CHAPTER 34

Queen Bee

Journal entry by Alex Woods

My emotions are starting to get the best of me today, and I'm beginning to feel that territorial jealousy seep under my skin again. It ticks me off that Lila's so reliant and accepting of Billy to re-join the team. And it still frustrates me that she went to him for help last Friday and not me. – I know now, <u>after</u> she explained everything, that she had actually come to my apartment first. But because I was avoiding her after our last fight and had agreed to lie to her about what she is, I stupidly pushed her into the helpful arms of another man.

Yep. – I'm just that idiotic.

This morning, I was so happy to see Lila giggling and having fun in the conference room, and my heart skipped a beat when she appeared on my lap and not Billy's, and then very cheekily got comfy on me. I was more than happy for that and loved every second of it.

And yes, I'm glad that Billy saved Lila from falling. But then watching her in his arms as they celebrated Lila creating her first fireball and hitting the target. – That part got to me. So after lunch, instead of heading off to the tree port with the group and saying goodbye to Isaac, Holly, Jordan, and Zera, I stormed up to the gym to work off some pent-up energy and try to calm down.

Nope. – It isn't working. – So plan B.

While taking calming breaths, I went back into my apartment to calm down, pouring myself a glass of water. – I need to calm down, so I focused on taking more slow breaths, standing in the kitchen, trying to remind myself of the love Lila has for me. – She's even said it to me. – Granted it wasn't direct, but she said it.

Suddenly, a repetitive knock banged at the apartment door, and it infuriated me, causing me to crush the glass in my hand. And when I pulled the door open, I angrily screamed, "WHAT!"

Aw Crap! – It's Lila.

My anger startled her, and she just stood at my door, staring at me, confused and slightly scared.

"Sorry..." she stuttered, backing away from the door. "I... I'll come back later."

"No, Lila, wait," I pleaded, rushing to stop her. "I'm sorry, I didn't mean that."

"Okay," she mumbled, still backing away. I think she was sensing my anger, and she started playing with her fingers as she explained, "Um... Katie and Jess have just found out a way to turn off the tracking devices. And I assumed you and Terrence would want to be the first to try it, so I came back as fast as I could to tell you... Terrence is already up in the conference room... But if you want, you can do yours in the next round."

She eyed the blood dripping from my hand and rushed to inspect it as she gasped, "Alex, you're bleeding... Is everything okay?"

I pulled my hand away and tried to casually explain that I accidentally broke a glass, and then said, "I'm fine... I'll head up to the conference room in a minute, okay."

The face she had on her was so sad and confused. She looked like she wanted to ask me a question, but instead just nodded and walked away. So now feeling like an even bigger idiot, I grumbled to myself, walking back into my apartment to clean up the broken glass while telling myself how idiotic and stupid I'm acting. – Lila was happy and having so much fun this morning, even through lunch. And she didn't let the almost-falling-to-her-death part ruin her mood. – But one second alone with me and her happiness shrivels.

I know I have to fix it and apologise. And I assumed she'd be up in the conference room with Terrence, but she wasn't. It was just Katie and Jess, shining a UV torch on the back of Terrence's neck and attaching a little node to the invisible marking.

I asked them where Lila was and the answer didn't thrill me when Terrence replied, "She's down in the lobby... Agent Green is making his weekly check-up. And Lila wanted to avoid any objections Green might have to what we're doing."

"Is Billy with her?" I huffed in slight disappointment. – Because I'm just that stupid and territorially dumb.

Terrence nodded and asked why, but I didn't answer, I just sat down and let Jess explain what they were planning to do.

"Okay, we've been researching the last bits of information Lila's tracking device recorded before it left her body... And from the looks of it, the device short-circuited. Probably because Lila was using so much of her body's energy that the device couldn't handle all the information and simply shut down... Her body must have then recognised that it was a foreign substance and treated it as an infection, trying to force it out of her system."

"So what have you got planned?" I asked, super worried that they had something stupidly painful in mind.

With a grin, Katie piped in, cheerfully saying, "We're going to electrocute you while you're running on the spot as fast as you can."

Yep. – Stupidly painful it is.

Terrence grew uncomfortable at that thought, shifting in his chair and asked, "Is that safe?"

"On humans, no," Jessica replied. "But guardians have the ability to endure a lot more pain and heal a lot faster. It should only hurt a bit."

Ah-huh. – In disbelief, I grumbled to myself while walking over to them, and then griped, "Alright... Let's just get this thing over with."

Journal entry insert by Billy Jonas

Alright, I've got to say it. – Lila looks incredibly sexy today. And it's not just because of the short red tennis-skirt and green and white top that shows off her amazingly strong body. – It's because she's happy, and she has a smile on her that I haven't seen on her since our date. – The smile she had before everything went wrong.

I still can't believe she pulled the puppy-dog eyes on me when she sprung the information that Isaac and Holly were leaving, and I am a little annoyed at her about it. I mean, honestly, she didn't even tell me that they wanted to leave in the first place. – It's not like she didn't have the chance, given the amount of late-night food deliveries I've been doing for her. And I know she was only calling me at 3am just to mess with me, because she always had the cheekiest grin on her when I brought up whatever random item she requested. – It got her to stay in the bed though, so I was happy to do it.

However, after we had said goodbye to Isaac and Holly, Lila had to rush back to the hotel to talk to Katie and Jess. And I assumed it was good news. But now Lila's happy demeanour has dramatically changed for some reason, and the meeting with her new government friend didn't start so well when he greeted us in the lobby. Especially when he eyed me standing next to Lila.

"Hello Ms Winters, I see you've gained another friend."

She smiled back at me, and then commented, "Yes, I'm quite good at finding new friends. Is there something I can help you with, Mr Green? I'm sensing that you want something from me that's not part of our usual arrangement."

His stance quickly changed, and he began to struggle with his words. "Yes... um. We've been following up on a few leads you've given us, and we wanted you to assist us... I've been sent here to personally oversee the mission."

Lila took a moment, staring at him before she replied, "Alright, we can look into it... But we're a little busy at the moment. You're going to need to wait."

Angered by the calm brush-off, Mr Green grabbed Lila's arm before she could walk away, and almost commanded her, "This mission has been given a deadline... We need you now."

I moved closer, ready to assist her, but Lila put her free hand up, signalling me to stop. I also noticed her grin — just a little — as she peered at me from the corner of her eye.

She then pulled her arm away from Mr Green, glancing around at the other patrons in the lobby walking past us, before calmly replying to him. "If that's the case then you'll need to find another team to complete the mission... I'm sorry, Mr Green."

"Yeah, see that's the problem," Mr Green replied still quite angry. "All of the guardians that were on Mission control's books are either still missing or have gone into hiding... Everyone else seems to end up here. I'm sure you can spare a few of them for a day or two."

Lila crossed her arms and delayed in her response before she reluctantly agreed. "I can talk to the team, see if anyone wants to volunteer. But..."

Suddenly, Lila stopped her speech, becoming distracted as a young man brushed past her arm, walking out of the lobby.

She followed him in a slightly confused panic, watching his movement. Then as he stepped out onto the street, in line with an oncoming bus, she raced at super-speed to pull him out of the way. And the bus screeched to a halt as it passed, narrowly missing both of them as they fell to the ground on the other side.

Holy Darns! — What just happened?

Mr Green and his other agents followed me out to see if they were okay, and I found Lila kneeling over the man who is now unconscious.

"What happened?" I asked, panicked and hoping Lila wasn't hurt either.

"I don't know." She looked up at me befuddled. "He just stepped out in front of the bus, and now he's stopped breathing."

"I'll call an ambulance," Mr Green added.

I stayed staring at Lila, and she clearly knew what I was worried about when she smiled at me. "I'm okay, Billy. I promise you can check the stitches later."

Well, that made me feel a little better, so I moved Lila back to start CPR on the man, and Lila stayed close to me but then looked around suspiciously.

"Somethings wrong," she mumbled, and I could hear the fear in her voice.

A second passed before the bus in front of us caught fire, and the bus doors weren't opening, trapping the passengers of young school students on an end-of-the-year field trip inside.

The kids started screaming, so Lila demanded, "Billy, you get the bus. I've got this."

She hurriedly swapped places with me and continued the CPR as I ordered the four government agents just standing there to help me. I forced the bus doors open, ushering the agents in to help the children, and I tried to tame the fire all while Adela raced out with the hotel's fire hose to douse the flames.

When the fire was out, I returned to where Lila was, only to find Mr Green standing around, looking dumfounded and confused, calling, "Ms Winters! Ms Winters! Lila!"

"Where is she?" I barked.

He stared back at me and stuttered, "I... I don't know... She just disappeared with some woman."

Darn Crap Buckets. — I lost her.

I searched the perimeter as fast as I could but found nothing and knew I needed to get help, so I returned up to the conference room to find Alex. Unfortunately, I found both Alex and Terrence lying on the floor being electrocuted by something attached to their necks, both with blood noses and a little busy.

Katie was studying them, watching as Alex's branding mark disappeared, and then shouted, "It worked" back to Jessica.

"Only hurt a little?" Alex sarcastically grumbled. Then he looked up at me and worriedly asked, "What's wrong?"

"Lila's gone... and I think Katherine took her."

Journal entry insert by Lila Winters

Well, isn't this just peachy. – I was having such a good day until I felt the presence of horrid-pure evil injecting me with a burning liquid that made me weak and drowsy before everything went dark.

Yep. – Just peachy.

Slowly I stirred awake again, and I'm not sure how long it's been but I still feel weak and unable to lift my arms. I took calm breaths and scanned my surroundings to realise that I'm in some dark, dirty cave with a small candle to light the area. And for some random reason, I'm naked, wearing nothing but my seed-stone bracelet that they've clearly tried to take off, and painfully failed, because I can feel my wrist blistering from what feels like a burn. – They've even taken off the bandages from my thigh and shoulder. Leaving the stitches of the stab wounds completely exposed to the elements.

What the Frac?

Now cold, confused, and angry, I looked around and found my clothes in a folded pile next to me with my necklace sitting on top, so I used what energy I could to command the vines in my stone bracelet to very discreetly grab my clothes. But the only thing I was able to get was my necklace before I heard her footsteps and sensed all the evil in her cold heart.

In a hurry, my vine bracelet retracted, weaving the necklace in amongst the vines so she couldn't see it when she entered the cave.

"Hello Katherine," I growled, undeterred by her creepy demeanour. "I hope you know you ruined my day."

She kneeled down where I lay, and I fumed that I'm still too weak to kick her obnoxious face as she replied, "Well... you ruined all of my fun too, Pumpkin. Threatening my empire and all... So I guess we're even."

"Empire?" I scoffed, rolling my eyes at her. "Katherine, what do you want?"

She stood up, circling me while creating a ring of fire around me. "Nothing much. I'm just conducting a little experiment... Two actually."

As she walked past my head, I stared at the blistered burn on Katherine's arm and realised, "You were the bird that attacked me at the hotel... I could have died."

"No, Pumpkin," she corrected. "You could have fallen. I had my men on standby ready to catch you. But instead your stupid little boyfriends had to mess things up again."

"What the hell is wrong with you?" I angrily grumbled. "And why am I naked! And why do you keep calling me Pumpkin?"

She kneeled down to look over the flames circling me, and tittered at my miserable attempt to at least cover my breasts as she answered, "Nothing's wrong with me, Pumpkin. And you're naked because I ordered it. And... I used to call you Pumpkin when I was pregnant with you... Don't tell me your dad calls you Honey-Bee. I told him not to call you that... It's too sweet and sickening."

Hating her even more, I mustered up enough strength to sit up, and then defiantly stated, "I like Honey Bees... Now what do you want from me? You know I won't tell you anything!"

"Oh, I know that. But I won't be getting the information from you. You are actually Keith's little project, and I'm sure you two will have so much fun... But mine is a little more intriguing... I've been watching you for a while now, Pumpkin. And well, I don't know if you've noticed it. But I certainly did..."

I rolled my eyes at her vexing stance over me, and sniggered. "Noticed what?"

She leaned in closer and ever so smugly explained, "Well, have you ever noticed that every guardian in your orbit tends to grow... let's call it an infatuation with you... And the longer these subjects spend time with you, the more they seem to care about you."

"It's called a friendship," I replied as I greasied her. "You know, it's a relationship between two or more people displaying a mutual affection for each other."

"I know the definition of friendship," she rebuffed – and wow, that is a shock. – Yet still she continued, "But it's more than that. These men hang off your every word, constantly seeking your approval. Doing anything for you. Some are even willing to die for you... You're like their queen bee, and while I can't have another queen running around, threatening the Dunstian empire, you've also piqued my curiosity because you act like their queen without even trying... And it took me years to master that little pheromone trick."

Dunstian Empire??? – What the frac is she on.

She stood up and started circling me again and spoke with so much evil in her. "You like science, don't you, Lila? Well, you married a scientist, so you must like it... Tell me, Pumpkin, what do you think happens to all the worker bees if their queen just... disappears?"

I huffed, contemplating staying silent but answered, "I don't know, but I have a feeling you're going to tell me anyway."

She grinned and did just that. "Most of the time it causes mass panic, then the bees begin to fight amongst each other, and eventually all the bees... die."

"What's your point?" I groaned, hoping that she'd get to it.

"Your little hive is well set up and I want to keep it that way," she answered while picking up my clothes from the other side of the flames.

Now baffled, I shook my head at Katherine's stupidity. "I thought you just said a hive needed their queen to function."

"You're right..." She grinned back at me again with a slight titter. "They do need a queen."

I then watched in pure horror as Katherine morphed into me before injecting me with the burning liquid again, and strutted out of the cave with all my clothes.

Aw Frac Biscuits. – I was having such a good day.

Journal entry insert by Billy Jonas

So now we have a problem. The one person I was confident could find Lila was Alex, and he's now lost his powers. He's also not taking the news of Lila being missing very well, seeing how we are now chasing Alex and Terrence down into the lobby to stop them from leaving.

"You can't... Alex, stop!" Jessica demanded, blocking them from the door. "Both of you don't have any of your abilities. It'll take you hours just to search the first block."

"Guardian or not, we need to do something," Terrence snapped, trying to move past her.

I thought I'd lend a hand and help stop them, seeing how they're both quite weak without their powers, and then suggested, "You could do as Lila asked and stay here. You know she'd be upset at you for even thinking about doing this... I'll keep looking for her. We will find her."

"How?" Alex bickered. "You're the one who lost her in the first place... Besides, what chance could you possibly have that will help us find Lila."

"HEY!" Adela yelled, storming up to the group from the reception desk. "You're causing a scene... Now, I know you're all upset about Lila, but you're not going to solve anything by arguing in the lobby. Now go back upstairs, brainstorm a search plan that makes everyone happy, and then go."

Alex and Terrence growled and grunted as Adela literally backed them into the elevator, not giving them any chance to argue. Then as we rode the elevator back upstairs, Alex started arguing with me again about who has a better chance of finding Lila. – And damn, he has a big head.

It got even bigger when Terrence chimed in, "Alex is right. You don't have any way of finding Lila except for searching Melbourne street by street, which in my opinion is a waste of time."

"You think you have a better idea, Nature boy?" I snickered, getting a little hot-tempered by their ego.

I mean seriously. – They're not the only ones that love Lila.

"Actually, I do," Terrence replied as the elevator door opened back onto the conference room floor. He showed us the matching bracelet Lila and him both wear. – The one with the purple stone thing in the middle. Then he explained, "This stone is one half of a tree stone, and Lila has the other half in her bracelet. It's what Lila and I use to communicate if we ever need to find each other."

Katie looked at it and nodded. "Yeah, that's what Lila used to track us to the government base the other week... But how are you going to use it? You don't have your powers."

"There's still one other Nature guardian in the hotel," Terrence replied. "And he would jump at the chance to help Lila."

"Good." Katie smiled then shot both Alex and Terrence in the back with Jessica's tranque gun.

I watched in an amused shock as they fell to the floor unconscious. Then I looked back up at Katie, a little puzzled as I made sure they were both okay, and with a chuckle, she just shrugged her shoulders at me.

"What...? Do you honestly think they were going to listen to any of us when we tell them to stay here?"

Well, she has a point there.

We met up with William and Tyme, and borrowed Terrence's bracelet, which was actually quite stubborn to remove because it clung to Terrence's wrist like it was his master. In the end, William had to command the vines to let go of Terrence's wrist. – And that is a seriously cool theft deterrent.

Without any more delays, Katie, Tyme, and I followed William and the stone on foot, running at super-speed out of the city and into a state national park in the middle of nowhere.

Well, this is just... great. – Not!

We're now in the middle of the woods with hills and trees everywhere. It's already hit nightfall which means we have to rely on our night vision and the purple stone that is glowing brighter as we walk. – And I'm going to assume that that is a good thing.

Suddenly, from the darkness of the trees, we heard Lila's scream not far from us, so we all raced through the woodland, looking for her. We ran through the thick shrubs, ducking and dodging low hanging tree branches, until William found her running towards us.

He grabbed hold of her, trying to calm her down as she kept screaming. But Lila mustn't have recognised him because she pulled away from him in a panic, elbowing him in the gut then in the low jaw to knock him out.

I quickly stood between her and William, putting my hands out in surrender. "Lila, stop! It's us!"

"Billy…" She breathed with relief, realising it was me and became ecstatic, leaping up to wrap her arms around me. "I'm so sorry… I thought you were him."

"Who?" I asked while holding on to her tightly.

She looked back into the trees, petrified. "Keith… he's out here."

The group went quiet as we listened to the rustling leaves around us. We could hear him lurking in the shadows, and I felt Lila tense in my arms as she shouted to the trees.

"Give it up, Keith. You've lost this round!"

Tyme was busy trying to wake William when Keith appeared in front of us, smiling at Lila as I held her close to me. Katie's hands became covered in fire, and I followed suit with my free hand. – And I kind of love the fact the Lila is light enough to be held up with one hand because I have no intentions of letting her go.

Keith glared at Lila and creepily grinned before taking off into the trees, clearly outnumbered at this point. Once we knew he was gone, I relaxed, placing Lila's feet back down on the ground when we heard the sound of William stirring awake.

Lila tried to leave the safety of my arms, but I held her tight, not ready to let her go yet. So she conceded and stayed put. And I appreciated that.

A little groggy as he woke up, William slowly stood to his feet when Lila asked if he was okay and worriedly spoke, "I'm really sorry, Dad. I didn't realise it was you."

He shook it off but groaned a little from the pain, and then confusedly sighed. "Er... yeah... That's okay, Lila."

Taking another breath, Lila then looked up at me and smiled. "Can we go home now, I'm starving."

Um? – Okay? – I had to laugh at her request, considering she ate almost an entire vegetarian pizza to herself at lunch, plus the garlic bread, and dessert.

CHAPTER 35

Don't Kiss And Tell

Journal entry by Matt Winters

Lila's been acting really weird all week. And she's been like that since she got back from her run-in with Keith at that state park over a fortnight ago.

I kind of felt bad for her. I mean, the night Lila came back, she seemed really rattled and out of sorts. – For some odd reason, she wouldn't let Billy check the stitches in her leg or arm or even change the bandages because they were covered in dirt. She wouldn't even let Terrence or Alex look at them, and instead demanded that all of them should just go, so she can rest. She then became confused about everything. She looked agitated at the fact that we were divorced but still live together. Then when she told me she was going to shower, Lila walked into my room, looking even more confused.

The next morning she was again confused to see Terrence in the kitchen making her breakfast. – Like he always does. – And she completely blew him off when he asked if she was going to help set up the Christmas tree down in his and Alex's apartment, stating that the kidnapping kind of soured her Christmas spirit.

Um. – How the hell is that possible? – She was kidnapped last year and was reported dead, and still loved everything there was about Christmas and its traditions.

A few days later, I came back from work early and found her tearing her bedroom apart, looking for her journal after first turning over the loungeroom and study. I told her I'd already cleaned the lounge and hadn't seen it, and that I'd keep an eye out for it. But she seemed determined to look anyway and has been searching for it ever since.

Add to that, she's been keeping some really odd hours, sneaking out in the middle of the night. I thought maybe she was going down to Billy's or Alex and Terrence's apartment, but none of them had any idea what I was talking about when I mentioned it to them.

The other odd thing I've noticed is that she never wears any of her jewellery anymore. – The necklace that she never takes off even when she's a wolf. As well as that glowing stone bracelet of hers. – She doesn't wear either of them anymore. – Terrence has been wanting to ask her about it, but for some reason Lila's always busy when he comes up to see her. – Which is strangely odd for her.

Yesterday, I confronted Lila about her odd behaviour, and she acted all cagey, trying to change the subject back to our relationship and was getting a little too close for our usual agreement. – She knows I have growing feelings for someone else. I don't understand this sudden change of desire she has towards me. And if she's ever feeling short on love, she knows exactly where to go to find it. – She even has her choice if she wanted.

Journal entry insert by William Knight

Today is Tyme's birthday, and it's now just over a week until Christmas. So to start the day, I opted to take him out for a late breakfast and enjoy marvelling at the Christmas decorations in the city. – It's Tyme's first Christmas in Melbourne. And I know he likes to experience the cultural differences of the cities he visits, and this is the perfect opportunity. – I tried asking Lila if she wanted to join us, but she seems determined to avoid me at the moment.

We chose one of the coffee shops in Melbourne Central so I could pick out a present for Tyme as well, and it feels really good to be able to do this with him. – Mainly because Tyme and his mother spent most of their years with their tribe while he was growing up. And while Time guardians aren't as rare as Nature guardians, they have always chosen to be more cautious and private to avoid being discovered by The Board. So being able to celebrate with Tyme in such a public area like this feels amazing.

To make things even better, tonight, he has a birthday party with all of his friends and his not-quite girlfriend, Adela. – Not entirely sure what they are yet. But either way, this is going to be a really good birthday for him.

As we sat and ate our usual cheese and tomato toastie, I opted for a coffee, but Tyme opted for the colder caffeinated variety, stating that it was Lila's favourite combination.

"Interesting," I mumbled. "I'm sorry she couldn't come out with us today... I think she might be avoiding me."

"Do you mean more than usual?" Tyme asked, seemingly unconcerned.

I suppose he's right in that sense. Lila and I haven't really gotten that far in our relationship aspect. But I thought, after everything we've been through this year, that I had at least gotten to basic speaking terms with her.

"I don't know." I shrugged, still a bit puzzled. "Something's just off with her."

"Why, has she said something to you?" Tyme asked again.

I leaned back in my chair, crossing my arms, feeling majorly displeased with the situation. "No... but that's the point. She hasn't said anything to me. And every time I see her, she quickly runs the other way."

Tyme went quiet for a second to think, and then stated, "Well, she has been a little different ever since Katherine came into the picture. I mean think about it, at the end of last year Lila thought both her parents were dead... Now at the end of this year, she discovers both her parents are alive, and thinks one willingly gave up on her, and the other is the devil incarnate... So no offence, Dad, but I can't blame her for wanting to avoid you at the moment."

I sat in silence, twiddling with my breakfast, feeling guilty that I was having this kind of conversation with my son on his birthday.

"Dad," Tyme said, pulling me from my trance. "I think it might be time you told Lila your side of the story. She thinks you just gave up on her... You need to tell her the truth."

I shook my head, feeling like a complete failure and a coward, "I can't... She'll never forgive me. Besides, she'll just think I'm trying to justify all of my horrible decisions."

Tyme sighed, slightly disappointed in me. I really think he was hoping we'd be one big happy family by now. And I was just about to apologise to him for souring his birthday when his not-quite girlfriend walked up to the table, looking for us. I picked up the sense that she really wanted to talk to Tyme about something but was feeling nervous.

Oh, young love. - It's so fickle and sweet.

"Hi Adela... have you come to join us for breakfast?" I asked, offering her a seat.

She looked at the seat then back at me. "In a way, yes... I was just out shopping with Lila, picking up a few last-minute things for tonight and thought I'd just pop in quickly...but..."

Pausing for a few seconds, Adela looked a little hesitant, then said, "I'm sorry, but I couldn't help but hear the last of your conversation. Lila's very smart and she has a really strong heart... She understands a lot more than you give her credit for."

"I didn't mean it like that," I tried to explain.

But she continued, "I know what you meant... trust me. I've hurt Lila and danced around that void as well. And I'm sure you already know Lila's code of second chances... But... look, please don't tell her I told you this. But ever since Hanna died, Lila has another code that she herself always sticks to... She always accepts responsibility of her actions be them good or bad. She'll apologise when she's wrong and defend when she's right. But she will never try to excuse or deny her actions, because a lie protects no one you love... I think maybe you need to take a page out of her book and at least give it a try."

Wow. – I have a really smart daughter if that's the morals she lives by. – Even after everything she's been through.

I nodded, reflecting on her words when Adela stated, "She's still here if you want to go talk to her... She was headed into one of the sporting stores when I left."

While thinking the idea through, I took one look back at Tyme's pleading eyes then agreed to at least try, and went to go find Lila.

I caught up with her just as she was coming out of one of the other coffee stores at the other end of the corridor, and I think she was on her way home when I found her.

"Lila... hi," I nervously uttered.

"Oh... hi." She smiled back me, starting to walk out of Melbourne central to cross the street.

Still a little nervous, I followed her, trying to spark up a conversation, "I didn't know you drink coffee now."

She looked at me as if I was crazy, leading me to point to the very strong scented coffee in her hand, and add, "It's just the last time you were at our apartment, you were groaning on about the horrible smell of coffee and how you would only ever drink hot chocolate. So, I was just wondering what changed your mind?"

She stayed silent and continued to walk, crossing the road into China Town, sending me a clear signal that she doesn't want to talk.

Right. – Let's try another angle then.

"Lila, I was wondering if you were interested in joining me for lunch today? To give us a chance to talk."

"Sorry, I can't... I'm actually really busy," she replied.

"Okay, what about tomorrow?"

She peered at me sideways, obviously getting the hint of my determination, and sighed, saying, "Sure, tomorrow... Bye, Dad." Then she turned down one of the alleys to get away from me.

"There... you did it again," I noted in confusion.

She stopped and turned back to me, seeming uneasy about what it was she did. And I walked towards her, staring at her, feeling really confused. "You just called me Dad."

"I'm sorry," she said looking around. And again, I felt this strange vibe around her as if she was hiding something when she explained, "It was a slip of the tongue. It won't happen again."

Again, Lila turned to walk up the alley, so I grabbed her arm about to beg her to stop and talk to me. But I quickly pulled away when I sensed her true nature, and it was one I knew all too well. In seeing my odd recoil, she stopped walking and looked back at me again, asking if I was okay.

"Yeah..." I nodded, trying to keep up the pretence. "I'm sorry for annoying you like this. I'll let you get back to whatever it was you were doing... See you tonight."

I acted all sad and disappointed as I walked off, determined not to look back. Then when I was out of her view, I ran at top speed into an alleyway a few blocks down to call Tyme and warn him. But as I dialled the number, she appeared in front of me again.

"Actually, Dad, I think we can talk now."

She knocked me to the ground, and as I fell, I hit my head on the lip of a window ledge, feeling way too dizzy to get up, and feeling the blood dripping from the throbbing gash at the back of my head.

While trying to shake off the dizziness, I heard Tyme's voice from the phone where it landed, so I yelled toward it. "Tyme... Lila's not—" But she hung up the phone before I could say anything else.

She stood there, staring at me, frustrated that I'd ruined her plans when we were unexpectedly joined by a young man as he walked into the alley, heading towards his car. The moment he saw me on the ground with blood dripping from my head wound, he confusedly hesitated and stared at us.

"Woah, sorry," he murmured. "Hey, is he alright?"

She looked at the young man before eyeing his car, and then randomly kissed him. The kiss became strangely passionate and his eyes glowed a pinkish-red colour as his entire body relaxed, becoming somewhat entranced by her. Then he just willingly did as she asked, shoving me into the boot of his car before knocking me unconscious with a monkey wrench.

Journal entry insert by Adela Eden

Okay, so I've been trying to work up the courage to ask Tyme out on a proper and official boyfriend and girlfriend date for weeks now. And I know he turned me down before because of his fear of making little hybrid babies with me. But I thought maybe because he and Lila are getting along so well now, that maybe Lila has softened him up for me around his qualms about the whole hybrid thing.

Before I could say anything though, he got this strange call from his dad on our way back to the hotel. So we thought we'd go a little faster than the average human, and made it back into the lobby just in time to catch Lila waiting for the elevator.

"Lila, hey... have you seen my dad?" Tyme asked a little puffed. - He really needs to go on more runs with us, and he definitely needs the practice.

"No, why?" she asked.

Oh Fruits. - I feel a bit disappointed. - I thought maybe William was actually going to talk to Lila this time. But it looks like he's chickened out, again.

Tyme stood straighter, still trying to catch his breath and explained, "I just got a weird phone call from him, and I thought he might have been with you."

"Um... well, I haven't seen him. But I'll let you know if I do," she replied, stepping into the elevator, and then held it open while looking at me. "Adela, are you still coming up to check on Alex and Terrence with me?"

I nodded and said goodbye to Tyme, suggesting he try calling his dad again as I stepped into the elevator with Lila.

When we got up to the conference room, there was a bit of a state to it with a broken office chair and a smashed *potted plant. Alex was sitting on one of the not broken chairs, getting his hand stitched up by Billy while Terrence was sitting on the other side of the table, icing a nasty bruise on his cheek. All the while Jess and Katie sat at the end of the table, writing notes and looking in the old journals they had borrowed from Lila.*

"What happened here?" Lila puzzled in disbelief.

Jess pulled her head up over the computer screen to answer, "Their frustration got the best of them, and they kind of took it out on each other."

I thought Lila would be mad at them, instead she smiled. "Right... and who won?"

"I did," Billy chimed in.

Lila's grin grew wider, as if she were enjoying the turf-war they were all having, and even encouraging it.

Strange. - Very, very strange.

"Urgh! It's been two weeks now. We should have gotten our powers back. Why isn't it working?" Alex grunted, and Billy had to demand he keep still to finish the last stitch.

"Maybe you have," Katie suggested, pulling her head up from one of the old journals. "Our powers are controlled by our emotions, right. What if you already have your powers back, but you just haven't needed to use them."

Jessica followed the same thought and agreed. "Right, so we just need to recreate the same emotional environment and trigger their natural responses... Alex, what's the emotion you felt when you first morphed into another animal?"

He peered back at Lila and smirked a little. "I was with Lila. She was trapped in the dreamland at the time."

"What do you mean trapped, by who?" Billy asked, completely baffled.

"By me," Terrence regretfully added, looking up at Lila apologetically. But Lila looked at him, almost confused herself.

"Seriously," Katie gasped. "You can do that? How?"

Again, Terrence regrettably sighed, leaning back in his chair. "It's kind of a difficult technique to do. But you can only use it on people who are of the same element as you. That's what makes the connection so strong. Then once Lila was trapped there, Adela was able to use her own element to enter the dreamland and keep her occupied... I used the same technique to keep Lila unconscious the night she got stabbed with the glass, and Billy needed to stitch her up."

Jess's scientific interest was piqued, murmuring, "Interesting, if you don't mind, I'd really like to document this..."

"Hey," Alex impatiently piped up. "We're getting off topic here."

"Wait a minute," Billy interrupted, looking at Terrence. "I remember Lila talking about this on our date. She said that Alex didn't know how to access the dreamland and needed her help to get in. So how did that happen if she was trapped."

Alex looked up at Lila, hoping she would answer, but she stayed silent, so he cagily answered, "Lila... pulled me in by kissing me."

"That's it!" Katie said, almost leaping from her chair. "What if it's love? If that's the case. Lila just needs to kiss him."

"Kiss who now?" Lila finally broke her silence, slightly out of sorts.

Her innocent act only caused Jessica to huff at the obvious longing each one of the boys have for Lila, before she untactfully explained, "Look, we all know Alex is in love with you. So if you kiss him, he should revert back to his animal ways."

Alex stood, looking very uncomfortable with the idea, slowly backing away from Katie and Jess. Then Katie frustratedly rolled her eyes as she bickered at him. "Alex, if you want to be the freaky animal man again, I suggest you at least try it."

He tentatively glanced at Lila, wanting her opinion, and she didn't hesitate in giving him an awkwardly quick peck on the lips.

"Aw, come on!" Katie shouted, frustratedly throwing her hands in the air. "You've totes got to put some effort into it... You need to really light the flames of passion for him."

We then all watched as Lila worked up the courage before slowly pulling her hands up around Alex's neck, running her fingers through his messy brown hair to pull him in for one hell of a kiss. It was long and very passionate, and Alex may have gotten a little too handsy, moving them to the more interesting curves of Lila's body, causing Billy and Terrence to get uncomfortable.

Oh fruits. - This was so not a good idea.

Yet Katie and Jess were both captivated and enjoyed finally getting to see Alex and Lila together. - It's only been like forever of both of them avoiding their feelings for each other.

I cleared my throat, subtly reminding them that they had an audience. Then surprisingly, Alex pulled Lila away from him, which must have been really hard to do.

"Well, that didn't work," Terrence grumbled. - Probably annoyed that he didn't get to do it.

"No, but it was totes fun to watch," Katie grinned.

Alex grew confused and started backing towards the door. "I'm sorry... I've got to go," he sighed, and then ran from the conference room.

From that, the experiment was over with Jess's phone ringing to break the tension. - It was reception looking for Terrence to tell him that his mother and sister were here.

Journal entry insert by Terrence Connors

Yeah. — So I've been avoiding my family since this whole mess of losing my powers occurred, and I was really hoping my abilities would have come back by now. The last thing I need is for Keith to find out that I'm the weak link in Lila's team. — I think that's why Lila's been avoiding me. And I know Izzy means well, but she can be a bit of a blabbermouth.

When I got down into the lobby, Izzy giddily ran up to hug me and squealed, "Terrence, I'm so happy to see you."

"I'm glad to see you too," I greeted and hugged her back.

She then stepped back from me, excitedly smiling. "You'll never believe this. Mum went to the doctors to get checked out, and she's been given a clean bill of health... She's cured and she remembers everything, even the times when we were little. Isn't that amazing?"

"Err...Yeah." I was stunned and nervous. "Wow, I didn't think that was possible."

Odele finally caught up with Izzy and stood next to us to greet me with a smile, and then added, "Neither did I, which is why I would really like to show my appreciation and offer my apologies to both you and Lila... I was hoping to invite both of you out for dinner tonight."

Yeah. — Um...

I think part of me is still a bit stand-offish and suspicious. — And probably overprotective, considering everything Odele is responsible for when it comes to Lila.

"Um... I can ask Lila, but I'm pretty sure she's busy tonight."

Both of them looked saddened, so I suggested, "But tomorrow night might work."

That seemed to perk up Izzy, and she started digging through her oversized designer handbag, excitedly mumbling, "That would be wonderful. I'll have Robert send you through the reservation plans?"

She then pulled Lila's journal out from her bag, the one Lila's been desperately looking for all week. "Lila left her journal at our house... You know, when everything happened. I promise you, no one has looked in it, not even me. I've guarded it very carefully. But can you give it back to her for me?"

I accepted the journal from her then said goodbye as they left the hotel. But I seriously felt weird about the whole thing. I'm really not used to Mother being so... um — appreciative and considerate and willing to negotiate over dinner plans, even before she got sick. — I mean she wasn't always so cold-hearted, but it grew that way over time.

I started looking for Lila to give her back her journal, and Shane said he had seen her going into Max's office, so I went to look for her there. I was about to knock on Maxwell's office door when I heard a scuffle from inside and Lila's voice, and she sounded angry.

"Maxwell, you're really starting to frustrate me... And you leave me with no choice."

I peered through the small gap in the door to see Lila lip-locked with Max and really going at it. Max's eyes then glowed some dark-reddish colour when Lila pulled away, seeming more frustrated as she scowled at him.

"Now let's try this again... where are the stones?" she forcefully ordered.

For a few seconds, there was silence until I heard Max's safe door open and then get slammed shut as Lila spoke. "Thank you. I'm also looking for my journal. Do you know where it is?"

Yeah — that's the journal I'm holding, and I clutched it tighter, holding it close to me while starting to freak out as she said very angrily, "That journal is very important to my plans... find it. Now!"

Um. — Yeah, something's definitely wrong here, and when she started storming out of the room, I didn't know what to do so I hid in the stairwell, listening to her as she waited for the elevator.

I heard her talking to someone on the phone, and I think it was Keith on the other end, but I couldn't really tell.

"I've got the Tree stones... No, I still can't find the island stone or her journal."

She sounded like she was getting more upset as she spoke. "How are you going with her? Has she given in yet or is she still holding out for more fun? ...Yeah, she really is a stubborn one... Keep at it... I love you too, Keith."

WHAT!?!

Her voice disappeared as the elevator doors closed. And my heart raced a mile a minute. — Lila and my brother.

Holy Crap. — He got to Lila.

In a frantic panic, I raced down the stairs and out of the hotel, making sure no one followed me. I really don't know what Keith has planned for Lila or her journal, but until I can figure it all out, this book has to disappear. And...

Yeah, not a chance. — There is no way I would even write down where I plan to hide this book.

When I came back to the hotel, I darted back up the stairs, hating my human fatigue and slowness as I raced to find Alex. He was in the apartment, getting ready for Tyme's birthday picnic when I burst through the door, wheezing, "Something's wrong... with Lila."

He didn't react the way I expected him to, he just asked what I meant by it.

"I think Keith may have gotten to her. I saw her kissing Max and looking for the stones and her journal... And as weird as that was, I heard her talking to Keith, and she said that she loves him."

He stopped getting ready and looked back at me. "Wait, do you know where her journal is?"

"No." I shook my head, baffled at his blasé attitude. "That's what you got from that whole explanation? It's Keith. How could Lila ever willingly love Keith? He's gotten to her, changed her somehow."

He doubtingly stared back at me then sighed, "Terrence, Lila loves everyone. You know that."

Oh Damn it.

The fear rose in me as I turned to see Lila walking out of Alex's room, wearing one of his t-shirts. And I really do not want to know what they were doing in there, but she doesn't have anything else on, so it's kind of easy to guess.

She stood at the bedroom door and smiled at me for the first time in weeks. But it was all wrong. — That's not the smile Lila usually has for me. She always bites her bottom lip with a cheeky sparkle in her eyes. But this smile is all wrong.

"He's right, I do love everyone." She grinned, staring back at Alex. But her smile disappeared when she looked at me and said, "Unfortunately, you're the wrong species for me."

"Lila, you need to fight this, you've been drugged," I stated before walking over to her.

Her blue eyes stared up into mine, and I ached all over as I stabbed an epi-pen into her thigh. I waited for some kind of reaction, but she just kept staring at me and huffed. "Are you finished?"

Seconds later, I blacked out.

Journal entry continued by Matt Winters

We were all gathered down in the rooftop garden for Tyme's dinner party, and the place looks amazing. Jess and Adela really outdid themselves this time. Shane and Katie were off playing with Danny and Ruby, and Tyme was talking with Adela and Jess when I went over to greet him and wish him a happy birthday.

We were just about to sit down for dinner, but Lila hadn't arrived, nor Alex or Terrence. Tyme's dad wasn't here either, but I just assumed he was respecting Lila's wishes and keeping his distance from the children.

When Lila did arrive, Tyme raced to hug her. "Lila, finally, I didn't think you were coming."

"And miss my little brother's first birthday with me..." She tittered while shaking her head. "I'd have to be locked in chains and held in a dark little cave to be kept from attending your birthday."

Eerr...? – That seems intense.

Tyme confusedly puzzled at her odd descriptive scene then changed the subject to something less dreary. "Um... okay... did you manage to see my dad on your way up?"

Lila shook her head, but before she said anything else, Danny ran up to give her a hug. She then stared down in what looks like confusion as Danny pulled away from her and ran back to me. But she shrugged her shoulder and just continued talking with Tyme and Alex without a care in the world. – And that was odd.

Seeming slightly rattled, Danny tugged on my hand, and I kneeled down to talk to him as he whispered, "Daddy, are you wearing a red shirt today?"

I glanced down at my blue-checked shirt and fearfully sighed, knowing what he meant by the question, yet replied calmly, "No, Sweetie, I'm wearing a blue shirt... But we can go and change it if you'd like."

He smiled and I told him to go get his sister as I discreetly went to talk to Lila, pulling her to the side of the garden. "Hey, Danny just asked me if I was wearing a red shirt."

She looked bewildered, staring at my shirt. "But your shirt is blue, he should know that."

Damn.

I very quickly realised that she had no idea what I was talking about. So I remembered the plan and stayed calm, not to give anything away.

"Yeah... I think he's not feeling well. I'm going to take him upstairs, let him have some rest. Can you apologise to Tyme for me?"

She nodded as I signalled Danny to come over with his sister, and we calmly walked out of the garden and into the elevator. I pushed the button to our floor apartment but got off on the floor below and walked the kids into the next elevator, taking that down to the basement to leave.

CHAPTER 36

Honey-Bee

Journal entry by William Knight

I've been trapped for hours in the trunk of this car, and it felt like it had turned down a dirt road when it finally stopped moving. I heard people talking outside the car, and then heard the sound of a man scream a long and fearful scream as if he were dying a slow and painful death. – Until the scream stopped, and there was silence.

A few seconds later the trunk door opened, and the glow of the moon shone on Keith's face as he injected me with some horrid-burning needle that made me feel like I had lost all my ability to stand. I groaned and protested as he dragged me out of the trunk, and then through the bushes, over large rocks and logs. I tried to ask the trees for help, but I couldn't sense them. I could just barely stay awake as he dragged me into some dark cave and dumped me down, creating a ring of fire around me before he left.

It ached all over my body, and whatever he gave me has weakened me to the point where I can't move. So for hours, I stared up at the roof of the cave as the circling flames flickered around me.

Eventually, I gained the strength to move, so I slowly lifted myself up onto my knees to look around the cave. It was dark, lit only by the fire surrounding me. But in the corner of the cave, resting in the dark was the soft glow of a young woman, curled into a ball, lying on the floor. She had nothing but a small blanket to cover her nakedness, and her hands were bound by chains embedded into the cave wall.

I tried to lift myself to get over the circling fire, but the flames grew hotter and when they did, the woman's tired face was illuminated.

Oh God. - It's my beautiful baby girl.

She looks just like she did back on the island. She's been tortured - again. Now covered from head to toe in bruises and lacerations, some older than others, and it looks like her arm's been dislocated. But what gutted me the most was that she lay so still in what looks like her own blood.

"Lila." I cried, falling to my knees, barely able to breathe with the fear in my heart. "Lila... please, my little Honey-Bee, open your eyes."

At the sound of my voice, she stirred and her eyes opened, but just barely as she peered up and moaned so weak in her breath. "Give it up, Katherine... I'm still not going to tell you anything."

That's my girl. - Keep those eyes open.

"Lila, it's me... It's William."

Moving ever so slowly, Lila turned her head toward me when I said my name. But she looked at me suspiciously and tiredly rasped, "When I first met you... at the hotel. What did you say to me?"

With confidence, I smiled because I knew she was testing me. The only other person who'd know this answer would be me. But before I could say anything, Keith appeared, towering over me and kicked me in the chest, winding me. I curled over in pain, but my fear heightened when I watched him move towards Lila.

"It's time for your medicine." He snickered almost too gleefully, holding a syringe in his hand filled with a dark-silver liquid.

She begged him not to. She pleaded and screamed as he dragged her towards the light of the flames, and stabbed the needle into her leg. Then as he stepped away, Lila's body went limp with a tear falling from her eye.

Mere seconds passed before Lila was screaming in agony as she unwillingly morphed into her white wolf form. The change must have been horrid for her because she still has the cuts and bruises and brokenness in her. But very slowly, her screams turned to a howl as she lay back down as a large white wolf.

No. – Please, Lila, please be alright.

Keith pulled the now too big shackles from Lila's injured and bloodied paws, when I noticed the stone bracelet on her front paw with her necklace chain woven in and around it. – I felt the tears start to burn in me, realising just how long my baby girl has been down here, hoping for her team to rescue her and saddened when no one came.

She growled as Keith cuffed a larger collar around her neck, and reattached the chains embedded in the wall before he scratched her behind the ear, saying, "Good girl."

"What did you do to her?" I seethed, struggling to stand.

"It's just a precaution..." He sniggered, turning back to me as he threw the empty syringe to the ground in front of me. "Recognise this?"

I looked down to see that the vial was labelled "Genirious." And yes, I recognise it, and it isn't good. – It means Lila is stuck as a wolf until someone gives her the antidote.

"Why?" I questioned.

He watched Lila as she lay on the ground, too weak to stand, and then scoffed, "To keep her from going home. It's not safe for a white wolf to roam the streets of Melbourne... She learnt that one the hard way."

In anger, I picked up the syringe and threw it against the cave wall behind Keith, originally aiming for his head, but my aim is off. "Why would you do this to her? What do you want with her?"

He walked around the circle of flames surrounding me, all cocky and smug, answering, "Katharine plans on using her to activate the tree stones."

"No," I fearfully gasped. "You can't, millions of people will die. Lila will never agree to that."

He then appeared in the circle of flames that trapped me, holding me up by the collar of my shirt and sneered, "You're right, she wouldn't. But you will... to save her... And very soon, I'll get the satisfaction of dragging the last Nature guardian in here to show him what's left of his little girlfriend... Tell me... How do you think Terrence will react when I tell him just how well I got to play with his girl? Do you think he'd still want to save her?"

My whole body burned with rage at the very thought of Keith touching my baby girl in such a disgusting and defiling way. – Knowing she wouldn't have wanted any of it.

"You're a monster," I spat, breaking out of his hold to punch him really hard in the face and push him back. I went to hit him again, but the flames grew higher around me the moment he stepped out of the circle.

Now angry and holding his face, Keith pulled a dagger from behind his back and appeared next to the wolf, clutching her neck and pressing the blade into the white fur of Lila's chest, so close to her heart. Yet she didn't move. She didn't even growl at him. It was like she had given up.

"No! Stop! Please!" I pleaded, sitting back down amongst the circling flames and conceding.

He let her go, throwing her back down to the ground, and then strutted out of the cave, boasting, "Huh... I thought so."

More hours passed as I sat and watched the white wolf just lying there, so sad in her whimpers. Her open wounds were weeping, and there are a lot of them, all over her, and the blood stained her white fur as it seeped from them.

When the sun's rays partially filled the cave and the sound of the morning birds chirped, Lila had regained some of her strength. She stood tall on all four then began to pull at the chain on the wall. Every time the chain pulled tight, she cringed and yelped to the pain. Yet still she kept pulling, almost choking herself in the process.

"Lila!" I begged. "Honey-Bee, stop. Please you're going to hurt yourself."

With so much mistrust in her eyes, Lila growled and barked at me. I don't know what it was I said, but she reacted badly. So I got up onto my knees and inched as close as I could to her, ignoring the heat from the flames to stare into her eyes as I spoke.

"That question you asked me before... it was a trick question. The first time I properly introduced myself to you, we were back at the Village islands... You were crying and I told you that my hugs were magical. And I will never forget that moment... because that was the first time in 26 years that my baby girl hugged me, making every moment of it magical... Now I know you're scared, but I promise you, it really is me."

With her dark eyes still sad and filled with pain, Lila continued to stare at me but stopped growling. So I took that as a good sign, watching as my baby girl very slowly rested her head back down on the ground, but still stared at me cautiously.

Taking a moment to breathe, I looked around at the cave walls and started to slowly regain my senses. I felt the trees growing above us and had an idea. "Lila... I'm going to do something, but it means you have to trust me."

She remained silent and watched as I gathered all the strength I had, and then punched my hand down into the rocky floor, ignoring the pain in my hand as I grabbed hold of a large tree root growing beneath us and asked for help.

One of the tree's roots then broke through the ground beneath Lila, wrapping around the collar. But she pulled away in a panic, growling as she lifted her head. Her eyes then stared along the chain that held her, at a metal box that surrounded the chain where it was embedded into the rock.

"You want me to crush that instead?" I questioned, a little hopeful that she trusted me.

She looked at me and then curled into a ball, bracing herself as if she were expecting to feel pain. I was a little worried, but I did as she asked, and she watched as my eyes glowed and the roots wrapped around the metal box, shattering it. When the box broke, an electrical current streamed down the chain and enveloped Lila, causing her to howl from the agony, and then went limp when the current disappeared.

"LILA!" I worriedly shouted.

I quickly pulled my hands from the ground when I saw Keith walking in, playing with a fireball with a smug grin as he boasted. "Well, I don't know about you. But I'm pretty eager to see what her lover boy has to say about saving her. Unfortunately, I'm supposed to ask you first... So tell me, Will, who are you going to save? The millions of pathetic humans... or your daughter."

Holding my breath, unsure what to do, I stared at Lila who was so still in her movements. But then I noticed her paw start to tense as Keith paced towards her, and a tiny bit of her claws peeked through. So I stood to my feet to answer with confidence.

"I choose my daughter."

At those words, Lila leapt to her feet with a fierce growl, charging towards Keith, pulling the chain from the wall. I couldn't take my eyes off her as she bit and clawed at Keith, hearing him scream from the pain. – But I'm positive his pain was nothing compared to what he did to Lila.

He eventually gained the upper hand, grasping one of Lila's injured paws to throw her against the wall and was about to throw a fireball at her. But through his distraction, I had broken free from my fiery prison, raising my hands to the ceiling and calling the trees to reach down and smack him into the cave walls, trapping him where he lay. – In his own bloody mess, aching from the pain.

At super-speed, I raced to Lila to slowly help her onto her paws, removing what was left of her chains while she angrily glared at Keith, growling at him. And I felt a wave of relief to see that she still had the energy and the fight in her.

"Come on, Honey... let's get you out of here."

Lila leaned on me as she limped out of the cave, finally getting to stand tall in the rays of the sun, and I saw a glimmer of happiness in her for a tiny second. But then she started sniffing the air around us and growled again, following a rocky trail through the trees.

I followed her, helping her to walk as we trekked for hours through the bushland. I could tell Lila was getting tired and asked where she was going, but she just growled at me more. So I kept walking as she led me to an old car that looked like Keith had been using for target practice. She then eagerly clawed at the trunk of the car.

Using extreme caution, I asked Lila to move away before I pulled it open to find Terrence, gagged and bound. His eyes squinted from the light of the sun, and he was frightened as he lifted his head. I helped him from the trunk, breaking his bindings when he quickly removed the gag and blurted, "William, we need to get back to the hotel! Lila's been compromised. Everyone's in danger."

"No, Terrence, she hasn't been compromised," I explained, turning him to face the large white wolf that he clearly missed. – Even though she's almost the same size as him. – Yet still I explained, "That's Lila... the woman at the hotel is Katherine."

Moving slowly, Lila limped forward, lifting her front paw up to show Terrence their matching bracelets and prove who she was.

"Lila," he cheered with excitement, wrapping his arms around her to hug her tightly. But it caused her to whimper, and I had to pull Terrence away.

"Careful... she's hurt pretty bad."

He turned back to me with fear in his eyes, almost afraid to ask the question as he saw the blood all over Lila's white fur, but he asked anyway. "How bad?"

I hesitated and peered across to Lila, but he asked again, and I sighed with so much sadness, "Worse than the island."

Tears filled Terrence's eyes, and he fell to his knees in front of Lila, gently holding his hand on the soft fur of her cheek as he wept, "I'm so sorry, Lila."

Seeing his sadness, a soft purr rumbled in Lila's throat as she limped closer to Terrence and rested her head on his shoulders, relaxing into his embrace as she comforted him.

Journal entry insert by Terrence Connors

I just can't believe it. And I can't stop crying, looking at Lila and the state of her beautiful white fur. — I can understand why she's angry, and why she's a wolf right now. And it infuriates me. I can see the pain in her eyes, and I'm honestly too afraid to touch her anywhere, worried I might hurt her more. But I happily welcomed her hug and held onto her while William thought of a plan. He disappeared for a while and returned upset, stating that he couldn't find the antidote and apologised to Lila, but he wouldn't tell me what he was talking about. He just went back to thinking of a different plan.

Eventually, William managed to get the old burnt-out car working, and we helped Lila to climb into the back of the car and asked her to stay low as we drove away. And in not caring about the car getting more damaged than it already is, William drove out of the bushland and onto the main road as fast as he could while I sat in the back next to Lila with her head resting on my lap, gently stroking the fur behind her ear to help her relax.

We drove for hours back towards the city, but when we got closer to the more built-up town areas, Lila fearfully growled at William. Neither of us could understand her, but we knew enough not to go any further. So William pulled into a petrol station to get food, petrol, and a map while Lila hid in the back seat with me.

We kind of did have an ulterior motive for hiding Lila because we didn't want her to stop William from doing what he needed to do. — No one was injured, and he used a baseball cap to hide his face. But none of us have any money at the moment, so he did what he had to, pick-pocketing the man from a few cars over then when the man walked into the centre to pay, William pretended that the man had dropped his wallet and returned it to him.

As he hurried back to the car, William placed bags of food in the back for Lila, and sat back in the front seat to look at the map and find the best area to go. — Other than the hotel that is.

Poor Lila teethed at the bags of chips on the seat, and I smiled at her cuteness as I opened them and started to feed her as William and I brainstormed ideas. After a few suggestions, Lila pulled her head up to look at the map, and I tried to pull her back down to keep her hidden, but she was determined. So instead I grabbed the map from William and placed it on the seat in front of her for her to see.

She took a second, staring at the map, and then slowly pulled her bloodstained paw up and held it on a small town not far from the city, called Greensborough.

"You want us to go there?" I asked, somewhat doubtful and reluctant. But when she pulled her head up and started licking my face, I think William understood that as a yes, and started the car up to head back onto the road with a fresh tank of stolen petrol and stolen food.

It was a bit of a long drive, but we drove out to Greensborough then waited until nightfall, letting Lila rest all snuggled up on my lap. Once it was dark enough and the locals had all returned to their homes, Lila left the car and slowly made her way down the streets. I think she knew travelling in that car would be too dangerous, so we followed her and let her lean on us as she limped.

She led us to a long street of suburban houses, all of them dark and quiet because of the hour.

"Where are we going?" I asked, scratching Lila behind her ear.

She stopped walking, staring across to both of us before tapping her paw on the ground. And William watched the tapping and sounded out. "S-T-A-Y"

"Stay?" I asked back confused.

Lila huffed, nodding her head then slowly limped into somebody's backyard, and a few seconds later walked back out with a torn red shirt in her mouth.

And Yeah — that is weird.

She handed it to me before she continued walking, leading us to the end of the street to one of the last houses, and then stared at the front door of the house. We stood next to her, staring at the house as well when I broke the silence. "Okay, another dumb question, what's with the shirt?"

Again, Lila tapped her paw in front of William. "K-N-O-C-K"

With great confusion yet still wanting to trust Lila, I silently groaned, asking Lila to stay behind William as I went up to knock on the door.

The woman who opened the door greeted me suspiciously but looked familiar, and I tried to figure it out as I spoke. "Err... Hi... my name is Terrence, and this is William. We're friends of Lila's and we're hoping you can help us."

Her eyes darted between William and mine then took one look at the red shirt in my hand and slammed the door. I looked back at Lila still standing behind William, wanting to know what to do next when the door jarred open again with Matt's face appearing through the crack. But he also had a gun in his hand, pointing it at me.

"What do you want?" he questioned.

I raised my hands, slowly showing him the red shirt and explained "There's a situation back at the hotel..."

"I know," he sniped. "How did you know about the red shirt?"

Still with my hands up, William and I stepped aside to reveal wolf-Lila, standing behind us, looking ever so patient and calm. — Even in her dishevelled, bloodied state.

"She gave it to me... and I assume you know what it means."

"Lila," Matt joyfully gasped, racing out to hug her. But we had to stop him, indicating to the many open wounds and injuries she had on her.

He nodded, briefly glancing at her 'not-white' fur then told us to come inside quickly, and locked the doors as he ushered us into the kitchen. He gave some lame excuse to his sister — Jane, and she accepted it, handing Matt the first aid kit and a stack of old towels before she went off to bed. We then got Matt to sit and comfort Lila as she lay on the dining room floor while William and I cleaned and bound her wounds closed with tape and bandages.

It's not the best. — But we can't stitch them while she's in her wolf form. — We'd risk skin distortion that may cause her more pain when she morphs back to her normal form.

After bandaging what we could, William sounded a little shaky in his voice as he leaned down to talk to Lila, gently patting her on the head. "Lila... I'm going to need to reset your arm now... And it's going to hurt. But you need to promise me to stay still... can you do that?"

She very gently nodded her head, and then through William's tears, he asked me to hold her down as he pushed her dislocated arm—paw back into place. Her little whimpers were so hard for all of us to hear, but she stuck to her promise and didn't move.

Once Lila was all cleaned up, she moved closer to me to rest her head on my lap again, and I was more than happy to comfort her as we all filled in the missing pieces of what each of us knew. — All except Lila.

William told us about the Genirious serum. Of how to keep her from going home, Lila was forced to morph into her wolf form, and that the transformation was excruciating for her. — Lila suddenly curled up a little closer to me, and snuggled in more when I asked William how many times she had to go through that.

"I'm not sure," he answered. "But when Lila saw Keith holding the syringe, she knew what it was. And she knew it was going to be painful."

My hand tightened into a ball at the thought of my brother causing Lila pain. "Okay... but she was human when you found her. So this is reversible, right?"

"Not without the antidote." He shook his head and sighed. "And I searched that cave and the surrounding area, and couldn't find anything... Chances are Katherine keeps it hidden somewhere. But those woods are massive, I could have spent hours searching and barely made a dent."

While sitting back in a bit of a sulk, William went on to explain what Katherine wants from Lila, which now explains why she wants the stones. Then when all was said and done, Matt set up some beds in the back loungeroom for us, next to the Christmas tree before he went off to bed himself.

Journal entry insert by Tyme Knight

For some reason I just can't get to sleep tonight. I tried, but I keep getting this horrible feeling that something is wrong. My dad missed my birthday last night and hasn't been seen all day. Add to that, Lila got some weird phone call this morning, disappearing for a couple of hours and didn't tell anyone where she went.

Alex and her have also become all lovey-dovey with each other, which has apparently caused Terrence to take off due to a broken heart. – Or at least that's what Lila said. – But she said it without showing any remorse for hurting Terrence's feelings.

Then this afternoon, we were all called to a mission brief that Lila agreed to help with for our government friends. But she didn't consult any of us first. – Nothing about Lila felt right. She just isn't acting like herself.

I grabbed my phone and hesitated in phoning Lila to talk about it but lost my temper, and from my frustration, I threw the phone at the wall way too hard as it tore a hole in the wall, landing in the middle of my neighbour's apartment bedroom. – And I'm really glad my neighbour is Katie. – And Shane when he sleeps over.

They looked through the hole in the wall and waved at me, and then a few seconds later, knocked at my door to return my shattered phone. I invited them in, and Shane sat down on the couch with Katie snuggling up next to him.

"Rough night?" Shane grinned sarcastically.

"Kind of," I replied. "Look, have you guys noticed anything... off lately."

They both looked at each other and pulled a face, shaking their heads to say no.

"I wouldn't stress, mate." Shane yawned. "I think you're just worried about your dad. He's a smart guy. He can take care of himself."

I shook my head with a long sigh. "Nah, he's probably just taking some time... Del must have struck a sour chord about Lila yesterday."

With a scowl, Katie sat up to gripe, "And what, that gives him an excuse to miss your birthday?"

"Yes," I answered, unknowingly scowling back at her.

She quickly dropped the subject, instead changing it to ask about me and Adela and our non-progressing relationship. I told Katie I didn't want to talk about it, but obviously Adela has talked to Katie about it because she knew way too much. Both of them did.

"Look, I get it," Katie insisted. "And I completely agree with you. But it doesn't mean you can't date each other. Take my mom and dad for example. Mom's a Fire guardian and my step-dad's an Animal guardian, and they managed to make it work without making any cute little hybrids. The only thing I had to do was call them both my step-parents out in public, that way people didn't think I was a hybrid."

"Wait... wouldn't that get confusing," I asked, trying to figure it out in my mind.

"Super confusing." She deviously grinned. "It's why I love doing it."

Shane stretched out on the couch and chimed in, "What's the worst that could happen anyway? So what if you make another hybrid baby... Lila's one and she turned out awesome. Hell, she's the strongest guardian I've met. I'd be proud to have a daughter like her... Worried like hell every day... but still be proud."

The conversation got derailed there when Katie got all mushy at the fact that Shane wants babies. – Oh gosh. – I took that as my cue to go back into my room and block my ears.

Journal entry insert by Terrence Connors

The sun started to rise on a new day, and neither Lila or I have slept. I was trying to sleep, but every now and then, I would glance across to see Lila limping back and forth across the floor of the kitchen with the Christmas tree lights illuminating her fur as she paced.

And yeah — it's very sad, that yet again it's nearly Christmas and we're again in this kind of mess. — I wish so badly that I could talk to her, to know what she's thinking or just hear her sweet voice again.

Eventually, William woke and peered over to see Lila still pacing, and I sadly and very quietly whispered to him, "She's been doing that all night."

"Has she slept at all?" he whispered back.

I shook my head, and he slouched back and disappointingly sighed. "I'm not surprised after what Keith did to her. It gives me nightmares just thinking about it."

My brows furrowed and I dreaded the answer as I looked at him and asked, "What did he do?"

His throat grumbled, watching Lila pace and replied, "All the wrong things... in all the wrong ways."

He looked back at me as I realised what he was talking about, and it felt like my heart's being ripped from my chest as I struggle to really come to terms with it. I mean I know my brother hates Lila and me, but how could he do <u>that</u>... to my best friend.

Very slowly, William inched towards Lila and kneeled to her level when she defensively growled at him with so much mistrust in her.

He stayed still and spoke quietly, "Lila, I'm going to go for a walk to get some breakfast. Would you like to come with me?"

She growled at him again then walked towards me and pawed at my hand. Then William stood up and smirked. "Looks like she wants you to come with us."

In hearing that, I quickly got to my feet to follow them.

We walked down to one of the local parks across the street from a small shopping strip with a bakery, news agency, and hairdressers. William borrowed — without permission — some money from Matt's wallet — fully intending to pay him back at a later date, and went into the bakery while Lila stayed with me, sitting under one of the park trees.

She sat very close to me, mistrustful of anyone who passed us or stared at how large she is and how not quite right she looks with all the bandages and tape on her. As she continued her watchful guard, I eyed the bracelet I gave her still tightly wrapped around her wrist or what is supposed to be her wrist, and I got a bit teary-eyed. I thought the reason why the other Lila wasn't wearing the bracelet was because she was disappointed in me. Because I was weak without my powers. — I should have known, Lila would never do that or think that of me. — I've failed her again.

I spotted her white-oak tree necklace, firmly tucked underneath the vines to keep it safe, but I noticed the ruby stone glowing in the centre of it. It's never done that before, and my curiosity piqued, trying to take it out to look at it. But Lila growled at me, seeming very protective of it, so I let it be. She then whimpered and nuzzled at the paw pendant sitting next to the tree pendant, and sulked on my knee.

"I know." I sighed, scratching her ear. "I'm worried about him too."

As William walked back towards us, Lila perked up and got really excited at what he was holding. He handed me two tomato and cheese toasties and a bottle of water, and then sat down next to us with a similar meal.

Lila eagerly nuzzled at her toastie bag, and I laughed at her impatience. "Hang on... It's too hot... You'll burn your tongue."

I broke both of our toasties into bite-sized pieces, and blew on each piece to cool them down before I fed some of the pieces to her. And I laughed more when she licked my cheek to say thank you.

My laugh fell silent though as I glanced over to see William lost in thought, watching a little girl playing on the playground with her mum and dad. His face turned sad as he let out a sigh and he returned to eating his breakfast.

"Can I ask a question?" I said, trying to keep my fingers from being bitten by a wolf's teeth. He looked back at me, nodding and kind of chuckled at the way Lila was eating from my hand when I asked, "How did Lila end up in the General's care... I mean, I remember you staring at her baby picture when you were my Elder. You clearly missed her?"

Suddenly, I felt Lila's sharp teeth as she bit my finger.

"Ow... Lila," I grumbled, staring at her eyes.

"I don't think she likes that question?" Will chuckled, shaking his head. But he answered it anyway. "When Lila was born, I was the happiest man in the world... I knew Lila was going to be a hybrid at the time. I just didn't know the extent... Katherine led me to believe that she was just an Animal guardian... Either way, I knew Lila was going to be in danger, and we had made plans to leave and go into hiding. But they came too soon. Following Hanna and Richard to our little hideout... I handed Lila to Hanna and begged her to run, wanting to go help Katherine defend our daughter, but I was too late to realise I had been tricked."

He stopped his explanation when he noticed Lila starting to limp away, so Will got up, helping me to stand before we followed Lila back down the street in silence.

When we got back to the house, Matt raced out to greet us, looking a little frazzled, "Um... I need you to hide in the garage."

He opened the garage door for us, and I confusedly looked at Lila then asked, "Why, is something wrong?"

Matt glanced back at us as we followed him in, and he created a space for us to sit, explaining, "No. It's just Jane's been organising a family get-together for weeks now, and all of my family will be arriving shortly."

He leaned his head down a little, looking so incredibly apologetic as he stared into Lila's eyes. Then Lila rested her furry-white head on Matt's shoulder, causing me to smile.

"I think she understands," I noted. "I'm sure it'd be hard explaining to your family why your ex-wife's a giant wolf."

"It's not that..." He stood up and cleared his throat. "Jane chose this day because it marked a very significant change in our family... This time last year all my family attended Lila's funeral."

Ah. — Yeah, I forgot about that.

I stood back and felt incredibly guilty, so when Matt turned to walk inside, I stopped him. "Matt, I never have gotten around to apologising to you for what I put you and the children through. If there's anything I can do or say..."

"There's nothing to be done," Matt huffed. "The damage is done, and it can't be changed."

I nodded, peering back at Lila who went to sit quietly in the corner. And again, I felt incredibly guilty, sitting down on a paint bucket next to her. But in seeing the sorrow on my face, Matt stood in front of me.

"Terrence, just remember... The actions from our past define who we are today, but our actions today define who we are in the future."

I smiled back up at Matt, agreeing with him when Will stood next to him and commented, "Those are really wise words."

"They're not my words," Matt replied, glancing down at Lila before he walked out of the garage.

"They're Lila's," I explained as the garage door closed.

She moved closer to me as I got comfortable next to her then she rested her head on my chest, wanting another hug from me.

CHAPTER 37

Evil Is as Evil Does

Journal entry by Alex Woods

Lila and I are finally in a good place in our relationship, and I'm over the moon with joy. Today we're heading off to our first mission with Phil Green, the guy from the government department that doesn't really exist. According to Phil's intel, John Lin – one of the CEOs of The Board, is doing his annual review around all the oil stations he owns. And he's set to visit one not far from the Western Australia coast for the next three days.

The problem is while we were on the flight over to Perth, my mind kept getting distracted by the unusual things I saw Lila doing. – This morning, she had completely forgotten that Matt was headed to his sisters for a family brunch to mark the day of her funeral last year and to celebrate a happier Christmas gathering. And she seemed really upset at that.

I asked her if she was okay and she just smiled and kissed me, and when she did, it felt like all my problems just disappeared in that kiss. But when we met up with Billy in the elevator, she made my blood boil, asking him if he also loved her like I did. Yet she spoke about herself in the third person, and then kissed him in front of me.

I felt a wave of jealousy course through me, but at the same time felt powerless to do anything. All I wanted to do in that moment was make Lila happy, so if she wants to kiss and love other guys, I need to be okay with that.

The problem I had after that, was she then pulled Billy off the mission, and asked him to go and look for Terrence and William because she was getting worried about them. – And since when has she been worried about William?

The weirdest part was when we got into the basement carpark where she met up with Keith of all people. – He's apparently now seen the errors of his ways and has asked Lila for her forgiveness. And because Lila is such an amazingly loving person, she welcomed him with open arms.

Yep. – That was just weird. – But if Lila wanted it, I just went with it.

We're getting closer to the private landing strip in Perth now. So Phil gathered what we had of our team around the front seats of the cabin where his team was sitting, to give us a final briefing with Lila, Adela, Katie, Tyme, and myself on main point.

"Remember, we need this to be a quiet operation... grab Mr Lin and get out. Does anyone have any questions?"

Adela shook her head, confused, looking at the mission intel we had, and enquired, "There are at least 16 guardians being held on the rig. We should help them."

"We can't..." Phil shook his head. "If The Board finds out the base has been compromised, they'll start looking for Mr Lin, and when they find out we are responsible, they'll enact the restart program on all of his assets."

"What's the restart program?" Tyme questioned.

That answer I knew, so I answered, "All of his passwords and files are destroyed, and the property or assets are given to the next in line."

Phil chimed in, adding, "And the last thing we want is a power struggle amongst the remaining Board members, at least not yet."

Adela didn't seem overly thrilled about the idea of not at least attempting a rescue, and pleaded, "Lila, you can't possibly agree with this."

Lila stayed quiet for a moment while staring at some of the files. "Agent Green is right, there's too much at stake here."

Again. – That is not the answer I was expecting from her.

For some reason, I started getting a really bad headache, so I walked to the back of the plane cabin to grab some water as the rest of our team stormed back to their seats in a huff. And it got me thinking. – This is the first mission Lila has ever taken us on, where 1- she didn't want to rescue anyone, and 2 - her team wasn't in complete agreement with the plan. And that's just not what Lila would do.

Hmm? – Something's wrong.

Journal entry insert by Terrence Connors

Matt's family gathering had started, and we could hear the ruckus of children playing and squealing in the backyard. Every time we heard Ruby squealing with glee, Lila's long wolfy ears would perk up, and she'd whimper just that little bit. I tried to comfort her, knowing just how much she missed and worried about them, and after two and a half weeks of not seeing them, she was probably aching inside.

I did find it slightly ironic though, that Will has now started pacing back and forth across the garage floor in front of Matt's car. All the while Lila had her head resting on my leg, slowly letting her fatigue get to her as I gave her long calming strokes along her neck.

"Now I know where Lila gets it from," I chuckled while looking at Will.

The large white wolf grumbled in her throat but still remained placid on my leg as I defended myself. "Well, it's true... You were doing the exact same thing this morning."

Her growling stopped, and she curiously perked her head up to look at Will.

"Sorry," he replied. "I was just thinking about what Matt said... Well, what Lila's saying was... to Matt."

He stopped pacing, seeming a bit confused at that statement, and then cleared his throat, kneeling down next to Lila and trying to find the courage to talk.

"Okay, here goes... Lila, I'm so sorry about abandoning you and leaving you to grow up with Richard as a father. There really is no excuse. I knew who he was when I left you with him... But he was just another grunt like me at the time. I didn't think he was going to use you to gain a foothold on The Board... And when I realised what he had done, there was no way you would have ever been safe anywhere else... I came to Victoria to take you away from Richard, but I didn't get far with you before he caught up with us and offered me an alternative that I should have never agreed to... I should have just kept running with you... But I wanted more to your life than just hiding in the shadows with me, and Richard offered that for you... He offered a school, protection, a chance to grow up and make friends. I wanted all of that for you. And I'm sorry, because I realised too late the cost that you had to pay each and every day to have that life."

His eyes teared up while Lila stared at him, listening to him sniffle. "I am so sorry, Lila... there's no excuse for what I did... But I really wish that you would let me try to be the dad that I should have been to you so many years ago... Please. I truly am sorry."

He broke into tears in front of Lila, and she sat up, looking at his saddened face, and then tapped her paw in front of him. He watched intently and sounded out, "H–N–E–B..."

A relieved smile appeared on Will's face, gazing into Lila's dark eyes. "Yeah... I used to call you Honey-Bee. My little Honey-Bee, to be precise... But you're not little anymore."

Still staring at him, Lila got up to slowly limp towards Will, and he kept his hands out to make sure she wouldn't fall. Then she rested her head on his shoulder and snuggled in for a cuddle, causing him to sob, holding her in his arms.

"If only I could hear you talk..." he cried. "I wish I knew how to fix this."

Slightly excited, Lila pulled away and wandered around the garage, looking at all the shelves then found an old school textbook and dropped it in front of us.

"A notebook?" Will puzzled, looking through the pages and staring at Lila for another clue.

But I understood her and clarified, "No, she wants her notebook. The other Lila... I mean, Katherine was looking for it back at the hotel." Lila turned to me as I got up onto my knees and asked, "Lila, is that what you want, do you want your journal?"

She nodded and my smile matched her excitement as I stared at her. "I know where it is... and it's not in the hotel."

With that news, Lila grew more excited, happily yet quietly barking at me, and then leapt up onto me and licked my face. But her excitement quickly stopped as she quietly growled at the garage door. Then in seconds, Will stood defensively next to her, whispering, "We've got company."

Journal entry insert by Matt Winters

The family gathering is going really well. We had finished our Christmas lunch and all the children have opened their presents from the aunts and uncles and are now off playing with their toys, running in and out of the back door.

I heard a knock at the front door and listened as the tone in Jane's voice changed. "Can I help you?"

I tensed up when I heard Billy's voice on the other side, and I was really hoping he knew the code. But he didn't. He just claimed that he was a friend and demanded to speak to me.

Jane stuck to the plan and told him I wasn't here. But then Danny raced past the door, chasing one of my cousin's little ones, and I just knew it was going to get worse from here.

Billy pushed through the door, looking for me, and I rushed over to ask him what he wanted, highlighting that he was interrupting a – human gathering, when he replied, "We have a situation back at the hotel. William and Terrence have gone missing... And Lila sent us to check up on you, and make sure you were safe."

"Us?" I questioned, slowly backing away as I followed Billy's gaze to see Terrence's brother Keith walk in the back door, holding my little Ruby's hand.

Um. – Shit.

Now filled with worry and fear, I held onto Jane's hand and screamed Lila's name as I ran with Jane to the back of the house where most of my family were sitting and chatting. Then as I ran toward the back lounge, I watched Lila as a giant wolf break through the back of the garage door and race into the house.

William soon appeared next to me and had snatched Ruby during the commotion of my family running at the sight of a giant wolf, and he held her close to him, making sure she didn't see her mummy going all angry wolf-momma on Keith. – But wow – her growls were loud and scary.

William helped me to usher my family into the safety of the back room and stood guarding us, but I couldn't find Danny. I hurriedly raced out to look for him and found him hiding in the kitchen in my nephew's arms, and spoke with great urgency. "Jake, go find your mum and don't let Danny go."

He inched past me and raced to the back room with Danny, and I was just about to follow him when Billy grabbed me around the neck, pinning me up against a wall. I tried to break free, kicking and punching him when Terrence ran in with one of Jake's old baseball bats and swung it hard onto Billy's back. But he was completely un-phased. That is until William, appeared next to Billy, tackling him to the ground, inevitably dropping me to the floor.

Terrence tried to help me and started hobbling me to the back room, but stopped when he saw Lila get thrown into a wall by his brother. Then amongst all of the commotion, Jane stormed out of the back room with my gun, aimlessly shooting at everything.

Instantly, William appeared behind us, pushing Terrence and me to the ground to protect us. Then when the gun had emptied, Keith and Billy fell to the ground as did a lot of art, glass and plaster.

Panic filled Terrence as he pulled away from William to find Lila, who was standing next to his brother, now lying on the floor with blood gushing from his stomach. Billy was also unconscious, not far from Lila with a black eye and a bullet in his shoulder.

Terrence rushed to aid his brother, trying to stop the bleeding, and he was crying as he begged, "We need to help him... Lila, what do I do?"

I'm sorry, what? — He seriously wants to help him?

Lila looked back at Will and barked before glancing at the back door. Then he disappeared and reappeared in the kitchen with a whole bunch of garden plants and a mixing bowl.

But now furious, Jane stood over me and yelled, "Matt, what the hell is going on?! Where's Lila?!"

The problem was she was also waving the gun around, pointing it back towards the rest of our family without a care. So in a hurry, I stood up, taking the gun from her as I replied. "It's classified."

"Like hell it's classified!" she shrieked. "These are Lila's friends, and that's Lila's dog, and they just made a mess of my house. Now, where the hell is Lila?!"

Her son Jake, quickly ran out of the backroom, leaving Danny and Ruby with my cousins and whispered, pointing to the wolf. "Mum... that is Lila."

How the hell does he know that?!?

The wolf barked at Jake and playfully shook her head as he rushed over to say hello, giving her a gentle pat with absolutely no fear. In shock, I glared at him, asking how he knew that fact. But he didn't answer because he was too busy watching William finish the blue-rose thing that Lila's team uses.

When William finished moving around at super-speed, he handed Terrence a glass of blue water then kneeled down next to Keith, using the narrow end of two butter knives to dig around in his stomach wound to pull out the bullet. He looked up to see Keith writhing in pain, and showed no ounce of care for him.

"Just be glad my baby girl has a big heart..." he bitterly seethed. "I would rather let you die for what you did to her."

Keith tried not to scream while trying to cope with the pain, waiting for William to pull the bullet out. Then when he had, William nodded to Terrence, signalling him to pour the blue water directly into the wound.

Knowing this was just going to go from bad to horribly worse, I glanced back to see Jane in shock, watching the bullet wound start to heal. — And there is no way I'm going to be able to explain any of this. — I'm still trying to figure out how Jake knows.

In a state of disbelief, Jane watched as William again disappeared and reappeared with the first aid kit in his hand, working at a ridiculous speed to clean and patch the wounds on both Keith and Billy.

"How... how did he do that?" Jane asked. "And don't tell me it's classified!"

Um...? — I still don't know how to answer that one.

While I was busy trying to think of an answer, William ran into the kitchen and came back out, handing Jane a glass of pink water. "Here drink this... it will calm your nerves."

She glared at him with suspicion, so he added, "It's just herbs... so drink up."

Clearly my sister's not afraid of herbs like she should be, and she took a large gulp of the water then fell asleep in William's arms. I stared at him and freaked out while asking what the hell he did to her.

"I gave her a sleeping tonic," he answered before laying her down on the floor. "It also has a mild hallucinogen, which makes everything that's happened in the past 24 hours seem like a dream."

"Oh, can you do that on him?" I asked, pointing back at Jake.

"Way ahead of you," he hurriedly answered while moving my sister to a more comfortable location, highlighting, "The pot on the stove has enough for your whole family."

"What?" Jake huffed still standing next to Lila without a care. "I get the rest of the family, but why me? I've known about Lila's secret for ages and haven't told anyone."

"I'm sorry, what? How?" I grumbled, getting all overprotective uncle on his butt.

"Um... I don't mean to be pushy," William interrupted, grabbing my arm. "But one of your family members just called the police... So we need to get these guys out of here."

He looked back at the state of the house, when Jake eagerly suggested, "They can come with me. I've got the key to the baseball club room at my school, you can hide out there."

"No!" I growled. "It's way too dangerous for you."

In response, Jake glared back at me with all his teenage attitude and sneered, "Have you got a better idea, Uncle Matt? Coz we're all ears."

I grew irked at not coming up with any other plan, and then handed Jake the keys to my car and warned, "But if you get hurt, your mother is going to kill me and then you... So if there is any fighting, any at all, you damn well stay behind that wolf, got it?"

He nodded with an eager smile, and then rushed to help me and the others drag Billy and Keith out into the garage, where we loaded them into the backseats of my Hyundai Imax.

I quickly opened the boot to let Lila sit in the back, but she suddenly heard the sound of the sirens as the garage door rolled open. She instantly knew what had to be done even though she was all bandaged up, and she leapt out to stand on the road, briefly glancing back at us before she ran towards the sirens, leading them away from the house.

William was about to chase after her until I stopped him. "William... Trust her, she knows what she's doing?"

I pulled him back to get him into the car, and Terrence quickly drove out of the driveway, speeding off in the other direction. All the while I stood there in the driveway, finally letting go of the breath I had been holding in for the last 20 minutes, fully aware that my sister is going to kill me when she wakes up.

Journal entry insert by Terrence Connors

Okay. — Right now we're in a crapload of trouble. We've just followed and helped Matt's teenage nephew break into a school sports locker room after running from the police. To make things worse, Lila still hasn't been seen, and its nearly nightfall which means she's been gone for more than 3 hours. But Jake said that Lila knew where the school is, so all we have to do is wait for her and hope that she's alright.

Billy and Keith are still unconscious, and Will tied them up in one of the shower stalls by using the plant vines from my bracelet. So now, Will's pacing the floor in front of them, trying really hard not to freak out. And Jake and I are standing guard not far from him, holding baseball bats as weapons.

I will add. — This is not what I expected to be doing the week before Christmas.

"You look nervous," Jake uttered with his eyes darting to me every now and then.

"A little," I replied, holding my baseball bat tighter.

It caused Jake to become nervous. "You... you can take 'em, right? If they wake up."

I hesitated and didn't want to answer him with the bad news, but he took my silence as a no and freaked out. "Aren't you like Lila?"

"Kind of," I whispered. "A few weeks ago I was a lab rat for one of my friend's science experiments, and I'm still trying to get my powers back."

"Well, what about him?" Jake questioned, pointing over at William still pacing around, lost in his own thoughts.

"Oh, he's a guardian," I replied. "But he's not like Lila... He's a... well, he's a scientist."

Fear and regret swept across Jake's face as he clarified, "So let me get this straight... if those guys wake up, the only thing stopping them from leaving... are two humans and a scientist."

As he said that, Keith stood to his feet, burning through his vines and strangling William until he fell to the floor. Then he deviously grinned at me. "Correction... the only thing stopping me from leaving is one human, and one weak-arse little brother."

Ah no. — I'm two months older than him.

But that's not the point. — So I stood in front of Jake to protect him and held my baseball bat high. And Keith laughed, slowly strutting towards us. "Huh-uh... You know I had this whole thing planned out of how I was going to kill you... slowly and painfully... watching your heart break into pieces as I shared with you all the very fun and exotic things I did with Lila... Of how she begged for it, just to save her own life."

"Oh god," I shuddered in repulsion. "You used the Salacio drug on her... Didn't you."

His horrifying grin was his answer, and the rage burned inside me. — He'd used the same sex drug that Lila was poisoned with at the beginning of the year. — Damn it, he makes me angry.

He stared across the room at me, yet kept his distance, goading me to respond. But I stayed in front of Jake, not wanting to play his game. Then he breathlessly whispered, "Hmm... she was such a wonderful plaything too."

Yeah. — That did it for me.

In anger, I charged at him and swung the bat. He caught the bat mid-swing and grabbed me around the throat, lifting my feet off the ground. When suddenly, we were both jolted sideways and I was thrown into the side of a locker, hearing a wolf growling and Jake shouting, "Alright, Lila!!"

Pretty soon Keith was on the floor next to me, unconscious and looking like a wolf had gone tropo on him again with bite marks and scratches all over him. I looked over at Lila to see Keith's blood dripping from her mouth, growling as she stood guard in front of Jake.

"Lila..." Jake ran to hug her and praised, "You have the most incredible timing."

I raced over to wake Will and check if he was okay, and he woke gasping for air, looking around.

"Um, guys!" Jake fearfully shouted. "She's bleeding! Lila's bleeding a lot!"

Will instantly appeared next to Lila, realising that all of her bandages had come loose or fallen off, and then found a bullet lodged in the back of her leg. "The police must have shot her to slow her down."

Jake raced away and brought back the gym's first aid kit and stuttered, "You... you can fix her... right? Like you did with those guys."

I took the first aid kit from him, grabbing what I needed to stop the bleeding as Will answered in a slight panic. "No... I don't know a healing recipe that can heal animals... I'm also not a doctor, and that bullet is lodged in pretty deep."

"So make her human again," Jake ordered.

"I can't. I don't know how," Will grunted again, holding back his tears.

He was completely panicking and so was Jake.

Lila huffed at both of them, trying to get them to calm down. And I saw her eyes roll at Will, causing me to let out a laugh, then I stood up realising what we needed. "We need her journal... I hid it at the Shrine of Remembrance. I need to go and get it."

Now broken from his panic-attack, Jake stood up, grabbing the keys, and shouted, "Well, what are we waiting for? Come on!"

Before I took another step, I looked back at Will and paused, watching Lila. She knew what I had to do, but she also knew I didn't want to leave her. Then clearly sensing the fear in me, she limped to stand next to Will and barked. And I knew what that meant, so I smiled before following Jake out to the van.

Journal entry continued by Alex Woods

Something definitely isn't right with Lila. We're now on a boat in the middle of the ocean, about to climb up onto an oil rig, and Lila isn't showing any signs of fear or hesitation. It's as if the water doesn't even affect her anymore.

Lila was the first to climb up onto the platform with Adela, Tyme, and Katie following. We couldn't stay in the time rift for this mission because I'm still just a human, but Lila had given Adela, Katie, and Tyme a different set of orders. They were on data recovery instead, and I was Lila's backup.

Tyme pulled Adela and Katie into the time rift as I followed Lila. But as we walked down a narrow hallway, I got this horrible feeling, getting images of Lila in her wolf form. She looked really angry and scared. I held my head in confusion, and Lila stopped and walked back to me.

"What's wrong?" she asked.

I cleared my throat, trying to shake the images, and answered, "I'm just a little confused. You are aware we're in the middle of the ocean, right?"

She looked at me and nodded, wanting more than that, so I added, "Aren't you afraid of the ocean?"

I saw the disappointment in her as she stepped back and took a long breath. "Damn... I was really starting to like you."

At full-speed, she pulled a gun hidden behind her back and shot me in the stomach. And I grunted, holding the bullet wound and staring at her in shock.

"Lila?" I croaked before collapsing into her arms.

She dragged me out of the corridor to hide me in one of the supply closets, and then shushed me. "Try not to move. It'll only make you die faster... Don't worry. I'll come back for you when I'm done... I still need you for my plan to work."

She stroked my cheek and grinned before closing the door on me, and I heard her footsteps disappear down the corridor. But I need to know what's going on with her, so I pushed out of the closet and followed her, leaning against the wall as I stepped.

My curiosity turned to shock when from a side hallway I watched Lila morph into Katherine, and I took a sharp intake of air, realising the horrible truth. If that isn't Lila – then Lila is still missing and has probably been missing this whole time.

Oh Crap. – Lila.

I tried to run and find the others, but I think I had lost too much blood because the next thing I knew, I was being dragged back towards the boat by Lila – or what looks like Lila. John Lin was in handcuffs being led by her as well, and I heard the sound of Adela shriek my name as I was lowered down onto the boat.

I was barely awake and too weak to speak, desperately wanting to warn them when the boat sped off away from the oil rig.

Journal entry insert by William Knight

Lila stood guard, watching Billy and Keith sleep, now tied up in even tighter vines, all while I try to gently clean off the excess blood from Lila's fur so she doesn't look as scary. She squirmed and wriggled, pulling her head away from me as I tried to wipe the blood off her face, and I chuckled a bit, feeling like I was washing a cranky toddler.

This is technically the first time I've bathed my daughter. - So I will most definitely remember this. - Even though she's a wolf at the moment.

"Keep still, Honey," I pleaded.

Hearing my plea, Lila moved her head toward me then tapped her foot on my knee, and I smiled at the message she gave me. I think she likes the fact that I know Morse-code, so I asked again with a grin. "Keep still... Honey-Bee."

She very happily did as I asked, staying still while I finished cleaning her. Then she laid on the ground next to me, resting while still watching our prisoners. But Lila's head perked up and her throat grumbled when she noticed Billy starting to stir.

I jumped to my feet, grabbing a baseball bat and inched towards him as he opened his eyes. He looked confused, staring at his bindings, and then grunted at the pain he felt from his freshly healed bullet wound, mumbling and asking where he was.

While standing ready to hit him, I sternly warned, "If you move, I will hurt you."

"What? Why? What's going on? Is that Lila?" he worriedly asked, looking back at Lila as she slowly limped towards him, growling.

She stood close to him and stared at him for a moment. Then her growling stopped and she licked his face, snuggling into his chest as she whimpered.

Right. – Well, it looks like he passed her test.

I raised my hands to loosen the vines around Billy, so he could hug her back. And it looked like a beautifully tender moment for them until he realised underneath all Lila's fur, she was covered in large open cuts and bruises. She whimpered louder when Billy's hands touched certain tender spots. – The large one along her back and another where the bullet was lodged.

"Who did this to you?" he asked while staring into her big black eyes.

To answer, Lila slowly lifted her head from Billy's chest then growled, looking over at Keith still unconscious and tied up. And a smile appeared on Billy as he looked at the extent and the type of Keith's injuries before giving Lila another hug.

"That's my feisty girl." He grinned.

"You don't know the half of it," I grumbled, putting the baseball bat down. "He deserves a lot worse than that... Lila was being soft on him, again."

Lila looked up at me with sad eyes, so I smiled at her. "But I'm still very proud of you for holding back... You've got a good heart."

She then relaxed back into Billy's embrace as I started questioning him. "What's the last thing you remember and when?"

"Um this morning, I guess... I met up with Lila to go on our first mission."

"That wasn't Lila," I interjected. "That was Katherine... Lila's been held prisoner since she went missing over two weeks ago."

"Two weeks ago?!" he repeated in shock, fearfully holding Lila tighter in his arms.

I nodded, understanding his shock then questioned further. "What's the last thing you remember the other Lila doing to you?"

Billy cringed as he thought then pulled a really sour and disgusted face.

"She kissed me?" He shuddered, looking like he was going to hurl.

Even Lila huffed in disgust. But it caused me to pace again, mumbling my thoughts aloud. "Huh... it must be a close reaction chemical that requires regular interaction with the subject... It probably explains why you've come to your senses now."

My thought was distracted when I heard Lila cry in Billy's arms and howled at the pain she felt. And just to make things really difficult for us, Billy spotted flashing red and blue lights shining through the window of the locker room.

"Stay here," I sighed, looking back at Lila and Billy.

But Lila growled while sniffing the air, and then hobbled to stand in front of me and huffed. I stared at her, and shook my head very insistently. "Honey-Bee, you're injured. I don't want you doing this."

Again, she huffed at me, staring back at Keith and used her head to nudge me back towards him, holding the baseball bat in her mouth to give to me. I grumbled with annoyance but trusted she knew what she was doing and let her limp out of the locker room.

But I am not a happy dad right now. – And I know she doesn't see me as her dad, but I still damn well worry about her.

I waited a few seconds, and then handed the bat to Billy and told him to guard the idiot while I climbed up onto one of the chairs to peer out the tall window and take a look.

There are four police cars outside, surrounding the large white wolf. And all the officers have their guns drawn, aimed at Lila, most likely scared of the state of her. – I mean she is quite large for a wolf, roughly the same height as most of them, if not bigger.

She's also still bleeding with blood staining her shiny white fur, which probably isn't helping the situation.

One of the officers slowly approached her, and she stood very still, staring at the officer pointing the gun at her. She didn't move and was very calm. But then I saw another man race out from behind the cars.

"Hold your fire!" he shouted as he moved the other officer's weapon out of Lila's line.

I took a great sigh of relief, watching the man approach her. I think I recognise him, but it's hard to see his face in the darkness. I then heard him call her by name and instantly knew who he was. It was George, Lila's detective friend. – But I'm not sure if this is good or bad, yet.

"Lila... is that you?" he asked, moving closer to her.

He stood so close and held out his empty hands towards her, claiming that he was unarmed. Then Lila leaned her large wolf head forward, and he copied, gently pressing his forehead against hers to show that he understands.

"Stand down," George ordered, turning to address the others. "She's a family pet, the owner is one of the men from the house shooting you were called to... She must have gotten scared and ran off."

All the officers then lowered their weapons as George followed Lila inside and told the others to wait at their cars. – Clearly, he holds some authority because they all listened.

I waited very anxiously as Lila limped back into the room, leaning against George. Then noticing her pain, Billy quickly appeared in front of Lila to let her lean on him as he greeted the detective.

"George? Man are we glad to see you. What the hell are you doing here?"

"There's a rumour going around my station that the force was on the hunt for the great white wolf... And I kind of figured it was her... Anyone care to fill me in?" he asked, casually looking back at Keith and getting slightly concerned. But he's taking most of this pretty well.

Since I had not yet filled in the gaps for Billy, he looked at me, hoping I would answer that lovely question, so I kept it short. "Over there is a very bad man, who has held Lila captive and tortured her for over two weeks now. Hence this..." I casually highlighted Lila's state before I continued. "We also have a foothold situation in the hotel, and we don't know who to trust."

George nodded, being surprisingly understanding for a human, and asked, "What about those healing things that Lila makes?"

I shook my head to answer, "It won't work on an animal and at the moment she's stuck this way... Terrence has gone off to find Lila's notebook, but even if we got the book, there's no way I'd be able to do anything here. We'd need light and a whole list of equipment. Plus... when she morphs back, she'll need a lot more medical attention."

"What about the hospital," George interrupted. "I can sneak her in, and keep guards posted at the corridor... Dr Ellis should be willing to help us."

I looked back at Lila and the state of her, strongly doubting George, and then asked how he plans to sneak a blood covered, large white wolf into the Royal Melbourne Hospital without anyone asking questions.

His lips peaked as he too looked at Lila then back at Keith, and replied, "Well, that man there needs medical attention... He will also need a police escort to the nearest hospital... And I know a paramedic who owes me a favour."

Journal entry continued by Alex Woods

The boat has been travelling for miles, and I'm starting to sweat and shiver from the blood loss. Adela and Katie have been trying to stop the bleeding all while fake Lila keeps her distance from me, looking through the files Adela's team had acquired. And damn it – I still haven't gained the strength to speak.

Tyme wanted to freeze me to give us more time to get back to dry land. But he couldn't do it with all of these humans around because his ability is still not well known to them, and all of us want to keep it that way. Instead, he pulled me into the rift, but it didn't help. It just caused more pain because I was human and couldn't handle the rift distortion in my weakened state. – It felt like I was getting a thousand needles at once.

So now feeling more helpless, Tyme lost his patience and yelled at who he thought to be his sister, demanding she do something.

The fake Lila stared at me and showed no remorse. Instead she nodded to the other agents who were accompanying Phil on the mission and guarding John Lin. The agents then turned their weapons on Tyme, Adela, and Katie, electrifying them with tasers and knocking them out cold.

Amongst all the commotion, I managed to make my escape, climbing over the railing and falling into the water. I swam down deep, so Katherine would think I had drowned and waited for the boat to disappear. But as I waited, I felt something move around me. It was cold and it grabbed hold of me, pulling me further down into the darkness of the icy water.

CHAPTER 38

A Scared Soul

Journal entry by Billy Jonas

By Golly Darn — We're actually getting away with this.

George had called and asked the hospital for a private room in the ER. Insisting on it because of what danger the patient is capable of, and surprisingly the cover story is working.

The moment the ambulance truck arrived at the hospital, I helped George's paramedic friend — Oscar, cart Keith's comatose body through the ER and into the room. William followed close behind us with George not far from him, ordering his officers to be posted at certain points of the corridor just outside the room before requesting Doctor Ellis to be paged immediately.

We hit the brakes on the trolley bed, and I heard Lila whimper, hiding beneath the blankets next to Keith. So as soon as William closed the doors and pulled the privacy curtains shut, I pulled back the blankets to see if Lila was okay. — I don't think she's overly happy being so close to Keith.

"It's okay, Lila… I'm gonna move him away right now for you."

I signalled Oscar to help me move Keith onto the room bed, and he grumbled as he did. "You know, when George asked me for a favour, I didn't think this was what he had in mind."

While Oscar was distracted with me and Keith, William moved at super-speed behind him to help make Lila more comfortable. She howled in pain, making me want to drop the idiot and race back to her, but I stayed focused on placing Keith down on the other med-bed.

"Doctor Ellis is on his way," George reported while storming into the room.

Oscar began to check Keith's vitals while hooking up the monitors and pressure cuff, and then griped, "Can anyone tell me what's so important about that bloody wolf?"

Err...?

We looked at George for that answer, who had to think on the spot. "She's... evidence... Sorry, but that's all I can tell you. Now I need you to go out there, and keep the ER doctors busy for me."

In a temper, Oscar eyed off George then left in frustration, agreeing to stall the other doctors for us. And as he left, Dr Ellis walked into the room a little distracted at the number of officers standing guard in the hallway.

"Sorry, I got held up..." he stated then jumped in fright. "What the hell is that?!"

"James, good to see you," George answered, hurriedly closing the door again. He then pulled the privacy curtain further over as he explained, "That would be our good friend Lila, and she's in pretty bad shape."

James struggled with his words, gawking at the giant blood-covered wolf on the trolley bed, but eventually spoke. "Seriously? Now this is a whole new level of weird... What the hell are you expecting me to do? I'm not a vet."

With an apologetic grin, George turned James towards Keith and said, "No, we actually need you to help him."

Taking one look at the deep wounds, lacerations, and bite marks all over Keith, James cautiously stared back at Lila, listening to George as he added, "Um... long story short, he picked a fight with Lila and lost. But according to William, he had it coming."

It took a moment but eventually James shook the shock from his face and ummed, "Eerr... He'll need surgery to clean out the wounds."

George agreed with whatever James needed but urged with great importance for the doctors to keep Keith sedated at all costs, for the safety of all the people in the hospital. And James nodded, realising the severity of all of this.

As James started looking Keith over, I heard Terrence yelling out in the hallway, arguing with a police officer, demanding to be let through. So I told George to go help him, and he led Terrence back into the room with a young man in tow.

The second they saw me standing next to Lila, they became scared and fearfully stared at me. But in noticing their fear, William appeared in front of Terrence, grabbing Lila's journal, and the bag of plant seeds from him, and then vouched for me.

"Don't worry. He passed Lila's test."

It did make it a bit easier for them when they saw Lila snuggling close to me as she sleepily watched William sit down on her bed and flick through her journal. There was a bit of silence as we waited for William to find the right antidote, but when he stopped on a page, he stood back up and looked at James.

"Right, I'm going to need some blood vials, some saline and a few sterile dishes," he demanded.

Without hesitation, James rushed out of the room, and William got to work, moving at full-speed to grow what he needed from the bag of seeds that Terrence had brought with him. And to be nice, Terrence and I begrudgingly helped to keep Keith from bleeding too much until James came back.

It didn't take long and when James returned, he carried with him the list of supplies and gawked at the speed William and I were moving at. But as Keith started to wake, the entire room paused when I appeared next to him, injecting a sedative into his thigh.

I peered up and noticed George stumble back a bit, fearfully aiming his gun at me while staring at my glowing red hand. "George, I'm a Fire guardian, remember? Put the gun away."

He wisely did as I asked, securing his gun as he tried to calm himself. But William didn't give anyone a second to stop with Terrence and his friend Jake being put on mixing duty, while my glowing hand was used to heat the saline in a metal bowl.

Once William had finished, he held up a 30ml syringe of a white, platinum-like liquid and sighed. "That's step one."

He then looked at Terrence and me and asked what blood type we were.

"O positive," Terrence said.

And I answered, "B positive, why?"

He didn't answer my question, he just moved on to his next mission, asking James to draw some blood from us. But again, James asked why as I sat down at the end of Lila's bed and let him draw some blood from me.

Still staying focused, William prepped the room, getting blankets ready to cover Lila when the time came as he explained, "There's currently a foreign substance in Lila's bloodstream that is suppressing all of Lila's natural abilities, including her immune system... I'm going to attempt to restart the immune system by aggravating it and kick it into overdrive."

I instantly figured out what he was planning on doing but so did James, and he stepped back, holding the syringe of my blood, and stated, "But Lila's O negative, she could get really sick from this... She could die if this doesn't work."

It's true, she could die, and I was a little nervous, staring back at William as he stopped his preparations and replied with fear. "Well, right now, it's the only way to help her."

Terrence didn't need any more convincing than that and sat on the end of the bed, ready for James to draw his blood. But James shook his head. "I can't do any more then. This breaches the code of ethics."

"I can do it," I sighed, understanding his position.

At super-speed, I grabbed what I needed and appeared back in front of Terrence, drawing the blood from his arm, and then took the syringe of my blood from James who surprisingly agreed to stay, just in case it all goes wrong.

Now that we had all the steps together, William readied to inject the white serum into the nape of the wolf's neck, then nervously explained to me, "It's going to take a few seconds for the tonic to spread. But when I tell you to, I need you to inject the bloods into one of the main arteries in her leg."

Alrighty. – That doesn't sound too hard to do. It just means I need to figure out how to find a wolf's vein in her leg that hasn't been severed. – No pressure here.

I had to ask William to give me a minute, and took some time to gently feel around the inside of Lila's thigh. But I caused her to whimper as I brushed past some of her more intense injuries, and I looked up at her, feeling so worried for her.

"Sorry, Lila... just give me a minute, okay."

I felt a little tense as everyone waited for me. But when I found a good vein, I nodded to William, and he pushed the large needle of white liquid into Lila's neck. He then waited until her body went limp and her breathing became shallow before signalling me. And I injected the bloods, praying that it works.

The room fell silent again as we all watched and waited for something to happen. Then without warning, Lila cringed and howled in pain then fearfully leapt from the bed, darting toward the door. I caught her, holding her close to me. – But she's huge and darn well strong, dragging me along the floor with her, all while Terrence and Jake stood in front of her trying to push her back.

We all held tight to her, and listened to Lila's howls slowly turn into a woman's agonising scream as she returned to her smaller, human-self, and then fell comatose in my arms. The only thing that didn't return to normal was her long white hair and elf ears.

At super-speed, William appeared over us with a blanket to shield Lila's nudity from the others before I carried her broken, bloodied, and bruised body back to the hospital bed. – And darn, just looking at the state of her made me want to kill Keith.

It's bad. – To the point where I'm shocked and glad that she's still alive.

One of the ER nurses ran in to inspect the commotion, causing James to break out of his shock and demand, "Nurse, I need two ORs prepped now... multiple lacerations to both and a GSW."

The nurse disappeared, rushing back out of the room as James moved to look at Lila's bullet wound, and the blood now seeping out of every laceration that covered her body, and then ordered, "We need to prep her for surgery."

"No!" William shouted. "She needs to finish the transition. She's still not human."

"She'll bleed out if we don't help her," James argued.

To help William, I stood between Lila and the doctor to explain, "And if anyone sees her like this, they're going to freak out and expose us all... Lila would never agree to that. I can do the surgery in here if you bring me what I need."

"You're seriously a doctor?" The teenager eagerly enquired.

And I'm still trying to figure out how Lila knows him, when I replied, "I'm still licenced, yes... But Lila's my only patient... Look, you can say I'm a specialist for all I care. But I'm not letting you take her anywhere. And the longer you hesitate, the less time we have."

In hearing my suggestion, James looked back at Lila's elf-like appearance and conceded to my request, "What do you need?"

I hurriedly wrote down a list, and he left, taking Keith and George with him. And Terrence followed behind them, and then shortly returned with everything I needed to save Lila.

Journal entry insert by William Knight

Billy worked at half-speed to help Lila, removing the bullet from her leg first. She had a dislocated shoulder again, and knee, as well as a broken arm and collar bone. She also has a fractured cheek and jaw bone with swelling surrounding them, and blistering burn marks on her wrist and ankles where the chains held her. But those will eventually mend themselves.

Once the bones were reset, Billy spent time slowly cleaning out and stitching up every open wound on her. But because there are so many, Terrence and I offered to help.

I think the worst wound was the one running down the length of Lila's back. It was ragged, as if her skin had been torn open to look at her spine before leaving her to heal on the dirt floor. I could see the rage building in Billy and Terrence as they worked together to clean and sew it up. But it was agonising for all of us to see her like this, because even though Lila lay so still and peaceful, on her face rested so much pain.

I was asked by Billy to take off Lila's vine bracelet, but when I tried, it wouldn't respond to my commands. It was like it was glued to her arm, even her necklace remained firmly trapped amongst the vines. – She clearly wanted to keep it on even in her comatose state, so we left it.

Throughout the night, Jake turned out to be really helpful, getting us whatever we needed, be it food or more dressings. And though it took many hours, by the end of the night – almost morning, we had finished, and now Lila's entire body is covered in stitches and loose dressings.

While we prepped Lila to move, Dr Ellis and George organised a private room adjacent for both patients so we can keep an eye on Keith while staying close to Lila. When Lila was settled, Billy received high praise from Dr Ellis for his handiwork as he sat by

Lila's bed to monitor her. - He's currently been given a visiting specialist pass with his name printed on it and everything. It was requested by Doctor Ellis in order for Billy to do what he needs for Lila without people asking too many questions.

We're all really appreciating the trust that both Doctor Ellis and George have given us with everything that's happening. And we understand the predicament we're placing on them at the moment, given that our situation is not exactly easy to explain to their human co-workers.

Now comes the hard part. - The part where we do nothing but wait for Lila to wake up.

While we waited, both Billy and Terrence asked me if I knew what had happened behind some of the injuries. I didn't think it was right to tell them what I knew, but I think they guessed a few in particular when they were stitching her up.

Terrence struggled to tell me what Keith said about him using the Salacio drug on Lila, and how he boasted about it. And Billy knew what that drug was and what it does, because Agronomique's was the company who made it. His breath was shaky, and it brought him to tears, trying not to think about it. And I could sense so much regret in both Billy and Terrence, knowing that all this time, Lila was being tortured and used, and they hadn't even been looking for her.

A few hours passed, and I went into the next room to check Keith's vitals, and they were slowly getting better. But to keep occupied, Billy had been looking through his blood work and noticed a hormonal imbalance that had actually started to level out after a second blood transfusion.

We both theorised that the hormonal imbalance was a side-effect of what might have been causing their infatuation with Katherine, so after Keith's third round of blood test came back somewhat normal for our kind, Billy suggested waking him up.

Since Terrence is technically his brother, Billy wanted him to make the call. So while Billy sat with Lila in the next room, I stood guard at the end of Keith's bed, just in case he really is that evil.

I nervously watched, holding my breath as Dr Ellis injected a stimulant into Keith's saline drip, and after a few minutes, he stirred awake. His first word was "Mother" and he sounded scared.

George stood cautiously nearby, readying his weapon as Dr Ellis checked Keith's vitals and spoke to him. "Welcome back, Mr Connors. My name is Dr Ellis and you're in the Royal Melbourne hospital."

Keith scanned around the room, confused, and then glanced at his brother. "Terrence? What happened? What am I doing here?"

Terrence couldn't answer him, he was too angry and sad, refusing to even look at Keith. He just sat there with his brows pinched, listening as George stood forward to introduce himself. "Mr Connors, can you tell us what the last thing you remember is?"

Keith looked uncomfortable with the question but answered, "I remember Lila and my brother... They destroyed my home... They... They blew it up."

His answer confused all of us, so George questioned further, "Mr Connors... that incident happened several months ago... Can you remember anything else between now and that date?"

Again, Keith looked back at Terrence, confused and worried and shook his head. "No."

That did it for Terrence, and he stormed out in a fuming mess. It was then Keith recognised me. "William... I don't understand, where's my mother?"

Oh, damn it. – I really wanted to hurt him, and I felt a lump of rage in my throat. But it was directed at the wrong person. This entire horrifying mess that my baby girl, my sweet little Honey-Bee is lying in. – It's all Katherine's doing. – But I don't understand why. Why would she do all of this to her own flesh and blood? – Does she feel no love for Lila at all? – Is she truly that evil?

Journal entry insert by Terrence Connors

I couldn't take any more of it. I was so furious at Keith. But that idiot doesn't even know why, and has no idea what he's done to Lila. I stormed back into Lila's hospital room, grumbling and groaning as I sat down in the chair next to her bed. She still hasn't woken up yet, and she still looks like an elf. But Billy's put a stretchy headband on her head and tucked her pointy ears underneath just in case someone walks in that isn't supposed to.

"I take it you heard?" I mumbled, looking seriously frustrated and angry.

Disappointingly nodding, Billy huffed, looking just as angry. "Looks like the only person who remembers what happened to Lila, is... her."

He gently brushed the white hair off Lila's swollen and bruised cheek, and looked like he wanted to cry. William was right, she looks worse than when she was being experimented on by Richard and his thug scientists. Her lips and face and everything else are swollen and discoloured from being hurt multiple times. And every time I look at her, I feel the tears welling in my eyes.

Billy had just finished hooking up another blood bag and was about to move on to checking the stitches when I asked, "Has there been any change?"

"A little," he answered, continuing to gently check the dressings. "The lacerations are healing nicely, and some of the bruising has started to fade... Her O2 sats have dropped though, so I've put the oxygen on for her... But she's a fighter. I think if we give her a few more hours, she might wake up."

I relaxed a little, and then looked around to realise we were one man short and asked, "Where's Jake gone?"

Billy stayed focused on checking and changing some of the dressing as he replied, "I sent him home... It's technically a school day for him, so he's going to fill Matt in on the details and return his car."

"Does he even have his driver's licence?" I questioned.

He hesitated and thought for a moment, "I think he's on his learners. So... no."

Whoops. — We just won't tell George about that. — Ever.

I sat forward in the chair to gently hold the only uninjured finger on Lila's hand. — Her pinkie. And yeah, I'm still wanting to cry. But then I noticed Billy's face ponder, so I asked, "What's wrong?"

He looked more confused when he answered, "These stitches on her leg... they're healing faster than before... And her blood looks like diamonds."

Curious of his statement, I stood up to have a look then noticed her skin begin to glisten, and I had to pull my hand away as I worriedly breathed. "Ow... She's really hot."

Billy placed his hand on Lila's forehead and around her neck and freaked. "She's burning up."

He raced to turn the oxygen off at the wall, and we stepped back and worriedly awed as her skin started to glow like a fiery diamond. Then in a panic, Billy shouted, "TERRENCE GET DOWN!"

I instantly dropped to the floor as Lila's body was engulfed in flames that started to fill the room. Then while lying on the floor, I peered up from underneath the hospital bed to see Billy desperately trying to contain the fire. Eventually he did and pulled it into a raging fireball in his hand to extinguish it. — But it wasn't easy.

In silence, we both stood at the end of the hospital bed, staring at Lila, and jumped in fright when she woke up in a panic, gasping for air. She sat up, looking around the room in fear then tried to get up and leave. We hurriedly moved to stop her and keep her on the bed, holding her hands. Then I pulled her closer to me and stared into her eyes, pleading, "No, Lila... Stop... You're safe here, I promise."

"Terry," she smilingly breathed, realising who I was and pulled me in for a way too strong hug.

Yeah... ouch. — It's good to see she hasn't lost her strength.

The problem is she was still holding Billy's hand and had not yet let go of it when she hugged me. So I peered up at him as he stood on the other side of the bed behind her, and awkwardly grinned as I felt his arm wrapped around me as well. But when Lila let go of me, her eyes followed the arm that she held to see Billy's face.

"Billy." She beamed with joy, leaping out of the bed and wrapping her arms and legs around him so excitedly as she sniffled. "You fixed me... I knew you could do it."

Very carefully, Billy held her, unsure of where to place his hands that wouldn't hurt her, but she didn't seem too worried about her injuries.

"Eerr... It actually looks like you fixed yourself," he remarked, gently putting her back down on the bed before slowly pulling away at some of the dressings to see the wounds completely healed, leaving just charred stitching thread amongst the scars. Then he gasped, "Lila, that's amazing."

She too started pulling away the dressings on her arms to look for herself, and saw only faint bruising and a lot of scars.

"Huh... well I guess I'm back to wearing skivvies and jumpers again," she grumbled, looking back at me all pouty faced. "And promise me, you and Alex won't force me to have any more horrid healing tonics to fix me... Please, Terry, don't ever make me relive any of this ever again."

I very happily nodded my head and agreed to the promise with certainty. But something clicked in her and her fear spiked when she felt Billy's hand on her thigh. He was kneeling down to remove the lower dressing on her legs to check that they had healed, when her whole body tensed, pulling away from him and inching backwards into my arms.

Oh Damn. — It hurts to see her scared like this.

We both knew why she was scared, so Billy stood up and gently apologised. "I'm sorry, Lila... I was just taking off the dressings, that's all."

Trembling in my arms, Lila timidly stared into Billy's eyes then moved back towards him, slowly and ever so cautiously holding his hand to rest it back down on her leg. She then took a long breath to stop her trembling before she nodded, leaning her head on Billy's chest as she sat quietly on the bed.

Taking that as a sign of permission, Billy kept one arm wrapped around Lila to stop her from falling, and then slowly removed the rest of the dressings and bandages with the other hand. The last thing he needed to do was to remove the bloodline and Saline drip. But he needed two hands for that, so he asked for my help and walked me through what to do.

Lila didn't move from Billy's arm the entire time, all curled up and very sleepy. Then when he had finished, he tried to step away, but she held onto his shirt, not wanting to let go. Instead, he stayed standing next to her, and I sat on the bed as she kept hold of my hand.

We sat for a while and I think Lila had almost gone to sleep on Billy's chest when Will stood at the door, confused at what he was looking at. I don't think he can see Lila from where he's standing. So I signalled him to come over, and he quietly walked to the end of the hospital bed, and looked like he was about to cry over his smile when Lila peeked up at him, rubbing the sleep from her eyes as she yawned.

"Hi Daddy," she sleepily whispered.

In seconds, he appeared sitting on the bed at Lila's feet and sniffled, "Hey Honey-Bee."

Her nose crinkled, and she smiled at him before wriggling down the bed to rest in his arms instead. And he held her so tightly as he studied the scars of her now healed skin and bones and everything, and then let some of the tears escape his eyes.

After a beautiful moment, Lila giggled. "Now all we need is Tyme, standing in the corner doing his little victory dance at the fact that I finally called you Dad."

That's when her smile disappeared and worry filled her face as she sat up from her hug. "Tyme... Alex... I almost forgot about them. They're still in danger."

She got up in a panic and raced around the bed towards the door, stating, "I need to go and rescue them."

Ah... No. — That is a terrible idea.

Thankfully, before she got anywhere near the door, Will appeared in front of her and acted all fatherly, trying to stop her. "You'll do no such thing."

He looked like he was preparing himself to give this long speech about not rushing into danger, but before he could do that, Lila fell into his arms. She clearly hasn't recovered yet, but she's determined to ignore it as she got back up to her feet, starting to sweat.

"Daddy... this is not the time to get all overprotective and crap. I'm hungry. And I'm dirty, wearing a hospital gown as clothes. I've been locked in a cave for weeks, trapped as a wolf for half that time, and the other half I never want to speak about... So right now, I'm angry and want to kick someone's arrogant and smug arse."

She glared at Will with her angered, teary eyes, waiting for him to move. But he stood tall, crossing his arms then replied, "Fine, I'll let you leave... On the condition that you get your doctor... the one you were using as a pillow not 10 minutes ago to give you the all-clear."

Will stared over at Billy who had gotten comfortable in the corner chair, and you could just tell he had no plans on giving Lila the all-clear yet. But while Lila was standing there giving her dad the death stare, her breathing became shallow and she held her head, wiping the beads of sweat off her brow.

"Billy," she rasped, struggling to speak. "Billy, something's wrong."

She tried to walk towards him but her legs gave way on her, so Billy raced to catch her before her head hit the ground, and cradled her in his arms.

"You're right..." he gently whispered. "Something is wrong... which means your dad's right. I'm not going to give you the all-clear to go and kick someone's arrogant and smug butt... Not yet anyway."

While gently placing Lila back on the bed, Billy started checking her over, focusing on her temperature and heart rate. Then he began to negotiate with her. — Because she loves that part of a battle.

"I'll make a deal with you... If you give me the time I need to fix you and you show me that you can walk at least 10 steps towards me without getting dizzy, I will let you go and kick someone's butt... I'll even help... deal?"

She looked up at him then silently growled, resting her head back down on his chest, scowling at the floor while pouting. "Do I have a choice?"

While trying really hard not to laugh, Billy glanced back at me to see that I was struggling just as much as he was. — It's not every day that you see Lila chucking a tantrum. And she's just so damn cute when she does. — Especially when she looks like an elf.

"Sorry... but doctor's orders," he answered trying to pull his smile back before he continued. "Now, we're going to start by ticking some of the things off your list... First off, and I hope you don't mind, but I'm going to ask your dad to read your journal and try to find something in there that will hopefully help you... Then, I'm going to send Terrence to go and buy you some clothes... And I am going to walk you into that bathroom so that you can get a shower... How does all that sound?"

Well, I've got to give him credit. — Billy's damn good at negotiating. — Maybe that's why Lila likes him.

We all stood silent and waited for Lila's answer as she continued to scowl at the floor then eventually huffed, "Fine... but they better be damn good clothes."
Now all in agreement with the plan, Billy handed me his wallet, and I left to hunt for some food and some 'damn good clothes' for Lila.

Journal entry continued by Billy Jonas

Lila's taking this whole doctor's orders thing pretty well. I mean, she knows I haven't been a practising doctor in years. But I appreciate the fact that she always respects and trusts me to help her.

After her dad and Terrence had left to get what they needed, I helped Lila into the bathroom to shower. But her heartrate spiked as soon as the door closed. I asked if she was okay, and she trembled as she timidly whispered, "I'm sorry... It's not easy being in small spaces at the moment."

I let out a sad breath, turning on the shower for her, and then turned to look at her with so much worry in me. "Do you still want to do this?"

She nodded, and I was about to walk out and leave the door open for her, so the bathroom didn't feel so small, when she pleaded with fear in her voice, "Please, don't leave me alone."

The sound of her fear got to me, and I could feel the ache in my chest, so I agreed to stay with her. I stood facing the door to give her some privacy, and she asked me to talk about something. – Anything to fill the silence.

I needed a moment to think then I talked to her about my home town back in Canada, and told her about my favourite place to visit called Rainbow Lake.

"The lake is small in comparison to all the others... but surrounding it are the most beautiful mountains and hills with lush green grass that grows up the side of the snowy peaks... And the hiking trails are always adventurous, constantly finding something new to discover."

"It sounds beautiful," she whispered, turning off the shower and standing behind me in just a towel.

I towel-dried her long white hair and put the sports headband back on to cover up her pointy ears. Then I gave her a fresh hospital gown, but she begged me not to make her wear it. And luckily enough, we could both hear Terrence waiting just outside on the bed for her.

It sounded like he had some bags with him, so I let Lila walk out of the bathroom in just her towel, and she instantly looked a lot happier when she saw Terrence holding hot chips and a lot of veggie burgers in his hands. So moving at half-speed, Lila got dressed and thanked Terrence for his good taste in clothes before very eagerly sitting on the bed, waiting for the food.

We all sat on the hospital bed and had a little picnic, sharing the food. I could still see the beads of sweat on Lila's skin and could tell her body was fighting an infection. But I'm positive all we need to do is give William enough time to find the right cure.

"So..." She grinned, looking at both of us. "Has anyone called Matt and told him I'm not a wolf anymore?"

Terrence and I both went quiet, thinking of what to say. But eventually I answered, "Um... we... sent Jake home with Matt's car to tell him the good news."

Her jaw dropped in shock. "But he doesn't have a driver's licence."

She then disappointingly shook her head at both of us, leaning over me and fondling my pocket to steal my phone and call Matt. But she still had a cute smile on her, looking at us while listening to the dial tone.

Darn. – I just love that smile.

Suddenly, her whole body stiffened, and her eyes went black when a female voice on the other end answered and said, "Hello Lila."

"Katherine," Lila angrily hissed. "What have you done with them?"

I listened in and heard the sounds of Danny and Ruby crying for their mother with Matt in the background screaming, "Don't do it, Lila. It's a trap!" before the phone was disconnected.

Very quickly, Lila went into a silent rage with her breathing short and shaky when Terrence worriedly asked, "What's wrong?"

"She has my kids." She angrily growled and her skin changed, turning to diamond as she seethed. "Keith."

Before I knew it, Lila was on her feet, storming toward the door. Terrence tried to stop her and even I tried to stop her. But somehow, she found the strength to throw both of us across the room. She then glared back at us and very sternly warned, "Do not try to stop me... this is not a fight you will win."

And wow, does she look scary as hell. – Even while she was hobbling out of her room and into Keith's.

I grunted from my pain while helping Terrence to stand as we chased after her into Keith's room, begging her to stop. But she didn't.

"Where is she?" Lila demanded, leaning on the end of Keith's hospital bed, just barely able to stand.

Keith looked at her, confused and completely clueless as to who she was talking about, shifting to sit up in the bed.

"Lila," Terrence worriedly begged, cautiously trying to get her attention. "Lila, stop! He doesn't know anything... He doesn't remember anything from the last six months. The last thing he remembers is us blowing up his house and running into some lady named Katty."

Taking a few steps back, Lila shook her head, staring up at William as he ran into the room. And she trembled, still struggling to breathe. "No. He... He killed Hanna... He burned my house... imprisoned me, tortured me for weeks, and he... he doesn't even remember?"

Moving carefully, William walked further into the room, gently holding Lila to comfort her. "I'm so sorry, Honey-Bee... but his blood work came back with faint traces of Neuritamine."

In anger, Lila pulled away from him, staring back at us and let out her screams of frustration, throwing a diamond fireball at the wall, and then fell to the ground sobbing. Her cries drew the attention of George who was talking in the hallway with Odele and Izzy, and they all came rushing in to see what was wrong.

"This was all her..." Lila tearfully mumbled. "Katherine, she did all of this to me. Why?"

Worried for her son, Odele cautiously walked into the room towards Keith, causing Lila to snap, moving at super-speed to steal George's gun. Then she angrily stood in the middle of the room, aiming it at Odele.

"You know why... don't you, Odele? You know why Katherine is just so evil."

I moved closer to Lila when I saw her struggle, sweating more as her breath laboured. But she glared at me again, warning me to stay back. And I did, but I also wanted so badly to hold her.

"How many times did it take you?" Lila asked, leering at Odele for the answer. But Odele stayed quiet, so Lila asked again, "How many times did you have to kill her before she turned? TELL ME!"

George put his hands out, slowly standing in front of Lila to plead, "Lila, put the gun down. You don't want to do this... This isn't you."

My chest ached as Lila's body trembled, and she spoke through her shivers. "I don't think you know me all that well anymore, George... Do you know what happens to a person when you bring them back from near death?"

She looked around the room, waiting for anyone to answer.

"No... Keith does," she cried, starting to weaken, and she leaned on the end of the bed. Yet she still had the gun squared on Odele as she angrily whimpered. "Or at least he did... Did you know, Odele, that for the last two or more weeks... I... well I lost count of the days that your son kept me prisoner? Every day, he tortured me. He did unspeakable things to me and caused me so much pain until I longed and begged for death to just take me away... But every time I got close to the end... He'd just bring me back, using my daddy's Knight serum to do it... The ones he stole from Dr Ellis."

Hearing that, William seethed in anger, briefly looking at Keith before his attention returned to Lila and her weakening, angered state.

"Oh, that's not all you should be angry about, Daddy. Because instead of using the full formula's dosage, Keith tainted it. He diluted it so he could use it again and again and again... So instead of healing me, the Knight serum only had enough strength to bring me back from the brink of death. Leaving me to do the rest... And Keith knew exactly what he was doing because he told me who he learnt it from... So tell them, Odele, what happens to a person when they experience death too many times?"

The room became very tense and quiet as we waited for Odele's answer, and she looked back at Keith and Izzy then regrettably sighed, staring at Lila's weakening state. "Your soul dies."

"That's right," Lila cried with sweat pooling on her skin as she put more of her weight on the end of the bed, still trying to hold the gun up as she spoke. "Every time you meet with death, little pieces of your soul is torn away. And it changes you... It changes every part of you. So tell me, Odele, how many times did you and The Board kill Katerina before she changed into the monster she is now?"

Again, Odele looked around the room at all the listening ears, and answered, "316 times."

Holy Darn Crap. – That's a lot.

Tittering just a little, Lila shook her head at Odele and rasped, "Then Katherine was weak... because I think Keith and I stopped counting after about 6 or 700... Apparently, I'm stubborn... and like my soul."

With sweat dripping off her, Lila lowered the gun, placing it on the bed before she turned to look at William with tears falling down her cheeks. I think she knew something was wrong with her and that it was going to go badly because she looked incredibly scared.

"Take care of Tyme for me, Daddy," she rasped then fell to the ground.

At super-speed, I rushed to scoop her up into my arms and her skin was boiling.

"She's burning up!" I shouted, moving at full-speed back into her room to rest her comatose body on the bed.

Dr Ellis and Terrence rushed in behind me and tried to help me wake her as I shouted her name and yelled, "No, Lila... You didn't give me enough time!"

Suddenly her eyes opened, glowing a furious bright green with her skin shining like diamonds. Then those beautiful blue eyes of hers looked at me one last time before they became distant and empty.

"No!" I cried. Then refusing to give up on her, I started CPR.

As James called a code blue, the nurses and respiratory team came rushing in with a crash cart, and James prepped the defib paddles. But before he could get near Lila, William ran into the room, aiming the gun at James and his staff and shouted, "Stop!!! Don't touch her!"

He clutched Lila's journal close to his chest as James's staff stepped back and waited, unsure what to do all while I continued with the CPR.

"Will, what are you doing?" I griped.

"If they shock her, she'll die... Look at her hand."

I peeked down at Lila's hands to see that she still had very faint diamond skin, then I looked back at James and demanded him to get out. He glared at me, confused and frustrated, so I explained, "He's right, if you shock her, she'll most likely conduct the energy and explode. Killing you and your entire team."

"But she'll die," he rebuffed.

I briefly glanced at William then back at James, starting to tire with the compressions as I asked, "Do you really want to argue with a father who's holding a gun?"

Realising he had lost the argument, James stood back, demanding everyone to get out. And once Terrence had ushered them out, he locked the door with a now broken curtain pole.

"I need you to leave," William demanded, looking at me.

"Like hell," I grunted back.

"Billy, after what she's been through, there's a strong chance she may not come back as the Lila we know."

"Which is why I'm staying," I rebuked, persisting with the compressions. "We are not going to let her go."

He conceded, and then looked back at Terrence who also refused to leave but looked as if he were on the brink of crying. Starting to tire more, I continued CPR while watching William as he placed Lila's journal on the bed, and he pulled out another long needle with platinum white liquid inside.

"I missed an ingredient last time and a very crucial step," he explained.

"What?" I wearily asked.

He held up the needle to give to me and answered, "Her... as she is now. This needs to be injected directly into her heart as soon as you stop compressions."

I took a breath, nodding in agreement, and as he counted down, I braced myself to move at super-speed in 3...2...1.

It was done.

I took another breath, pulling the empty syringe from Lila's chest and waited. — And waited for what felt like forever. But nothing happened and William shook his head, confused.

"No, that should have worked."

Panicked and worried, I leaned in to check Lila's pulse. And as I did, she opened her dark black eyes and clawed her diamond hand around my neck as she stood to her feet, lifting me from the ground. She didn't look like herself. — Her eyes were filled with so much hate.

"Lila... Stop," I choked. "Fight it, Lila... Fight it! Remember who you are... You are the woman... we love."

"I know... And I hate it." She hissed with so much anger, and then threw me across the room towards William, knocking both of us to the ground.

Looking back up, I watched as she effortlessly blasted a hole through the hospital window that is several floors up from ground level, and climbed up readying herself to leave.

"LILA!" Terrence worriedly shouted. "Where are you going?"

"To get what's mine," she sneered back at him as she stepped out onto a platform of leaves.

As she pulled away from the window, I heard her screams of pain when the stone-bracelet and necklace she wore on her wrist began to glow a furious green colour, causing her to rip it from her arm and throw it to the ground.

The next thing I saw was Lila flying off and Terrence leaping out of the window towards her as William screamed, "NO! TERRENCE... DON'T DO IT!"

Continue the adventure in
Journals of the Earth Guardians – Series 4

www.ingramcontent.com/pod-product-compliance
Lightning Source LLC
Chambersburg PA
CBHW050057120726

47904CB00004B/1117